Deep *in the* Heart
of Trouble

Books by
Deeanne Gist

A Bride Most Begrudging

The Measure of a Lady

Courting Trouble

Deep in the Heart of Trouble

Deep *in the* Heart *of* Trouble

A Novel

DEEANNE GIST

BETHANY HOUSE PUBLISHERS
Minneapolis, Minnesota

Published by Bethany House Publishers
11400 Hampshire Avenue South
Bloomington, Minnesota 55438

Bethany House Publishers is a division of
Baker Publishing Group, Grand Rapids, Michigan.

Printed in the United States of America

Library of Congress Cataloging-in-Publication Data

Gist, Deeanne.
    Deep in the heart of trouble / Deeanne Gist.
      p. cm.
    ISBN 978-0-7642-0524-8 (alk. paper) — ISBN 978-0-7642-0226-1 (pbk. : alk. paper) 1. Single women—Fiction. 2. Oil well drilling—Fiction. 3. Corsicana (Tex.)—History—19th century—Fiction. I. Title.

PS3607.I55D44   2008
813'.6—dc22

                                                          2008002398

To Gary and Carol Johnson,
whose contributions to the Christian Fiction genre
have had an immeasurable impact
on the furthering of God's kingdom.
May He bless you a hundredfold to how you
have blessed me and so many others.

DEEANNE GIST has a background in education and journalism. Her credits include *People, Parents, Parenting, Family Fun,* and the *Houston Chronicle*. She has a line of parenting products called I Did It® Productions and a degree from Texas A&M. She and her husband have four children—two in college, two in high school. They live in Houston, Texas, and Deeanne loves to hear from her readers at her Web site, *www.deeannegist.com*.

ACKNOWLEDGMENTS

I am so thankful for the support I receive from fellow writers Meg Moseley and J. Mark Bertrand, who see my work in its rawest form, then faithfully critique it for me one chapter at a time. I am forever grateful to you both. Thank you for the time commitment and the sharing of your expertise.

Once I finish my novel, I have my "go-to" readers who give the manuscript a fresh read from start to finish, then offer excellent feedback and suggestions. They include: my parents, Harold and Veranne Graham; my sister, Gayle Evers, who also thought of the title, *Deep in the Heart of Trouble* (You go, girl!); and my beloved friend and comrade, Allison Smythe.

Finally, I humbly turn the manuscript in to my editors, David Long and Julie Klassen, who then take it and put it through a refining fire. How blessed I am to have them.

Thus, the book you hold in your hands is the offering I give to you and to our gracious God. It is my fervent hope that it be worthy of you both.

"When I saw you on your wheel, sweet Lenore
Oh my brain did never reel so before.
You were clad in knickerbocks
And you wore such brilliant sox
I could see 'em twenty blocks, maybe more.

"I but gave a passing glance, sweet Lenore
At the natty sawed-off pants which you wore,
Then the cruel ground I hit
I had fallen in a fit,
And I've not recovered yet, sweet Lenore."

—Anonymous

PROLOGUE

ESSIE SPRECKELMEYER didn't have a man, nor did she need one. She had her own arms and legs, a head full of sense, and a hearty constitution. Furthermore, if she'd married and multiplied—thus fulfilling her moral and physiological destiny—then she'd never have been able to travel to New York City alone and enter her bicycle costume in the *Herald*'s competition.

Hundreds of people had gathered to celebrate this first day of New York's cycling season. The stately grounds of Central Park contrasted sharply with the hustle and bustle of the city's streets, yet Essie found herself unable to enjoy her surroundings. Moisture collected on her palms, and her stomach tensed, for the newspaper editor on the podium was winding down his speech and preparing to announce the contest winner.

With one hand, she smoothed the full yellow bodice of her costume, which fastened on the right side under a ruffle of cream lisse. With the other, she plucked at bloomers that drooped deeply upon gaiters of cloth to match.

Glancing at the crowd of bicycle enthusiasts packed in and around her, she took a deep breath. Her solo train trip across the country had scandalized everyone back home in Corsicana, Texas. If she won this competition, though, it would go a long way in soothing their sense of propriety. There was nothing Texans liked more than to prove they could do things better than their northern compatriots. In Essie's mind her only real competition was a woman from Boston, whose costume was both appealing to the eye and extremely practical. But the lady's plain brown hat fell quite short of the mark.

Essie checked the hat perched atop her tightly twisted blond tresses, hoping the extravagant design of her own invention would tip the scales in her favor. The straw confection held two lines of yellow roses, with a frill of laced leaves towering well above the crown.

The speaker recaptured Essie's attention. "So without further ado, ladies and gentlemen, the winner of the *New York Herald*'s contest for Best Bicycle Costume goes to . . . Miss Esther Spreck-elmeyer of Corsicana, Texas!"

At the sound of her name, Essie trembled with a mix of elation and disbelief. Excusing herself, she wove through the murmuring crowd and toward the festooned podium. Heads craned to catch a glimpse of her approach. The masses parted like clouds making way for a tiny beam of light.

"Congratulations, dear," said an elegant woman wearing a hat of rose-pink chiffon with a sheer polka-dot veil. A swarthy man in white knickerbockers and matching jacket touched his beret. A young police officer took Essie's elbow and waved the crowd back.

And then she was at the podium, where the newspaper editor, who couldn't weigh more than a hundred twenty pounds soaking wet, handed her the giant first-place wreath. It was half again as big as she and almost as heavy.

A bouquet of luscious aromas from the roses, gardenias, and carnations decorating the wreath filled her nose.

"Thank you," she said.

The editor beheld her prizewinning costume, then turned to the crowd with a flourish of his elegant little hand. "I give you Miss Spreckelmeyer, owner and president of the Corsicana Velocipede Club."

Straightening her posture, she slipped the pleated cuff of her gigot sleeve through the wreath and held it to the side so the crowd could take another look at the costume that had been voted to victory.

Men cheered. Women clapped, their gloved hands sounding like the rapid flapping of birds' wings. Out of the corner of her eye, she caught sight of an illustrator just as he flipped back a page in his sketchbook.

He poised his charcoal on a fresh sheet of paper and shouted, "Miss Spreckelmeyer, look this way!"

Startled, she glanced at him, amazed as he quickly swept his charcoal pencil in large arcs across his pad, his movements culminating in a rough outline of her holding the wreath. The crowd quieted and she returned her attention to the waiting audience.

The confident words she had rehearsed in her daydreams fled from her mind. In a panic, she looked to her right and left as if she might miraculously discover the content of her acceptance speech hanging from the grand oaks lining the park.

She cleared her throat. "Ladies and gentlemen wheelers. I, um, I cannot begin to find the words to express how very much this honor means to me."

A smattering of applause.

"I wish to thank—"

"Hey, lady!" A large man in a black summer jacket, black Derby, and black boots pushed his way to the front. "I'm a member of the Anti-Bloomer Brigade, and we don't approve of this emancipation movement you lady wheelers are pushing on our female population.

We believe that a lady should look like a lady. What are you thinking to parade in an outfit like that, and in front of an assembly like this? Why, you're shaming God, our country, and the entire fair sex."

The crowd hushed and the illustrator hastily flipped over a new page, sketching the heckler.

"I do not belong to any special dress-reform movement, sir," she said. "I simply wear bloomers because they are the most sensible attire for a lady cycler."

"Well, you might as well be wearing men's trousers!" He leaped up onto the stage.

Essie stumbled back. Gasps rose from the crowd.

The diminutive editor-in-chief would be no match for the burly man, and she saw no sign of the officer who had escorted her to the podium.

"I've taken an oath," the man said, lumbering toward her. "An oath to do everything I can to put a stop to this immorality. And I intend to do just that!"

He grabbed Essie's arm. Three men standing close to the front scrambled onto the platform.

"Now, see here," shouted one of them. "Unhand that woman!"

His words had the effect of a battle cry. And the most defining moment of Essie's cycling career reduced itself into an all-out brawl.

chapter ONE

THE YEARS hadn't been good to Norris Tubbs. His back curved like a bow. Long white hairs grew from his ears in a tangled mess. His nose had increased in width and depth. And his eyes were glassy—but earnestly focused.

"Your father told me I could have Anna," he said.

"Have Anna?" Tony Morgan asked, taking a sip of coffee.

"Yes. As my wife."

Tony sucked in his breath, taking the coffee down the wrong pipe, choking himself and burning his throat.

Tubbs thumped him on the back. "Everything was settled."

"Everything?" he asked, eyes watering.

"Except for informing Anna, of course."

"Of course." Still regaining his composure, Tony scanned the group of mourners filling his family's parlor and caught sight of his sister accepting condolences from the governor of Texas.

Though she wore black from head to foot, the cut and style of her gown was anything but harsh, particularly on her. A modest hat sat upon piles of dark hair, and the form-fitting bodice accentuated her feminine assets.

Tony sighed. With her nineteenth birthday just a week or so away, he wasn't surprised his father had been considering offers for her hand. But, Norris Tubbs?

Tubbs followed Tony's line of vision. "I assume you will honor your father's wishes?"

Pulling his attention back to the part owner of the H&TC Railroad, Tony tried to rein in his exasperation. Once his father's will was read, he expected to be placed at the helm of Morgan Oil while his older brother ran the more profitable Morgan interests. Therefore, it wouldn't do to alienate Tubbs.

"Dad never said a thing to me about this."

"No? Well, I'm sure he intended to, but he just didn't figure on dropping dead last week."

Tony smoothed the edges of his moustache. "No, I imagine he didn't. Nevertheless, Anna will be in mourning for a year, so there's no need to rush into anything."

"Now, Tony, it's almost the twentieth century. Folks aren't nearly as particular as they used to be about that kind of thing."

"Maybe some folks aren't," he said. "But I am."

Tubbs stiffened. "Well, perhaps it's Darius I should be speaking to about this anyway. He's the oldest, after all."

Tony set his cup on the tray of a passing servant and reminded himself there was more than one railroad coming through Beaumont.

"You can speak to Darius all you want to, Norris," he said, "but you're forgetting that he is only her half brother. I'm her full brother, and I can assure you that her hand will not be awarded to anyone without my express permission."

The Morgans' longtime friend and family lawyer, Nathaniel Walker, murmured a few words of condolence to Mother, then ushered her inside his office. Tony led Anna by the arm, leaving Darius to bring up the rear. His half brother crossed to the far side of the room and installed himself in a wing chair. Tony, along with his mother and sister, made do with a small, uncomfortable black-and-white cowhide settee. Horns from about six steers acted as a cushion for their backs.

Walker fished his watch from a vest pocket, confirmed the hour, then pulled a sheaf of pages from a drawer in his grand mahogany desk. The silence, while he fixed a pair of gold-rimmed spectacles to his nose, was awkward and charged.

"I will now read the Last Will and Testament of Blake Huntley Morgan," he announced.

He began in a strong, even voice, but the farther he went, the slower he read. After a while, the words began to recede into the background, supplanted by the thumping in Tony's head.

"There must be some mistake," he finally blurted out, interrupting Walker.

The lawyer looked up. "I'm sorry, Tony. There's no mistake."

"But what you've read makes no sense. It sounds as if Dad only married Mother to have someone to take care of Darius. Like Anna and I don't even matter. Or Mother either."

"Yes," Walker said softly.

Mother whimpered. Anna placed a black handkerchief to her mouth.

The smell of leather, musty books, and tobacco pressed against Tony's lungs. He caught his nails against the grain of the settee's coarse hair. Darius shifted in his chair but showed no visible reaction to the news.

"I don't understand," Mother whispered.

Walker cleared his throat. "Leah, you will be allowed to reside in the mansion and awarded a generous stipend for the duration of your life. Anna may also remain at home until she weds, at which time she will receive a respectable dowry."

"What about Tony?"

"I was just getting to that." Peering through his spectacles, he looked down at the papers on his desk and took a deep breath. " 'I bequest to my son, Anthony Bryant Morgan . . . nothing. No portion of my estate, real, personal, or mixed is bequeathed to him.' "

Nothing? Tony thought. *Nothing?*

Mother squeezed his hand. Bit by bit, her grip tightened until he was sure her wedding band would leave an imprint on his fingers.

" 'Anthony will be endowed with the most valuable gift of all: an education. I charge him to take his knowledge and go higher and farther than even I have.' "

The windows were barely cracked, leaving the room stuffy and hot. A droplet of sweat trickled down Tony's back.

" 'I hereby declare that after Anthony has reached his majority, my wife is not to share her bequest with him or she will forfeit all monies and inheritance provided herewith.' "

After he reached his majority? At twenty-eight, he was well past that.

As Walker read on, Tony tried to comprehend how his father could have intentionally left him penniless. Unless his brother died, that is, in which case Tony would be the subsequent beneficiary. But the likelihood of that happening anytime soon was extremely improbable. Darius was thirty-one and in excellent health.

Tony glanced at his mother, noting a fine sheen of moisture around her graying hairline. Both she and Anna had worn black serge suits. Mother was prone to fainting, and given the situation and the extreme heat, he was surprised she'd not succumbed already.

Walker finished, turned over the last page of the will and looked at Tony. "Are you all right, son?"

Tight-chested, he kept his voice calm and level. "When? When did he change it?"

Walker straightened the stack he'd made in front of him on the desk. "He didn't change it. It has been like this for years."

Tony nodded. "How many years?"

"Since you children were born." He hesitated. "Well, no, that's not quite true. He did revise it that time Darius had the fever as a boy. He wasn't sure Darius would survive and wanted provisions in place."

Since they were born? His father had disinherited him from the moment of birth? Only making provisions for him in the case of Darius's premature death?

Bile rose in the back of Tony's throat as he thought of the countless times he'd tried to earn his dad's approval. How pathetic.

"Why didn't you tell me, Nathaniel?" Mother asked, choking.

"It was not my place."

"Our families have known each other for three generations."

He removed his glasses, then slowly folded them. "I took an oath, Leah. Would you have me break it?"

"Couldn't you have convinced him to offer Tony some kind of settlement, to give him a start?"

Walker rubbed his nose where his glasses had been, then directed his answer to Tony. "I'm sorry. Blake said he started with nothing. He wants you to do the same. I will say, however, that as the years passed, he had every faith you would rise to the occasion and then some."

The tick in Tony's jaw began to pulse. "I see."

Darius, who had observed the proceedings in cold silence, finally rose. "Is there anything else, Mr. Walker?"

"No, I believe that is all."

Tony watched his half brother cross the room. Apart from Darius's lack of facial hair, the two brothers looked alike. The same olive skin, the same brown eyes, the same tall, lean, and hard physiques.

But they could not have been more different in temperament. Darius had no time for other men's ethical codes. From the start, he'd been out to please himself. Leaving the Morgan Oil enterprise in his hands was as good as feeding it to the wolves.

But his father had loved his first family and merely tolerated his second. No matter how hard Tony had tried to measure up, obviously nothing had ever changed that.

Beads of sweat glistened above Darius's mouth. "Thank you for your time, Walker. I'll be in touch. Would you give us a moment?"

Walker nodded, gathered his papers and stepped out of the office.

Darius moved behind the desk. "Anna," he said, leaning back in the cavernous calf-skin chair, "clearly there was no love lost between you and Dad. So you should have no objection to cutting the grieving process short. Moping about in unrelieved black will do nothing to advance your chances for matrimony."

Mother paled even more. "You mean to marry her off before the mourning period has been observed?"

"I most certainly do. You, Tony," he said, shifting his focus, "will be gone by morning."

Mother gasped. "Darius! Don't be ridiculous. He must have time to make a plan, to prepare."

Tony took several slow, deep breaths.

Darius looked at his stepmother with neither malice nor cruelty, merely disinterest. "I'm afraid you have nothing to say about the matter. Everything now belongs to me, and no one is welcome unless I say he is welcome."

Tony jumped up from the sofa. "Mother, Anna, leave us."

Anna immediately stood, slipping her arm around Mother and helping her vacate the room. Their skirts rustled, muffling his mother's sobs. But Tony heard them. And his anger swelled.

As soon as the door clicked shut behind the women, he advanced toward the desk. He had not struck Darius in years. Not since childhood.

Tony spread both palms on top of the massive desk and leaned over as far as it would allow. "If you try to marry Anna off before a year has passed, or if anything happens to her or Mother while I'm gone, you will answer to me."

Surprise brightened Darius's eyes for a moment, then he relaxed. "Don't be melodramatic, Tony. I have no ill will toward Leah or Anna. We hardly see each other as it is, what with them in the opposite wing of the house."

"That will all change when you take over Dad's rooms. Mother has been in the chamber that connects to his for thirty years. Where are you going to put her?"

Darius pursed his lips. "Well, if it will ease your mind, I'll allow her to choose whatever room she likes for herself."

"Very generous of you." The bite in Tony's tone belied the charitable words.

"Thank you."

Tony did not remove his hands or his bulk from the desk.

Darius cocked an eyebrow. "Do you mind?"

With slow deliberation, Tony straightened, turned and strode from the room.

⁓⁓

Standing on the porch of the dilapidated gable-front house, Tony knocked again. The wooden door opened a crack, revealing a small blond girl shorter than the doorknob.

"Hi there, Miss Myrtle. Is your papa home?"

She said nothing. Just stood there, looking through the crack with big brown eyes.

"How 'bout your mama? Can you tell your mama Uncle Tony's here?"

She stuck her thumb in her mouth.

He rubbed his jaw. He usually brought Russ's kids a licorice stick, but with all that had happened, he'd come empty-handed.

Setting his suitcase down, he squatted so he'd be eye level with her, then crossed his arms over his chest, slapped his thighs and clapped his hands to the rhythm of his words. "Miss Myr-tle . . . ?"

He extended his hands, palms up, in front of her. Smiling around her thumb, Myrtle slipped out the door and tapped her free hand against one of his at each repeating word.

" . . . Mac, Mac, Mac," he continued. "All dressed in black, black, black. With sil-ver buttons, buttons, buttons. All down her back, back, back."

Opening his arms, he waited. She came into them and he kissed her downy hair, the smell of dishwater and milk bringing a smile to his face. The door opened behind her.

"Mercy, Tony. You oughta know you can come right on in without waiting for an engraved invitation. How long has she kept you out here for?"

Tony stood, ruffling Myrtle's head. "I just got here, Iva. Is Russ home?"

"Sure, sure. Come on in." Shifting the baby boy on her hip, she widened the door, hollered for her husband, then frowned at his suitcase. "You all right?"

He slipped his hands into his pockets. "I've been better, I guess."

He'd known Iva all his life, though she was closer to Anna's age than his. Russ had claimed her just as soon as her red braids had been released and twisted up in a bun, and then wasted no time in filling up his house with their little ones.

The apron she had tied around the waist of her linsey-woolsey might have started out white but now held smudges of dirt across its entire breadth. Her strawberry hair stood in disarray, long since coming loose from its pins, but her cheeks were rosy and her eyes bright.

The little one on her hip blinked at him and blew bubbles through his lips. Tony reached out and tickled the boy's chin, causing him to giggle and swat at Tony's hand.

"You shaved off your moustache," Iva said.

He swiped his hand across his mouth, still trying to get used to having a clean-shaven face. "Feels funny."

"Looks nice, though. You have a right handsome face, Tony."

He smiled.

"I'm sorry about your pa," she said.

"Thanks."

"Well, are you comin' in or not?"

Picking up the suitcase, he crossed the threshold just as his best friend rounded the corner, his large body filling the hall. Russ had one boy wrapped around his leg, the other on his shoulders.

"My turn, Pa! My turn!" the one on his leg yelled.

Russ's face sobered and he lifted Grady off his shoulders. No sooner had Grady's feet hit the floor than they pumped as fast as they could to Tony.

"Unk Tony! Unk Tony!"

Tony lifted him up, throwing him high into the air before catching him and lowering him to the ground. Tony briefly remembered jumping into his own dad's arms once, but his dad hadn't caught him.

Let that be a lesson to you, boy," his father had said. *"Never trust anybody. Not even me."*

Tony felt a tug on his trouser.

"Me too! Me too!" Jason had released Russ's leg and now stood beside Tony with arms up. Tony repeated the ritual with Jason amidst squeals of not exactly fright, but not exactly delight, either.

"Okay, you two," Russ said. "Go on to the kitchen with your mama."

Iva shooed the boys toward the back. "Step lively, now, I've just sliced up some juicy peaches."

All but Myrtle ran to the kitchen.

Russ glanced at the suitcase. "It's true, then?"

"What have you heard?"

"That your daddy left you with nothing but the clothes on your back."

"That about sums it up."

Russ ran his fingers through his sandy hair. It had begun thinning at an alarming rate, leaving him with half the amount he'd had just last year. "I can't believe it. Why?"

Tony shrugged. "Darius has always been the favorite. We've known that from as far back as our memories take us."

And the memories stretched clear back to their one-room school days, when during lunch Tony had miss-kicked a ball outside, nearly knocking a painter off his ladder. The teenaged painter had come after Tony, cursing and whacking him with his paint paddle.

Darius had done nothing more than watch and laugh. Russ, big even then for his age, grabbed the teener and shoved him clear to kingdom come, promising more if the fella didn't leave Tony alone.

They'd been inseparable ever since. Didn't matter that Russ's family lived across the tracks. The two boys were either at Russ's place or Tony's or somewhere in between.

"I came to say good-bye," Tony said.

"Good-bye?" Russ's eyebrows lifted. "You in a rush or do you have time to sit a spell?"

Tony checked his pocket watch. "I've a ticket on the noon train. That leaves me a little less than an hour."

"Well, come on, then."

The two men stepped onto the front porch and settled into a couple of rockers, Myrtle right behind them. She crawled up into her daddy's lap and curled into a ball, sucking vigorously on her thumb.

"What are you going to do?" Russ asked.

"I'm not sure, really." Pulling out his pocketknife, he flipped it open and began to clean his fingernails. "I bought a ticket up to Corsicana. Thought I'd try to see if I could get hired on as a cable-tool worker for Sullivan Oil."

"A toolie! For Sullivan Spreckelmeyer? You gotta be joshing me. You don't know the first thing about it. Do you have any idea how the boys treat rookies? They'd eat you alive."

Tony looked out over the yard. Iva kept it swept, neat, and orderly. No grass, but the azaleas around the house's foundation would rival any in the pampered gardens around the mansion he'd built for his father.

He sighed thinking about all the work he'd put into supervising the construction of that monstrosity, hoping to earn his father's approval. Instead, his father made him pay rent just to live within its walls.

"Are you listening to me, Tony? You know nothing about working in the oil field."

Closing the knife, he returned it to his pocket and set his chair to rocking. "I've been doing the bookkeeping for Morgan Oil since its inception. I've handled its shipments, inspected deliveries, corrected bills, paid bills, recorded payments. If I can do all that, I figure I can manage working in the fields."

"It's nothing like sitting behind that desk of yours. A driller is judged on his ability to fight first and hold his liquor second. What do you think those boys are gonna do when they find out you don't drink?"

"Fight me?" Tony hooked his hands behind his head, leaning back as far as the rocker would allow. "Sure am glad you taught me how to fight, Russ. 'Course, I can't handle a bullwhip the way you can, but I'm plenty good with my fists. So, if that's what they judge a man on first, maybe I'll be exempt from the other. Besides, I'm not qualified to be a driller. I'll have to start on the bottom rung. Nobody's gonna pay any attention to some lowly rope choker."

Russ rested his chin against Myrtle's head. "They will if his last name is Morgan."

"My last name isn't Morgan anymore. I'm going by Mother's maiden name. From here on out, I'm Tony Bryant." He rubbed the skin below his nose. "Besides, I shaved off my moustache. Nobody will recognize me."

Russ shook his head. "I saw that, and ridding yourself of that colossal mess must have taken a good ten pounds off of ya. But moustache or no, it's a small world, the oil business. Everyone is gonna know who you are."

"I don't think so. I never went out to Dad's fields. I spent my time either behind my desk or at the rail station."

"Which brings us back to my point. You aren't cut out for this kinda work. We work from can-see to cain't-see. It's brutal, dangerous, rough, and dirty. You talk like an educated man, but the boys have a vocabulary all their own."

Tony smirked. "You think because I spent my youth sweeping out the church and my adulthood adding up numbers that I don't have the stamina for outdoor labor?"

"I think *you* think you can."

"I'm not afraid of hard work, Russ. And it's not like I can't tell the difference between a Stillson wrench and a pair of chain tongs. Morgan Oil doesn't own one single tool that I haven't inspected and logged in first."

"But do you know what they're used for?"

"I'm a fast learner."

Myrtle began to squirm. Russ set her down, pointed her toward the door and gave her bottom a soft pat. "Go on, Myrtie. Mama's in the kitchen."

They watched her toddle to the door, then struggle to open it. Russ got up, opened it for her and let her inside before returning to his seat. "Maybe I better go with you."

"No, Russ. Thanks, but I need to do this on my own. Besides, you have Iva and the kids. You can't be leaving them."

"And just how long do you suppose Darius will keep me on, do you think? Not long, I'd wager."

Tony popped open his pocket watch and stood. "You're the best driller in the entire state of Texas. And Darius may be a shoddy businessman, but he's no fool. He's gonna need somebody in charge who knows what he's doing."

"But don't you resent it?" Russ asked. "Wouldn't you like to see Morgan Oil go down in flames and Darius with it?"

Not a question Tony wanted to examine too closely. "What I want is to build a bigger and better oil company than Darius ever dreamed of. To do that, I need to know all there is to know about the business. Starting with how to work a rig."

"Maybe I oughta give you my hat. It's splattered with slush from the pits, and no decent driller would be seen without one."

Tony laughed. "I may be a six-footer, but your hat would still swallow me whole. Besides, what would a toolie be doing wearing a driller's hat? Wouldn't be right, somehow." He stuck out his hand.

Russ grasped it. "Do you suppose you'll meet Spreckelmeyer's daughter?"

"What daughter?"

"The bloomer-gal," Russ said, rolling his eyes. "The one that caused such a ruckus up in New York City and had her name plas-tered in all the papers."

"Bloomer-girls," Tony scoffed. "They are nothing but a roly-poly avalanche of knickerbockers."

Russ chuckled. "You better not let your new boss hear you say so. I hear he sets quite a store on that gal of his."

"I figure that unless bloomer girls have suddenly decided to roustabout in those trousers of theirs, then I won't be running into much of the fair sex—seeing as I'll be working from dawn to dusk." He picked up his suitcase.

"Well, you take care of yourself, you hear?" Russ said, slapping him on the shoulder.

"Will do." He'd made it halfway to the gate when Russ's deep bass voice came floating to him in a parody of a popular nursery song.

"Sing a song of bloomers out fer a ride,
With four and twenty bad boys runnin' at her side,
While the maid was coastin', the boys began to sing,
'Get on to her shape, you know,' and that sort of thing."

chapter TWO

TONY CHECKED up and down Bilberry Street. This had to be it. The fellow at the train station had said Sullivan Spreck-elmeyer lived northwest of town in a two-story Georgian, shaded by giant pecan trees on a spacious lot and surrounded by a white picket fence.

It was nothing like the ostentatious Morgan mansion, but the place had all the makings of a well-to-do, respectable family home.

Giving his Stetson a determined tug, Tony opened the gate and approached the front porch that ran the entire width of the house, its cedar posts enhanced with carved appliqués. He paused a moment to admire the work, then took the steps two at a time and allowed himself a quick peek through the screen door.

An open dogtrot ran clear to the back of the house, with rooms on either side and a set of stairs just inside the threshold. He raised his hand to knock, then paused, noticing in the darkness at the top of the stairs a creeping figure looking to the left and right.

Tony jumped back out of sight, then peered around the edge of the door. The figure at the top of the stairs straddled the banister and rode it down, flying off the end and landing with a thump on both feet, arms flung into the air.

Tony lunged forward instinctively, pushing open the screen door, expecting to cushion the fall of a misbehaving boy, but stopped in shock when he found himself facing the back of a woman.

Her infernal knickerbockers—along with the means by which she'd decided to descend the stairs—initially misled him as to her gender. But this was no young lad. This was a fully grown woman. Complete with hat, pinned-up hair, tiny waist, and pointy boots.

Her landing looked perfect at first, but then something on her left side gave, an ankle maybe, and with a squeak, the woman crumbled.

She hit the floor before he could react. Kneeling down, he helped her to a sitting position. "Are you all right, ma'am?"

"My stars and garters," she said, a feather from her hat poking him in the eye. "Would you just look at this?"

Repositioning himself, Tony watched as she propped her left foot onto her right knee, wiggling the heel of her boot. It hung like a loose tooth that should have long since been pulled.

"These are brand-new," she said. "Straight out of the Montgomery Ward catalogue. Can you even imagine?"

What he couldn't imagine was how that hat of hers stayed attached. One-and-a-half times as tall as her entire head, this haberdasher's nightmare had steel buckles, looped ribbons, feathers, foliage, and even a bluebird. The only evidence it gave of her fall was a slight tilt to the left.

She thrust out her arm for assistance. He took her hand and placed his other beneath her elbow, helping her stand.

"Well, you'd think a pair of boots that came clear from Michigan Avenue could hold up a little better than that." She brushed the front of her skirt, then raised her gaze to his.

Thou shalt not covet thy neighbor's wife.

The commandment popped into his head just as he noticed the blue of her eyes, the dimples carved into her cheeks, and the peach color of her heart-shaped lips. He'd thought Spreckelmeyer's wife was deceased. But clearly he was mistaken, for here she was—alive, healthy, and fine looking. He'd had no idea she was so young. And a wheeler, as well. Though it made sense, since the daughter was such an avid cyclist.

He whipped off his hat. "Are you all right, ma'am?"

Narrowing her eyes, she brushed off her backside and glanced at him, the screen door, and back again. "How long have you been standing there?"

"I was just fixing to knock when you, uh, fell."

She touched her hand to her mouth. "You saw me?"

"I saw you fall, ma'am."

She studied him for several seconds before a smile crept up. "I reckon that's not all you saw, is it?"

He answered her smile. "I have no idea what you mean."

She chuckled. "Well, sir. I do apologize and thank you for helping me up."

" 'Twas no trouble. Are you all right?"

"Fine, fine. Heavens, I've taken much worse tumbles than that. Now, is there something I can help you with?"

"Yes, ma'am. I was here to ask your husband if he had any need for a cable-tool worker."

"Ah." Her grin widened. "If you're wanting to speak to my husband, you're going to have one *loooong* wait. But, now, if you wanted to speak with my father, well, you'd find him right through there." She indicated a closed door along the wall.

He felt a surge of blood rush to his face. "I beg your pardon, miss."

"No need to worry yourself." She twirled her hand in a dismissive gesture. "Now, what's your name, son?"

Son? "Tony Bryant, miss."

"Come on, then, Mr. Bryant, and I'll introduce you to Papa." She hobbled a few steps, then came up short and turned back to face him. "You, uh, you won't tell, will you?"

"Tell?"

"About . . . you know." She nodded toward the banister, the bird in her hat coming perilously close to losing its perch.

"I didn't see a thing." He licked his finger, crossed his heart and winked.

"Oh, thank you," she said, her laugh sounding like bell chimes.

She knocked and poked her head inside a door, mumbling something, then threw it open, inviting Tony in with a sweep of her hand.

"Papa? This is Mr. Tony Bryant of . . . ?"

"Beaumont," Tony offered.

"Beaumont," she repeated. "Mr. Bryant, this is my father, Judge Spreckelmeyer."

"Judge?" Tony asked.

"Of the Thirty-fifth Judicial District," she confirmed.

"Come in, come in," Spreckelmeyer said. The robust man with a full gray-and-white beard, and blue eyes just like his daughter's, placed his pen in an ornate brass holder. If his brown worsted suit had been red, the man could have been Santa Claus.

"Would you fetch us some coffee, Esther?" Spreckelmeyer asked.

"I'll bring it right in," she answered, then turned to go.

"Essie?"

She paused at the open door, her hand on the knob.

"Are you limping?" her father asked.

She glanced quickly at Tony before looking down at her feet. "Oh, it's my new boots. The heel snapped right off. Just as I was about to answer the door."

"Those bicycle boots you ordered?"

"Yes. Can you imagine? They just don't make things the way they used to."

"Well, you must take it to the cobbler at once."

"And so I shall. Now, if you will excuse me?"

She backed out of the room and closed the door.

Judge Spreckelmeyer stared after her for a long moment, his frown becoming more and more pronounced. "Surely she didn't slide . . . naw," he muttered, then with a shake of his head, he stood and offered Tony a hand. "Mr. Bryant, please have a seat."

Tony settled into a heavily stuffed wing chair and glanced out a large bay window. The view outside was blocked by a massive oil derrick taking up almost the entire backyard. Nearly every home he'd passed had one.

Corsicana couldn't be more than two square miles, yet it was full to bursting with thousands of oilmen and at least that many derricks, allowing no relief from the pungent odor of gas.

"Now, what can I help you with, young man?"

Tony set his hat on the chair beside him. "I'd like a job as a toolie, sir."

"You ever worked in the patch?"

"Only on the supply end. Never in the actual field. But I've a strong back, a quick mind, and you won't find a harder worker anywhere in the state."

Spreckelmeyer glanced down at some papers on his desk, then moved them to the side. "What do you mean, 'the supply end'?"

"I used to oversee the ordering and shipping of tools and supplies for Morgan Oil."

"What happened?"

"Mr. Morgan died last week and the younger Morgan decided he no longer needed my services."

"You said your name is Bryant?"

"Yes, sir. Tony Bryant."

The judge looked up over the rim of his glasses. "Is that short for Anthony?"

"It is."

"And your age?"

"Twenty-eight."

"Really." He leaned back in his chair. "Interesting."

Before Tony could ask him what he meant, Miss Spreckelmeyer entered with a tray of coffee. Gone were the broken boots, replaced by bicycle shoes covered with gaiters. Tony and Spreckelmeyer rose to their feet.

"Oh, please, sit down. I'll just be a minute." She placed the tray on an oak sideboard and began to pour.

Spreckelmeyer sat. Tony remained standing.

"Do you take cream, Mr. Bryant?" she asked, her back still to him, the bird in her hat wobbling.

"No, thank you."

"Sugar?"

"Yes, ma'am."

"One lump or two?"

"Two, please."

"Ahh. Seems we have us a man with a sweet tooth like yours, Papa."

The affection on Spreckelmeyer's face while he watched her surprised Tony. No wonder people talked about how he doted on his daughter. His own father never would have allowed his feelings to be so transparent.

She turned and handed Tony a cup. "Tsk, tsk. I thought I told you to sit, sir."

"I don't mind standing." He wondered how he ever could have mistaken her for Spreckelmeyer's wife. She was far too young. But it was hardly unheard of for a man to marry a much younger woman. Hadn't his father done the same?

Sipping the coffee, he tried to gauge how old she was but found it difficult. Well past marrying age, that was for certain. Yet she had a fine figure. Barely any lines around the eyes, and none at all around her mouth. He felt sure she was somewhere in her thirties, but beyond that, he couldn't tell.

She set her father's cup and saucer on the desk.

"Why don't you join us, Essie," Spreckelmeyer said. "Mr. Bryant here is interested in working in our fields."

Our fields? Did the man actually include his daughter in his business dealings?

She poured herself a cup—with three lumps, he noticed—picked up his hat and carried it to a coatrack before settling herself in the upholstered chair next to his. Only then did he sit back down.

"What kind of experience do you have, Mr. Bryant?" she asked.

He hesitated, taken aback by her question. Yet Spreckelmeyer seemed perfectly willing to let her take over the interview. "I was just telling your father that I'd cataloged tools and supplies for Morgan Oil before Morgan Senior died."

Her brow furrowed. "We heard about his death. So unexpected. Did you know him at all?"

"I knew him, though we were never close."

"No, of course not." She blew on her coffee. "So you have no experience in the field whatsoever?"

"No, ma'am. Not yet. But I aim to—whether with Sullivan Oil or somebody else."

She exchanged a glance with her father. "Your lack of experience is going to be a problem, I'm afraid. Working in the field is quite a bit different from cataloging tools."

He narrowed his eyes. It was one thing for Russ, an experienced driller, to doubt his abilities, but to sit here and be questioned by a female with birds in her hair was something else altogether.

"Does it look to you like I can't handle it?" he asked, his tone sharper than he'd intended.

And though he'd meant the question rhetorically, she gave him a thorough sizing-up, like she could appraise his merits then and there. In spite of his irritation, he straightened his shoulders.

"You needn't get defensive, Mr. Bryant. There is nothing lacking in your physique. It's your gumption that I'm concerned about."

"I beg your pardon?"

"The fields require a man who can keep calm in the face of danger. I can tell by looking that you're strong, but I've no way of measuring your courage."

He set his cup on the edge of the mahogany desk, careful not to rattle the china. "Are you questioning my manhood, Miss Spreckelmeyer?"

She sighed. "It's nothing personal, just a requisite for the job."

His jaw began to tick. In spite of his troubles, he'd still grown up a Morgan. He might have his hat in hand right now, but he had more mettle in his little finger than this gal could possibly have from the top of her ridiculous hat to the tip of her bicycle shoe-clad toes.

All those newspaper articles he'd read about her came back to him now. He leaned toward her. "There is a difference," he said, "between wearing trousers and being a man."

Her breath hitched, and for the first time since he'd met her, she seemed at a loss for words. She recovered almost at once, however, dabbing at the corner of her mouth with her handkerchief.

"Nevertheless, the oil field is no place for novices. Seasoned oilmen can be killed or crippled in a day's work." She shrugged. "I'm afraid we can't help you."

Tony speared Spreckelmeyer with a questioning stare. Surely the man wasn't going to allow her to make such a decision for him?

But the expression on the old judge's face was unreadable. He held Tony's gaze a moment, then shifted in his chair to address his daughter. "What about that well out on Fourth and Collin, Essie? We could use another man out there."

Her head was shaking before he got the words out. "But he has no experience at all."

"Neither did Jeremy, and look at him now. A derrickman at the ripe old age of eighteen."

"That was different," she said. "That was back in the old days."

Spreckelmeyer chuckled. "Four years ago hardly qualifies as 'the old days.' "

"In the oil patch it does."

The judge said nothing. Tony could not believe this woman held the kind of power she did. Oh, but he'd like to take her down a peg or two. Instead, he kept quiet and waited.

She cocked her head to the side. "Do you really wish to give him a try, Papa?"

Spreckelmeyer shrugged. "He's certainly a strapping fellow."

"And yet he would have us believe he did desk work for a major competitor. He'd have to have had schooling for that."

Tony leaned back in his chair, forcing himself to assume a casual air. Clearly, his trouser comment had hit its mark. He knew he ought to leave well enough alone, but temptation overrode caution.

"Would you like to see my grade-school cards, Miss Spreckelmeyer?" He patted his pockets as if he always kept them at hand. "Or perhaps you could write for references to the schoolmarm from my hometown?"

It was on the tip of his tongue to reveal he'd learned Spencerian penmanship, bookkeeping, banking, and business ethics at no less an establishment than the Bryant & Stratton Commercial College. But those kind of credentials didn't measure an oilman's fortitude.

She stood imperiously, like she was ready to shake the dust of Tony Bryant off her fancy bicycle shoes. He rose politely in response.

"Do what you want, Papa," she said. "But I won't take responsibility for hiring this one."

There was no mystery now as to why this woman had never married. He watched her bloomer-clad body stride out of the room, the blue bird in her hat quivering.

Good, he thought. Now he and the judge could talk man-to-man.

As soon as the door clicked shut, Spreckelmeyer smiled. "Think you could work for a woman, Mr. Bryant?"

"That one?"

The glint in the judge's eye spoke volumes. "None other."

"How much will you pay me?"

chapter THREE

SWEAT DRIPPED into Tony's eyes but he never slowed his pace on the grinding wheel. Pumping his foot to keep the grindstone spinning, he pulled the drill bit across the wheel's surface again and again, raising a burr on the stone that set off an explosion of sparks.

The wheel sat within calling distance of the rig but far enough away to quit grinding if the crew smelled gas. All it would take to blow them to smithereens was a single spark. Over his shoulder, Tony could see the cable-tool boys bailing out the hole. Soon they'd be finished and would need the drill he was sharpening.

Pulling his foot from the pedal and the chisel-like bit from the stone, he dipped the tool in and out of a water bucket to cool the steel. The grindstone whirred almost to a stop before he started it up again and laid the chisel flat on the stone, rubbing it side to side.

After a week on the job, he'd been expecting to have his mettle tested any time, but according to the others, "Grandpa" didn't allow any hazing, harassing, or fighting on the oil patch.

Grandpa, the driller in charge of the rig at Fourth and Collin, was thirty years old and got his nickname from the way he hunched over when he walked. Skilled and proficient, he was a patient teacher, and Tony had made up his mind to be the best hand Grandpa had ever brought up through the ranks.

Most of the other men working the rigs were boomers—here today, yonder tomorrow. All they wanted was a place to sleep, food to eat, and plenty of good whiskey to wash it down. He smiled to himself. A couple just wanted the whiskey.

Not me, he thought. He had a business to build. A mother and sister he still felt responsible for. It killed him that they had to rely on his half brother's mercy, so Tony was determined to provide for them as soon as he could. He would work harder than any man in the patch and move up the chain of command accordingly.

Just a few more rubs and the bit would be ready.

"Ain't ya through with that drill yet, Rope Choker?"

"I'm coming, Gramps," Tony hollered over the sound of the wheel, giving the chisel a couple more swipes before dousing it in water.

"Wall, whatchya been doin' all this time?"

Once the steel cooled properly, Tony jogged to the eighty-two-foot rig, holding the bit in two hands. Three cables ran up and over a pulley system in the crown block at the top of the derrick. One cable was the drilling line, one was for the bailer, and the third to lower and pull casing.

Jeremy Gillespie stood high up on the double board about thirty-five feet above the derrick floor. The eighteen-year-old was wiry, quick, and exceptionally strong. What impressed Tony most, though, was the boy's sense of timing.

Grandpa worked fast, expecting Jeremy to handle those cables and to run or pull pipe without missing a stand. The youth took his trips with a semi-controlled madness that made him as competent an attic hand as a person could be. Not surprisingly, he was no boomer, but a local Corsicanan.

Below him on the derrick floor stood a structure that looked like a giant seesaw. An upright post acted as fulcrum for a horizontal timber. One end of the timber extended over a band wheel. The other end extended into the derrick as far as the center of the floor. Grandpa waited there to inspect the bit.

"Good as new," Tony said, holding the bit while Grandpa attached it to a drilling cable suspended from the timber.

"There we are. You can let her go now."

Tony pulled his hands back and watched Grandpa gently lower the bit into a hole until it rested on the bottom. Once the cable showed some slack, he put a mark on the line three or so feet above the floor and put the rocking beam in motion, raising and dropping the bit as it pounded away at the bottom of the hole.

The chisel would only break up three feet of the black gummy soil before they'd have to stop and bail out all the rock and shale. It was nigh on noon and they'd only drilled about twenty feet.

Tony rubbed the stubble growing on his jaw and thought again of the water-well drillers from the Dakotas. The men were brothers and claimed their rotary drill could go a thousand feet in three days.

They'd set up their contraption in Beaumont and given Tony a demonstration. From all accounts, it looked as if the thing just might be as good as the brothers claimed, but before Tony could commission them, his father had died.

He couldn't help wondering, though, if Darius had followed up. Or if Spreckelmeyer had even heard of them. Maybe he'd go to the judge's house after work and ask him about it.

A man dressed in black with a boy in tow approached Paul Wilson, who was stacking pipe on the north side of the rig. The salty old roughneck was stout in the back, weak in the head, and had the biggest hands Tony had ever seen. He stretched one of them out and shook with the stranger.

"That's Preacher Wortham," Grandpa said, taking hold of the drilling line in order to judge what was going on down in the well. "Good fella."

"Kinda young for a preacher, isn't he?"

Grandpa glanced over at him. "Same age as us, I reckon."

"Exactly."

The driller shrugged. "Don't see why God cain't use him same as some old geezer."

Tony studied Wortham more carefully. Nothing about him looked like any preacher he'd ever known. This one was quick to smile, broad as an ox and probably just as strong.

"That his kid?"

"He's not married. That little fellow's an orphan who was adopted by a local couple a few years back."

The preacher caught sight of the derrickman up in the attic and gave a wave. "What's the weather like up there, Jeremy?" he hollered.

"Purty near perfect, Preacher. You wanna come up and see for yourself?"

"That's a little too high for my liking, I'm afraid."

"Shoot. You've climbed plenty o' trees in your day. This ain't no different."

"The difference is I got older and wiser and prefer to keep my feet planted on solid ground."

Jeremy grabbed the casing line and leaned out over the men, dangling above them. "Well, I got older, too."

"What about wiser?" Wortham asked.

"Married me the prettiest gal in the county, didn't I?"

The preacher chuckled. "That you did, Jeremy Gillespie. That you did."

"Hey there, Harley. What you doin' out here?" Jeremy asked the kid.

The boy cracked a smile, revealing a chipped front tooth. He hooked his thumbs in the straps of his overalls and squinted up at Jeremy. "Preacher's gonna take me fishin' after he's done savin' a few souls."

"It's a good day fer it. Bet they'll be biting."

"The fish or the souls?" Harley asked.

Jeremy laughed. "Both, I reckon."

Stepping up onto the derrick floor, the preacher nodded at Grandpa and offered a hand to Tony. "Howdy. I'm Ewing Wortham, pastor of the First Christian Church on Sixth Street."

"Tony Bryant."

"You're new around here. Where you from?"

"Beaumont."

"Well, welcome to town. You have a wife? Kids?"

"A mother and sister, sir."

"Well, I'd sure like to see y'all join us on Sunday morning. Mr. Alfrey here attends our services. I'm sure he'd make room for you on the pews."

"Sure, Bryant. You come on out with me and the missus." Grandpa adjusted the drilling line, taking up some of the slack so it wouldn't spring up and kink.

"Where's your family staying?" Wortham asked. "I'd love to call on your mother and sister."

"He don't have no family here," young Harley said. "He stays in Mrs. Potter's boardinghouse and keeps purty much to himself. I ain't never seen him go to a saloon even once."

Tony gave the youngster a closer look. He appeared to be about ten, well fed, and with big brown eyes that, apparently, didn't miss much.

"I don't believe we've met," Tony said, extending a hand.

"Howdy. I'm Harley Vandervoort." He pumped Tony's hand. "I have a ma and pa. If'n you come to church, you'd be able to meet 'em."

Tony looked up at the preacher, but Wortham simply smiled.

" 'Courst," Harley continued, "if'n you ever go to the Slap Out, you'd see my pa there. He plays checkers near every day. 'Cept Sunday, of course. You play checkers, Mr. Bryant?"

Tony nodded. "I've been known to play a time or two."

"Well, if'n you come out to the store after supper tomorrow, I'll play you a game. But don't feel bad if you lose. I'm the second-best player in town."

The preacher chuckled and slapped Tony on the back. "Well, then. It's all settled. Checkers on Wednesday. Church on Sunday." Leaning in, he gave Tony's shoulder a squeeze. "Though I'd wager you'll find Sunday more to your liking. We got us some right pretty women all dressed up in their Sunday-go-to-meeting clothes and smelling of rose water. That's sure to be a nice change from looking at these crusty old fellows."

Grandpa shook his head. "Everybody's old to you. Except maybe Jeremy up there. Now go on with you. I got me a rig to run."

Smiling, Wortham tugged on his hat. "See you Sunday." He sauntered across the field toward the rig next door, Harley skipping behind him.

Tony had seen the mercantile called the Slap Out over on Collin Street. A game of checkers would get him out of that cramped boardinghouse and maybe even help clear his mind. He supposed it wouldn't hurt any to visit the First Christian Church either, but he had no intention of tangling with the young ladies there. His mother and sister were counting on him. He had no time for distractions.

"Quit yer squinting at the sun, Rope Choker," Grandpa said. "I've got me some tools over there that still need sharpening."

Taking his cue, Tony returned to the grindstone and started on the next drill bit.

∽

Marrying "down" had certainly agreed with Shirley Bunting Gillespie. The banker's daughter had always been an attractive girl, but after her nuptials to Jeremy—a boy from the other side of the tracks—she'd come into full bloom.

Essie moved away from the refreshment table and signaled the girl with a slight nod.

Immediately, Shirley rapped her gavel on the lectern to get the group's attention. Although she'd dressed in a no-nonsense shirtwaist of starched white cotton, trying to look more the authority figure, nothing could disguise her youthful exuberance. "It is time to resume the meeting of the Corsicana Velocipede Club, ladies."

After making announcements, having the minutes of the last meeting read, and receiving the balance sheet—which showed the club to be in a flourishing condition both financially and numerically—Shirley had adjourned for a short break. At the sound of the gavel, the women began to make their way back to their chairs in the seed-house-turned-bicycle-club.

When the club held its weekly meeting, chairs were arranged facing the bandstand on the north wall of the massive structure, just overlooking the wooden rink that dominated the room. Bleachers flanked the rink down the length of the western wall, and on the opposite side of the building were small rooms set aside for selling bicycles and bicycle parts, along with ready-made clothing and patterns. There was also a small repair shop and an office for the staff.

"As you are all aware," Shirley said, watching the ladies settle, "Mrs. Crook is unable to attend this evening's meeting due to the birth of her twin baby boys a few weeks ago."

A swelling of voices ensued as the ladies shared comments about that celebrated event.

It was sometimes difficult for the women to get away in the evenings, but with the discovery of oil, Corsicana had gone from a quiet farming community to an oil boomtown. And with that growth had come a swell of new "businesses" on the east side of Beaton Street.

And though the bicycle club had many male members, they'd not been able to attend any of the daytime meetings. In an effort to accommodate the men's schedules—and to lure them away from the public houses—the Velocipede Club changed their Tuesday morning meetings to Tuesday evenings. Yet no men came, and the women had long since quit expecting them to.

Shirley struck the lectern three more times. "Please."

They quieted.

"Since Mrs. Crook isn't here to make the introductions, it is my pleasure, as your treasurer, to present our teacher, the founding member and owner of the Corsicana Velocipede Club, Miss Essie Spreckelmeyer. She is going to lead us today in a discussion about a rather delicate matter."

The ladies tittered behind their gloved hands, not daring to speculate aloud as to what that matter might be. Shirley gave Essie an encouraging smile.

When she reached the front of the assembly, Essie placed a basket at her feet. She hadn't braved the topic of bicycle fashion since that debacle in New York. In spite of the effusive compliments she'd received from club members for winning first place, Essie knew many of the ladies had been shocked by the newspaper accounts, most of which were grossly inaccurate.

There were only three reasons a woman's name should ever appear in the Corsicana newspaper: being born, getting married, and keeling over dead. To provoke a full article not just in the *Corsicana Weekly* but in newspapers scattered across the country was nothing short of appalling.

So instead of coming home a reigning queen, she had slinked back with her tail between her legs. But it had been almost three weeks now. She decided it was time to quit her cowering. Steeling herself, she faced her peers.

"Life in a corset is one long suicide," she began. "But nothing short of death will get us to admit it."

The fidgeting stopped. As if everyone were playing a game of freeze tag, no one breathed, or even blinked.

"Ours is a living death, though. Fainting. Indigestion. Restriction of movement. Shortage of breath." She placed a hand against her stomach. "Worse, it can endanger not only a woman who is quickening, but it can harm her unborn child, as well."

She paused to make eye contact with several women in the audience. "Is an hourglass figure really worth all that?"

The murmuring started in the back, and before long many of the women were leaning sideways to whisper with a neighbor. Shirley pretended not to notice and gave Essie another encouraging smile.

Usually, Essie addressed this topic individually with her students during private lessons. Never before had she spoken so openly to the group.

Whether their rumblings were due to the injustice of the corset or the boldness of the topic, she did not know.

"Dr. Weller Van Hook of Chicago recommends cycling for women because it requires the discarding of 'the murderous corset,' as he calls it."

She heard an audible gasp. Glancing over, she saw Mrs. Bogart, the retired preacher's wife, turning an alarming shade of red.

"I'm not suggesting we throw our corsets out altogether," Essie continued. "I do, however, strongly recommend the use of a modified corset while riding."

She reached into her basket and held up a white eyelet bicycle corset. At the sight of the garment, several matrons in the audience covered their mouths and lowered their eyes. Mrs. Bogart sat rigid with shock.

Essie paid them no mind. "Notice its shortened length for easy bending at the waist?" She pulled until the side panels began to stretch. "See that? These panels are made of a new stretchable fabric called elastic, so it's even more flexible. The American Lady Corset Company is offering free bicycle accident insurance for every garment purchased."

At the sound of a bargain, some of the murmuring stopped and a couple of the ladies in the back craned their necks for a better look. Essie continued as if she were discussing something as ordinary as how to fry a chicken. She unfurled a new advertising poster that read, "Pretty Women Who Ride Should Wear Smith's Corsets."

She quoted excerpts from medical journals cautioning women not to cycle in traditional corsets. She even went to the dress form she'd brought from the back room and demonstrated how to lace the corset so it wouldn't cut off the wearer's breath.

"An article in *Lady Cyclist* last week cautioned that a host of sufferings arise from 'interference with the circulation of the blood and the prevention of the full play of the breathing organs,' " she said.

In conclusion, she offered ten percent off any bicycle corsets purchased at tonight's meeting. By the time the evening was over, she had sold a half dozen new corsets.

Mrs. Lockhart approached her afterward and gave her a pat on the arm. "Quite an informative lecture, my dear."

A few short years ago, the petite, elderly widow had worn unrelieved black from head to toe. A more traditional lady couldn't have been found. Since learning to ride the bike, however, she had embraced the modified corset and split skirt—going so far as to wear them even when she wasn't out cycling.

"Thank you, ma'am," Essie said.

"What do you plan to discuss next week?"

"Bicycle Etiquette for Courting Couples."

"Excellent. I shall look forward to it. And how is our young racer coming along?"

Essie smiled. "Splendidly. Mr. Sharpley trains with me five evenings a week. He is quite proficient on the wheel and I think this might be the year for Sullivan Oil to claim the trophy. Wouldn't it be something if Corsicana's hometown oil company won?"

"The townsfolk would be ecstatic. Might even name a street after you."

Essie flushed with pleasure.

Mrs. Lockhart paused in the midst of pulling on her gloves and peered at Essie over the rim of her glasses. "But you're training Mr.

Sharpley five evenings a week, you say? That is quite a bit of time to be spending with a young man without chaperone."

"He's barely eighteen," Essie said, reining in her exasperation. "I hardly think it qualifies."

Mrs. Lockhart buttoned her gloves thoughtfully. "Jeremy married our little Shirley this year, and he's eighteen."

"And Shirley is twenty," Essie whispered, hoping none of the other ladies could overhear. "I, as you well know, am almost twice that."

"Tut-tut. You're merely thirty-three. Plenty of time left yet for breeding."

Essie rolled her eyes. She'd turn thirty-four next week but did not feel inclined to mention that fact. "Good night, Mrs. Lockhart. I shall see you later in the week for your lesson."

After the last of the women shuffled out, she and Shirley began to place the chairs against the wall. They'd barely cleared the first row when Jeremy stuck his head inside the door.

"Is it safe?" he asked in an exaggerated whisper that echoed off the cavernous walls.

"Jeremy!" Shirley squealed, hurrying to him. "We were just straightening up."

The young man strode in with a cocky grin and eyes for nothing but his bride. "I came to walk you home."

"How long have you been out there?"

"Long enough to be glad I wasn't in here with all them harpies."

Shirley swatted his arm. "For shame. Those ladies are the life and soul of this place. Now, come help me and Miss Essie."

"Howdy, Miss Essie," he said, tipping his mud-caked hat. As an oilman's point of honor, his hat stayed filthy, but the rest of him was clean as could be. His starched and pressed blue cotton shirt fit taut across his wide shoulders. He'd cinched his denim trousers with a store-bought belt—which was a good thing, since there was nothing in the south end of his frame to hold those pants up. With the young man's help, they quickly finished storing away the tables and chairs.

"I'll do the sweeping," Essie said. "You two go on."

"Are you sure?" Shirley asked.

"Of course."

"Thank ya, Miss Essie," Jeremy said, grabbing Shirley's hand. "Good night."

She watched the two hurry out, a smile on her lips. Such an unlikely couple. One just never could tell.

Humming to herself, she began to sweep the yawning floor when the hinges on the door squeaked once more.

"Did you forget something?" she asked, looking up.

But it wasn't Jeremy or Shirley or even one of her club members in the doorway. It was the new toolie her father had hired the previous week.

chapter FOUR

"WHY, MR. Bryant. What brings you here?" Essie asked.

The new hire stood in the threshold of her clubhouse, dressed much the way Jeremy had been, but the effect was entirely different. Jeremy had the shoulders, but this man had the chest, forearms, and legs to go with it.

"May I come in?" he asked.

"Yes, of course."

Closing the door behind him, he took off his hat and revealed a thick mat of brown tousled hair. She noted that this past week in the sun had added a bit of color to his face.

"Is there something I can do for you?" she asked.

He glanced over the rink as he moved toward her, obviously impressed by the size of the place. His black boots tracked mud across her floor, but she knew better than to scold him. Oilmen put as much stock in slush-marked boots as they did their hats.

At least she hadn't swept that part of the floor yet. Perhaps she'd make him do it. The thought made her smile.

He took stock of her Parisian toque hat and the cherry velvet bows decorating her chest, elbows, and waist. Stopping at the edge of her skirt with its full four-yard sweep, he tapped his hat against his thigh.

"Miss Spreckelmeyer, are you aware your operation is just about ready for the boneyard? All the boys in Pennsylvania have switched from cable-tool rigs to rotary drills. If you don't make improvements, you'll be obsolete before the year is out."

Her lips parted.

"I've already spoken to your father about it," he continued, giving her no chance to reply. "But he said you were in charge of deciding what supplies he needed and when. So I've come to discuss it with you."

Staring at him, she had no idea how to respond.

He put his hat back on his head and rested his hands on his hips. "You do know what a cable tool and rotary drill are, don't you?"

Good heavens. "Mr. Bryant. How on earth did those Morgans let a man of your qualities slip through their fingers?"

"They shouldn't have."

She arched a brow. "Perhaps I'm mistaken, but last time I checked, you were a toolie with no field experience."

"It doesn't take much experience to see the obvious."

"Well, it's pretty obvious to me that a newly hired employee with nothing to recommend him should know better than to challenge the boss his first week on the job."

"It's not the boss I'm talking to," he said. "It's his daughter. Besides, this isn't a challenge. I'm trying to help you."

She drew up to her full height. "I regret to inform you, sir, that I am not only your boss, I am also part owner of Sullivan Oil and have all the power that goes along with it. Furthermore, we don't need any help."

"You need more than help," he said, looking her over from top to bottom. "You could use an entire overhaul."

She clenched the broom handle. "Just what is that supposed to mean?"

"It means that a rotary can drill almost a thousand feet in three days."

A thousand feet? In three *days?* Impossible. It took their cable-tool rigs at least three weeks to go that deep.

"How would you know?" she asked.

"I've seen them."

"In Pennsylvania? You've been to Pennsylvania?"

"No. I saw a demonstration down in Beaumont."

"A demonstration. I see. And what guarantee would I have that this rotary could drill into the black Corsicana soil? It's nearly unbreakable and gummy, to boot."

He shrugged. "Those Baker boys up in the Dakotas have been using rotaries to drill for water in all that hard rock they call ground. I don't know how successful they were at finding water, but I can tell you they were plenty successful at drilling."

"And what magical principle makes this rotary drill bore so quickly?"

"A mule."

"A mule?"

"Rotaries are completely different from cable tools," he explained. "It's kind of like a giant screw. Here, give me your broom." Plucking it from her hand, he clamped his fist around the handle. "You attach a gripping device to a very strong rod with a cutting tool at its tip." Spinning the broom upside down, he ground it against a knot in the floorboard. "Then rotate it. The tip cuts into the ground as it turns."

"Where does the mule come in?"

"You put an extension on the rod, then attach it to the mule. The mule goes round and round and round in the same small circle. Basically, he rotates the cutting tool."

What he said made sense. Her grandfather used to have a maple syrup mill that ran much the same way. And she could see Bryant believed in this new method. But a thousand feet in three days? That was awfully hard to take seriously. "How much are they?"

"Around six hundred dollars, I believe."

"Six hundred dollars! Do you have any idea how many wells Sullivan Oil has? We can't replace all our cable tools at that price when there is absolutely nothing operationally wrong with the rigs we have."

"If you don't, then you're done for. Morgan's just a couple hundred miles away with money and slow-producing wells. If he commissions the Baker boys first, his wells will start producing at a rate you couldn't possibly compete with. But if Morgan hasn't hired them yet, you could. Morgan's oil isn't as pure as yours, and if you convert to rotaries, you'll leave him and everybody else in the dust."

She pursed her lips. With her trip to New York and then the accompanying scandal, she'd had her mind on other things recently. Sullivan Oil's competition had never been a big concern and, therefore, made his dire predictions rather hard to believe.

She studied his face. For all his exasperating presumption, he at least seemed honest. But for a clerk to hire on for field work, then come back a week later with news like this . . . something just didn't add up.

"And why exactly are you so bent on Sullivan Oil having the upper hand?" she asked.

He shrugged. "Because it's in my best interest for you to succeed."

"Oh really?"

"Keeps my belly and pockets full."

"Well, if we spend all our money and have to borrow more just to buy all these new drills, then more bellies than yours will go empty. Pockets too."

"Don't you understand what I'm saying? This decision isn't something that can be put off. It could make or break Sullivan Oil's entire future." He tunneled his fingers through his hair. "I cannot believe your father is leaving this up to you."

"Be careful, Mr. Bryant, lest you find yourself with no job at all. Then what will happen to your belly and pockets?"

"What's the matter? Is your feminine constitution too fragile to take a business risk?"

"That is quite enough, sir."

He stepped back, letting go of the broom. Too late, she reached out to catch it, but it slapped to the floor, the sound echoing off the walls.

"You're the one trying to move within a man's world, *Miss* Spreckelmeyer. And men don't sugarcoat the facts or run away from a chance to grow and expand their businesses. We face challenges head on. And we do so without fear of losing our jobs. If you don't want to take this small-time operation and turn it into something that rivals the companies up in Pennsylvania, then get yourself back in the kitchen where you belong."

She bent down and snatched up the broom. "I won't be going back to the kitchen, sir, but you will be looking for a new employer. You're fired."

His eyes darkened with anger. "Now, that's exactly what I'm talking about. You let a woman wear the britches and she gets way too big for 'em."

She took a step forward, but he did not retreat. "I will have you know, Mr. Bryant, that Sullivan Oil is the largest producer of oil in this entire state."

"Not for long. Not if you refuse to recognize progress when you see it."

"Get out."

"No. You need me. Now, get off your high horse and let's talk about this—man-to-man."

"You don't seem to have grasped the situation, sir. You are no longer an employee of Sullivan Oil. So there is no need for us to talk. Man-to-man or otherwise."

He stared at her for several seconds. The patch of skin under his sunburned nose was burned more than the rest of his face, making him look like a child who'd drank too much cherry juice.

But there was nothing childlike about his thick neck. His piercing gaze. His lips and square jaw. Nor the hollow beside his mouth that formed a deep groove when he smiled.

He heaved a sigh, his animosity falling away like a collapsing crinoline. "I can't afford to lose my job."

"You should have thought about that earlier."

"Your father is too busy with his judicial duties to give the oil company the attention it needs, and you spend most of your time in here," he said, stretching his arm out in a gesture that encompassed everything from the wooden floor to the rafters above.

"You've worked in the fields for one week, Mr. Bryant. You barely even look the part. How can you possibly presume to know enough to advise me?"

"And just how many hours have *you* worked in the field?"

Ignoring him, she returned to her sweeping.

"It's not only the rotary drills, Miss Spreckelmeyer," he continued, following behind her. "There's other changes that need to take place, as well. And soon."

"My stars and garters," she mumbled.

He gently clasped the broom handle, stopping her. "Don't let your pride stand in the way of the good of your father's company. 'Dare to be wise.' "

Was he quoting Horace to her? Surely not.

" 'It is not wise to be wiser than is necessary,' " she responded.

He raised his left brow. " 'Some folks are wise and some are otherwise.' "

Jerking the handle away from him, she touched the bristles of her broom against his boots as if she could perhaps sweep him away. "The door is that way, Mr. Bryant. Good night."

He bucked the bristles with his foot, a tick in his jaw setting up a rapid pace. After the slightest of hesitations, he strode to the door and slammed it behind him.

The following afternoon, Sheriff Melvin Dunn and Deputy Billy John Howard stepped through Essie's back door and into the kitchen.

"Hey, darlin'," the sheriff said. "How's my girl?"

Cracking an egg into a small bowl, Essie looked at her uncle. "I'm all right. I suppose you came by to check on Papa?"

"I did. How's he holding up?"

She began to whip the egg, thinking of how surprised the law-breakers would be to discover their big, husky sheriff had a heart as soft as butter. It was the two-year anniversary of Mother's death, and grief over her passing continued to plague Papa. And though Uncle Melvin came by on the pretense of seeing him, she knew he grieved for his only sister as well.

"He's sequestered himself back in his study," she said.

He hung his hat on a peg, revealing a head of hair with more gray than brown. "Something smells mighty good in here," he said, giving her a kiss on the cheek. "How come you're doing the cooking? Where's Mrs. Carmichael?"

"Her rheumatism was bothering her again, so Papa sent her on home. I was just whipping up some veal soup. Would you like to stay for supper?"

He patted his belly, which had grown rounder over the last couple of years. "Better not. I'm watching my girlish figure. Besides, Verdie's expecting me home any minute." He headed toward Papa's study. "Be back in a minute."

The clacking of her eggbeater sounded loud in the sudden quiet. She knew she should acknowledge Deputy Howard, but she was loathe to encourage even polite conversation.

He stood just inside the door, tracking her every move. He was small in stature and had the face of an angel, but in the six months since Uncle Melvin had deputized him, he'd enjoyed the power of his badge just a little too much for her liking.

Her uncle was blinded to the deputy's shortcomings, though, for Billy John Howard was grandson to a close friend—who also happened to be the Texas secretary of state.

Without bothering to remove his hat, Deputy Howard sauntered to the stove and lifted the lid off her cast-iron pot. "Ummmm. I sure do love veal soup." He dipped his finger in the broth, then licked it off. "And I'm not growing soft in the middle like your uncle."

The thought of his grimy finger fouling her supper curdled her stomach. She strode to the stove and poured the egg into the pot, ignoring his attempt to finagle an invitation.

He leaned in toward her and inhaled deeply. "I do believe I smell dessert. I always like a little something sweet after my meals, don't you?"

She placed her fingertips on his chest and pushed. "You're crowding me. Do you mind?"

Capturing her hand, he brought it to his lips. "Not at all. I don't mind in the least little bit."

She snatched her hand out of his grasp. "Deputy Howard, you are making me uncomfortable."

"Call me Billy John. Come on now, sweetheart, let me hear you say my name just once."

"That is quite enough!"

"Uh-oh," Uncle Melvin said, coming back through the archway. "What've you gone and done now, Billy John?"

Deputy Howard took a casual step back and removed his hat. "Oh, I'm just teasin' her some. Telling her how a bowl of veal soup would cure me of my ailment, but she got mighty prickly about it."

Uncle Melvin chuckled. "Now, Essie, don't be so hard on him. It's been a month of Sundays since that boy's had himself a home-cooked meal."

"I thought that *boy* had dinner with you and Aunt Verdie last week?"

"Well, that's not quite the same, is it, Deputy?"

Howard turned up his smile. "I do enjoy Mrs. Dunn's cookin', sir, but having a meal put together by Miss Spreckelmeyer surely does sound right nice."

She poured a cup of milk into the soup. "Perhaps another time."

Replacing his hat on his head, he nodded. "I'll be countin' on it, ma'am."

Uncle Melvin opened the door. Deputy Howard passed through it, his footfalls heavy as he made his way off the porch.

When the door remained open, she looked back over her shoulder.

Uncle Melvin stood puzzled, his hand on the knob. "What is it about him that rubs you so raw?"

"How much time do you have?"

He chuckled. "Oh, I know you told him to leave you be, and if he doesn't, you just tell me and I'll talk to him. But, girl, he really has taken a shine to you."

"I'm not interested."

"You're nearly thirty-four, Essie. He's a good man, and if you don't take him, you might not ever—"

She slammed the lid on the pot. "I'm not interested."

He held up his hands. "All right. All right."

Sighing, she wiped a spot of milk off the stove with her apron. "How was Papa?"

"Struggling. Tonight's supper won't be easy." He gave her a sad smile, retrieved his hat and quietly closed the door behind him.

Essie slumped against the stove. When it came to his deputy, Uncle Melvin wore blinders. She couldn't understand how such a shrewd judge of character could be as deluded as Melvin was to Mr. Howard's true nature. She'd begged Papa to intervene, but he always demurred.

"If you've heard rumors about the man, then you can be sure Melvin has, too. If he chooses not to credit them, then we ought to respect that. No amount of arguing will change his mind."

"So you won't say anything?"

"Essie," he'd said. *"Is it the stories about the deputy that bother you, or is it the fact that he's intrigued by you?"*

She moved to the washbowl, dipped a rag into it, then wrung out the water. Perhaps her father was right. If the townsfolk told tales about Deputy Howard, goodness knows they told more about Essie herself. Perhaps the rumors about Howard were as false as the ones about her.

But why couldn't the deputy pursue some other woman? As Uncle Melvin had reminded her, she was well into her thirties and had another birthday fast approaching. She might not have a man, but she didn't want one, nor did she need one.

Her work in the bicycle club brought great satisfaction, and she enjoyed helping Papa with Sullivan Oil. Her neighbors and friends had known her all her life and loved her. She attended a thriving church. She had a wonderful God.

No, she didn't need a man to make her whole. She was whole already. Picking up the egg bowl, she wiped it clean, then placed it on the shelf.

Her only wish was for a close female friend. She knew plenty of women and most all of them cared for her and would help her if she were in need. But she didn't have a confidante.

Now that her mother was gone, she found herself longing for another woman who could give her an opinion on which hat would best suit her new outfit. Or someone she could play a duet with on the piano. Someone to go bike riding with. Someone to share a cup of coffee with.

For a while, Essie thought perhaps Shirley would fill that role. But her helper at the club was almost fifteen years younger than she, a new bride and a bit too whimsical to suit Essie's taste. They were friends, but the intimate rapport she longed for had yet to materialize.

She gave the soup a stir and tried to recall ever having a girl chum. But even as a child, her friends were always boys. And she got along with them famously.

Didn't matter the age, the occupation, or even how long she'd known them. If they were male, she had something in common with them.

Boys loved the outdoors. They didn't play catty games with each other. They spoke their minds. They were everything she'd ever wanted in a friend. Even now, in spite of the many women who had embraced the Velocipede Club, she was closest to Mr. Sharpley, the young man she was training for the Corsicana Oil & Gas Bicycle Invitational.

Yet lately she found she'd rather stitch a sampler than climb a tree. Or read a book of poetry instead of hunt snakes. Oh, she still enjoyed the outdoors, but having a man for a chum simply wasn't practical at this juncture of her life. Besides, she couldn't whisper secrets and press flowers or discuss facial creams with a man. There were some things only a woman could understand.

Picking up a teakettle, she put some water on to boil. It didn't do to dwell on such thoughts. God knew her heart's desire for a friend. She would wait on Him, and He would bring it to pass. It was only a matter of time.

chapter **FIVE**

ESSIE DISHED veal soup into two bowls, then called her father to the table. She hoped Uncle Melvin's visit had brought Papa some comfort. He stepped into the kitchen, his eyes puffy.

She set down their ice tea glasses and walked into his arms. He wrapped them clear around her shoulders, squeezing her so tightly she couldn't breathe.

"I don't think I can eat in here tonight, Squirt. Would you mind if we ate on the porch instead?"

She patted his back. "Of course not, Papa. We're having soup, so it'll be no trouble to move outside."

He released her and pinched a napkin against his tea glass in one hand, then tucked his spoon and bowl in the other.

From the porch, they could look across the flat, coastal plain of East Texas where the town of Corsicana resided. Black silhouettes of derricks too numerous to count stretched to the sky, the smell of oil riding on the breeze. Dusk coated the blue above them, frosting it with deep navy clouds. Magenta fired the clouds out on the far horizon and glazed those closer to them.

Crickets chattered, toads bleated, whippoorwills sang out their names over and over. The creaking of Papa's rocker joined in, his napkin riding the slope of his stomach, his bowl resting in his lap, untouched.

A large, broad man, he held a commanding presence and had earned the respect of most everyone in town, garnering their votes election after election. Essie hated to see him in such a dolorous state.

"I heard you fired the new toolie last night," he said finally.

She hesitated a moment before finishing her bite. "Yes."

"Grandpa was none too happy when he found out. According to him, Bryant was the soul of courtesy—fearless, punctual, and hardworking."

She scooped up slices of potato and onion.

"You gonna tell me about it or not?" he asked.

She dabbed her lips. "You gonna eat or not?"

He placed a spoonful of soup in his mouth.

"Mr. Bryant barged into the club after everyone had left and started ordering me around," she said.

"Ordering you around? How so?"

"He demanded we convert all our rigs to rotaries, or else."

"Or else what?"

"Or else we'd become obsolete."

"He said that?"

"More or less." She waved her spoon at his bowl.

He took another bite. "I talked at length about the rotary drills with Mr. Bryant before I sent him out to see you. I'd been reading about them and was actually toying with the idea of updating."

She set her empty bowl on the small round table between them. "Well, heavens. You've not said a word. Why didn't you tell me?"

"I was going to, but I've been . . . distracted." His gaze roved over the sky. There was only the barest hint of magenta left.

Her heart squeezed and she laid a hand on his arm. "I'm sorry, Papa. I know this month has been hard on you."

His beard quivered.

"The rotary drills are terribly expensive," she said, "but if you'd like for me to write up an assessment, I can."

"Please," he whispered, rubbing his eyes with his thumb and finger.

She placed her napkin on the table, gathered her skirts and knelt before him. His hand now rested against his entire face.

She removed the bowl from his lap and placed it on the table. "I'll write up a report first thing tomorrow."

He nodded. "Would you re-hire Bryant also, please?"

She bit her lower lip. "I'd rather not."

Papa lowered his hand and looked at her, his expression turning protective. "Was he fast with you?"

"No, no. Just . . . officious."

"I imagine he's not very used to discussing business with a woman."

"What's he doing discussing business with either one of us? He's a toolie, for heaven's sake. And a novice at that."

"Don't kid yourself, Essie," he said. "He knows the oil business. Somehow he secured a higher-up position for himself in Morgan Oil without ever having to get his hands dirty. He's a pencil pusher, not a rope choker. Doesn't mean he's ignorant."

"I don't like him."

"I don't think he much likes you, either."

"I stopped caring a long time ago what men think of me," she said. "Anyway, he's probably already left town."

"I saw him at the Slap Out playing checkers with young Harley just before I came home for supper."

She took his hands into hers. "Why is he so important to you, Papa?"

"Why's he so repugnant to you? It's not as if you've never had to tangle with a fella who didn't like the idea of taking orders from a female."

Full dark had descended and she could no longer distinguish his features. "He said I was too big for my britches."

Papa chuckled. "And so you are."

She started to pull away, but he squeezed her hands. "Now, Squirt, you know there's a bit of truth to that. And what does it matter one way or the other? Bottom line is, you're his boss. He'll come around."

If he'd asked on any other day, she'd have put up more resistance. But she simply didn't have the heart to argue with him tonight. "Will you hire him back, Papa, so I don't have to?"

Standing, he brought her to her feet, as well. "I'd rather you do it. I'd like to be alone for a while, if it's all right with you."

She frowned. "You mean, you want me to go find him right now? This minute? And leave you alone in the house?"

"Yes, please."

"Can't it wait until tomorrow?"

"He's leaving at first light."

"But what if he's left the Slap Out already? I wouldn't have a clue as to where he might go. He could be anywhere."

"You'll find him." The words came out a croak. And she realized Papa truly did need to be alone with his memories without worrying she might overhear him grieving.

"Very well," she sighed. "You sure you'll be all right?"

He pulled her into another hug but gave her no assurances.

❧

Tony could not believe he was being trounced in checkers by a ten-year-old. They'd been playing for best out of five, but when Tony went down early by two games, he'd convinced Harley to play the best out of seven. It was three to one. Harley.

The child's shiny black hair had been parted on the side but would not stay slicked down. The barrel that the checkerboard rested on came up to his chest.

He jumped two of Tony's pieces before landing on his king row, then leaned against his cane chair. "Crown, please," he said with a smirk.

The door to the Slap Out—where Corsicanans came if they were slap outta something—was propped open by a basket of oranges, giving Tony a view of the darkening sky. The smell of stale coffee, tobacco, and vinegar wrestled for dominance over the mercantile. Mr. Crook, the slim and fastidious man who owned the store, began to prepare for closing.

"How'd you learn to play checkers so well?" Tony asked.

"Miss Essie taught me."

"Miss Essie?" Tony asked, his finger poised on the checker he was fixing to move. "Miss Essie Spreckelmeyer?"

"Yep."

The boy's grin irritated Tony. Because of that pompous, short-tempered woman, he'd be heading over to Powell's oil patch in the morning looking for another job. "You play checkers with her?"

Harley shook his head. "Not if I can help it. I cain't hardly ever beat her."

Tony slid his piece into a position to jump one of Harley's blacks.

The boy leaned forward and studied the board. "Me and her go way back."

Way back? The boy was only ten. "You're friends, then?"

"Thicker 'n calf splatter."

"She fired me yesterday." Tony couldn't keep the edge from his voice.

Harley snorted. "What'd ya do? Kick a dog or somethin'?"

"No. I told her she needed to update her father's rigs."

The boy looked up from the board. "Told her or askt her?"

"Told her."

The shopkeeper, sweeping between two tables, began to chuckle.

Harley shook his head. "She don't like to be told what to do. But she's a square shooter and once you're her friend, she'd back you 'til Sittin' Bull stood up."

"That a fact?"

"Sure is." Harley moved his piece out of harm's way.

The unmistakable sound of a lady's bootheels approached the open door, then stopped. Tony looked up. Speak of the devil.

"Good evening, Hamilton," Miss Spreckelmeyer said to the shopkeeper. "I was afraid you might be closed already."

Crook set his broom aside. "No. Katherine has ladies from the Benevolent Society upstairs fawning over the twins. I thought I'd hide out here for a while longer."

Tony couldn't help staring, though she paid him no mind. She could pretend all she wanted that she hadn't noticed him there, but he knew better.

She wore a simple skirt and white shirtwaist with a relatively plain straw hat. Her entire countenance had mellowed the moment she'd seen Crook, and mention of the babies had provoked a tender expression.

"They're so adorable, Hamilton," she said. "I could gobble them right up."

Crook pushed his spectacles farther up onto his nose. "Yes, they're something special, all right." His expression sobered. "I've been thinking about you today. How's your father?"

The softness about her melted into melancholy. "It's been a difficult day for us both."

"I'm sorry," Crook said. "What brings you to the store at this hour?"

She looked somewhat at a loss, then noticed the basket of oranges holding open the door. "I'd like one of these, please."

"An orange? You came all the way out here for an orange?"

"Yes, please." She picked one up and gently squeezed it. "Can you put it on our tab?"

Crook eyed her curiously but didn't argue.

"Your turn, Mr. Bryant," Harley said.

Tony turned his attention back to the board, but he could see Miss Spreckelmeyer out of the corner of his eye. She made a show of noticing them for the first time, then approached the barrelhead slowly, her boots tapping the floorboards.

"Good evening, Harley," she said.

"Hey, Miss Essie. Sorry you're havin' a bad time. What's the matter?"

She gave the boy a sad smile. "My mother died two years ago today."

Harley's face collapsed. "I'd forgotten it was today. The judge all right?"

"As good as can be expected, I suppose."

Tony had learned Mrs. Spreckelmeyer was deceased, but, of course, had no idea this was the anniversary. The anger he felt toward Essie dulled a bit in light of the circumstances.

She turned to him. "Mr. Bryant."

He stood, snagging Harley by the shirt collar and lifting him to his feet, as well.

"Miss Spreckelmeyer," he said. "I'm sorry for your loss." Harley squirmed away from Tony's grip.

"Thank you," she said. "And, please, don't mind me. Go ahead and resume your game."

He grabbed a chair from beside the potbellied stove and brought it to the barrel, holding it in readiness. Smoothing her skirts beneath her, she sat. He and the boy followed suit.

"Who's black?" she asked.

"I am," Harley replied.

"Hmmm." She and Harley exchanged a smile.

Tony frowned at the board.

"Shouldn't you be home having supper?" she asked Harley while cutting into the orange's skin with her thumbnail.

"Ma, Brianna, and a couple of ladies are upstairs fussin' over Mrs. Crook's babies. Ma told me to wait here for her."

"Brianna's here?" Essie asked, glancing at a curtain that led to a back room. "Brianna Pennington?"

"Yep."

"I heard you've been teaching her how to fish."

Harley scratched his chest. "Reckon you heard right."

Essie cocked her head. "How's she doing?"

"She won't put worms on her hook. Thinks it's mean. So I'm gonna take her snake hunting. No killin' involved in snake hunting."

Tony glanced at Essie, waiting for her to raise an objection to Harley doing something so foolhardy—particularly with a girl in tow. But she didn't so much as bat an eye.

"Who's Brianna?" he asked.

"You know," Harley said. "She's one of them Pennington girls. There's a whole passel of 'em, aren't there, Miss Essie?"

"There sure are." She turned to Tony. "Bri's the youngest of the cooper's eight daughters. Her mother died about three years ago."

Nodding, Tony moved his piece. Essie paused in the peeling of her orange to assess his move and again gave Harley the slightest of smiles.

"We're playing best of seven," Harley said. "I've already won three out of four."

Tony stiffened. Essie might have been irascible last night due to her distress over her mother's anniversary, but that was no call to fire him, nor to gloat over him being beaten by this kid in knee pants.

She split open the orange, and its fresh smell filled their corner of the store.

"Hadn't seen ya around much lately," Harley said.

She offered him a sliver of fruit. "I've been busy training Mr. Sharpley for the bicycle race."

She offered Tony a piece, too, but he declined with a wave of the hand.

Harley popped his slice into his mouth. "How come you're not trainin' him tonight?"

"I had planned to spend the evening with Papa, but he retired early."

"I hear Sharpley's purty fast." He slid a black piece onto a square that would allow him to jump one of Tony's, unless Tony jumped him first.

Tony propped his elbows on his knees, trying to figure out if it was a trap.

"I have high hopes for Mr. Sharpley," she said. "You should come by one evening and see him for yourself."

"Sure. That is, if Ma will let me."

"I'll speak to her for you."

The boy beamed. "See?" he said to Tony. "I done told you she was a good egg."

Her gaze touched Tony's before skittering away. Just then, several chattering women poured through a curtained partition at the back of the store, disrupting their concentration.

Essie moved to greet them. Tony stood.

"Hello, Essie, dear. Have you seen the babies yet? Precious, simply precious."

"Yes, Mrs. Vandervoort. They are indeed adorable. How do you do, Mrs. Tyner, Mrs. Whiteselle?"

The women greeted Essie with warmth, then swept past her and Crook, pulling on their gloves while continuing to extol the virtues of the babies they'd been to visit.

"Hey, Harley," said a girl of about eight with reddish brown braids. "Whatchya doin'?"

"Climbin' a tree. What does it look like I'm doin'?"

Scrunching up her nose, she stuck her tongue out at him.

Mrs. Vandervoort, a woman with salt-and-pepper hair and shaped like a cracker barrel, signaled the children.

"I gotta go, Mr. Bryant. Miss Essie can take my place for me."

"Oh, I'm sure—" he began.

"I'd be glad to finish up the game for you, Harley," Essie said.

Smiling, the boy nodded. "Come on, Bri." He waved to Tony and ran out the door to catch up with Mrs. Vandervoort, who looked better suited to be his grandmother than his mother. Brianna scampered behind him, braids bouncing.

Essie settled into Harley's seat and took a small bite of orange. A drop of juice formed at the corner of her mouth. Without ever taking her attention off the board, she pressed the butt of her hand to the liquid, stopping its descent.

"I'm afraid Harley has you in a pickle, Mr. Bryant. Would you like to cry uncle?"

He had no interest whatsoever in playing checkers or anything else with this woman. But he'd be hornswoggling something fierce before he gave up, especially to her. "I'm not sure all is lost just yet."

"Whose turn is it?"

"Mine." Reclaiming his chair, he jumped the disc Harley left open.

She quickly moved a piece on the other side of the board. The store owner carried the carton of oranges inside, allowing the door to slam shut behind him.

"Your turn," she said.

She studied him with eyes the color of bluebells, disconcertingly direct. Having a ten-year-old flounce him was humiliating enough. He wasn't about to let Essie Spreckelmeyer do the same. Tony needed time to examine the board, but after she'd moved her piece so quickly, he'd look like a fool if he dawdled.

He slid a disc into her king row. She crowned it and moved one of her pieces toward the center.

"I'm calling it a day, Essie," Crook said, removing his apron. "Will you turn down the lantern when you're done and go out the back?"

"Of course." She twisted around. "Are you sure you don't mind?"

He smiled. "You know I don't. Just make sure this fella goes with you when you leave."

"Will do. Good night, Hamilton."

"Good night, Essie." He nodded toward Tony. "Bryant."

Crook's footsteps clunked on a set of stairs behind the partition before the sound of a door opening and closing sealed off the silence in the mercantile.

"You and Mr. Crook must be pretty good friends for him to let you stay in here after hours."

"I used to work here, is all. He knows I'll leave everything in its proper place. It's your turn."

Of his four pieces left, he could only move his crowned one safely. He headed it in the direction of one of her more vulnerable blacks, trying to figure out why she had offered to finish out the game for Harley. From all indications, she didn't care for his company any more than he cared for hers.

She slid her king into an attacking position. Tony would have no choice but to move out of her way or be jumped.

"Why did you stay just now, Miss Spreckelmeyer? Why didn't you leave when Harley and the others did?"

Her lips flattened a bit. "Actually, I was looking for you."

"Me?" Surprise tinted his voice.

"Yes." She struggled for a moment, clearly unhappy with whatever it was she had to say, then straightened her spine and gave him her full attention. "Papa wants me to reinstate you."

Leaning back in his chair, he hooked an arm over the backrest. *Well, well, well. What do you know about that?* "He was in here just before sunset. Why didn't he say something?"

"He wanted to discuss it with me first."

"And what happened when the vote was one in favor and one against?"

She rent the last two slivers of orange in two. "I conceded under duress."

"Duress?"

"I didn't want to upset Papa by arguing with him tonight. But rest assured, had it been any other night, you would be on your way out of town."

He leaned his chair back on two legs. "What makes you so all-fired sure I still even want to work for Sullivan Oil?"

Hope kindled within her eyes. "You don't have to if you don't want to."

He dropped his chair to the floor and slid his checker to a safer square. She finished off her orange, then bullied another of his discs with a different king. Their pieces danced for several more moves—hers charging his, then his charging hers.

"Are you going to switch to rotary drills?" he asked.

She took so long to answer, he thought she was going to ignore the question.

"We're considering it," she finally conceded.

The woman clearly did not like to eat crow. And if he were a betting man, he'd guess she didn't do it often.

He faced off his king against hers. "I'll expect a raise, of course."

Her mouth slackened. "A raise? Don't you think that's a bit precipitous?"

"I think it's the least you can do."

She puckered her lips. "You may have your old job back, Mr. Bryant, at the same rate as before." Reaching for a single black disc, she jumped all four of his remaining markers. "Take it or leave it."

chapter SIX

TONY STOMPED on his shovel, sinking it into the gummy soil, then hoisted up a load of dirt. As soon as he'd returned to the rig, Grandpa promoted him from toolie to roustabout, and he'd spent the morning picking up broken rods, junk pipe, and connections so the men wouldn't stumble as they scurried around the well. He'd discharged the lines to safeguard against leaks. He'd put new clamps on a broken sucker rod. And now he was digging a ditch for the saltwater that had accumulated in the stock tank. Once he filled the ditch with the water, he'd have to figure out how to make the liquid evaporate.

Arching his back, he glanced up at Jeremy on the double board. The boy was juggling elevators—resting one pipe on a device used to lift and lower drill pipe while fitting a collared pipe to a second device, pulling some pipe, then shifting a giant hook back to the other elevator. The process was tedious and the greatest crusher of fingers ever invented, yet Jeremy never missed a beat.

Paul Wilson, their roughneck, had made a visit out to the old pecan tree thirty yards east of the rig and was hotfooting it back. Tony smiled, thinking that what the old fellow lacked in brain power, he made up for in brawn.

Instead of returning to the pipe he was stacking, though, Wilson snatched up his knuckleduster and bullets, then hurried back to the tree.

Tony tossed down his shovel and jogged after him. "What is it, Wilson?"

"I spotted a squirrel up in that there pea-can tree and I mean to get me a piece of it," he hollered over his shoulder.

Tony slowed, coming to a stop several yards behind Wilson. Toolies, roughnecks, roustabouts, and pipeliners from the surrounding rigs left their posts. All work came to a standstill as they watched Wilson shoot up a box of twenty shells.

For ten minutes he and the squirrel played chase. Men cheered poor Wilson on while simultaneously making bets against him. When he'd fired his last shot, the untouched squirrel eyeballed him from the edge of a branch, flicked his tail, then jumped to another tree and darted out of sight.

Throwing down the empty box of ammunition, Wilson cursed the varmint. Red-faced, he plowed through the crowd and headed back toward the pipe he'd been stacking.

The fellas slapped him on the shoulder as he went through their gauntlet. "Didn't know you was such a crackshot, Wilson."

"Where'd ya learn to shoot? At Lady Pinkham's School of Charm?"

"I'm thinking ol' Crackshot would've had a better chance of finding hair on a frog than pullin' that squirrel's picket pin."

"Maybe you oughter join up with Miss Spreckelmeyer's shootin' class fer ladies. Now, there's a gal that could fill a hide so full o' holes it wouldn't hold hay."

Tony tried to pinpoint who'd called out that last remark, but the crowd was too dense.

"Back to work, fellas," Moss hollered. "We ain't being paid to laze around in the sun."

As tool pushers go, Moss was a whopdowner—hard, mean, and ugly. He didn't put up with any lip or lollygagging. No one openly criticized him, though, because he had a few loyalists who would frail your knob if you low-rated him. He looked after all of Sullivan Oil's rigs and had the stroke to hire and fire.

Catching Tony's attention, he motioned him over. "I see the old bicyclette changed her mind about you."

"It's the judge who's responsible for me being here."

"I wouldn't put any money on it if I were you." Moss had a laugh that sounded more like a growl. "The lady of the house wields a mighty sword and you'd best be remembering it."

Someone from a rig up the way called for Moss, and the tool pusher headed his direction.

"He's right, ya know," Jeremy said, falling into step beside Tony. "Miss Essie pretty much runs the place. Even Moss reports directly to her."

"Why?" Tony asked. "Why doesn't the judge manage it?"

"He kinda lost interest when his wife died. So Miss Essie took over and it's been that way ever since."

They reached the sump Tony was digging and paused. "Is it true what that fellow said?" Tony asked. "About Miss Spreckelmeyer being an accurate shot?"

Jeremy smiled broadly. "It shore is."

"And she teaches other women how to use a gun?"

"My missus takes lessons from her every Thursday mornin', " Jeremy said, "along with a passel o' others."

"What possible use could a woman have for shooting?"

Chuckling, Jeremy placed a hand on Tony's shoulder. "Don't let Miss Essie hear ya askt such a thing. She'll wear yer ear out giving ya reasons."

Grandpa barked out Jeremy's name. The boy hustled up the rig to his spot on the double board leaving Tony to try and make sense of Miss Spreckelmeyer. Checker champion. Marksman. Wheeler. Banister-slider. And worst of all . . . boss.

∞

By the time Tony had been to the bathhouse and washed off all the drilling mud, the shale, the ditch, and the compound used to grease the pipe with, he'd barely made it to Castle's Drug Store for dinner. He took his time over the meal, though, regardless of the fact that the "boss" wanted to see him first thing after work.

Taking a swallow of genuine Coca-Cola, he listened along with the other men as Mr. Castle read aloud the latest news of the war. The boys cheered and whistled upon hearing the marines had captured Guantánamo Bay and seventeen thousand troops had landed just east of Santiago.

Setting his coins on the counter, Tony wiped his mouth and slipped out. The streets were congested with men heading east toward the saloons. A ninety-foot gas tower at the corner of Beaton and Collin threw out enough illumination to get by on, though from here he couldn't see the abandoned seed house Miss Spreckelmeyer had converted into a bicycle club. Still, he'd have no trouble finding it in the dark. It was just northeast of town, not far from Whiteselle's Lumber Yard.

He skirted the red-light district, passed Frost's Wagon Yard and the Central Blacksmith Shop. He wound behind the city pound and set a few dogs barking until he was a good distance away.

When he got within sight of the club, gaslight from its high horizontal windows guided him to the doorstep. He knocked, but no one answered, so he pushed the door open.

"Quicker, Mr. Sharpley. You must keep your eye on the ball. Now, let's try again."

In the middle of the vast room, Miss Spreckelmeyer faced a young man who wore a quarter-sleeve shirt with exercise tights as snug as a pair of long johns.

Bunching her skirt in her fists, she raised her hem and tapped a ball back and forth between her booted feet as she moved toward Mr. Sharpley. The full skirt and white shirtwaist she wore were more suited to a stroll through town than a ball drill.

It was the first time he'd seen her without a hat, though. Her hair had wilted, its twist no more than a suggestion of its former glory. Hunks of blond hair swirled across her face, over her shoulder and down her back.

Sharpley crouched, bounced on his toes, and kicked at the ball when she drew near, but only succeeded in stirring her skirts.

She easily passed him, then stopped the ball with her toe. "You lunged again. I'll get by you every time if you jump in like that."

"I don't see what this has to do with ridin' bikes. Just put me on the bicycle and I'll go faster than any of the rest of 'em. I swear I will."

She brushed a strand of hair from her eyes. "There is a difference between being fast and being quick. I will admit you are fast. But if something happens during the race that requires you to respond quickly, you will not fare well."

Tony settled his shoulder comfortably against the south wall, ankles crossed and hat in hand. They went through the exercise two more times, and he could see their frustration mounting. Sharpley did lunge, but she also outplayed him. Even if the boy used proper technique, he'd be hard pressed to win the ball from her.

"Perhaps I can be of assistance?" Tony suggested.

Miss Spreckelmeyer squeaked and whirled around. "What are you doing here?"

"You sent for me."

"I sent for you hours ago."

"And here I am." He pulled away from the wall and gave a mock bow.

"Well, I'm busy now. You will have to come back in a hour or so."

He strode onto the court. "Surely that won't be necessary. I can't imagine you needing me for very long and it looks like your young charge could use a rest."

"He can't have a rest. I'm trying to build up his stamina."

"By trouncing him at football?" He extended his hand toward the boy. "You must be Sharpley. My name's Bryant."

Sharpley grinned. "You work with Crackshot."

Tony smiled at the mention of Wilson's new nickname. "I surely do."

"Who's Crackshot?" Essie asked.

"Nobody," Tony answered, turning toward her. "If you'd like, I would be glad to help you show Sharpley what it is you want him to do—with the football, that is."

He bent over and pulled off his cowboy boots.

"Mr. Bryant! Stop that at once. What do you think you are doing?"

"You can't very well expect me to play football in my boots." He removed both socks and stuffed them in his boots.

She stared at his feet. He wiggled his toes.

"Oh, my goodness." She clasped her hands together, red flooding her face. "This really isn't at all proper, and I'm not dressed for an actual match. I was merely demonstrating."

He walked to the ball, flipped it high into the air with his feet, juggled it with his knees, dropped it in front of him and passed it to her. "Watch closely, Sharpley, and I'll show you how to tame your opponent."

She trapped the ball with her instep, a spark firing her eyes. "I'm really not dressed for this," she said again.

He neither encouraged nor discouraged her, just held her gaze.

She worried her bottom lip, then looked from him to the ball and back up to him. "Where's the goal?" she asked.

"I'll take the bandstand, you can have the entire south wall."

She rolled the ball back to him. "I won't need the entire wall."

Allowing himself a slow grin, he again passed the ball to her. "Oh yes, you will. And . . . ladies first."

She didn't stop the ball as he'd expected, but lifted her skirts, kicked the ball as it slid past her, then sprinted after it. He had no trouble catching up and stealing it back.

Instead of racing to his goal, though, he toyed with her—changing directions, faking a kick, cutting across the ball. But when he tried to backheel it, she intercepted the ball and skirted around him.

He took her on again. Planting her left foot, she lunged to the right, then abruptly to the left, catching him off balance. She attempted a shot on the goal, but he managed to knock the ball into the bleachers before she made contact. Sharpley ran after it.

"Here!" she cried, jogging south. Sharpley threw it her direction.

She pulled the ball back toward her body, forcing Tony to step up and open his legs, then she kicked it between his feet, maintaining possession.

They parried for another minute before Tony acted as if he was going to turn, but stepped over the ball instead and headed in the other direction, breaking away. A few feet short of the bandstand, he struck the ball and scored his goal.

Essie held her waist and tried to catch her breath, droplets of moisture clinging to her skin. Playing football in a tight corset was not terribly wise, but she took satisfaction in the fact that Mr. Bryant was panting just as hard as she. Sweat plastered his shirt to his chest and back, accentuating the muscles beneath.

A smile played on his lips. "A good match, Miss Spreckelmeyer. I'm impressed. Too bad you lost."

She wondered how well he'd fare running up and down the length of the building strapped into a corset, but, of course, she could not plead her case.

"What?" he said. "Nothing to say?"

Inhaling, she squeezed her side. "That was fun."

His eyebrows shot up and his smile grew. "So it was. How is it that a judge's daughter knows how to play a game popular only with the lower, working classes?"

"It's a beautiful game," she breathed. "A couple of years ago we had a group of oilmen who used to play every Sunday. I'd go and watch them—from a distance, of course."

"Of course."

"Then I secretly played here with Jeremy Gillespie and practiced until I could duplicate what they did. But this is the first time I've ever played with anyone other than him or Mr. Sharpley." She propped her hands on her knees, trying to suck in more air.

His smile began to fade. "Are you all right?"

She nodded.

"Sharpley, go get some water for Miss Spreckelmeyer."

"No, no. I'm fine." She straightened and the room began to spin. "Uh-oh."

Tony rushed to her and grasped her elbow. "Perhaps you should come sit on the bleachers."

Her vision dimmed. The room began to fade.

Tony scooped her up into his arms. "Keep your eyes open, Miss Spreckelmeyer." He glanced at Sharpley. "Is there somewhere she can lie down?"

"Over here," Sharpley answered. "There's an office."

Weak. She felt so weak.

"Do not faint. Do you hear me? I won't have it."

Chagrined at the panic in his voice, she tried to keep her eyes open and focused, but all went dark.

chapter SEVEN

TONY FOUND the office door ajar and kicked it wide. "Get everything off that desk, Sharpley, and be quick about it."

The tiny office held an old teacher's desk, a bookshelf, a stove, and two ladder-back chairs. Sharpley grabbed the books littering the desk and pushed all the papers to the side so Tony could lay Miss Spreckelmeyer on top. He glanced around for something to prop her head on.

"There's some ready-mades two rooms down," Sharpley said, reading Tony's mind.

"Good. Grab the first thing you see."

She lay still and limp. He gently squeezed her wrist, relieved to feel a strong pulse, yet wondering what he would do if she didn't come to.

What had he been thinking to challenge her to a game of football? If she suffered some serious injury and word got out that he had pitted himself against her in a one-on-one match, a scandal would follow for sure and he would permanently lose his job. The men in the patch might think she was eccentric, but they were protective of her.

He combed his fingers through his hair, admitting to himself exactly why he had challenged her. Because he knew he could beat her. He, Russ, and a group of immigrant boys from across the tracks used to spend many an hour playing football. When his father had found out he'd participated in that "workingman's game," he'd taken a strap to Tony. But it hadn't kept him from playing.

It wasn't worth losing his job over now, though. Instead of trying to prove himself to this woman, he needed to start focusing on his goals.

He glanced at the door. What was taking Sharpley so long? A B. F. Goodrich Company advertisement tacked on her wall caught his eye. *Cycling produces Health. Health produces Honesty. Honesty impels Cyclists to ride licensed SINGLE TUBE TIRES!*

Sharpley returned with two pairs of bloomers. "It's all I could find."

"You're kidding me," Tony said, but took them anyway. "Now go get a pitcher of water and some cloths."

He wadded up one pair of bloomers and put them under her knees. The other pair he placed beneath her head.

Blond hair spilled over the navy fabric and across her face. Hooking a tendril with his finger, he pulled it free of her mouth. Then brushed another strand from her forehead.

Her sandy-colored eyebrows arched gracefully above her eyes. Long, long lashes lay still against her pale cheeks. Cheeks that usually held such color and life. Her perfect, rosebud lips were bleached white.

"Miss Spreckelmeyer?" He ran his thumb along her brow. "Wake up. You need to wake up."

Sharpley zoomed around the corner with a bowl of water. "I can't find any cloths."

Tony grabbed Essie's left wrist and slipped his finger inside her cuff, snagging the handkerchief hidden within its folds. Taking the bowl, he dipped the frilly piece of cotton inside, then brushed it against her forehead, cheeks, and lips.

"Can you hear me, Miss Spreckelmeyer?"

Her eyelids quivered.

"I think she's coming around." He dipped the hanky again and bathed her chin, the back of her neck, and up behind her ears.

She blinked her eyes open, then let them fall closed again.

"No," he said, his voice clipped. "Do not go back to sleep. Open your eyes, Miss Spreckelmeyer. This instant!"

She opened her eyes, her brows crinkling.

He took a deep breath. "That's better. Now keep them open."

She obeyed, though the blue orbs were clouded with confusion and fatigue. Her body was still as flimsy as jelly.

"Go see if you can find a glass or at least a smaller bowl than this, Sharpley, and fill it with water so I can give her something to drink."

Wrapping the hanky around two fingers, he dipped it again. "You about scared me to death."

Her expression didn't so much as flicker. He slid his cloth-encased fingers down each side of her nose, beneath her cheekbones, and across her upper and lower lips.

The wet fabric provided no barrier between his skin and hers. She was so soft. As soft as a goose-down pillow. Swallowing, he glanced up and suspended his ministrations. Her blue, blue eyes had cleared and were fixed on him.

They held waves of royal blue and sky blue and a blue so light it was almost white, all captured within a fine ring of deep navy.

"Found one," Sharpley said, entering the room with a glass of water.

Tony jerked his hand away from her mouth. "Good. That's real good." He slid his hand beneath her head. "I want you to take a little sip now."

He brought the glass to her lips, tipping it slightly. She swallowed. A tiny rivulet missed her mouth and plunged down her chin and neck.

He captured it with the handkerchief. "Your color is starting to come back. Do you feel any better?"

"Yes," she whispered. "I've never fainted before in my life. I'm so terribly sorry."

"It wasn't your fault, it was mine. Are you able to take a proper breath yet?"

A splash of color momentarily touched her pale face. "Yes, thank you. I'd like to try to sit up now."

He placed a staying hand against her shoulder. "Not so fast. There's no rush." He looked over at Sharpley. "I think the danger's passed, son. It would probably be best if you called it an evening, though. I don't think she'll be up to training you any further tonight. Were there any laps you needed to do or anything?"

"No, sir. We usually do the football drill last."

"Very well. Report back here tomorrow night as usual unless she sends word otherwise. I imagine she'll be back to herself within the hour, though."

"Yes, sir. You'll make sure she gets home all right?"

"I will."

He turned to leave.

"Sharpley?"

The boy paused.

"You're not to say a word about this to anyone. As part owner of Sullivan Oil it would cause her a good deal of embarrassment if the boys were to blow this thing all out of proportion. I'll have your word that you'll keep your trap shut about both the football match and her fainting."

"You have it, sir. I wouldn't never do nothin' to hurt Miss Spreckelmeyer."

"Thank you, Sharpley." He gave the youth a nod of approval and listened as he moved to the entrance and let himself out.

The lantern in the room hissed. Retrieving the water glass, Tony propped her up again. "Let's have another sip now."

She brought her hand to the glass, her fingers resting against his as she swallowed.

"Excellent." He laid her down and smoothed the hair away from her forehead. "How are you feeling?"

"Lethargic."

"That will pass."

"I'm terribly embarrassed. I'm not some weak, simpering female."

"And nobody thinks that you are. As a matter of fact, I heard today that you're one of the best shots in town."

"Who told you that?"

He relayed Crackshot's story, pleased to see the color return to her lips and cheeks as she smiled over the tale. She had a nice smile, with white teeth and dimples on both sides.

"If today is any indication, I'm afraid Wilson's gonna be forever known as Crackshot," he said.

She started to push herself up, and Tony reached to support her shoulders.

"Are you sure you're ready?" he asked.

"I'm feeling much better."

"Sit here on the desk for a minute before you try to stand." He removed the bloomers propping up her knees and took hold of her calves, gently swiveling her around so her legs dangled off the side of the desk before realizing what he'd done.

Snatching his hands back, he slid them into his pockets, looked at the floor and discovered he was still barefoot. "Do you recall why you sent for me today?"

"Yes, of course," she said, catching her breath.

He glanced up to make sure she wasn't faint again, but her cheeks weren't pale, they were burning with embarrassment. He felt his own begin to heat. What in the blazes had he been thinking to manhandle her just now?

"It was just a small thing, really," she said, "but I didn't have time to get out to the fields today and didn't want to wait until tomorrow."

He said nothing, not sure how to respond.

"I, um, I wanted to find out the names again of the men who sell those rotary drills and how to contact them," she said.

"Baker. M.C. and C.E. Baker. I'm not sure where they are, though. I know someone I can telegraph over in Beaumont to find out if they're still there or if they've taken a job out of town."

"Would you mind?"

"Not at all."

"If they are there, do you think you could ask if they would come to Corsicana and give me a demonstration?"

"Yes, ma'am."

"I'd appreciate that, Mr. Bryant. Thank you."

"You're welcome."

He waited, but she said nothing more.

That's it? he thought. *That's all she wanted? All of this for one simple question?* He suppressed his irritation, then realized that as a female, she probably avoided coming out to the fields if she could.

She'd only shown up at his rig once since he'd started, and all work had come to a complete standstill. If she tried to do anything, someone would jump in and do it for her. All the while, Grandpa and Jeremy did what they could to get her away from the patch. He wondered if she was aware of the effect she had on them.

He curled his toes beneath the hem of his denims. "Do you think you'll be all right if I go out and get my boots?"

"Oh yes. I think I'm ready to go now, actually."

Frowning, he pointed a finger, stopping her. "No, ma'am. Don't you move from there until I get back."

"I'm fine, Mr. Bryant."

"I mean it, Miss Spreckelmeyer. I want you to stay put. Tell me you'll stay put."

She shooed him out with her hands. "I'm fine."

He didn't budge. "Say it."

"Oh, for heaven's sake." She sighed. "All right. I'll stay put."

He wasted no time in grabbing his boots and heading back to her office. She'd stayed where he'd left her, as promised.

Plopping down into a chair, he pulled on his socks and boots, then slapped his hands on his knees.

"Well," she said. "I guess we'd better call it a night."

He jumped up to help her off the desk, holding tightly to her elbow.

"I'm really all right, Mr. Bryant. You can let go now."

"I'll just hang on awhile longer, if you don't mind."

When they left the office, he tried to guide her toward the exit, but she tugged in the opposite direction.

"Where do you think you're going?" he asked.

"I need to turn out the lights."

"I'll do it. You want to sit down?"

"No. And please, all this mollycoddling is not necessary."

"Listen, you plum scared the living daylights out of me and I'm not anxious for a relapse. Now, can you stand on your own or do you want a chair?"

"I can stand on my own."

He eyed her skeptically, but her color was better and she seemed to have her wits about her. Still, he wasted no time turning out all the lights except for the one by the front door.

"Okay, nice and slow, now," he said, returning to take her elbow.

At the entrance he lifted her shawl off a hook, draped it over her shoulders, turned out the final lamp and locked the door behind them.

Essie had become so used to the smell of oil permeating town that she hardly ever noticed it anymore. But now, as she and Mr.

Bryant stepped outside the club and the familiar fumes rushed up on her, her stomach lurched and her knees wobbled.

He pulled her close, allowing her to lean more heavily onto him. "There's a wagonyard just around the corner," he said. "Would you like to go there instead and get something to ride home in?"

"No, thank you. Walking is fine."

"Are you sure?" he asked, slowing their pace to a stroll.

"Yes. I'm positive."

Darkness shrouded them. With the sun gone, the worst of the heat had dissipated, but its stickiness lingered, leaving the air thick with humidity.

Her pride urged her to pull away from Mr. Bryant, but common sense insisted otherwise. She was not as surefooted as she'd pretended, and she didn't want to risk humiliating herself again. Though his ministrations had been swift and efficient, thrusting him into the role of caretaker had been too unsettling by half.

She was his boss. His superior. But now he'd beaten her at her own game and had also taken charge of her. To make matters worse, she'd participated in a rather physical match with a man—a barefooted man—and then allowed him to see to her personal needs. If anyone found out, there would be the devil to pay.

His parting words to Mr. Sharpley had surprised her, though. The field men loved telling tales, and tonight's episode would have been embellished, laughed over, and retold for weeks. It could have damaged her standing in the community and embarrassed Papa. That Mr. Bryant had made certain her privacy and reputation remained intact had taken her completely off guard.

She risked a surreptitious glance in his direction, but it was too dark to see more than a faint silhouette. Cowboy hat. Straight nose. Defined chin. Powerful chest.

A few years back she might have pretended they were a couple. A young married couple strolling for the sheer pleasure of enjoying each other's company.

But she'd learned the hard way that ill-founded fantasies and manipulations brought nothing but pain and heartache. No, she knew exactly who she was and who she was walking home with and why. She had no illusions whatsoever.

Still, the man no longer fit so neatly into the mold she'd originally placed him in. "Do you have a family, Mr. Bryant?"

The muscles supporting her arm tensed slightly, then eased. "Yes, ma'am. A mother and a sister."

"In Beaumont?"

"That's right."

"Have you lived there all your life?"

"More or less. What about you? Have you lived here all your life?"

"Yes. I used to go out to my grandparents' farm in Quitman every summer as a child. Other than that, I've been right here in Corsicana."

"Guess it's changed a lot in the last few years."

"Oh my, yes. We went from being a small, struggling cotton community to an overpopulated oil boomtown almost overnight. We are still trying to adjust to the growing pains."

To reach her house, they would need to cross through town. Instead of taking her the shortest—and more public—route, Mr. Bryant kept them on the abandoned streets that edged the city limits. It would double their walking time but would keep curious eyes from speculating about her disheveled appearance and her choice of escort.

"I heard you give shooting lessons to the ladies in town every Thursday morning," he said, interrupting the quiet. "Is that true?"

"Yes, it is."

He said nothing for the longest time, their leisurely footfalls muffled by the dirt in the street.

"Why would a bicycle club offer shooting lessons?"

She allowed herself a small smile. "Women are unaccustomed to being without escort or chaperone. I think it wise, therefore, to give my students the skills needed to protect themselves from any threats they may encounter while out bicycling alone."

"Threats of the four-legged kind or the two-legged?" he asked, a touch of humor in his voice.

"Both, I suppose."

"Are you telling me, then, that the ladies of Corsicana ride their wheels with six-shooters strapped to their bloomers?"

"No, of course not," she said with a short huff of amusement.

"Then, why learn how to shoot a gun if you aren't going to carry one?"

"I never said we weren't carrying pistols. Just that we don't strap them to our bloomers."

He pulled her to a stop, clearly appalled. "Are you packing a pistol right now?"

"I am not."

He took a moment to absorb her answer. The moonlight behind him silhouetted his head, hiding the nuances of his expression, but it did not disguise his thorough perusal of her. "Where do you put it when you are carrying, then?"

She shook her head. "I shall not discuss such a delicate matter with you, Mr. Bryant."

"Delicate?" he asked, a hint of astonishment in his voice. "You carry it someplace delicate? Do you think that wise? What if it went off?"

She started toward home again. "I cover safety precautions in my instruction."

He caught up to her and recaptured her elbow.

"I feel steadier now," she said. "I can walk without assistance."

"All the same." He held her firmly. "Who is allowed to take lessons?"

"Any of my club members."

"Are all your members female?"

"No, no. I have a vast number of men in my club. But their work keeps them from utilizing as many of the privileges as the women."

"What other privileges do you offer?"

"Our members can receive private instruction on bicycle riding and repair, etiquette, fashion, health, and a number of other things. We also have weekly lectures, monthly group rides, service projects, and an annual ball and supper. We are going to have a huge group ride on the Fourth of July that is open to the public, regardless of membership status."

They turned in a westerly direction toward the residential part of town. The clouds hovering earlier in the day had dispersed, leaving a palette of stars too numerous to count.

"You do all that and run Sullivan Oil, too?"

She hesitated, wondering if it was surprise or appreciation she detected in his tone. "Papa makes all the major decisions for the oil company. I have more of an administrative role."

"That's not what I heard."

She glanced up at him. "What have you heard?"

"That you pretty much run the company."

"That's not true. Papa is the majority owner and I couldn't possibly manage it without him."

A scream rent the air. It came from somewhere deep in the woods, a long, piercing wail that stopped Essie in her tracks, then sent her racing toward the sound, skirts lifted just high enough to clear the ground.

She forgot about her earlier ordeal as a surge of energy shot through her. Whoever was screaming was either terrified or in a great deal of pain—perhaps both.

She'd spent the better part of her childhood cavorting in these woods and knew them backwards and forwards. The lack of light didn't slow her down, but she could hear Mr. Bryant stumbling through the underbrush behind her.

Harley Vandervoort burst through some trees in front of them. "Miss Essie! Brianna got bit by a snake!"

"Lead us to her," Mr. Bryant said, catching up to them. Harley wasted no time. He turned and bolted deeper into the forest.

"What kind of snake?" Essie shouted, racing after him.

"A rattler!"

They found the girl writhing on the ground in a damp clearing lit by a full moon. She grasped her wounded leg and kicked out frantically with the other.

"My foot! My foot!" she screamed.

Several yards away lay a three-foot rattler with a severed head and a bulge in his middle from a recent meal.

chapter EIGHT

TONY KNELT in the damp leaves to lift the girl up. He wasn't sure exactly how far from town they were, but he'd run the whole way if he had to, with the struggling girl in his arms. He slid his arm under her, but Essie pushed him back.

"Leave her be," Essie said.

She crouched over the girl's hurt leg, trying to grab the calf, but the little thing kicked free.

"Hold still!" Essie snapped.

"I can't. I can't." The girl whimpered, tears coursing down her face, her reddish brown braids mussed and filled with leaves and dirt.

"Grab hold of her, Tony, and keep her from thrashing."

"We've got to get her back to town," he said.

"There's no time! Hold her!"

He pulled the girl onto his lap and wrapped his arms around her, crushing her to his chest. "Hush, now," he said. "It'll be all right."

Essie reached across to him. "I need a knife."

"No!" Brianna screamed, twisting frantically and almost breaking free of his hold.

"Keep her still, I said!"

Anchoring the girl against him with one arm, he quickly pulled his knife from his pocket and tried to open the larger blade, but Brianna kept jostling his hold.

"Here," Essie said. "Let me." She took the knife from his hand and flipped it open.

Brianna fought with renewed vigor, screaming, squirming, and kicking her feet. A spot of blood stained the girl's stocking above the ankle.

"Shhhhh," Tony said, tucking the girl's head and knees against his chest. "Hold still, honey, and let Miss Essie have a look."

"I'm just going to cut your shoe off, Brianna," Essie said, her voice a little calmer now that she had the knife in hand. "But you must hold still so I don't cut you instead."

"We were snake hunting," Harley said, his thin voice choking on the words. "Not fer rattlers, o' courst, but that's what we found when we poked under that bush over yonder."

"Snake hunting?" Tony asked. "With a girl? And at this time of night? What were you thinking?" And what were her parents going to say when they found out, he wondered, though he didn't say so aloud.

Harley puffed out his chest. "The snake wasn't expectin' us to go peeking in its hidey-hole or it would've warned us away with its rattle. But we didn't know it was there 'til Bri lifted that branch. She started screamin' and carryin' on and scared the blasted thing so bad that it bit her. I killed it right quick, then ran fer help."

The boy sounded defensive, and Tony regretted saying anything. He watched Essie slice the buttons off the girl's shoe and rip open her stocking. Amid the cuts and scratches on the girl's ankle, he spotted two oozing fang bites.

Essie took one look at the injury and turned to the boy. "Go get a horse, Harley, and bring it to the edge of the woods."

Harley tore off in the direction of the nearest house. Tony tried to maneuver Brianna so that a beam of moonlight fell across her ankle. He knew what was coming. They'd need all the light they could get.

"It's burning, it's burning," she sobbed.

Tony kissed her head and stroked her hair. "I know, honey. Try to take some deep breaths, if you can."

She took a shaky breath, then moaned.

Essie tossed up her own hem, ripped the ruffle clean off her petticoat, then split it into two strips. She quickly tied one strip above the bite and one below.

"You need me to tighten those?" he asked.

She shook her head. "I'm just trying to slow down the venom, not cut off her blood flow." She wedged two fingers beneath the cotton bands, making sure the strips weren't too tight.

He'd seen plenty of snakes in his day but had never actually seen someone who'd suffered from a bite. He had a gleaning knowledge of what had to be done but wouldn't have trusted himself to do it when he could just as easily have taken her to a doctor.

But Essie had no hesitation in her actions. Picking up his knife, she pantomimed a firm, rigid hug.

Nodding, he gathered Brianna to him and clamped down. "Hold real still now, sweetheart. Essie's gonna have a look at the bite and I don't want you to kick her. All right?"

Brianna moaned in answer and stiffened in his arms.

With quick proficiency, Essie made an incision across each wound. Brianna screamed. Tony held her firmly in place.

Tossing the knife down, Essie grabbed the girl's leg like it was a piece of corn on the cob and began to suck at the wounds, then spit out blood.

The girl cried out in protest, struggling anew, but Tony held her secure, watching in wonder as Essie sucked and spit, sucked and spit.

He knew of grown men who wouldn't have the stomach to do what she was doing, yet there was no wavering in her task. On and on she went. How long would she continue?

"Stop, stop. Please. It hurts!"

He buried his nose in Brianna's hair, shushing her, whispering to her, all the while Essie tried to pull the venom from the girl.

"You need a break?" he asked. "You want me to do that for a while?"

She swiped her mouth with her sleeve. "I won't be able to hold her still. Besides, every minute counts. We've only a few left for this to be effective."

Essie checked the tightness of the bands, then bent to her task again. The girl was trembling all over and sobbing uncontrollably now. Her leg was beginning to swell.

Wasn't it dangerous for Essie to suck the venom into her mouth like that? What if she swallowed some of it? Could both she and the girl die?

His stomach started to gurgle and he took several deep breaths.

Harley exploded back into the clearing. "I got two of Mr. Peeples' horses tied to a tree. He said he'd get word to Doc Gulick to meet you at the Penningtons'."

Essie surged to her feet. "Come on. We need to hurry."

As Tony ran with the girl in his arms, he could feel all the fight bouncing out of her. When they reached the horses, Essie held out her arms for Brianna. The girl was no longer thrashing but lay limp, sweating profusely and keening in a high, mournful voice.

Tony grabbed the mane of a cinnamon-colored horse and pulled himself onto it. He hadn't ridden bareback since he was a kid. At least Harley had taken the time to bridle her.

Slipping off his jacket, he wrapped it around Brianna and took her from Essie's raised arms. Harley made a stirrup with his hands, giving Essie a boost up onto her mare.

Without so much as a word, she straddled the horse like a man and kicked the animal's sides.

⁓

The Penningtons lived in a house on West Jackson Avenue. It had three large rooms, a kitchen, and a center hall leading to a back porch, where Tony and Harley waited for word about Brianna.

A full moon hanging high in a bed of stars threw muted light onto the yard. Nearby crickets performed a syncopated symphony.

"You should see this place in the day," Harley said, sitting on the top porch step, his back against a post. "Miss Katy loves to work in the garden and she has flowers almost solid from here to the fence out front. Blue ones, purple ones, red ones, pink ones, every color you could name."

Tony set his chair to rocking. After arriving, he remembered what Essie had said back in the Slap Out about there being no Mrs. Pennington. She'd died and left behind a husband and eight girls. The cooper and his oldest daughter had met them at the door and whisked Brianna into a room off the central hallway. The doctor and Essie followed, but Tony and Harley had been consigned to the back porch. Which was just fine with Tony.

"Which one is Miss Katy?" he asked.

"One of the older ones."

Tony had seen four of the sisters since arriving. The one that had greeted them at the door and three others running between the kitchen and the room they had taken Brianna into.

"Did Brianna's father know you'd taken her snake hunting?"

"O' courst. My pa would whup me good if'n I took her without permission."

"Aren't your parents wondering what's keeping you now?"

"They might be. But I ain't leavin' 'til I know Bri's gonna be all right."

A distant coyote gave a yapping howl, ending with a shrill, scream-like sound. Harley repositioned himself on the step.

"You do this often?" Tony asked. "Snake hunting, I mean?"

"Yeah, I guess. I caught me a yellow-bellied water snake a few weeks back out by the old watershed. It was a good four feet long and this big around." He made a circle the size of a silver dollar with his fingers.

Tony whistled in appreciation. "You still have it?"

"Naw. My pa made me let it loose 'cause I snuck up on Lexie Davis and scared her with it." Harley gave Tony a conspiring grin. "She shore did squeal something fierce, though."

Tony chuckled. "How do you know which snakes are poisonous and which are friendly?"

"Miss Essie showed me."

Tony stopped his rocker. "Essie? Our Essie?"

Harley gave him a funny look. "You know any others?"

"She *showed* you?"

"Well, at first, she just tol' me that if it had a flat head instead of a round, pointy one, that it would be poisonous. Then when we would run acrost a copperhead or cottonmouth or something, she'd tell me what it was."

"Do you and Essie make a habit of running across snakes?"

Harley laughed. "Well, yeah. Wouldn't be much use in huntin' snakes if we never ran acrost any."

"You and Essie hunt snakes?"

"Why, shore. She's the one what taught me how."

Tony rubbed a hand across his mouth. He didn't know why he was surprised. Nothing about that woman should surprise him anymore. "How often do you go hunting with her?"

"Not so much anymore. She's always busy with her bicycle stuff."

The screen door opened and Essie stepped outside. Tony and Harley came to their feet.

"She's going to be fine," Essie said.

Tony let out his breath and Harley slumped against the porch rail.

"What did the doctor say?" Tony asked.

"That the swelling should go away in another two or three weeks and then she'll be back to normal."

"You extracted all the venom, then, when you were, um, treating her?" Tony asked.

"Well, I don't imagine there was all that much to begin with. It was apparent the snake had eaten recently, which would have used up most of its poison."

"No, Miss Essie," Harley said. "You saved her life." He pitched himself against her skirts and hugged her tightly. "I don't know what I would've done if somethin' had happened to Bri."

Essie smoothed her hand over his head. "Well, she's fine now, so no need to worry yourself. And I'm surprised you're still here. Hadn't you better be getting on home?"

He pulled away from her and swiped his nose with his sleeve. "Can I see Bri?"

"Not tonight, Harley. Maybe tomorrow."

He glanced at the back door, then slumped his shoulders. "Well, if yer sure she's gonna be all right?"

"I'm sure. Now go on with you."

He waved good-bye to Tony, clomped down the steps, then disappeared around the corner and into the night. Essie moved to the porch railing, leaned her hands against it and looked out at the moonlit sky.

Tony wished he had a lantern. Her hair had come completely unbound. It was wild and thick and clear down to her waist. Her blouse was twisted, its sleeve stained with blood. Her torn skirt fell limply about her slim hips.

"You okay?" he asked.

"It's been a long night," she said, looking at him over her shoulder. A breeze swept across the porch, stirring her hair and causing her to shiver.

"You left your shawl in the woods," he said, slipping off his jacket and hooking it on her shoulders. The coat trapped her hair beneath it, cutting all but the top from his view.

She pulled the collar tighter around her neck. "I left your knife behind also," she said.

Patting his pockets, he realized she was right. "I'll have Harley fetch them for us tomorrow. I'd do it myself, but I don't think I could find the spot."

"I hope your knife doesn't rust being left out overnight. It was such an unusual one."

"It'll be fine. I'm more worried about you."

She waved her hand in a gesture of dismissal. "I'm just tired, is all."

"Why don't you let me walk you home, then. Surely you've done all you can."

Keeping her back to him, she scanned the yard and the shadows beyond it. "Yes. Dr. Gulick is almost finished, and Brianna's sisters will take good care of her. But you needn't walk me home. I'm sure you're just as anxious to get some rest as I am, and morning will come awfully early for you."

Moonlight gilded her hair, and his jacket hung on her like a burlap sack, shrouding her form. He tried to recall the reasons he'd held contempt for her just a few short hours ago, but could not. Instead, he kept seeing her in his mind's eye crouched over that little girl, desperately trying to save her life—and succeeding.

Then he pictured her sliding down a banister, playing football, hugging Harley, smiling.

He took a deep breath. He was no stranger to the feelings stirring inside him. But this time they were unwelcome. He had a purpose to fulfill, a mother and a sister to provide for.

There was no room in his life for distractions. Essie had offered an excuse, and he knew he should accept it and put as much distance between them as he could.

She lowered her chin and began to pick at the wood on the railing. Her hair bunched along the back of the jacket's collar. Reaching up, he scooped the golden mane into his hand and pulled it free from its confinement. The silky strands glided through his fingers and fell against her back.

She spun around, her skirts catching against the railing and twisting round her legs. She lifted her hands to her hair, causing the jacket to fall off, then swiftly fished out some pins from a skirt pocket and placed them in her mouth. She finger-combed her hair, banded it together, and twirled it against her head with quick, efficient movements.

While her hands were full and occupied, he drew the pins from her mouth. She stilled and lifted her gaze to his.

He handed her a pin. She took it from him, careful to keep her fingers from brushing his, and tucked it into her hair. He doled the pins out one at a time until she reached for the last one. He squeezed it, keeping her from taking it.

They stood suspended, linked not by touch, but by opposite ends of the pin. What would she do if he tugged on his end? Would she let go or would she come to him?

Releasing the pin, he stepped away, retrieved his jacket from the floor of the porch and held it open. "Ready?"

Patting her hair, she presented her back to him. He hooked the jacket on her shoulders and offered her his arm.

After a slight hesitation, she slipped a hand out from the folds of his jacket.

On the street, he adjusted his stride to hers. The fabric of her skirt swished when she walked and brushed against his leg. Neither of them uttered a word the entire way home.

At Bilberry Street they took a right and she gently removed her hand from his arm. He opened the gate leading to her house. There were no lights coming from the windows. Hadn't her father wondered where she was? Did she come home late so often that he didn't even bother to wait up for her?

The giant pecan trees on either side of the walkway shadowed the porch, making it almost impossible to see. Taking her elbow, he guided her up the steps, then reached for the door.

She placed a restraining hand on his arm. "Thank you for seeing me home, Tony."

He straightened. "You're welcome."

Darkness surrounded them. He could make out her silhouette, but little else.

Shrugging his jacket from her shoulders, she handed it to him. "Thank you."

He nodded and slung it over his arm, but made no move to leave. A lonely bird some distance off called out, but received no answer.

"Well," she said.

"Well," he repeated, backing up a step. "I guess I'd better be going."

"Yes." But she made no move to go inside. "When do you think the Bakers will be able to come to Corsicana?"

"Who? Oh! The Baker brothers. Yes, well, I'm not sure. It depends on whether or not they're still in Beaumont. I could shoot my friend a telegram first thing in the morning, but it would mean I'd be a little late for work."

"I'll tell Mr. Moss."

"Then I'll take care of it and let you know when I hear from them." He backed up another step.

"Be careful. I think the stairs are right behind you."

He glanced over his shoulder. "Right. Yes. Thank you. Don't suppose it would be good if I fell down the stairs after everything else that's happened tonight."

She made no response. He wished he could see her expression, then thought better of it. After another second's hesitation, he tugged the brim of his hat, then strode down the steps, across the yard, out the gate and back toward town.

chapter NINE

ROLLING PEGASUS out of the shed, Essie walked her bike to the street, pointed it toward town and smoothly mounted. The cloudless day offered no breeze or relief from the sun's intense rays, but Essie took little notice of it, her mind fully occupied with thoughts of Mr. Bryant.

Something had changed, though she couldn't pinpoint what exactly. When he'd gathered her hair into his hands, she'd briefly remembered another man doing the same thing. And much as she'd enjoyed those moments, there was a wealth of hurt in the memories, too.

Turning onto Fourth Street, she waved at the men working a series of Sullivan Oil rigs. Work on the derricks ceased. The men doffed their hats, waved back and waited for her to pass before resuming their duties.

When she'd first met Tony, he had bristled with resentment. When had his feelings changed, she wondered. After she re-hired him? After the football match? Brianna's tragedy? Whenever it happened, there was no question the animosity had slowly melted away like bubbles in a washtub. What troubled Essie was what the change meant.

Approaching Collin Street her heart began to hammer. In another minute or two, she'd be passing the rig Tony worked on. Releasing one handlebar, she touched her hair and hat, assuring herself all was in place. She smoothed her collar, pinched her cheeks, then ran a hand across her stomach.

Turning the corner, she immediately spotted his rig several hundred yards ahead. Should she look for him? Pretend she didn't notice him? Wave? Smile? Do nothing?

Before she could decide, she was upon them. Again the men stopped and she raised a hand to wave. Her tire hit a rut in the road, throwing her off-balance. She grasped the handlebars with both hands as if they were the horns of a bull wrenching its head from side to side.

The bike pitched to the left, and she only kept upright by kicking out her foot and pushing against the road. But she overcompensated and had to do the same with her other foot before regaining control.

Heat rushed to her face. Were they still watching her? Had Tony seen? She knew the answer without looking.

Mortified, she kept her eyes straight ahead and did not wave to any other rigs or acknowledge them in any way. Experienced wheelers fell off of their machines all the time, she told herself. It was part of the sport. Nothing to be embarrassed about.

Her stomach refused to calm, however, so she cleared her mind of all thoughts and concentrated on reaching the sanctuary of the jailhouse.

At the south end of Jefferson Avenue, she rolled to a stop, jumped off Peg and leaned her against the red bricks of the sheriff's office. The handlebars of her bike knocked loose a bit of grout, sprinkling the boardwalk with flakes of gray.

Adjusting her straw hat, she took a moment to compose herself, then tiptoed underneath the oversized five-pointed star hanging above the open door and peeked into a building that was as familiar to her as her own home. She could tolerate the deputy if Uncle Melvin was there to run interference, but she didn't relish being caught alone with the man.

Nothing stirred inside the vacant room. "Uncle Melvin?"

Two desks filled the space between the door and the empty cells running along the back wall. Moving to the desk closest to the door, she fingered a Wanted poster frayed at the edges, and examined the vacant eyes of Saw Dust Charlie, horse thief, wondering what led a man into a life of crime.

Oil leases, tax records, and licensing documents littered the left side of the scarred wooden desk, rings of black ink stained the other. A hollowed-out groove cradled her uncle's Easterbrook pen.

Accidentally brushing his papers, she recoiled at the discovery of a postcard with the corpse of a badly beaten man in shredded clothes hanging from a rope while onlookers gawked. She flipped the offending card over, but its image still branded itself in her mind.

She scanned the printed inscription, *Wichita, Texas*. A note scribbled in coarse letters slashed the expanse above it.

Melvin,
    If this can happen in my town, it can happen in yours. When my deputies interrupted the proceedings, they were imprisoned by the mob. Something's got to be done.
                                Herbert

Covering the note back up, she tried to quell the sickness in her stomach. She'd heard of lynchings in neighboring counties, but nothing like that would ever happen in Corsicana. And the local merchants certainly wouldn't sell postcards glorifying them.

Her gaze moved to a delicate china figurine tucked beside an unlit kerosene lamp, the sight of it bringing a touch of normalcy and comfort. The six-inch woman was lifting her porcelain face to the sun while hugging a basket of wild flowers to her waist with one hand. The other hand was plastered to her head in an attempt to keep a hold on her wide-brimmed straw bonnet. Her back was arched, her laughing face enchanted.

Essie remembered the first time she'd seen it prominently displayed in the window of the Flour, Feed and Liquor Store. She couldn't have been more than eight or nine years old. The figurine had captured her imagination and she'd saved up her money for weeks. Not for herself, but for one of the most important persons in her young life. She'd never forget Uncle Melvin's surprise when she proudly presented the little statuette to him on his birthday.

The following morning, she'd all but burst from pride upon entering the jailhouse to see her gift prominently displayed on his desk. And it had been there ever since.

She smiled at the memory, then started as the town stray, Cat, jumped up onto the wooden surface, scattering a stack of oil leases to and fro.

Picking up the tabby, she curled it against her chest and rubbed her nose against its head. "Where is everybody, hmmmm?"

Cat raised her chin, and Essie obligingly scratched it. "What's the matter? You looking for Uncle Melvin, too?"

The words had hardly left her mouth before she sensed someone else in the room. She glanced behind her.

Deputy Billy John Howard leaned against the open doorframe of the storage room where all weapons and supplies were kept under lock and key. She wondered how long he'd been standing there.

His petite frame never failed to surprise her, especially considering how quick he was with his fists—too quick. In the six months he'd been deputy, those fists had made many enemies and actually killed a man who'd challenged his authority. All in the name of maintaining law and order.

"Have you finally come to your senses, Essie?" he asked. "Come to accept my suit?"

"I'm afraid not."

"I promise not to disappoint."

"All the same, no thank you."

"As you wish," he said, his eyes hooded.

"What were you doing in there?"

"We got us a leak and had to move all the spare rifles to your uncle's house. So he's been pestering me to fix the ceiling."

Pushing away from the doorframe, he locked the storage room, sauntered to her and reached for her arm. She jumped back, dropping Cat between them. Howling, the animal streaked out the front door.

Deputy Howard's hand veered to Uncle Melvin's top drawer—as if that had always been his destination—and dropped the key inside. "A bit jumpy, aren't we?"

"Where's Uncle Melvin?"

"Here and there."

She edged back, keeping the desk between them, but he followed her step for step.

"What brings you here?" he asked.

"I have a message for my uncle."

Howard hooked one hip on the edge of the sheriff's desk. "You can leave the message with me. I'll be sure he gets it."

She began backing toward the door. "If it's all the same to you, I'll just check back later."

"The Fourth of July celebration is next week," he said, standing, then hitching up his trousers. "I figured I'd pick you up around ten."

"My bicycle club sponsors a group ride that morning. And even if it didn't, I'm afraid I would have to decline. Now, if you'll excuse me?"

She didn't have time to so much as turn around before he'd closed the distance between them and grabbed her arm.

"You goin' with somebody else?"

"No," she said, trying to pull away. "Now, let me go. You're hurting me."

He increased the pressure on her arm ever so slightly before releasing her. "My apologies. I'm just gettin' a little tired of your excuses."

"They aren't excuses, Mr. Howard. They are outright refusals. I am not going to the celebration with you or anyone else. Is that clear?"

His eyes flickered. "Clear as a bell, Miss Spreckelmeyer. I guess if you won't let me escort you, then I'll just have to settle fer seein' you there."

⌘

Tony pushed away a plate piled with chicken bones, then pulled the napkin from his neck. He caught Castle's eye and laid a nickel on the counter. The proprietor strolled over, wiping his hands on his apron, and snatched the coin up with a nod of thanks.

A boomer two stools down from him pointed a drumstick at the man sitting beside him. "I'm tellin' ya, pulling all this oil from the ground ain't gonna do a lick o' good lessen we have a refinery of our own. Just ain't right the way we send all our slick up to them Yanks."

"It'd take a lot o' cartwheels to do it ourselves," his partner responded. "Why, we'd need to build a refinery first, along with gatherin' lines, pipin', heavy steel, and I don't know what all."

The door jingled, signaling the entrance of two young women. The men draped along the counter straightened, tracking the ladies' progress. Those wandering about the drugstore removed their hats.

Tony didn't recognize the girls, but he smiled politely, then slipped out the door. Harley had promised to return Tony's pocket-knife to him at the Slap Out in exchange for a game of checkers, and he didn't want to be late.

The sun had long since set, and oilmen filled the walkways and road, jostling Tony and kicking up dirt. Pulling his handkerchief from his pocket, Tony sneezed and wiped his nose. The dirt never settled in this town, coating him with a film of grime every time he stepped outside.

Like a trout moving upstream, he wove through the press of men and crossed Main Street, then over to Collin Street. A man in overalls and a straw hat strode into the store while another man stepped out of the mercantile, swung up onto his horse and headed in the opposite direction.

Tony climbed the steps and made his way back to where the stove was. Harley leaned against the chair of an old man whittling on a piece of wood, a pile of shavings between his feet. Two other gaffers divided their attention between the game of checkers they played and the man whittling. The carver held up his piece of wood and said something Tony couldn't quite catch, causing the group to guffaw.

"Howdy, Mr. Tony," Harley hollered, noticing him. "Come look here at what Pa's a-whittlin'. "

The man stopped working and greeted Tony. His nose was as wide as it was long and the texture of tree bark. Bushy gray eyebrows shaded little bitty blue eyes.

"I'm Ludwig Vandervoort. Harley's pa. That there is Owen and Jenkins." He looked Tony up and down. "You the feller what left his knife exposed to the elements?"

Tony flushed at the censure in his tone.

"I done told ya, Pa," Harley said, "we was helping the womenfolk after Bri got bit. And womenfolk is way more important than knives. Ain't that so, Mr. Tony?"

The three old-timers waited for Tony's response.

"A knife is an important tool, Harley," Tony said, "and a man shouldn't be leaving it behind like that."

The men nodded.

"But what about the women?" Harley asked.

Tony put his hand on the boy's shoulder. "In my book, the women are definitely more important than a pocketknife."

Harley gave his father a triumphant look, but the man had propped his elbows on his knees and continued to whittle . . . with Tony's knife.

"You keep 'er good and sharp," Vandervoort said, making no apologies for testing it out. "I'll give ya that."

From what Tony could tell, the carving was almost finished. Vandervoort shaved very small pieces around the figure's shoulders, then blew on it. "Well, that just about does it."

Pressing the back of the blade against his trouser leg, Vandervoort snapped the knife closed and handed it to Tony. "Much obliged."

Tony ran his fingers along the stag handle, then slipped it into his pocket. He wanted to inspect it for damage from the previous night but decided to do that without an audience.

Harley held out his hands and his father placed the figure into them. The boy turned the carving over, a smile splitting across his face.

"Lookit," he said, handing it to Tony.

The real-life features of the three-inch figure impressed him. A hat hid the eyes of the statue and rested on an oversized nose. Thin lips formed a smile that looked more like a leer.

"Turn it over," Harley said, delight in his voice.

Tony flipped the figure over, expecting to find its back but instead discovered it was another man. The eyes on this one, though, were visible with eyebrows drawn into an angry V. The lips were curled and the hands formed exaggerated fists.

"It's the deputy!" Harley exclaimed. "See?" He took the carving from Tony, holding up the smiling side. "This is how he acts in front of the sheriff and the ladies." He flipped it over. "But this is what he's really like. Ain't he, Pa?"

Vandervoort shot a stream of tobacco into a spittoon. "It's just a carving, son. Not meant to be anybody in particular."

Harley's face registered shock. He started to say something, then must have thought better about contradicting his father.

"Where'd ya get a knife like that?" Vandervoort asked.

"My father gave it to me."

"How come the top of it's shaped like a dog bone?"

Tony hesitated, recalling the long-ago day a mean-looking dog had chased him home from school. After outrunning the beast, he'd burst into his father's study with tears streaming down his face.

"Come 'ere," his father had said, laughing at the tale and motioning Tony forward. He rummaged through his desk and produced the oddly shaped knife. *"Here's a weapon fit for you, Dogbone."* He chuckled at the nickname, amused at his own joke. *"If that dog comes looking for you again, you can throw this at him."*

Tony fingered the memento in his pocket. "My dad liked unusual things, I guess."

Vandervoort spit again. "Well, I ain't never seen nothing like it."

Tony nodded. "Me neither, sir. Me neither."

"Guess what I did, Mr. Tony?" Harley asked.

"What's that?"

"I got to watch Miss Essie train Mr. Sharpley."

"That a fact?"

"Sure is. And you should see 'im. He takes off like the first rattle outta the box. Everybody's saying we're gonna win the race this year, ain't they, Pa?"

Vandervoort cracked his knuckles one at a time. "If what the peddler man says is true, then we just might have a shot."

"The peddler man said the fella over at Alamo Oil is purty fast," Harley explained, "but he thinks Sharpley might have the edge on him."

113

Owen jumped his opponent's checker, then looked up from his game. "The boys have a kitty going if you want in on it, Bryant."

Tony smiled. "I'll keep that in mind, sir."

Jenkins rubbed his bald head and slumped back in his chair, having lost his last checker. "Well, that's it fer me."

He and Owen stood.

"Y'all leavin'?" Vandervoort asked.

"Reckon so."

Vandervoort pushed himself into a standing position. "We'll go with ya." He looked at Harley. "You ready?"

"I was hopin' to play a game with Mr. Tony first. Can I stay a little longer?"

"I dunno, son," he said, scratching his cheek. "Yer ma's gonna want ya home soon."

"I won't go easy on him this time, Pa, so it won't be a long game."

Tony frowned.

"Well, all right, then," Vandervoort said, patting Harley's back. "But come straight home when yer finished."

"Yes, sir. I will."

The men shuffled out and Harley began setting up the game.

"How's Brianna?" Tony asked, pouring himself a cup of coffee.

"Madder 'n a hornet."

"Mad? What about?"

"Her pa ain't gonna let her go to the Fourth of July celebration."

Tony settled into the ladder-back chair. "That's a pity. How's she doing otherwise?"

"Okay, I guess. She doesn't have to do no chores."

"Ah. A silver lining." Tony took a sip of coffee.

Harley moved first. "I still feel bad for her. The whole town will be there and we're gonna have sack races, a marble contest, and everything."

"Brianna plays marbles?" Tony asked, pushing his piece forward.

"Naw. She's all upset about that dumb box-supper auction. You know, where the fellers buy up food they could get fer free if they'd just eat with their ma instead o' some girl?"

Tony chuckled. "Isn't Brianna a bit young to be putting her box up?"

"Oh, she don't do it yet, but she wants to somethin' fierce. She still likes to see who buys whose, though. It's all her and her sisters been talkin' about." He jumped two of Tony's pieces.

"Maybe you could bring a bit of the celebration to her."

"How do you figure that?" Harley asked, moving onto Tony's king row.

"Well, you could ask your mother to help you make a box tied up with some little gewgaw of Brianna's. Then, when the auction starts, you could take it to her house, pretend like it was hers, bid on it, and then share it with her."

Harley smiled, positioning his king so that it threatened three of Tony's pieces. "She'd like that fer shore. And I bet my ma would like makin' a box, too."

Tony refocused on the checkerboard, dismayed to see any move he made would put him in harm's way. He looked at Harley.

The boy shrugged. "You gotta learn to talk and play at the same time."

In the next few minutes of silence, Harley claimed all of Tony's pieces.

chapter TEN

WITH A telegram from driller M.C. Baker in his pocket, Tony headed to the Corsicana Velocipede Club. He'd sent a message to Russ and received a reply from Baker himself. The brothers were still in Beaumont and free to come to Corsicana in a couple of weeks.

He lengthened his stride, wondering what kind of paces Essie was putting Sharpley through this time and if he could coax her into letting him participate.

He'd thought of her often over the last few days and had tried to glean a bit of information by covertly pumping the boys in the patch. But he hadn't learned anything new, other than a few specifics that confirmed what he already suspected. If the judge was head of the company, then Essie was its hands and feet.

Reaching the club, he knocked, then pushed open the door. Instead of Sharpley, though, he found a group of about twenty-five women gossiping around a table with cookies and punch. Some were young and in their twenties, but most were matrons. Essie was not among them.

He scanned the building and spotted her up on the bandstand, flipping through a sheaf of papers. She wore a blue gown with poofy sleeves that narrowed sharply to a skin-tight fit outlining elbows and lower arms. An extremely wide sash hugged her tiny waist, emphasizing curves both above and below. The brim of her hat protruded well past her forehead, while the back was pinched up, her blond hair piled underneath with a collection of curls at its center.

With her head bent over her papers, he noted for the first time the length of her long, lovely neck.

"Well, now, who have we here?" a petite, elderly woman asked, approaching with a cane.

He stifled his surprise at the woman's attire. She was wearing bloomers rather than a gown. Her trousers were baggy at the knees, abnormally full about the pockets, and considerably loose where one strikes a match.

He doffed his hat. "I was wanting to speak with Miss Spreckelmeyer, ma'am."

"Were you, now?" Through wire-rimmed spectacles, she looked him up and down with frank appreciation.

He felt his cheeks warm. "I can see she's busy, though. I'll just come back another time."

"Are you a member, Mr. . . . ?"

"Bryant." He nodded. "Tony Bryant. And you are?"

"Mrs. Penelope Lockhart."

"A pleasure, Mrs. Lockhart. And, no, I'm not a member."

"Would you like to be?"

He hesitated. "I'm . . . Is it . . . Are visitors allowed?"

Her skin folded like an accordion as she smiled. "Indeed they are. But in order to attend a meeting, you must come as a guest of one of the members."

"Well, I didn't really come to attend the meeting."

"Of course you did." She glanced quickly over her shoulder. "But we're supposed to register our guests ahead of time," she whispered. "We could just pretend I forgot all about that. Would you like to attend as my guest?" Her eyes were alight with appeal.

Despite his better judgment, he found himself responding to her less-than-subtle petition. "Won't your husband mind?" he asked in mock undertone.

She looked at him over her spectacles. "Not likely. He's been dead almost twenty years now."

He choked back a laugh, having no notion of what to say.

"Tonight's topic is Bicycle Etiquette for Courting Couples," Mrs. Lockhart said, then leaned in close. "I do not believe Miss Spreckelmeyer has ever discussed this particular topic in front of a, um, mixed crowd."

The touch of mischief in her eyes was unmistakable. He glanced again at Essie. She was giving lessons on *etiquette*? But the woman on the stage was not the ball-playing, snake-hunting, disheveled tomboy he'd walked home earlier this week. This Essie was every inch the proper, elegant, refined lady, and he found himself wondering what this side of her was like.

Returning his attention to the old woman before him, he offered her his arm. "It would be my honor to have such a lovely lady at my side this evening, Mrs. Lockhart."

Her eyes lit up. Hooking her cane over her elbow, she placed her hand on his arm. "Come, I'll introduce you to the girls."

Satisfied with the arrangement of her notes on the lectern, Essie decided it was time for Shirley to call the meeting of the Corsicana Velocipede Club to order. As she looked for Shirley, the sound of deep male laughter filled the room.

She moved her attention to the refreshment table. Tony, with a coffee cup in one hand and Mrs. Lockhart on his arm, stood surrounded by the ladies of the Velocipede Club.

He looked up, caught her watching him and telegraphed her a private hello. She experienced a quick rush of pleasure.

After careful consideration over the last few days, she finally realized why Tony had bucked her authority before. When she'd looked at him, all she'd seen was a toolie, not a man.

She smoothed the hair at the nape of her neck. She admitted to herself that she'd definitely noticed the *man* the other night, though. And she was sure he knew it—just like she knew he'd taken notice of her.

At the moment, Mrs. McCabe, the coroner's wife, held Tony's attention. She was a jolly, large-chested woman with a wicked sense of humor that did not suit her husband's occupation. Essie could not hear what the woman was saying, but her eyes were glowing and when she finished speaking, she whipped open her fan and put it to rapid use.

Tony threw back his head in laughter. The younger ladies giggled, though their eyes were downcast. The matrons, chuckling good-naturedly, exchanged knowing looks with one another.

Essie quickly left the stage and headed toward the group.

"You'll find Mr. Bunting a fine, civic-minded banker," Mrs. Blanchard, secretary of the bicycle club, interjected. She was a stout woman of fine form and looked as if she'd come right out of a Rubens painting. "Now, were you to visit Mr. Delk's bank, he'd say that he'd be happy to help carry the load. But what he means is for you to carry the piano and him to carry the sheet music."

Tony smiled. "Sounds as if Mr. Bunting's bank is the place to entrust my money, then?"

"I think so, yes."

"Ah," said Mrs. Lockhart, "here comes our teacher."

The ladies made room for Essie.

"My dear, this is my guest, Mr. Bryant. Mr. Bryant, this is the owner of the Velocipede Club, Miss Spreckelmeyer."

He tipped his head. "I've had an opportunity to become acquainted with Miss Spreckelmeyer already, as I'm a roustabout for Sullivan Oil."

The women *ahhhhed* in understanding.

"Hello, Mr. Bryant," Essie said. "Was there something you needed to see me about?"

"No, no," Mrs. Lockhart answered for him. "He is considering membership in the club and wanted to attend tonight's lecture on bicycle courtship."

Essie looked at him in surprise. Mrs. Lockhart was a consummate matchmaker. Had she decided he would do nicely for one of the younger girls and brought him here to promote her agenda? Was he party to her shenanigans?

"I don't recall seeing any guests listed on the register," she said.

"Oh my." Mrs. Lockhart brought a gloved hand to her lips. "I confess I completely forgot to sign him up in advance. Will you forgive me, dear?"

Something wasn't quite right, but Essie couldn't determine what it was. "Of course. Had I known he was coming, though, I might have chosen a more suitable topic."

He covered Mrs. Lockhart's hand with his. "Perhaps it would be best if I came another time."

"No, no," the woman responded. "We wouldn't hear of it. Would we, Essie?"

"Don't answer, Miss Spreckelmeyer," he said. "I have no wish to make you uncomfortable." He kissed Mrs. Lockhart's cheek. "Thank you, ma'am. It's been a pleasure."

"Tony," Essie said, stopping him before he could withdraw. "Don't be silly. You are more than welcome to stay."

He shook his head. "Thank you, but—"

"I insist."

Mrs. Lockhart latched on to his elbow. "There. All settled." She gave Essie a pointed look. "Isn't it time we start?"

"Yes, ma'am." She made eye contact with Shirley, and the girl hastened to the stage.

Tony glanced at Essie and, with a pained look, mouthed, *I'm sorry.*

She waved her hand in a dismissive gesture, but Mrs. Lockhart had already commandeered his attention as she directed him to the spot she sat every week. Right on the very first row.

Having a gentleman in the house electrified the women. Some tittered, some preened, while others laughed a little too loud. The younger women cast inviting glances Tony's direction, but he had eyes for Mrs. Lockhart alone.

Leaning much closer than was proper, he whispered something in her ear, earning himself a wicked chortle and a halfhearted slap on the arm.

Essie's stomach fluttered. How on earth would she convey tonight's message with Tony sitting directly in her line of vision? He towered almost a foot above the women.

She sighed. It could be worse, she supposed. He could have come to last week's lecture on corsets. She felt ill just thinking about it.

A spattering of applause commenced and Shirley looked at her expectantly. Essie jumped to her feet. Good heavens. She'd missed her own introduction.

Stepping up to the lectern, she silently read the first line of her notes. She believed her opening statement would set the tone for the entire evening and she'd given careful thought to its wording.

The charming and fascinating power of serpents over birds is as nothing compared with what a woman can wield over a man.

She couldn't say that now. Not with Tony sitting right there. She scanned down to the next paragraph.

A woman who once starts a man's love can get out of him, and do with him, anything possible she pleases.

Warmth began to bedevil her cheeks. She'd lifted that statement right out of the Social Manual her mother had given her. But how could she, a thirty-four-year-old unmarried woman with more failed relationships than she cared to admit, present such an argument?

She'd thought nothing of it before when she wrote her speech. But having a man present changed everything.

Perhaps she should skip the introduction and move directly to the point at hand. She flipped her first page over. The ladies began to fidget, disrupting the stillness of the vast room with a slight fluttering of skirts as they shifted in their chairs.

Panicked at how long she'd been standing there without saying a word, Essie simply picked a sentence and started. "Marriage very rarely mends a man's manners."

Good heavens. She took a calming breath and pressed forward. "Goldsmith says that 'love is often an involuntary passion placed upon our companions without our consent, and frequently conferred without even our previous esteem.' "

She knew only too well that statement was true.

"The first point to be considered on this subject is a careful choice of associates, which will often, in the end, save future unhappiness and discomfort."

Memories of the drifter who had stolen much more than her heart the summer of '94 swept through her, giving an urgency to her message. There were young, impressionable girls in her audience who could become the next ne'er-do-well's victim.

"An unsuitable acquaintance, friendship, or alliance is more embarrassing and more painful for the woman than the man. Wealth, charm, and genius mean nothing if the character of the man is flawed."

She looked from her papers to her club members. "The bicycle is responsible for much promiscuous acquaintanceship. Many elderly chaperones find it too difficult to keep up with their young charges. And if we are not very, very careful, the people lobbying to have bicycling outlawed for females will get their way."

She had them now. Every eye was focused on her. No outdoor pastime could be more independently pursued than bicycling. None of these women wanted to give up that freedom.

Tony, however, gazed back at her, not with rapt attention but with a touch of amusement, and it hurt her feelings, then ignited her sense of injustice. Men could walk away unscathed from a licentious relationship. Women were left ruined. Stripped of their reputations, their options, their very virtue.

"Just remember this, ladies," she said. "You cannot come to any harm unless you get *off* your bicycle."

Murmurs of agreement flitted through the room. Faint laugh lines formed at the corners of Tony's eyes.

Had she been wrong about him? Was he, in fact, simply passing through town, looking for a woman desperate enough to believe his quiet words and soft gestures?

Old wounds long since buried rose to the surface, surprising her with how swiftly and painfully they struck.

She made her next statement looking straight at him. "A man's duty to the woman who rides could be turned into a long sermon. But long sermons are never popular. So I will briefly state that he must always be on the alert to assist his fair companion in every way possible."

Mrs. Lockhart looked at him and he nodded at her with mock sobriety.

"He must be clever enough to repair any slight damage to her machine. He must assist her in mounting and dismounting. Pick her up when she has a tumble. And make himself generally useful. Incidentally ornamental. And quintessentially agreeable."

He chuckled. Not out loud, of course, but he bit the insides of his cheeks, and his shoulders shook. Mrs. Lockhart gave him a stern frown.

Essie gripped the lectern. "Lastly, he is to ride at her left in order to give her the more guarded place."

She stomped down from the bandstand and grabbed one of the two bicycles she'd had waiting in readiness for her demonstration. The wheels stood side by side, center front.

Originally, Shirley had agreed to assist her, but now that they had a bona fide "gentleman" in their midst, there would be no need for Shirley's help.

"In mounting, he holds her wheel." She thrust the machine toward him. "Mr. Bryant? Would you be so kind?"

He jumped to his feet. "It would be my honor." He turned to Mrs. Lockhart. "Please excuse me."

Mrs. Lockhart nodded and he stepped to the front, taking hold of the bike's handlebar.

Essie lifted her chin. "The lady stands on the left side of the machine and puts her right foot across the frame to the right pedal, which at the time must be up." Her skirts were far too long and full for riding. She'd never meant to actually mount, just to take the women through the steps verbally. But her entire speech had gone awry.

Giving him a brisk nod, she shooed him away. "You may see to your wheel now, Mr. Bryant." She edged the hem of her skirt up so it wouldn't get caught in the spokes or chains. "The lady rider starts ahead."

She pushed the right pedal, causing her machine to start and then with her left foot in place began to move forward. "She must go slowly at first, in order to give her cavalier time to mount his wheel, which he will do in the briefest possible time."

She glanced over her shoulder, hoping against hope that he would be slow and clumsy. But he was already upon his bike and taking up his position on her left side.

They kept to the perimeter of the seated assembly. She clutched at her skirts to keep them from becoming entangled. He made no effort to avert his gaze from the show of her ankle.

Halfway around the circle, she turned her attention to her members. "When the end of the ride is reached, the man quickly dismounts and is at his companion's side to assist her."

The women twisted and turned, trying to keep Essie and Tony within their view. Approaching the final leg of her journey, she prepared for dismounting.

"The most approved style of alighting from one's machine is when the left pedal is on the rise, the weight of the body is thrown onto it, and the right foot is crossed over the frame of the bike. Then, with an assisting hand, the rider easily steps to the ground."

Before she had finished speaking, he was there. Hand out, seeing her smoothly to the ground.

They stood facing each other, the silence in the room palpable.

He grazed her gloved knuckles with his thumb. "The pleasure was all mine, Miss Spreckelmeyer."

A collective sigh issued forth from the audience.

Essie snatched her hand from his. "Thank you for your assistance, sir."

He took her machine, parked it next to his and returned to his seat. The women started chattering at once, sharing their thoughts on what they'd seen and learned.

Essie reached the lectern and noted with a start that Tony's attention had never strayed from her. Mrs. Lockhart was speaking to him, but he paid her no heed. Instead, he stared intently at Essie.

It was not a flirtatious look he gave her. Or even a suggestive look. It was the look he'd given her when they played tug-of-war with her hairpin.

She swallowed and tugged her gloves more securely onto her hands. One thing was certain: His intentions toward her, honorable or otherwise, would be discernable soon enough.

chapter ELEVEN

MRS. LOCKHART pedaled her bike slowly, allowing Tony to keep up as he walked her home.

"So, Mr. Bryant," she said, her bloomers rustling, "why did you *really* come to the bicycle club tonight?"

He shot her a glance. "I had some business to discuss with Miss Spreckelmeyer."

"Business?" The wheels of her machine crunched against the gravel and dirt. "What kind of business?"

"Oil business."

"At such a late hour?"

"I work until sundown, ma'am. By the time I clean up, eat, and walk out to the club, the hands on the clock have done some spinning."

"Why not speak with the judge?"

Tony adjusted his hat. He wasn't sure if the townsfolk knew exactly how involved Essie was in the running of things. "I probably should have done that, now that you mention it."

A smile flitted across her face. "No. You did the right thing. Whatever you wanted, I'm sure Sullivan would have told you to go ask Essie."

They took a right on Decatur Street. A door closed in the distance. As they passed a house on the corner, the lantern hanging in its window went out.

"You like Essie, don't you?" Mrs. Lockhart asked.

He missed a step. "Uh, yes, ma'am. The Spreckelmeyers are good folks."

"That's not what I meant, sir."

He remained silent, wondering how much farther it was to her home.

"Well, then, where are you from, Mr. Bryant?"

"Beaumont."

"Beaumont. A very nice town. Do you still have family there?"

"Yes, ma'am. A mother and sister."

"I have family there, too. A daughter and a son-in-law."

He smiled in acknowledgment.

"I don't rightly recall any Bryants, though." She squinted her eyes, searching her memory. "Of course, there's Leah Bryant. You know, Blake Morgan's widow?"

He kept his face carefully blank.

"Would you be related to those Bryants?"

He pulled a handkerchief from his pocket and wiped his neck. "I imagine we're all related one way or another. What's your daughter's married name?"

"Otter. Mrs. Archibald Otter."

His heart began to hammer. Archie Otter was Morgan Oil's tool pusher. His wife, Leslie, was an intimate friend of Anna's, and the couple often sat with Tony's family on the porch while Archie picked his banjo.

He cleared his throat. "Do you have opportunity to visit your daughter very often?"

"Yes. Quite often. Her husband works for the Morgans. Who did you work for while you were there?"

"The same."

"Really? Then you must have known Archie." She lowered her voice. "He's very high up in the company, you know."

"Yes, ma'am. Everybody knows who Mr. Otter is."

She hit a hole in the road, causing her bike to wobble.

He reached out and steadied her.

"My son-in-law was always singing the praises of Tony Morgan, one of Mr. Morgan's sons." She sighed. "According to Archie, though, Mr. Morgan disappeared after being disinherited by his father. Actually, that happened right about the time you arrived in town."

He studied her face, trying to decide if she was baiting him.

She slowed in front of a hipped-roof bungalow surrounded by a white picket fence. "I shall have to tell Archie I've made your acquaintance." She looked him directly in the eyes. "He never forgets a name or face."

She knew who he was. No question about it. Perhaps they had even met when he was with the Otters, but he could not recall one way or the other.

He assisted her off her bike.

"Won't you come in for a refreshment, Mr. Bryant?"

He handed her cane to her and opened the gate. "I'm afraid I can't, ma'am. It's awfully late and I have to be out on the fields at first light."

She walked through, then waited while he retrieved her bike and brought it inside the yard.

"Where would you like me to put this?" he asked.

"Come, I'll show you."

The grass crunched beneath his boots as they headed to the back of her house.

"Are you returning to the club to discuss . . . *business* with Essie?"

"I might swing by on my way home and see if she's still there."

Mrs. Lockhart nodded. "She wears her spinsterhood like a suit of armor, you know."

"I beg your pardon?"

"It'll take a man with great skill to find the chinks."

He stopped, but the old woman kept going. She was much more intuitive than he'd given her credit for and in order to keep her quiet about his identity, he would need to cultivate a relationship of some sort with her.

That aside, he was willing to admit he wanted to find the chinks in Essie's armor but didn't think it wise. Not while his family relied on the goodwill of Darius. Instead, he should be working his way up through Sullivan Oil, learning everything he could about the business.

He'd been working hard during the day, sleeping hard at night. He'd been keeping an eye out for men who would make good partners and good investors. He'd been saving every penny he earned. And when the time was right, he planned to branch out on his own, build up his business and send for his mother and sister.

But that would take months yet. Years, even. His mother would probably be all right, but what about Anna? He decided to write another letter home. His sister must observe the customary year of mourning. Not just because it was the respectful thing to do, but because her very future depended on it.

"Take Monday, for example," Mrs. Lockhart said, pulling Tony back into the present. He quickly caught up to her.

"If you were wanting to escort Essie to the Fourth of July celebration, you'd certainly have your work cut out for you."

"You think so?"

"I know so."

They rounded the house and came face-to-face with the silhouette of a giant derrick in her backyard. For houses in these parts, derricks had become as common as chimneys over the past few years—he'd seen the same thing happen in Beaumont, though he was a little surprised to find Mrs. Lockhart living under the shadow of such a monstrosity.

"You can prop Hilda right there," she said.

Hilda? He leaned her machine against the derrick's legs. The familiar smell of oil enveloped them. He figured he could find every derrick in Corsicana blindfolded just by sniffing for fumes.

"Are you going to ask our Essie to the celebration?"

A rabbit leaped from underneath a bush, then disappeared into the tree line. He cupped Mrs. Lockhart's elbow and helped her onto the back porch. "I hadn't thought much about it."

"Perhaps you should."

He considered her suggestion. Essie was already disrupting his schedule and his efforts to remain focused. He thought about her constantly. And tonight she'd looked so, well, pretty. Maybe taking her to this one event would relieve some of his pent-up tension.

"You think Miss Spreckelmeyer would tell me no?" he asked.

"I'm sure of it."

He removed his hat. "You have any suggestions?"

Mrs. Lockhart smiled. "Yes. As a matter of fact, I do. Would you like to come in?"

He hesitated. "Only for a minute, ma'am."

⌒

After such an unsettling evening, Essie wanted nothing so much as to be alone, so she had sent Shirley home. Without help, it would take twice as long to close up, but the quietness of the club at night never failed to soothe her.

She loved the vastness of the room and the way it magnified even the slightest of sounds. In the lamplight, the vaulted roof seemed closer somehow, and the stillness reminded her of church. Staying here when everyone else had gone gave her a sense of keeping vigil, and she loved sharing her thoughts with God when no one else was around.

One by one she began to extinguish the sconces along the far wall, each sputtering as she snuffed out their amber glow. At the sound of the door opening, she turned. Tony stepped through, searched the shadows until he found her, then pushed the door shut behind him. The latch clicked into place.

Light from the remaining lamps glazed the left side of his silhouette with gold. He tipped his hat back, then swaggered toward her, his footsteps echoing through the building.

As he approached, he studied her from hat to head, shoulder to waist, waist to toe, and back up again. The slow survey awakened in her long-forgotten—and certainly forbidden—desires.

He came to a stop just inches from her.

Not wanting to be in the dark with him, she twisted the metal knob on the lamp at her shoulder until the hissing flame bathed them both in light. His eyes shone, his whole face seemed to glow.

"I didn't expect to see you again this evening," she said. "Was there something you needed?"

"I received a telegram from the Baker brothers."

He spoke quietly, his words saying one thing but the look on his face another. She hardly knew which overture to answer.

"What did it say?" she asked.

He slipped his hand behind his lapel, digging inside his shirt pocket. The blue cotton stretched tight across his chest, until he found and withdrew a crumpled piece of paper.

Pinching the edge with one hand, he unfurled it between the thumb and finger of his other, one slow stroke at a time. The parchment crackled, opening like a flower.

"M.C. is going to come in a few weeks," he said, handing her the telegram.

She took hold of the message, but when she tried to draw it near, he didn't let go. She waited, eyes down. He'd released her hairpin that night on Brianna's porch. Surely he would release the paper now.

But he did not.

She tugged again.

"Essie?" he whispered.

She let go and took a step back.

He held the telegram suspended between them before finally reaching for her hand. He pressed the crumpled paper in her palm and gently squeezed before releasing her.

She curled her fist around the telegram, the paper rough against her skin. "What else does it say?"

"Read it."

She opened her hand, but the note remained crumpled. Placing it against her stomach, she flattened it, then made the mistake of looking up.

She wished she'd left the lantern off. Tony's eyes were dark. Intense. His nostrils flared.

She held the telegram up to the light, confirming that M.C. Baker would be here the fourteenth of July. "Thank you for arranging this."

"You're welcome."

She handed him back the telegram. "Would it be too much to ask you to accompany me to the train station when he comes? That way you could point him out and make the introductions?"

He folded the paper into fourths, creasing each fold between thumb and fingernail. "It would be my pleasure."

She moistened her lips. "Yes. Well. Thank you again."

"You're welcome again."

He tucked the paper back into his shirt pocket.

She waited, but he said no more.

"Was there something else?" she asked.

He hesitated, then took a deep breath. "Is anyone taking you to the Fourth of July celebration?"

Her lips parted. "No."

"I'd like to take you, Essie. Will you go with me?"

She ran her fingers along the skirt pleats at her waist. "My father usually escorts me to such events."

He removed his hat, then tapped it against his leg. The light caught and highlighted the richness of his hair.

"Tony, I . . . How old are you?"

He lifted his brows. "Twenty-eight. Why?"

"Because I am a good deal older than you." She gave a quick twist to the knob of the lamp, plunging them into darkness. "I'm afraid I must respectfully decline."

She headed to the next sconce.

He followed. "I'm only six years younger. That's nothing."

She spun around. "How do you know my age?"

"Mrs. Lockhart told me."

"Mrs. Lockhart told you? Why would she do a thing like that?"

She started toward the sconce again, but he touched her arm, stopping her. "She said you still have plenty of years left in you."

"Mr. Bryant!"

He held up his hands. "She said it, not me."

She yanked on her cuffs. "The two of you gossiped about me?"

"Not in the way you mean. Mrs. Lockhart has a way of getting a fella to spill out more information than he has a mind to. By the time I got her home, she'd learned I was planning to ask you to the festivities." He pulled on his ear. "Once she found that out, she gave me all kinds of tips and advice."

Essie stiffened. "Like what?"

"She said you'd hide behind your spinsterhood—"

"I'm not hiding!"

"She said you'd worry over what people would think—"

"Well, of course I'd worry what people would think. I have a business to run and a reputation to uphold. I can't be acting like a schoolgirl. Every one of my business acquaintances will be there."

"She said you'd not want to step out with an employee—"

"And she's absolutely right! That would be the height of stupidity."

"She said your eyes shoot out sparks when you feel passionately about something." His voice dropped and he took a step closer. "I can see she's right."

Essie retreated a step. "The answer is still no. Thank you for asking."

She continued turning out lanterns all the way around the room. He didn't move or say a thing. One more sconce left. The one at the entrance.

"Are you coming, Mr. Bryant?" Her voice sounded shrill, even to her own ears.

He settled his hat on his head. "Yes, ma'am."

He took his time, then instead of heading to the door, he removed her shawl from its hook and held it open for her.

Swallowing, she turned her back. He draped it across her shoulders, turned out the final lamp, opened the door and waited.

"You are not walking me home."

He said nothing. Just held the door.

She hurried outside, but no matter how fast she walked, he stayed by her side. She suppressed a groan, chagrined that she'd allowed things to come to this.

She was still shocked by the objections he'd heard from Mrs. Lockhart. No doubt he had expected her to disown them, coming from his lips, but they had the opposite effect. Whatever attraction she might have felt for him, whatever scruples she'd been thinking to set aside before, the objections made perfect sense. After all, she was the boss and he was the worker. She had wealth and standing in the community, he had nothing.

What would people say if they saw him courting her? They would laugh at the difference in age and station. They would whisper behind her back about how desperate she'd become. They'd say he was after her wealth or, worse, her virtue.

And for all she knew, they'd be right. She could hardly trust her own judgment when it came to matters of the heart.

No. She had long since reconciled herself to being unmarried. Once she had finally embraced singleness, she found it suited her quite nicely. She must keep that at the forefront of her mind.

Tony never would have made his offer if Mrs. Lockhart hadn't put him up to it, and now that Essie had refused, he ought to be grateful. It went against all his principles to complicate his personal mission by pursuing a woman. Instead, however, her refusal roused a deep-seated instinct to hunt, capture and conquer.

Essie was churning up dust just ahead of him, dragging him along like a fish on a hook. He lengthened his stride to keep up with her. The faster she bolted, the more he wanted to stop her, but they were almost halfway to her house and he still didn't know what he'd say if he did.

Still, he reached out, gently grabbing her elbow. "Slow down. You're moving faster than a deacon taking up a collection."

She yanked herself free and spun to face him. "I wouldn't be going so fast if you would leave me be."

Her chest was heaving. A few bits of hair had slipped loose of the fancy twist decorating the back of her head, and he wondered what she'd do if he reached over and took the pins out to let it fall.

"I like your hat," he said.

A bit of the starch immediately left her. "Th-thank you."

"You're welcome."

She touched the back of her head and discovered her disheveled hair. With jerky movements, she stuffed bits and pieces into place.

"Why won't you go with me?" he asked.

She closed her eyes for a moment before answering. "Because I'm your boss. It is simply out of the question."

"I don't believe you."

Surprise followed by a look of wariness crossed over her face.

He clasped her hand. "Why won't you go with me?"

Her eyes welled up. "I can't," she whispered. "I can't do this again. Please don't ask it of me."

He stroked her inner wrist with his thumb, catching part glove and part skin. "Can't do what again?"

She tugged on her hand.

He interlocked their fingers. "Tell me."

"We've an entire town of young, pretty girls much more suited to your age. I'm sure any one of them would be thrilled to accompany you."

"I don't want to go with them."

"Why not?"

"Because I want to go with you."

"Why?"

"Why?" He hesitated, stumbling over his thoughts. "Why do I want to go with you? You're asking me why?"

"Yes." She looked straight at him, a touch of confusion in her expression and not a little vulnerability.

In a whoosh, his pulse calmed, his vision cleared, the tension left him. "Because, Essie, you have real pretty eyes. You're nicely put together. You're not flighty and giggly like all those young girls you seem so anxious to thrust upon me. You showed an incredible amount of strength and character when Brianna was bitten by that snake. And when you smile, you have two dimples that I noticed the very first time I saw you. Remember? You'd just fallen off the banister."

She'd gone stone still. "I didn't fall off. My heel broke."

"Go with me, Essie."

"No."

"Why?"

"It's . . . complicated."

"It's not. It's the simplest of things and it's done every day by men and women all over God's creation."

"Not by me. And I won't change my mind. So will you please let me go?"

He studied her. She meant every word. He dropped his hold.

She tucked her arm against her waist, well out of his reach. "Good night, Mr. Bryant."

"I'm walking you home, Essie."

"Please don't."

He swept his hand in an "after you" gesture.

The pace she set was not exactly breakneck, but it wasn't leisurely, either. He wanted to take her elbow but reconciled himself to simply walking beside her. They approached her house and he opened the gate.

"Thank you for seeing me home, Mr. Bryant. I believe I can make it to the door by myself."

He tugged the rim of his hat. "As you wish, ma'am."

She backed through the gate, then spun and raced up her sidewalk and into the safety of her home.

chapter TWELVE

THE FOURTH of July dawned full of promise. After breakfast, Tony went out on the streets, which were already packed with people. The whole of Corsicana was outdoors, basking under sunny skies punctuated by the occasional cloud.

He set a jaunty pace, falling into step with the people around him. Children darted through the crowds, and a morning breeze blew down the lane, rustling ladies' skirts. At Beaton Street, he paused while a marching band passed through the intersection, serenading the town with patriotic tunes.

He eyed a taffy vendor urging him to buy, but he shook his head. He couldn't afford such frivolities. Every penny counted.

A pang of homesickness washed over him and he wondered if his mother and Anna would be attending Beaumont's celebration. In years past, he'd always been their escort. Now they'd be adrift in the crowds—or worse, they would be under Darius's thumb.

He'd only received one letter from them, a quick note conveying Mother's relief that he'd found some work and her chagrin over Darius's disregard for showing proper respect for the dead. At the time, though, both she and Anna were still in black.

A stray tabby wove between Tony's legs. He stroked its matted fur, then followed the band as they made their way to the Velocipede

Club. Essie was hosting a public ride and he aimed to witness the spectacle firsthand.

On the way, he saw familiar faces from the rigs. Most of his working buddies had started their celebration in the saloons and would not find their way out for at least another hour. A few of the oilmen, however, had already imbibed and were ready to commence with the day's activities.

Females of every age, size, and shape came bedecked in all their finery. He watched them kick up the back of their skirts as they strolled on the arms of their husbands, fathers, and beaus.

He wondered what Essie was wearing and how much it would cost to win her box supper. Slipping his hand in his pocket, he ran his fingers over the coins jingling there. He'd have to set himself a limit—not so low as to be insulting, but not so high he couldn't part with the money.

If someone else outbid him, he'd just have to live with it. He would bid, though, for as long as he could, on whatever basket matched her clothing.

⌇

The care and planning that went into a woman's Fourth of July outfit was second only to her Easter attire. For Essie, the burden was greater, because she had a reputation to maintain, and she no longer had her mother to conspire with. As she approached the bandstand of the Velocipede Club, she glanced down at her white dotted-swiss gown one last time hoping she had achieved her desired effect. The front of her skirt was pleated in, its folds caught with a series of blue bows, each held by a fancy button.

She smoothed her bodice of blue accordion-pleated mousseline de soie and straightened her fancy straw hat. It held a cluster of red roses on the left side, surrounded by loops of blue ribbon and white lace.

The club was filled to capacity. Looking out at the crowd, she saw new members, established members, and plenty of adventurers, too, willing to give the bicycle a try just this once. The bleachers burst with spectators in an array of colorful attire, calling down cheerfully to the riders as they prepared.

The Collin Street Bakery provided refreshments at a table in the back. Bicyclers stood about the rink visiting with each other as they waited for the music to start. Attendance this year was even higher than the last. She decided she would most likely have to hold two public rides in '99.

"The band's about settled there on the platform," Uncle Melvin said, his sheriff's badge winking. "You ready to get this thing goin'?"

"I'm ready," she said, tucking her hand into his elbow and noting he'd curled and waxed the ends of his bushy gray moustache.

He assisted her onto the stage, then let out a piercing whistle that cut through the crowd, silencing them.

"Here's the rules," Uncle Melvin shouted. "No chewin'. No spittin'. No walkin' across the rink. Food and drinks are free. If you're of a mind to give one of these machines a twirl, then don't cut anybody off. Don't run anybody over. And don't park in the middle o' the track. Any questions?"

None were forthcoming.

"Essie-girl?" he said. "You got anything you wanna say?"

She stepped to the front. "Welcome to the Fourth Annual Corsicana Velocipede Club's Group Ride. We're so very glad you're here." She turned to the band director. "Mr. Creiz?"

The conductor held up his baton, bringing the band to attention, then commenced on the downstroke, starting the event off with their traditional "Bicycle Built for Two."

The wheelers mounted their bikes and began whizzing around the track, singing to the music while friends and family joined in from the bleachers. Mr. Peeples, an employee of the Anheuser-Busch

Brewing Company, wobbled back and forth on his machine, had a near miss but, to his credit, kept his balance and avoided taking a spill.

"You go on ahead, honey," Melvin hollered in her ear. "I see Deputy Howard signaling me."

He gave her a peck on the cheek, then headed to the other side of the stage. Lifting her skirts, she started down the stairs, accepting a hand that shot out to assist her before realizing it belonged to Tony.

His appearance made her pause. Gone were the blue denim trousers, rawhide boots, and cowboy hat. In their place stood a gentleman in the very latest of summer fashions.

He wore a blue pincheck four-button coat that fit his broad shoulders so well it could not possibly have been borrowed. She'd developed an eye for such details after working in Hamilton Crook's mercantile.

She noted at once that the fine dress shirt, celluloid collar, and cuffs Tony wore were of the very best quality. The silk tie around his neck had been knotted by an experienced hand. Even the brown Derby on his head seemed particularly fine. How could a roustabout afford such fine clothing? What's more, how could he wear them with such ease?

He said something to her, but the music swallowed his words.

From the corner of her eye, she saw Mr. Peeples accidentally cut off Mr. Davis. Essie couldn't catch Mr. Davis's words as he swerved to the side, but she had an inkling as the man's face turned red and he shook his fist.

Mr. Peeples smiled and waved, fully confident in his newfound ability.

She continued down the steps, then stood before Tony. His gaze traveled over her hat, her new gown, her face.

"You look beautiful," he said, bending close so she could hear him.

"Thank you." She kept her voice neutral.

"Will you ride with me?"

"I'm sorry. I've hostess duties to attend to."

As if verifying the truth of her words, a loud shriek, followed by a sharp, "Look out!" caused her to whirl around.

Mr. Peeples jerked his handlebars sharply to the left to avoid running into one matron, only to, instead, broadside another.

Lifting her skirts just above the toes, Essie hurried to the collision.

⌇

Tony stood on the periphery of the bicycle club watching Essie welcome guests, soothe ruffled feathers, manage crises, calm drunks, enroll new members and sell bicycle accessories. He was content to watch her work until Deputy Billy John Howard approached her.

The crowd drifted away as the deputy moved in. People in Corsicana tended to give the small man a wide berth. All the rumors Tony had heard about Howard came back to him.

He was surprised at how familiar the man was with Essie. As a protégé of her Uncle Melvin, it was natural that they'd be acquainted, but the way she stiffened as he hovered near her—and the way she bobbed and weaved to avoid his covertly straying hands—put Tony on his guard.

What was the deputy playing at? If he'd been courting Essie, Mrs. Lockhart would have said, and it was obvious from Essie's reactions that Howard's attentions were unwelcome.

Several times, Tony started forward to intervene, then stopped himself. It was none of his business, after all. And if Essie was a distraction from his purpose, then trouble with a deputy was even worse.

Howard settled his hand on Essie's waist, and all Tony's reasoning evaporated. He headed toward them. She twisted from Howard's touch, but he immediately returned it to the curve of her back and leaned over to whisper something in her ear.

He couldn't tell what the man was saying, but whatever it was caused Essie to flush.

The band finished up the last chorus of "A Hot Time in the Old Town." Spectators clapped. Wheelers continued to ride.

" . . . so what do you say?" Howard asked.

"If you would excuse me, I have things to attend to," Essie said in undertones, once again shoving aside his hand.

He grabbed her wrist, careful to keep it hidden in the folds of her skirt. "You listen here, missy. I've had just about enough—"

"Miss Spreckelmeyer?" Tony said, joining them. "Mrs. Gillespie needs your assistance."

The deputy puffed out his chest, making sure Tony saw the star pinned to his vest. "She'll be along in a minute."

"She's needed now." Tony kept his posture relaxed but allowed a bit of steel to enter his voice.

Howard narrowed his eyes. "I don't believe we've—"

"Billy John," said Preacher Wortham, stepping to their circle and extending his hand.

The deputy had no choice but to let go of Essie or leave Wortham's hand hanging in the air.

"I've been meaning to talk to you about the appalling amount of liquor consumed within our town," the preacher said, placing a hand on Howard's shoulder and turning him toward the door. "You don't mind if I steal the deputy for a moment, do you, Essie?"

Tony saw a look pass between the preacher and Essie, leaving him no doubt as to Wortham's motivations. The preacher had done what Tony could not.

"Mr. Bryant here said Shirley was in need of me." She turned to Tony. "Lead the way."

Cupping Essie's elbow, Tony escorted her toward a table in the far corner where a German man and his partner were giving out slices of fruitcake.

"What was all that about?" Tony asked.

"Nothing."

"Didn't look like 'nothing' to me. How long has he been bothering you?"

"Just a bit longer than you have."

He let go of her. "You view me the same way you do him?"

She paused, looking startled at the suggestion. "No, of course not. I meant no offense." She looked around. "I don't see Shirley over here."

Taking a deep breath, he decided to ignore the sting of her careless remark. "Mrs. Gillespie doesn't need you. I made that up."

"*Did* you?" She took a moment to study him, her guard slipping a bit as she considered his gesture. "Well, thank you, then—for coming to my assistance. I appreciate it."

He picked up a slice of fruitcake, broke a piece off and handed it to her.

She popped it into her mouth. "Ummm. That's good. I didn't realize how hungry I was."

He started to ask her about Howard again but realized this wasn't the place.

"Well." She brushed the crumbs from her fingers. "I'm afraid you'll have to excuse me. I see Mrs. Tyner is waving me over."

He nodded his head in acknowledgment, but she had already walked away, slipping him as quickly as she had the deputy.

∽

Beneath an old wooden pavilion, Tony strolled past the tables lining the auctioneer's dais, each of them bowed with the weight of box suppers. Not a one of them held frippery to match Essie's outfit.

Tony once again surveyed the collection of baskets, ribbons, bunting, bows, and gewgaws. Where in the blazes was her box?

"Quite a selection, isn't it?" the preacher said, joining him. "Do you see one that takes your fancy?"

"Not just yet, I'm afraid," Tony answered.

The preacher stuck out his hand, and Tony clasped it.

"Good to see you again," Wortham said. "What did you think of the service on Sunday?"

"I enjoyed it very much."

The preacher wasn't the only one of Essie's patrons to have arrived at the red-white-and-blue-festooned pavilion. Most of the others, having concluded their group ride, milled about the fairgrounds with other locals in anticipation of the box-supper auction.

"So," Wortham said, "are you looking for any basket in particular?"

"Matter of fact, I am. What about you? Is your wife's box somewhere in here?"

Wortham smiled. "I'm afraid hers might be a bit difficult to find seeing as how I haven't got a wife."

Tony nodded, remembering Grandpa had mentioned that the time Wortham and Harley came out to the patch. Tony didn't think he'd ever met a preacher with no wife. Those two things just went together like ham and eggs.

"Which one are you going to bid on, then?" Tony asked.

"Oh, I don't have a particular one in mind this year. What about you?"

Tony scanned the box suppers. "I was looking for Miss Spreckelmeyer's."

"Were you, now?" Wortham lifted his brows. "Well, what do you know about that. Is she aware you want to bid on it?"

"She might have some inkling. How much competition do you think I'll have?"

A mischievous smile grew on the preacher's face. "Considering who she's been sharing her basket with for the past four years, I'd say you have some mighty big competition."

Tony's chest tightened.

Chuckling, Wortham slapped him on the shoulder. "Don't worry. It's nobody you need concern yourself with."

"It's not the deputy, is it?"

"Goodness, no." Wortham's frown made his distaste for the deputy plain, but he disguised it quickly enough.

Tony rubbed his mouth. "Do you know what was going on this afternoon when you interrupted Howard and her?"

"I aim to find out."

"You interested in Miss Spreckelmeyer?" Tony asked, narrowing his eyes.

The preacher gave him a long look. "I was at one time. But she turned me down."

She seemed to make a habit of rebuffing suitors, Tony thought. He wondered if Wortham had given up on her yet.

"You bidding on her box supper today, Preacher?"

"No, I'm not."

Tony released a pent-up breath. He'd never been one to share his thoughts with strangers, even if they were preachers, but he figured Wortham could answer some of the questions rattling around in his head. "So how long have you known her?"

"Essie? A long time." Wortham smiled. "We've been friends for as far back as I can remember."

"That so?"

"She was a grand playmate. She taught me how to fish, shoot, swim, climb trees, and gig frogs. I was half in love with her before I ever reached adolescence."

Gig frogs? "So what happened?"

"She turned me down flat. Said I was too much like a little brother. Kinda takes the starch out of a fellow, if you know what I mean."

Tony smiled. "Well, don't feel bad. She's fighting me tooth and nail, as well."

As soon as he said the words, he regretted them. He hadn't meant to make light of his feelings toward her, even if he didn't exactly know what they were.

The preacher picked up on the false note in Tony's voice. The man's posture never changed, but his tone turned colder than a well chain in December.

"Just make sure you don't hurt her, Bryant, or else you'll answer to me."

Tony shook his head. "I'd never hurt her, sir."

For the first time, he sized Wortham up as a man, not a preacher. He was short, but he was no weakling. The way he filled out his jacket was nothing to scoff at. Tony figured he could throw a good punch if he had a mind to.

The crowd had grown in anticipation of the auction, gathering tightly within the pavilion. A group of young ladies clustered together, giggling and trying hard not to see if the fellow of their choosing was lingering nearby. Essie was nowhere in sight.

Wortham took Tony by the shoulders and turned him so he was facing east. "She's up there. Under that big oak tree."

A couple hundred yards away on the crest of a green hill, a massive oak tree dwarfed Essie while providing an abundance of shade beneath its outstretched branches.

"And her basket isn't for sale," he added. "It's been off the market for a long time. If'n you want to share it with her, you'll have to do some mighty slick talking. Good luck."

Pushing the rim of his hat back, Tony took in the sight. Young boys rolled down the slope, racing to see who could reach bottom first, with no regard for the clumps of yellow wild flowers they crushed along the way. But Essie kept her head down, paying them no attention.

He wove through the crowd, greeting several of the men he worked with. To his surprise, many of the women he'd met at the Velocipede Club last week stopped and introduced him to their husbands. Mrs. Bunert was married to a harness maker. Mrs. Fowler, the blacksmith. Mrs. Garitty, the Opera House president. And Mrs. Whiteselle, the mayor. By the time he made it to Essie's hill, the auction in the pavilion was in full swing.

The farther up the incline he moved, the better he could see. With her white skirt billowing out around her, she scribbled in a journal of some sort that she'd propped on her lap. Beside her lay her gloves, hat, and box supper. She'd decorated her basket to match the ribbons in her hat and the bows on her skirt.

As he drew closer, he half expected to be overtaken by a rival. He looked around and saw no one, but his imagination still ran rampant. What would he do if a man stepped out from behind the tree and took his place beside Essie, neatly edging Tony out?

A blue-checkered cloth covering her meal had been nudged aside, and she occasionally removed bits and pieces of the basket's contents, absently nibbling on them. So caught up was she in her writings that she didn't hear him approach. Didn't know he was there until his shadow fell across her blanket.

Shading her eyes, she looked up. "Mr. Bryant!" She slammed her journal shut. "I didn't expect . . . I thought you were . . ." She took a deep breath. "How do you do?"

He removed his hat. "How do *you* do?"

"I'm fine. Thank you."

"May I?" he asked, indicating the blanket.

"Well, um, actually, I was, um, saving it, sort of."

"Saving it?" He looked around. "For whom?"

She placed her pencil atop her journal. "For the person I usually share my box supper with."

Disappointment gripped him. "And who would that be?"

"Christ."

He blinked. "Christ? You mean, *Jesus* Christ?"

"The very same."

"You share your box supper with Jesus Christ?"

"Yes. I do."

Relief poured through him. No suitor would intercept him, after all. He knelt on the blanket, then settled down beside her.

"As it happens," he said, "the Lord and I are very close. I'm sure He wouldn't mind if I were to join the two of you."

"I'm sure He wouldn't."

He placed his hat next to hers.

"I, on the other hand, mind very much."

He froze.

"I cherish this time I spend with Him. The nice thing about all this is that if you would like to take your meal with Him, He can be in two places at once."

He could not believe he was having this conversation. "Essie, it's you I want to have supper with."

"I'm sorry. Perhaps if you hurry, you can acquire one of the boxes up for auction."

"I don't want any of those boxes. I want yours." He sighed. "Is my company really that repulsive?"

She looked away. "It's not you personally, Tony."

"Then what is it?"

"You're my employee. It would be unseemly."

Couples began to trickle out from the pavilion as suppers were auctioned off. Mothers put their youngsters down on blankets for naps. A group of older men sharing stories and a liquor jug clustered together on the edges of the fairgrounds. Up on the hill, it all seemed so far away.

Rubbing the back of his neck, he glanced at her lap. "What were you writing?"

She kept the pages of her journal firmly closed within her grip. "Nothing."

"Something, surely?"

"Nothing that need concern you."

His stomach growled. He glanced at her supper. "You know, I was really looking forward to today because I haven't had anything to eat since I arrived other than the fare Mr. Castle serves up in his drugstore."

Her brow crinkled for the briefest of moments.

He picked up his hat and started to rise.

"Mr. Castle's meals aren't so bad," she said.

"Not if you like to eat the same thing over and over every three days."

"There are other restaurants in town."

"Not that a roustabout can afford."

After a slight hesitation, she moistened her lips, then gently tugged the covering off her basket. Fried chicken, green corn patties, cheese wafers, potato croquettes, hard-boiled eggs, two fluffy biscuits, and a broken-off fig tart. His mouth watered.

"Somebody's sampled the dessert already," he said, making no effort to disguise the teasing in his voice. "Was that you or the Lord?"

She studied him for a moment, then moved the basket between them. "Just remember, Eli's sons both dropped dead when they ate food prepared for God."

He smiled and settled back down on the blanket. "That was a consecrated offering. And made before Christ came to abolish the law. Besides, I've already sent up a quick prayer asking if He'd mind."

She gave a slight smile. "And what did He say?"

"To help myself."

She huffed, but he could see her heart wasn't in the resistance. He peeled a bite off a chicken breast with his teeth, the crispy crust a perfect foil for the tender meat.

Back in the pavilion, a heated competition had commenced, the shouting so loud it nearly drowned out the auctioneer's voice. At the climax of the proceedings, everyone burst into applause.

Tony ate another piece of chicken, plus a sampling of corn, cheese, and potatoes before Essie finally joined in.

"Harley tells me Brianna is doing better," he said. "Have you seen her?"

"Yes. And every day the swelling goes down a little bit more. Today will be hard on her, though. Her father wouldn't let her come to the festivities."

"That's what Harley told me," he said. "But he and I came up with a scheme to cheer her up."

"What scheme?" she asked.

"Harley had his mother make up a box supper for him. He's going to take it over to Brianna's and pretend like it's hers, then 'buy' it from an imaginary auctioneer." He scanned the park. "As a matter of fact, I haven't seen him in a while, so it wouldn't surprise me if that's where he is now."

Essie's lips parted, her eyes softening. "I know Harley didn't think of that. Was it your idea?"

He shrugged. "It was the only thing I could come up with."

"It was wonderfully sweet."

He chuckled. "It oughta earn Harley a star or two." He reached for the half-eaten fig tart.

"What are you doing?" she asked.

"Having my half of dessert."

"That's not your half. That's my half."

He removed the partially eaten confection. "There were at least two portions of everything but the fig tart. So either you've eaten one and a half tarts, or you forgot to provide Christ with dessert."

"I made Him one."

"Then where is it?"

She didn't answer.

He wagged his finger at her. "You ate it already, didn't you? You ate the Lord's dessert and half of your own, and now you want the rest of mine?"

She eyed the tart longingly. "They're my favorite. And I didn't know you were coming."

"All right, then," he said, winking. "What will you give me for it?"

Her back went ramrod straight. "I'll not play those games with you, Mr. Bryant."

He started to laugh, but her stern, unwavering glare said she was serious.

"You may take the fig tart and go." Her voice was sharp, clipped.

"Whoa, there, girl. I was only kidding." He placed the tart back in the basket, then motioned for her to take it, but she remained stubbornly still.

"I was just teasing, Essie. I didn't mean anything by it."

"Didn't you?" She held up her hand, cutting off his denial. "I know exactly how men like you work. A charming word. A gallant gesture. Then you cast out some harmless bait—only it isn't harmless once it is taken. But by then it is too late. The damage is done."

She wadded up the checkered cloth and tossed it into her basket, along with her journal and pencil.

Tony sat still, stunned by the force behind her words, by the anger that surged up like a newly tapped well. And like a gusher, it had drenched everything around it, including him.

He placed a hand on her gloves before she could reach for them. "I'm sorry. I meant no offense. I have no idea what you thought I intended, but it wasn't dishonorable. You have my word."

"And just how do I know if your word is any good?"

He sucked in his breath. "Now, wait just a minute. What's that supposed to mean? You think I'd lie?"

She plucked up her gloves.

"Don't leave," he said, standing. "I'll be on my way. I never intended to chase you from the celebration. I know you've worked really hard today with your group ride and all. And I want you to enjoy yourself. Please."

She stilled, her hand on the basket handle, never once meeting his gaze.

"Thank you for the meal, Essie. It was the best I've had in a long while. You have a nice evening, now."

Placing his hat on his head, he headed down the hill without a single backward glance.

chapter THIRTEEN

SNAPPING THE blanket in the air, Essie shook loose the dirt and debris. She should never have shared her lunch with Tony. She loved spending this time with the Lord and had no desire to replace it with a man simply because he couldn't afford a decent meal.

Folding the blanket in half and then fourths, she glanced at Tony's retreating figure. He'd reached the bottom of the hill and was making his way toward a game of horseshoes. Even from here the expensive cut of his clothes struck her.

His was no new outfit purchased for the holiday. The jacket, though brushed and well taken care of, draped his shoulders like a dear old friend. Only a man accustomed to wearing costly clothes could move in them with such ease.

She recalled Mr. Zimpelman attending his daughter's wedding in a suit clear from New York City, his work boots peeking out from the wool trousers puddling at his feet. His jacket had ridden too low, his vest too high. He'd tugged on his collar, tripped on his pant legs and soiled his ascot.

She smoothed the creases along the folds of her blanket. Tony didn't even seem to notice his fine clothes. He wore them with casual indifference, as if he were born to them.

Not for the first time, she wondered who his kin were and why he wasn't with them. She sighed. Whomever he was, he'd obviously come down in the world.

Perhaps she should have been a bit more sensitive to his plight, though she didn't regret sending him on his way. She'd celebrated her thirty-fourth birthday with her father, aunt, and uncle just last week. She had no interest in romantic pursuits.

Tony handed his jacket to another man, rolled up his sleeves and pitched a horseshoe. From where she was, she couldn't see how close he'd come to the stake, but judging by the amount of backslapping the other men gave him, he'd come mighty close.

She studied him for a moment more. The townsfolk were usually very reticent about accepting newcomers into the fold. Even with the boom, there was a clear delineation between the boomers and the native Corsicanans. Yet Tony had won over Mrs. Lockhart, the women of the Velocipede Club, and, if the game of horseshoes was any indication, several of the old-timers, as well.

Picking up her basket, she shook Tony from her thoughts, turned her mind to the many tasks awaiting her in her father's study, and made her way toward the sanctuary of home.

∞

Darkness ushered in the much-anticipated Fourth of July dance. Crowds began drifting in the direction of the pavilion around dusk, but Tony hung back until the sound of fiddlers sawing on their instruments to foot-stomping music became irresistible.

He ducked inside. Strings of Japanese lanterns lined the covered area, splashing light on the festivities and attracting every bug in Corsicana. Tony tapped his toe, unused to attending a dance where he didn't know most everyone present.

He tried to stick to the sidelines, but no place was safe from the dancers. He jumped out of the way as an enthusiastic couple whirled by.

In their wake, a grandfatherly man glided with smooth finesse around the floor, his arm unable to reach around his partner—a large, elderly woman as wide as she was tall. A father stood in the center of the dancers, swaying to the music, his baby daughter in his arms. And a young man with a day's worth of beer in his belly coaxed a flushed young lady into an intimate embrace as he spun her across the floor.

The novelty of being just another oilman, as opposed to a "mighty Morgan," was both refreshing and disconcerting. Tony's anonymity provided him with a viewpoint he'd never experienced before. Still, he missed his family and the camaraderie of friends and neighbors who had known him for years.

"Good evening, Mr. Bryant."

Tony smiled at Mrs. Lockhart's greeting, tugged on his hat, and made room for her beside him. "Ma'am."

"I saw you shared a supper with Miss Spreckelmeyer."

His jovial mood dimmed a bit. "Yes, ma'am."

"How did it go?"

"Not too well. She ran me out on a rail, then left the celebration by herself and never came back."

"What happened?"

"I'm not exactly sure." He scratched the back of his head. "One minute we were carrying on a conversation, the next she was as sore as a frog on a hot skillet."

"Tell me exactly what you said."

"I can't really remember." He watched the dancers without seeing them, trying to recall what had caused Essie to ignite. "I just wanted my half of the fig tart and she started screeching at me."

Mrs. Lockhart tapped her finger against her cane, deep in thought. "Come by my house tomorrow night after dinner. I'll serve you up some coffee and sweets and we'll see if we can piece together where you went wrong."

"Sweets? Well, ma'am, you have yourself a date." He removed his hat and bowed. "Until then, may I have this dance?"

Hooking her cane on her elbow, she stepped into his arms and looked at him over her glasses. "Just try to keep up."

With that, she attempted to lead him around the floor, but he admonished her with a stern look and stiff arms, until, laughing, she acquiesced and followed his lead.

∽

"Please come in," Mrs. Lockhart said, pulling the door open.

She smiled, causing the rice powder frescoing her face to congregate in the hollows of her wrinkles. A cameo brooch decorated her throat. The pearl gray gown she wore was dated but very finely made with gold-embroidered trim. Long, tight sleeves covered her arms, bracelets jangling against one wrist. No cane in sight.

Swiping his hat from his head, Tony offered up a quick prayer of thanksgiving that he'd "dressed" for the occasion. On a hunch that Mrs. Lockhart would entertain in high style, he'd taken special care with his toilette. Then he'd thoroughly brushed his clothes, blackened his shoes, and attached spotless cuffs, collar, and handkerchief.

Taking her hand, he raised it to his lips. "How enchanting you look this evening, ma'am."

She took his hat and hooked it on an ornate hall tree, then beckoned him inside. When she turned, he was surprised to find a bustle swinging from side to side. He couldn't remember the last time he'd seen anyone wear one.

Entering the drawing room, he took note of the ornaments, bric-a-brac, and gadgets covering every inch of available space. Framed photographs lined the walls as thickly as wallpaper. A piano sat at the far end of the room, bookcases on either side.

She led him to two upholstered easy chairs with fringe skirting their arms and feet. A tray with china cups and a sterling coffeepot graced the table next to her chair, along with two small plates of fancy cake. She poured him a cup and he settled in across from her.

"Do you play, Mrs. Lockhart?" he asked, indicating the piano.

"Certainly. But I won't be persuaded to do so this evening. We've much more serious pursuits planned." Picking up a tiny pair of silver tongs, she looked at him. "Sugar? Cream?"

"Sugar, please," he answered, willing to let her lead the conversation. She obviously knew who he was, and his main purpose for the visit was to ensure no one else did. If he had to endure her instruction on how to woo Essie in exchange for silence about his identity, he could think of worse prices to pay.

"First," she said, "I think it's time you come clean."

Leaning forward, he accepted the cup and plate of fancy cake she offered. "I'm Tony Bryant Morgan. Son of Blake and Leah Morgan."

Her facial features relaxed, losing some of their sternness. "And why are you pretending to be otherwise?"

"My father disinherited me, so I have dropped his name and carry my mother's instead. I'm not pretending to be anything other than who I am."

"Dropping your father's name does not make you any less a Morgan than you were before."

The tick in his jaw began to pulse. "It does to me."

She poured a dollop of cream into her coffee. "Who all knows?"

"About my being here? My mother, my sister, and my best friend in Beaumont."

"No one here in town?"

"No, ma'am. Not unless you've told them."

She shook her head. "No, no. I haven't said a word."

Relieved, he began to relax. "I'd like to keep it that way, if you don't mind."

"You're going to be found out."

"Eventually, perhaps. For now, though, I'd like to remain anonymous."

Picking up a spoon, she swished it in her drink, then tapped it against the edge of her cup. "Very well. We'll talk about that later. Tell me, instead, exactly what happened yesterday with Essie."

He hesitated. "The whole thing was a mistake, actually. I'd really rather not talk about it."

"Nonsense. What happened?"

He took a deep breath. "Do you know who Essie usually shares her box supper with?"

"Yes, of course. The whole town knows. And though no one would say anything to her face, plenty is said behind her back."

Mrs. Lockhart's words evoked an unexpected surge of protectiveness in Tony. It was one thing for him to think of Essie's picnic with the Lord as a bit unconventional. It was another thing for the townsfolk to make fun of her over it.

"The fact that she shared her supper with you did not go unnoticed, though," Mrs. Lockhart added.

"How long has it been since she put her box up for auction?"

"Three—no, four years now. But that's neither here nor there. I want to know why she chased you off."

"Like I told you last night, I'm not really sure. And it doesn't really matter anyway." He took a bite of cake.

"You had to have said or done something."

He shrugged. "I teased her a little bit about eating most of the dessert, then asked her what the last fig tart was worth to her. That's all I can remember."

"Ahhhh. You hinted that you'd let her have the last tart if she were to pay some kind of forfeit?"

"I never said that at all."

"No. Of course you didn't. But games of forfeit are a risky gambit. Take, for example, *Repented at Leisure,* where Mr. Flexmore robbed

Miss Kite of her innocence through clever games. Perhaps Essie was simply being cautious."

Tony blinked. "I beg your pardon? Mr. Who did *what*?"

"Mr. Flexmore. According to Mrs. Bertha Clay, he has a face no one can look into without admiration, one that irresistibly attracts man, woman, and child alike, and he uses it shamelessly."

Tony set down his empty plate, cake crumbs decorating its surface. "And who is Mr. Flexmore?"

"He's head of one of the oldest families in England."

"And he did something to Essie?"

Mrs. Lockhart rolled her eyes. "No. For heaven's sake, he's a fictional character."

Tony rubbed his forehead. "What exactly are you talking about, ma'am?"

The elderly woman began to rise. Tony jumped up and assisted her to her feet.

"Come," she said. "I'll show you."

She led him to the bookshelves on the far wall and began running her finger along the spines of books, her bracelets tinkling as she searched for one volume in particular. He scanned several of the titles. *Lady Damer's Secret. Foiled by Love. A Fiery Ordeal.*

Incredulous, he could only stare. The entire bookcase was filled with romance novels, rows and rows of them. He quickly looked for just one classic or tome of learning or even a dialogue or recitation. Instead, he found *Evelyn's Folly, A Crooked Path, A Pair of Blue Eyes.*

"Ah," she said, pulling a volume from the shelf. "Here we are. *Repented at Leisure.*" She thumbed through the book, stopped about a third of the way through and held it up to him. "There. You see?"

Looking over her shoulder, he glanced at the chapter heading. *Weaving the Spell.*

"This is where Mr. Flexmore uses his charm to engage Miss Kite's affections." She flipped to the next chapter.

Deeper and Deeper Still.

"Here he convinces her that her parents' motives for keeping them apart are self-serving." She turns to yet another chapter, sighs and shakes her head. "This is where Miss Kite's downfall occurs."

How the Plot Succeeded.

She snapped the book closed. "So you see? In order for a young lady to guard herself from such things, she must be always on the alert." She pushed the novel back onto the shelf. "Essie is a smart girl. Very conscientious. At the first hint of such shenanigans, I've no doubt she would squash the man's pursuit immediately."

Tony straightened his spine. "Are you comparing me to Mr. Flexmore?"

"No, no," she said, waving her hand in the air and making her way back to her chair. "I'm simply suggesting Essie might have."

"Essie's read *Repented at Leisure?*" he asked, appalled.

Mrs. Lockhart lowered herself into the chair, her bustle keeping her from sitting very far back on the cushion. "I'm afraid not." She shook her head with regret. "I lend my books to her all the time, but she never reads them. Prefers highfalutin authors like Mr. Dumas and Mr. Twain—though they obviously haven't taught her a thing about the human heart, or she'd have long since been married."

She poured Tony a fresh cup of coffee. "No, my books are the ticket. And since Essie won't listen to these authorities, you must. Otherwise, all hope for her is lost."

He sat down, the books once again drawing his attention. Hundreds. There were hundreds of them.

"I think what you need to do, Mr. Mor—Bryant, is to ask Essie's father for permission to court her."

Having just accepted the cup of coffee, he'd been taking a swallow and ended up singeing his tongue. "Court her?"

"Like in *The Squire's Darling*," she continued. "The squire falls in love with Lady Carline—only he isn't a squire at all. Ends up, he was in reality of noble birth, only he wanted to be loved for himself, not his position or title. So he disguised himself as a squire. Like you."

"Like me?" He was having difficulty keeping up with the conversation.

"That's kind of what you are doing, isn't it? You being a Morgan, yet pretending to be a boomer." She nodded, satisfied with her conclusion. "Yes. It's perfect. You must ask Sullivan for permission as soon as possible."

He had no notion of what to say. She was citing her romance novels the way a Latin tutor invoked Cicero. Yet he had to admit, asking Essie's father for permission to court her was something he'd already considered.

The fact that he could achieve his goals much more quickly by marrying into his empire instead of building it was not lost on him, though that wasn't his motivation. But if Essie were to learn of his identity, she might mistake his intentions completely. And it was for precisely that reason that he should suppress his interest in her.

"I'm afraid this match won't work, Mrs. Lockhart," he said. "I can't afford to pay court to Essie anyway. As I said before, my father disinherited me."

She reached over and patted his knee. "I am sorry about that, Mr. Bryant. It must be extremely difficult to go from being heir apparent one day to a nobody the next."

He raised a brow. "I'm not sure I consider myself a 'nobody' just yet."

"That's because deep down you are still a Morgan. In the meanwhile, there are many ways to court a young lady without spending money. Why, Mr. Kent courted Miss Awdrey with long walks in the park, quiet moments on the porch, and Sunday dinners with her family."

"Are they married now?"

"Oh my, yes. And very happily, I might add."

"Do they live here in Corsicana?"

"No, no. They were the two in Mrs. Barrie's *When a Man's Single*."

He cleared his throat. "I see." Finishing his drink, he stood. "Thank you for the refreshments and the . . . enlightening conversation, ma'am. I'm afraid, however, I must take my leave now."

He assisted her up. Before she walked him to the door, she moved to the bookcase and pulled out a novel.

"Essie will be extremely easy to court without money." She made her way to the entry hall and handed him his hat. "All you need do is ask her to go fishing, and you'll win her heart for certain. Meanwhile," she said, tucking the novel into his hand, "it would profit you to study Mr. Chester's speech in chapter five and meditate on his words."

Out of politeness, he accepted the volume. Once he made it down her sidewalk and onto the street, he glanced at the title.

When False Tongues Speak.

chapter FOURTEEN

PAPA BLESSED the food, served himself up a portion of mashed potatoes, then passed them across the kitchen table to Essie.

"Tony Bryant asked if he could court you," he said.

Essie plunked the bowl of potatoes on the table. Papa paid her no attention, just kept piling his dinner plate with food as if he'd merely mentioned what the phase of tonight's moon would be.

"I beg your pardon?"

"You heard me."

"And how did you respond?"

He sawed a piece of roast beef on his plate, jabbed it with his fork and stuck it in his mouth. "Said it was up to you."

"Well, then." She took a sip of ice tea. "You can tell him I'm not interested."

"You'll have to tell him yourself." He dunked his bread in his gravy.

She looked up. "What do you mean?"

"You're old enough now to make up your own mind about such things," he said around his mouthful. "No need for the fellas to be coming to me anymore. And that's exactly what I told Bryant. So I guess it's you he'll be asking permission from next. You can tell him your decision then."

"He's our employee."

"Yep."

She set down her glass. "Papa, you know how I feel about this subject."

He met her gaze for the first time. "What's past is past, Essie. Let it go. And in the meanwhile, I'm getting too old and soft to keep breaking these boys' hearts. You can just do it yourself if you're so bent on it."

"I hardly think anyone's heart has been broken on my account."

"Just the same, I've made my decision."

She crinkled the napkin in her lap. "But don't you see? By giving no answer at all, you are in essence giving your permission."

"If you tell him no, I'll stand behind you."

"I don't want you to stand behind me, I want you to stand *in front* of me. It's the father's job to refuse suits of this sort, not the daughter's."

He shook his head. "If you want to get particular, the father's job is to decide what's best for his daughter. So if you want me to do the answering, you'll have to let me do the deciding, too. And you may not like my decision."

"That's blackmail."

A shadow from the oil rig in the backyard moved across the room as the sun began to set, casting her father in momentary darkness as he softly burped into his napkin, then continued to eat.

"Papa, I'm too old. If I step out with a young, handsome man like Mr. Bryant, the whole town will laugh."

"Yep."

Her jaw slackened, stung that he hadn't contradicted her. "Don't you care?"

"Nope. And you don't, either, when it suits you. If you want to wear bloomers or ride a train to New York City by yourself, you don't seem bothered by what the townsfolk have to say about it. So don't go picking a fight with me just because you're scared of anything that wears trousers."

She shoved back her chair. "I'm not scared."

"No? Then where are you running off to?"

Her stomach tightened. "All this talk has made me lose my appetite, is all."

"You needn't eat if you don't want to, but I'd like you to stay and keep me company. I get lonesome when I have to eat by myself."

She forced herself to take a deep breath. Wearing bloomers and going to New York City were nothing like being courted by a man. Papa was comparing apples to oranges. But she would not disrespect him by running to her room like a spoiled child. She scooted her chair back up, picked up her fork and glanced across the table.

He smiled politely. There would be no changing his mind. He really was going to make her be the one to turn Tony down.

✑

Tony looked up from the grindstone and saw that work all around him had stopped. Up in the derrick, the men stood still, shielding their eyes from the sun to glance off to the west, and on the ground they left what they were doing to wander in that direction. Tony stepped back, placed his hands on his head and twisted from side to side before jogging over to see what the fuss was about.

"What is it?" he asked a man in back.

"They're saying somebody fell from the Tarrant Street rig."

"Is he all right?" Tony asked, but no one seemed to know.

He pushed his way through to where Grandpa stood wiping his brow with a soiled handkerchief.

"Who was it?" Tony asked him.

Grandpa frowned. "Sharpley," he said, "the derrickman over on Tarrant Street. Lost his footing and plunged from the double board to the ground."

Just then Jeremy came running from the direction of Sharpley's rig. He pulled up next to Grandpa out of breath.

"Is he dead?" Grandpa asked.

"Naw," Jeremy said with a shake of his head. "But the ones who seen him land said his leg was all stuck out like this." He laid his arm over his leg, forming a hideous contortion. "They stopped the work and Moss is bringing him this way in the wagon."

A few moments later, the wagon creaked by with the company's tool pusher on the buckboard and the pitiful Sharpley laid out back.

Tony couldn't get a good look at him, but he could hear the boy's moans, then an outright shriek when Moss hit a rut in the road. The same rut that had caused Essie to lose her balance before and thus reinforce the nickname the men had long since given to her: Errant Essie.

A few minutes later, Essie herself zoomed by on her bike. She stood in the stirrups of her machine, her skirt and petticoats flapping as she pumped the pedals.

The men stopped again, but she paid them no mind. Her straw hat bounced against her back, held on by the ribbons straining at her neck. Snippets of long blond hair slapped her shoulder as she circumvented the pothole.

Tony remembered her racing to Brianna's rescue and doing everything she could to keep the girl alive. He knew she'd do no less for Sharpley.

Tony tracked Essie's progress down the road until she was swallowed by dust and the other traffic.

"He'll be all right," Grandpa said, squeezing Tony's shoulder.

Tony roused himself, realizing the driller was referring to Sharpley. But Tony was every bit as worried about Essie as he was the derrickman. She'd take the boy's injury hard and it didn't set well with Tony that Moss would be the one at her side.

"Does Sharpley have family here?" Tony asked.

"Not that I know of," Grandpa answered. "But the Spreckel-meyers take care of their own. He'll be in good hands."

Tony strengthened his resolve to win a higher position in Sullivan Oil. If he were tool pusher, it would be him driving that wagon, him making sure that boy was all right, and him comforting Essie in her distress.

෴

Essie pounded on the lectern with her gavel, calling the emergency meeting of the Velocipede Club to order. Townsfolk had turned out in grand numbers, forcing most of the gentlemen to stand at the rear due to lack of seating.

Only Mrs. Lockhart had taken time to dress for the meeting. Most of the women wore their linsey-woolsies along with simple straw hats. The men wore their denims. Essie had done no more than splash water on her face and re-twist her hair. All were frantically conferring with one another, bringing the volume to horrendous heights.

The one person whose attention she held was the one whose she didn't want—Mr. Tony Bryant. He stood in the back, his white shirt unbuttoned at the collar, his hat in hand, his eyes on her. This was her first sight of him since the Fourth of July celebration three days earlier.

She looked away and rapped again on the wooden lectern. "Ladies and gentlemen. Please."

They shushed each other, which ended up being even louder than their talking. Finally they began to settle.

"As you know," Essie began, speaking over them, "we have convened this evening to discuss what action to take concerning our entry in the Corsicana Oil & Gas Bicycle Invitational. It is but one month away, and as a club we voted to sponsor the Sullivan Oil rider, Mr. Lucas Sharpley."

Murmurs of agreement filtered throughout the room.

"This morning Mr. Sharpley fell from the double board of his rig, snapped his leg in two and broke three ribs. The Benevolent Society has set up a schedule for visitations with Mr. Sharpley as he recovers in the home of Mr. and Mrs. Blanchard. Ladies, if you haven't had a chance to sign up, please see Mrs. Whiteselle after our meeting."

Essie tucked a loose piece of hair behind her ear. "Sullivan Oil has asked the Velocipede Club to find a replacement for their bicycle race. And though we mean no disrespect to Mr. Sharpley's circumstances, we dare not delay our decision for even a day or our team will be in jeopardy of forfeiting."

Old Widow Yarbrough raised her hand. "My son, Finis, could stand in for Mr. Sharpley."

"Finis Yarbrough is sixty years old if he's a day," one of the men from the back yelled. "He'd be no match for those young fellas the other oil companies have."

Barks of agreement followed.

Essie banged on the lectern. "Thank you for that nomination, Mrs. Yarbrough. And may I remind the gallery that comments are restricted to Velocipede Club members only." She wrote Finis's name on a piece of octavo amidst the grumbling of the townsfolk who'd yet to join the club. "Does anyone else have a name they'd like for us to consider?"

Victoria Davis stood up—young, fresh, and pretty as spring. "What about Preacher Wortham?"

Victoria had been sweet on Ewing for two summers now, and though many of the men her own age had expressed interest in her, she'd set her sights on the preacher.

Mrs. Bogart struggled to her feet, her skin drooping in folds about her eyes, cheeks, and neck. "Impossible," she said, out of breath from either the effort of standing or from outrage. "Neither the elders nor the congregation will stand for it. I insist Preacher Wortham's name be stricken from the list."

Ewing, having taken the pulpit from the retired Mr. Bogart, stepped forward. "Though I appreciate the nomination, I'm afraid any free time I have will need to be used for more charitable pursuits."

Essie scratched Ewing's name from the list. Victoria sent him a smile, then resumed her seat.

Several more names were offered up, but the members found fault with every recommendation. The man in question was either too old, too young, too unfit, too reckless, too lazy, too unfamiliar, too free with his liquor consumption, or too something.

Essie had just about given up when Mrs. Lockhart stood. "What about Mr. Bryant?"

The crowd twisted around to look at him.

He was clearly stunned.

"He ain't even from Corsicana," someone yelled.

"Neither is Mr. Sharpley," Mrs. Lockhart said. "But Mr. Bryant lives here now, he is an employee of Sullivan Oil, he is in excellent physical condition and, from what I understand, handles himself very well on a bicycle."

One by one, the members—particularly the women members—began endorsing the nomination. They praised Mrs. Lockhart for seeing what was right before their noses and encouraged Tony to step up for the good of the club.

Essie began to panic. True, he was the best candidate so far, but if the club elected him as their racer, they'd expect her to train him. Five evenings a week. More if she were to get him ready in time.

Mrs. Lockhart smiled. The proverbial cat who got the cream. Essie tamped down a groan. The old biddy was nothing more than a frustrated romantic who didn't have enough sense to fill a salt spoon.

Essie frantically searched her mind for another, more suitable candidate. None came to mind.

A speculative gleam entered Tony's eye. Had he, too, realized he'd be forced to spend most every minute of his time off with her?

The men around him pushed him toward the bandstand, encouraging him to accept the nomination. He circled around and made his way to the front.

Stepping up onto the platform, he addressed the crowd. "I would be most honored to represent the Corsicana Velocipede Club and Sullivan Oil in the Corsicana Oil & Gas Bicycle Invitational. That is, unless there is some objection?"

He directed this last question at Essie. And what could she say? That he was an employee? Well, so was Sharpley. That he didn't have the physical stamina? Anyone with eyes could see he did. That she wanted a chaperone during their training sessions? They'd think she was a delusional old maid and laugh behind their hands.

A swelling of excited voices filled the room.

"Take a vote, Miss Spreckelmeyer," Mrs. Lockhart said over the crowd, punctuating her demand with a thump of her cane. "And start with Mr. Bryant's name. I have a feeling you won't need to go any further on your list."

Silence fell like a guillotine.

Essie cleared her throat. "Were there any other nominations?"

Not so much as a murmur.

She swallowed. "Very well, then. All in favor of electing Mr. Tony Bryant as Sullivan Oil's representative in the Corsicana Oil & Gas Bicycle Invitational, please raise your hand."

Unanimous amongst the women. Well, almost unanimous. Mrs. Yarbrough was still holding out for her son. And a majority of the men members voted in the affirmative, as well.

Essie gripped the lectern. She must not let anyone—most of all Mrs. Lockhart or Tony himself—see her distress.

Pasting a smile on her face, she turned to him. "Congratulations, Mr. Bryant. It seems you are our new contestant."

chapter FIFTEEN

ESSIE WORKED Tony twice as hard as she'd ever worked Sharpley. She made him do twice as many laps, twice as many sit-ups, twice as many push-ups, twice as many bell pulls, twice as many sprints, twice as many jumps of the rope, twice as many everything.

She wanted to make certain that when the session was finished, he didn't have enough energy left for amorous pursuits.

He took to the regimen without complaint. How he had the strength after putting in a full day on the rig, she could not imagine. But he did.

As the days passed, and she observed his remarkable stamina, she grew optimistic. They just might have a chance of placing in the bicycle race, after all. They might not take first, but they certainly had a shot at the second- or third-place trophies.

Holding Tony's feet to the floor, she gave the final countdown for his three hundred sit-ups. "Five, four, three, two, and one."

He fell back, flinging his arms above him. Sweat saturated his sleeveless shirt, his chest pumping as he sucked in air. The light-weight navy fabric stuck to his torso, outlining the shape beneath it. Even relaxed, his muscles bulged.

Dark hair matted the pits of his arms. Skin a few shades paler than the rest lay bare along the underside of his outstretched limbs. His fingers curled in repose.

She released his feet. He'd refused to wear the tights so many men preferred when exercising and she'd been extremely relieved. Those tights left little to the imagination.

She unscrewed the lid of a water canteen and handed it to him. Pushing himself up, he lifted it to his mouth, the muscles in his arm flexing. He guzzled the liquid, ignoring the rivulets seeping from the corners of his mouth. They streamed around his jaw, down his neck and into his shirt.

"Not too fast, Tony," she cautioned. "I don't want you getting sick."

He lowered the canteen, swiping his mouth with his forearm, his chest still heaving. The richness of his deep brown eyes struck her again.

He hadn't said a word about what had happened after their meal on the Fourth or what he'd talked with her father about. And though the words had remained unspoken, she'd caught him staring at places he oughtn't. He tried to cover his indiscretions, but he made no apologies for them.

"You ready for our football drill?" she asked.

He scratched the stubble on his jaw. "I dunno if I want to waste my time kicking the ball with some female who doesn't have the constitution to play a match without fainting."

After her embarrassing episode with him and Sharpley, she'd been careful to dress more appropriately for the training sessions. But Tony never ceased to tease her about her one lapse.

"Careful, sir. Don't you know that pride is the never-failing vice of fools?"

He rose to his feet and offered her his hand. " 'If we had no pride we should not complain of that of others.' "

She allowed him to help her stand, then fetched the ball. At first they passed it back and forth, giving her a chance to get her blood flowing.

"M.C. Baker's coming in on the three-o'clock train tomorrow," he said. "If you'd like, I can come round and pick you up at the house on my way."

She leaned back, giving the ball a lift. He caught it with his knee, allowed it to drop, then passed it back.

"That'll be fine," she said.

"I'll pick you up at two, then."

"Don't you think that's a bit early?"

"I told Moss I'd take some tools to the smithy for repair on our way." Putting a spin on the ball, he kicked it past her and took off running.

For the next fifteen minutes they raced up and down the building, fighting for advantage. And though Essie tried to keep up, Tony was not only better with his foot skills, but he also outmatched her in size and speed. The fourth time he scored, he lifted his fists in the air like a pugilist and bounced up and down.

She propped her hands on her waist. "That's not very gentlemanly of you. The conduct of the winner should be modest and dignified."

He slowly lowered his arms. "Modest and dignified? Who was it that stuck her tongue out when she scored a few moments ago?"

"I wasn't gloating. I was trying to see which way the wind was blowing."

A slow grin crept onto his face. "Inside the seed house?"

"This is not a seed house, Mr. Bryant. It is a bicycle club."

"And your undue liveliness during our match, Miss Spreckelmeyer, was improper by anyone's standards."

She picked up the ball and returned it to its bin. "Well, maybe it was. I almost scored two off of you tonight, though. You're slipping, sir."

Without asking, he helped her put away jump ropes, dumbbells, Indian clubs, and his bicycle. Mr. Sharpley had never thought to do that for her.

After they put the lights out, he draped her shawl over her shoulders and followed her through the door. He locked it, then handed her the key.

Their walks home were her favorite part of the evening. She had protested at first, but Tony wouldn't hear of any objections. He would walk with her whether she consented or not.

"Suppose some snakebitten child should need assistance," he said, "and there you'd be without a knife."

"Yes, but I usually pack a pistol, don't forget," she teased.

"A pistol's not much use to a snakebite victim."

So she had acquiesced and then grown to enjoy the company. Something Mr. Sharpley had also never offered.

Earlier in the week they had talked of the transatlantic steamers filled with Americans sailing to Europe. Last night, of Napoleon Bonaparte's invasion of Egypt a hundred years ago, a subject on which Tony seemed remarkably well informed. Often they discussed the latest developments in the war with Spain, but when he fell to discussing tactics, he lost her entirely.

Tonight they deliberated over Thomas Stevens' three-year trip around the world on his Columbia highwheeler back in 1884, a trek Essie had researched for a recent lecture.

"Can you even imagine?" she asked. "Velocipedes were so cumbersome and heavy back then."

"And the roads rough and poorly formed."

"How marvelous to be a man, though," she sighed. "To embark on such an adventure. Meeting princes. Seeing the Taj Mahal. Riding alongside a caravan of three hundred camels."

Tony shook his head. "You forget his supplies were limited to socks, a spare shirt, and a slicker that doubled as a tent and bedroll."

"Still, I'd give anything to do something like that."

They reached her house and he placed his hand on the gate's latch. "For what it's worth, Essie, I'm glad you're not a man."

She pulled herself out of her musings. He stood close. Too close.

The hinges squeaked as he pushed open the gate. "I'll pick you up at two o'clock. Don't forget."

"I won't forget." Slipping past him, she hurried into the house.

∽

Mrs. Lockhart opened the door before Tony had a chance to knock. She took one look at his exercise clothes and frowned.

"Quickly," she said. "Before someone sees you."

He slipped into the darkened entry hall. Mrs. Lockhart clasped his hand and led him blindly down a hall and into another room before releasing him. He stood where he was while she lit a lantern.

Light spilled onto a square table, revealing a typical kitchen with a braided rug, a woodburning stove, and a water pump in the corner. The smell of coffee coming from the stove filled the room. Two mugs sat in waiting beside it.

Grabbing a towel, Mrs. Lockhart poured coffee into the cups. She wore a black shirtwaist and skirt, no bustle, no rice powder. She'd twisted her white hair up so tightly, bits of pink scalp peeked through.

He glanced at the red-checkered curtains hanging still as stone above the water pump, indicating a secured window and explaining why no breeze circulated through the room. The tightly closed curtains would also keep light from seeping out and curious eyes from peeking in.

"Why all the secrecy?" he asked.

She added sugar to his cup, cream to hers. "A gentleman caller at this hour? What would people say?"

He came up behind her and pecked her cheek. "They'd say I was sparkin' my favorite gal."

Blushing, she pushed him away and indicated he take a seat. "Get on with you, now."

She picked up their cups and he followed her to the table, then pulled out her chair.

"I received your note," she said, settling herself. "What has happened?"

Sitting across from her, he grabbed the corner of his shirt-sleeve and wiped his forehead. "Sorry I didn't have time to clean up before I came."

She waved away his concern. "You did the right thing. If you'd gone back to Mrs. Potter's and then left again all spruced up, eyebrows would have raised for certain. Now, tell me what has brought you to my doorstep at this late hour."

He took a sip of coffee. "Am I keeping you from your beauty rest?"

She leaned forward, light capturing the sparkle in her eyes. "I haven't had this much fun since Mr. Dubois ran off with Lord Wynton's daughter."

He suppressed a smile. "How shocking. And when did this perfidy occur?"

"Several summers ago in *A Young Girl's Love*."

Tony leaned back onto two legs of his chair. "I read *When False Tongues Speak*."

Mrs. Lockhart glowed with delight, the pleasure taking ten years off her face. "And what did you think of Mr. Chester's speech?"

"The man was a fool."

"Never say so!"

"He'd have completely gotten away with his scheme if he'd simply kept his mouth shut. That speech was his undoing."

Mrs. Lockhart raised a finger in protest. "But what of Miss Laura?"

He gave a disgusted snort. "Miss Laura? She led him around like a bull with a ring in his nose. What did he see in such a spoiled little miss anyway? Mrs. Neville of Neville's Cross, however—" He smiled with lazy appreciation. "Now, that is what I call a woman."

Mrs. Lockhart sat stunned. "You are deceived, Mr. Bryant. You have completely turned things around. Why, I never would have suggested you read the book if I thought—" She slowly narrowed her eyes. "You are teasing me."

He took a sip of coffee.

She chuckled. "You are a wicked man, Mr. Tony Bryant Morgan."

Dropping the legs of his chair on the floor, he placed his mug on the table. "I received a letter from my mother."

Mrs. Lockhart sobered. "What's happened?"

Tony hesitated one last time, questioning the wisdom of sharing confidences with Mrs. Lockhart. He'd stopped by her home several times now and discovered she knew much more about his family situation than he'd first realized. Though, it wasn't all that surprising, what with her daughter being such an intimate friend of Anna's and her son-in-law, Morgan Oil's tool pusher.

He took a deep breath. "Darius had all of Anna's mourning clothes removed from her armoire and replaced them with gowns suited for a debutante's first season. She has no choice but to wear them or remain hidden in her room indefinitely."

"Why would he do such a thing?"

"He wants to marry her off."

"Why?"

"To increase his wealth and standing in the community."

"But the Morgans are already wealthy and quite powerful in these parts."

"Not enough to suit, evidently. Mother said he has been parading Anna in front of senators and railroad men." He combed a hand through his hair. "Including old Norris Tubbs."

Mrs. Lockhart removed her glasses. "Anna simply cannot marry for at least a year. It would be downright scandalous."

"I agree. But there is no one who has the gumption to stand up to Darius other than me. Yet I don't know what to do. Knocking his teeth down his throat would be extremely satisfying but won't really solve anything."

She rubbed her eyes. "What if you brought Anna here to Corsicana?"

"How? I can barely support myself. And if I brought her here, the Spreckelmeyers would find out I'm a Morgan and I'd lose my job." He shook his head. "Not only that, Darius would find some way to sabotage her inheritance and keep it for himself. Then where would Anna be?"

"Let's tackle one thing at a time. First, Judge Spreckelmeyer is a reasonable fellow. And he knew Blake quite well, so he'd be sympathetic to your situation."

Tony blanched. "He knew my father?"

"Oh my, yes. When the railroads first started coming into Texas, your father tried to use his influence to push regulations through the state congress that Judge Spreckelmeyer opposed." She held her glasses up to her mouth, huffed onto their lenses, then wiped them with a napkin. "The judge didn't have the money your father did, but he had the support of many who, combined, were quite powerful. I don't remember the particulars other than the regulations your father was pushing for were not passed."

Propping his elbows on the table, Tony dropped his head into his hands. "Spreckelmeyer knows. He has to. I'm the spitting image of my father."

Mrs. Lockhart put her glasses back on. "I think it is quite possible you are correct."

He jerked his gaze up. "Do you think Essie knows?"

She shook her head. "I doubt it. She's not nearly as good at hiding her feelings as the judge. If she knew who you were, she'd have been much more antagonistic toward you."

"Why do you think Spreckelmeyer hasn't said anything?"

She considered his question. "You could always ask him."

Tony tapped his fist against his mouth. "It just doesn't make any sense. If Spreckelmeyer knows who I am, why would he have granted me permission to court Essie?"

Mrs. Lockhart lit up. "You're courting Essie? Why, no one has said a word!"

"That's because I haven't stepped out with her yet. I'm still undecided about the whole thing."

"Why? She'd be a wonderful catch for any man."

"It's not that."

"Then, what is it?"

Lowering his gaze, he ran his finger along the rim of his cup. "She's Spreckelmeyer's sole heir."

"So?"

"So don't you think it looks a bit suspicious for the disinherited son of Blake Morgan to suddenly take an interest in the spinster daughter of the largest producer of oil in Texas?"

Mrs. Lockhart pursed her lips. "In *Wooed and Married*, Mr. Tayne pursued the Lady Conyngham. She, too, was a spinster—and every bit as attractive as our Essie. Yet all of England opposed the match, claiming the second son of the new baron simply wanted to increase his family's lands and wealth. But it was a love match, and after Mr. Tayne had slain a dragon or two—figuratively speaking, of course—"

"Of course," Tony said.

"—love conquered all and the young people married and went on to live a full and happy life."

He drained the last of his coffee. "That's all well and good, Mrs. Lockhart, but I can't court Essie simply because Mr. Tayne courted Lady What's-Her-Name."

"Conyngham."

"Exactly."

"What if you confess all to the judge and reassure him that your motives are honorable?" she asked.

"Why? He's already given me permission, of a sort, to court Essie."

"What do you mean, 'of a sort'?"

Tony rubbed his neck. "He said I had to ask Essie directly for permission and if she agreed, he would be favorable to the match."

Mrs. Lockhart rolled her eyes. "For the love of Peter. That man has not been the same since Doreen passed." She picked up their cups and moved to the washbowl. "Tell me this, Mr. Bryant. Are your motives pure?"

He stiffened, then sighed. "The advantages of marrying her are not lost on me. But my . . . interest . . . has nothing to do with that. I intend to earn my position in life and not have it handed to me—by inheritance or marriage."

Mrs. Lockhart nodded. "Well, I recommend you court her as planned and if you find yourself more interested in the inheritance than the woman herself, then you can simply bow out gracefully."

"That would hardly be fair to Essie."

"It would be better than marrying her for the wrong reasons."

He nodded. "What about Anna?"

The elderly woman picked up the lantern and headed out of the kitchen and over to the parlor, Tony following.

"I think it is too early to make any moves on that front," she said. "So long as nothing official has been announced, you still have time." She slipped a book from the shelf. "Now, I'd like you to read this and we will discuss it when next we meet."

He glanced at the title. *Marjorie's Fate.*

"Mrs. Lockhart, I really don't think—"

"Pay particular attention to the strategy employed by the down-on-his-luck earl who thwarted his wicked brother's scheme to steal his lady love."

She handed him his hat. He took it, knowing he'd read her book, if for no other reason than to have an excuse to come back and spend time with someone who knew who he was and liked him anyway.

Squeezing her elbow, he whispered, "Next time we meet, I'll come in the back door."

Her eyes sparkled with delight just before she extinguished the lantern and shooed him out the door.

chapter SIXTEEN

ESSIE TOLD herself she chose her Worth gown and her favorite tall walking hat to make a favorable impression on Mr. Baker. But it wasn't Mr. Baker's reaction she pictured in her mind.

She checked her gown in the mirror. The stamped linen fit her close as a sheath, the maroon design standing out on the lighter background. A wide revers of white plush narrowly massed on her shoulders, then knotted in the middle of her back above full pleats. Tasteful, yet eye-catching.

A week had passed since Tony asked for Papa's permission. Yet he'd said nothing at all to her about courtship. Had he changed his mind?

She ran her finger over a new wrinkle between her eyebrows that she didn't remember seeing before, then sighed. The more time she spent with him, the more she enjoyed his company, his wit, and his willingness to discuss anything with her—whether it be politics, gas versus electricity, or Mr. Ford's motorized carriage.

He was courteous, hardworking, and attractive, and he could ride a bike with the best of them. Most of all, he didn't seem to mind her independent ways anymore. If he truly did want to step out with her, what could it hurt?

But she knew all too well what it could hurt. The real question was if courting him was worth the risk. Worth the risk of rousing talk in town. Worth the risk of making herself vulnerable. Worth the risk of being rejected.

The clock chimed two. Pinching her cheeks, she headed down the stairs. Tony crossed the porch just as she reached the entryway. He wore a silk vest, gray trousers, and summer jacket. They stared at each other through the screen door.

"The first time I saw you through this door, you were sliding down the banister," he said.

"Shhhhh." She glanced over her shoulder, then quickly opened the screen. "Papa might hear you."

"You were wearing knickerbockers and a hat that reached clear to here." He held his hand level with his nose. "And then you looked at me and I thought you were just about the prettiest thing I ever had seen."

She raised a brow. "You thought I was married to my father."

"And I was jealous of him."

Her stomach somersaulted.

"You ready?" he asked.

"Yes. Let me just poke my head into Papa's study and tell him I'm leaving."

When she returned to the entryway, Tony stood holding the door open. She stepped out onto the porch and hesitated at seeing a Studebaker carriage parked in front of the house. The buckboard held a front and backseat with a natural wood finish and green cloth trimmings.

"We aren't walking?" she asked.

Riding through town all dressed up like this would look too much like courting, and she certainly didn't care to have her employees or the townspeople misinterpreting the reason for her excursion.

"I'm taking some tools to the Central Blacksmith Shop," he said. "Plus, M.C. will have a trunk with him. I figured a carriage would be best."

She glanced at the boot of the vehicle. Sure enough, a box of tools had been stowed there behind the second seat. Not seeing any way around it, she allowed him to escort her down the sidewalk and assist her into the buckboard.

Shaking out her skirts, she noted he'd replaced his mud-splattered work boots with his Sunday boots. The expensive kind the cowboys called Wellingtons.

Once again she wondered what had happened to change his circumstances. He enjoyed playing a card game or two with the boys, but she couldn't imagine him gambling away his life's fortune. He simply didn't strike her as the type. But looks and charm and good manners meant nothing, really. It was what was on the inside that counted.

"You look awfully fetching, Essie. Is that a new hat?"

She glanced at him. "No. It's not new, exactly. I just don't wear it too often."

"Well, it's very nice."

Despite herself, she was pleased. With its tall, willowy plumage, maroon satin ribbon, and butter-colored lace, it was one of her very favorites.

She tipped her face up to the sky. It offered no clouds to temper the sun's penetrating rays, but a steady breeze kept her from getting hot in the open carriage.

Mr. Drake's towering pecan tree—whose branches had provided her with hours of quiet reading as a child—spread beyond his yard and stretched out over the road. Warblers and songbirds that had poured into town after crossing the Gulf of Mexico flitted through its branches, each trying to outdo the other in song. Mrs. Davis's rose garden thrived, showing off blooms of white, yellow, and pink.

They reached the smithy's in no time. Tony jumped down from the seat, instructed her to stay put and toted the box inside. Moments later he rejoined her.

It couldn't be more than ten after two. What in the world would they do for the next fifty minutes while they waited for the train to arrive?

Clicking his tongue, Tony pointed the buckboard south.

"Where are we going?"

"We've some time to kill, so I thought a ride out to Two Bit Creek would be nice."

"Why?"

He looked at her. "Why not?"

"I'm not sure it's such a good idea, is all."

"Why not?" he asked again, making no move to redirect the horses.

"Because in order to get there we will have to pass many of my rigs and the men will see us together."

"So?"

"So," she said, scrambling for a delicate way to point out the obvious. "It might produce some talk."

"What kind of talk?"

"You know exactly what kind of talk."

Pushing up the rim of his hat, he leaned back against the seat. "Yes, ma'am. I guess I do."

Now, what is that supposed to mean? "Well, I'm not sure I care to stir up any talk."

He chuckled. "Essie, there isn't a woman in town who defies convention more than you. You own one business. Run another for your father. Wear bloomers. Travel clear to New York City by yourself, only to get your name plastered in the papers from here to kingdom come. You ride all over Corsicana on that bicycle and hold weekly shooting lessons for the women in this town. And now you expect me to believe a little ride out to Two Bit Creek is gonna upset your apple cart?"

Good heavens. Put like that, she sounded like an eccentric old maid. But what some thought of as eccentric, others took for something else entirely.

"It doesn't mean I'm loose, Tony," she said, fiddling with the gathers in her skirt.

He yanked the horses to a stop. Right there in the middle of Fifth Street. She had to grab on to the rail to keep herself from pitching forward. She glanced up and down the street, relieved to find no one else coming or going.

The muscles in his forearm swelled against his sleeve as he held the reins tightly wrapped in his right fist. "Look at me."

She lifted her gaze.

His brown eyes conveyed acute displeasure. "I never, ever, for one single minute thought that you were anything other than the respectable woman you are."

Swallowing, she nodded.

"Furthermore," he continued, "I was not taking you out to Two Bit Creek for some prurient purpose. The train's not due in for almost an hour, and you were looking so pretty in your dress and gloves and hat that I just wanted to take you for a ride."

She opened her mouth to reply, but he wasn't quite through.

"And you wanna know something else?" he asked, whipping off his hat. "I'm sick and tired of you assigning motives to me that I don't have. First you question my integrity. Now you question my morals." He twisted to face her. "I don't know what makes you think otherwise, but let me assure you I'm not about to risk my job by playing fast with the boss's daughter."

She moistened her lips, refusing to be cowed. "I see. And if I wasn't the boss's daughter? Would you play fast with me then?"

"Take the deuce, woman!" A tick in his jaw hammered. "Sometimes you make me so mad I could strangle your pretty little neck.

And no. I do not make a habit of playing fast with *any* women. Boss's daughters. Farmer's daughters. Any kind of daughters. You got that?"

The very fact that he was so insulted soothed many of her concerns. "Yes. I believe I do."

"Good." He slammed his hat back on his head. "Now. Do you think you can ride out to Two Bit Creek without finding fault every step of the way?"

She bit the insides of her cheeks. Never had she heard a more hostile invitation from someone who, she was beginning to realize, truly didn't have some ulterior motive. "I shall do my best to steer my thinking in a more positive manner."

"Fine." He slapped the reins, and the buckboard lurched forward. "You do that."

The horses shook their heads in protest and slowed to a walk after only a few yards. Essie's mind backtracked, filtering through Tony's exasperation and honing in on what he'd actually said.

"You were looking so pretty in your dress and gloves and hat that I just wanted to take you for a ride."

She allowed his words to wash over her, seep inside and settle. In the past, she'd have waved off a declaration of that sort, assuming the speaker was simply being polite.

But Tony hadn't been spouting platitudes. He'd meant what he said. He was attracted to her and wanted to ride out with her. So simple, yet so complicated.

She'd already admitted to herself that she found him attractive, as well. But so far she'd been very careful not to dwell on it.

She glanced at his hands as they loosely held the reins. Blue veins crisscrossed his tan skin, drawing her eyes to defined knuckles, masculine fingers and nails that, though scrubbed, still held a slight stain of oil.

"I'm sorry I lost my temper," he said.

She pushed a tendril of hair back up into her hat. "It's all right. I seem to have that effect on people."

Squinting, he searched the horizon. "You have no idea of the effect you have on me."

She lifted her gaze.

He swallowed, causing his Adam's apple to jump up, then roll back down his throat. "I'd like to court you, Essie."

She caught her breath.

"I asked your father, but he said I must appeal to you directly."

"Why?"

"I don't know. That's just what he told me."

"No, I mean, why do you want to court me?"

He frowned. "What kind of question is that? The same reason any man goes courting."

"Why *do* men go courting?"

He appeared at a total loss. "Because."

"Because why?"

"Because they just do." He turned the team west, taking the long way around in order to avoid passing any of Sullivan Oil's rigs.

She grabbed on to the wing to steady herself. "Let me rephrase it, then: What are your intentions?"

"Are you trying to make me mad on purpose? This is the last time I'm going to tell you. They're completely honorable."

She sighed. "I don't want to know what *kind* of intentions you have. I want to know what they *are*. If you can't tell me, then the answer is no."

He slipped a finger in his collar and gently tugged. She understood his discomfort but did not want to misinterpret or mistake what he was asking her. At this point in her life, there was only one acceptable reason for a man to go courting, and that was if he was considering marriage.

The longer he took to respond, the more she realized she had her answer.

"It's all right, Tony," she said. "Let's forget you ever mentioned it."

"No," he said, panic lining his voice. "I just don't know what to say."

"It's a simple question."

"It's not."

On the outskirts of town he guided the horses off the road and onto a lightly worn trail that led to the creek. Sand and grass muffled the horses' hooves. The wheels creaked with each turn.

He sat up straighter. "I would like to see you more often in a more intimate setting so that I can get to know you better." He let out a *whoosh* of air.

"You're all alone with me every night."

"That's different. We're working. Training. You're bossing me around the whole time." He shook his head. "I want to take you somewhere. Like the soda shop or fishing, even. I want to pick you up at your house knowing that you'd put on your finery for me—and only me. I want to go where there is no boss or trainer. I want to go somewhere with just you and me."

The trees grew thicker. The sound of water churning reached her ears. Loamy smells stirred from the earth.

She toyed with her gloved fingers. "And what," she whispered, "would all that lead to?"

The creek came into view, its contents chafing against the banks, racing toward an unseen goal.

He pulled the carriage to a stop, anchored the reins and turned toward her, placing his arm along the seat back. "Well, ideally, I suppose it would lead to marriage. Occasionally, however, I've seen it lead to heartache."

She nodded. "Tony?"

"Hmmm?"

"What if I knew right now that it would lead to heartache. Would you still want to pursue this, um, courtship?"

He frowned in confusion. "What makes you so certain our courtship would lead to heartache?"

"Because," she said, taking a deep breath. "If your feelings for me were to grow to the point of making an offer, I would be honor bound to reveal some things about me that might cause you to change your mind. And that would then lead to heartache."

An expression of skepticism crossed his face before he realized she was serious. After a moment of thought, he rubbed his mouth. "Would you like to tell me about them now and get it over with?"

She clasped her hands together. The last time a man had asked to court her, she'd laid all her past transgressions on the table before proceeding. But she wasn't the same person now as she'd been then.

For the past four years she'd learned to embrace her singleness. Enjoy it. Be proud of it.

Mrs. Lockhart's words to Tony flitted through her mind.

"She hides behind her spinsterhood. . . . She worries about what people think. . . . She won't want to step out with an employee."

A fish jumped above the surface of the creek, the sun catching its silver scales in a moment of brilliance before it disappeared back into the safety of its home. She scanned the water, waiting for some of its companions to do the same, but no other fish appeared.

Was she like that? Did she stay below the surface where it was safe? Never risking a journey out into the sunlight?

"Essie?" he said, placing a finger beneath her chin and bringing her face around. "How 'bout we just take our chances and see how it goes?"

She worried her lip.

"It'll be all right. If things progress, there will be time enough for you to tell me your secrets and for me to tell you mine."

She searched his brown eyes and found no censure there.

Long ago she'd learned that she was a whole person without a man. That all she needed was Jesus Christ. Had she somehow taken that blessing and pushed God out of it? Made it about her instead of Him? About her being single and successful?

She thought of the virtue she'd so carelessly gifted to a man who wasn't her husband. Had she accepted God's forgiveness, then subconsciously built a wall around herself that no man could possibly scale? What if God had a man for her after all?

Is this your will, Lord?

She waited, but He gave no answer. Not so much as an inkling as to what His thoughts were. Her heart began to hammer. Was she willing to let Him knock down that wall?

Tony ran his thumb along her jaw. "What do you say, Essie? Will you accept my offer?"

It was a risk. A huge risk. But deep down, she wanted to tell him yes. This time, however, she wanted to do it the Lord's way.

Will you show me how to knock down that wall, Lord? Will you show me how to court a man?

But she didn't need an answer. She knew He would.

Taking a deep breath, she nodded. "Yes, Tony. Yes, I will."

A gorgeous grin split across his face. His fingers tightened on her chin.

He's going to kiss me.

After the slightest hesitation, however, he let her go and pulled his watch from his pocket. "We need to head back. With all the stopping and starting and detouring, it took longer to get here than I estimated."

"All right."

He gave her a sideways look. "If we take the more direct route back, we'll pass all the boys."

Her palms dampened.

"I can't think of an easier way to announce our courtship," he said. "Can you?"

Arranging her skirts, she shook her head.

"Well, then. Let's make it official."

chapter SEVENTEEN

TONY CUT their buckboard right through the heart of the oil patch, passing rig after rig after rig. Most of them belonged to Sullivan Oil.

The men stopped their work. They pulled off their hats and waved, then shouted a greeting and glanced speculatively between Tony and Essie.

He kept one arm along the seat back, so there'd be no mistaking his claim. Essie looked neither left nor right but sat rigidly beside him, face flushed, eyes on the road.

For an awful moment back there, he'd thought she was going to refuse him. He wondered what social faux pas she'd committed in her past to make her think he would back out. Any woman who'd been so outlandish as to have been in the newspapers was sure to have made a spectacle of herself more than once.

But if he reached the point of wanting to marry her, he couldn't fathom this imagined sin of hers being something he wouldn't be able to overlook. How bad could it be?

Besides, any secrets she had would pale in comparison to the fact that he'd lied to her about his identity. No telling what her reaction was going to be when he revealed himself as a Morgan. When he revealed that just a train ride away his own flesh and blood owned and operated Sullivan Oil's most adverse competition.

He clucked at the horses, urging them to pick up their pace. He really ought to go ahead and tell her. But if she found out now who he was, she might question his motives. He needed to keep his identity a secret at least a little while longer. But time was running out. M.C. knew who he was, as did Mrs. Lockhart and quite possibly Judge Spreckelmeyer. He only hoped he could convince M.C. to keep his knowledge to himself.

Essie squirmed, becoming even more agitated now that they'd reached town. The boomers gave them no more than a passing glance, but the more established citizens gaped, tracking their progress down Main and making even Tony uncomfortable. What was the matter with everybody?

He removed his arm from behind her and urged the horses onward. "Giddyup, there."

When they finally reached the railroad station, he felt as if he'd run a gauntlet. "What in tarnation was that all about?"

"What?" she asked, placing her hands on his shoulders while he lifted her from the seat by her elbows.

"You can't mean you didn't notice," he said, indicating the town with a nod of his head.

"Oh. That." She took a step back. "Well, what did you expect? You're now courting the town's old maid."

He cringed. "Don't call yourself that."

"It's true. I'm not ashamed of it."

"Well, I don't want you saying it anymore. You hear?"

She shrugged and started toward the train platform.

He grabbed her elbow. "Whoa, there. We're together. Remember? That means so long as you're with me, you don't go anywhere unless it's on my arm."

"Even during the day?"

"Especially during the day." He extended his bent arm.

"Why especially?" she asked, slipping her hand in the crook of his elbow.

"Because there are only three reasons a man would give his arm to a lady during the day. If she was a close relative, if her safety required it, or if she was the gal he was sparkin'. "

She swallowed. "I see. Well, you needn't worry. I'm perfectly aware of how to conduct myself on the street."

He let her rebuke pass. She might know the proper etiquette, but she'd been going her own way for a long time. He wondered just how willingly she'd give up that independence.

A train whistle pierced the air while the rumbling of the oncoming locomotive shook the ground. Metal screamed as the conductor put on the brake, the smell of burnt wood and clashing steel reaching the depot even before the railcars did.

A blue-green iron boiler with gleaming brass handrails, silver road assemblies, and ornamental stag's horns barreled toward them, pitch black smoke pouring from its cabbage stack.

Tony would need to get M.C. alone before introducing him to Essie. He wanted to make sure the rotary man didn't accidentally give him away.

He ran his gaze down the rainbow-colored cars. The russet baggage car rolled by first, pulling a red car behind it, where the nicer compartments were housed. A yellow car held the express passengers, and the Jim Crow section brought up the rear in a bright green car.

The train stopped with a smoky sigh. Corsicana's depot provided a wooden platform for passengers so they wouldn't have to step out onto the dirt beside the tracks like so many other train stops Tony had seen. Men, women, and children milled about, searching the railcar windows for friends and loved ones.

Tony spotted M.C. jumping off the express car. He wore a baggy ready-made suit one size too big, the sleeves falling clear to his knuckles. His short blond hair stuck out in sporadic tufts across his balding head.

"You stay put," he said to Essie. "I'll be right back."

Weaving through the crowd, he hollered out to M.C., capturing the man's attention.

"Tony! Good to see you. Where in the world did your moustache run off to?"

Shaking hands, Tony clapped him on the shoulder. "I shaved her clean off. What'd you think?"

"Doesn't look right. Doesn't look right a'tall. And say, I'm sorry about your pa."

"Thank you." Tony never quite knew which of M.C.'s eyes to look at because one went to the east and the other went to the west and he never could tell exactly which one was looking at him. "Speaking of my father, I need to ask a favor. After he disinherited me, I dropped the name Morgan and started going by my mother's name, Bryant."

M.C. scratched the back of his neck. "Well, I'd heard what your pa did and couldn't quite credit it. Strange doings, that's for sure."

"Be that as it may, I'm sure you can imagine that in Sullivan Oil country, having the last name of Morgan wouldn't earn a body any trust. So no one knows who I am and I'd like to keep it that way."

"You're fooling me."

"I'm deadly serious."

"How could they not know? You look just like him."

"I don't think Corsicana was a place he frequented, if at all."

"Well, I'll be." M.C. shook his head. "I don't much like the idea of hoodwinking people, Tony. Even ones I don't know. I'm a God-fearing man and it just don't sit well."

"He disinherited me, M.C. As far as I'm concerned, he's not my father anymore, so you wouldn't be hoodwinking anybody."

"Your pa is Blake Morgan, son. Ain't no piece o' paper or different last name that can change that."

"Doesn't mean I have to claim him."

"You're gonna be found out. Cain't keep a secret like that. It's too big."

"I agree. I'd just like for folks to find out later rather than sooner. So will you hold your tongue?"

Sighing, M.C.'s shoulders slumped. "Well, all right, then. I won't go volunteerin' the information, but if somebody asks me straight out, I ain't gonna lie about it, neither."

"Fair enough, and I appreciate it, M.C. I surely do. Now, where's your trunk?" Tony looked around and caught sight of Deputy Howard talking to Essie.

"I imagine it's over by the baggage car."

"What? Oh. Right. Well, you head on over there. I'm going to fetch Spreckelmeyer's daughter."

M.C. swiveled his head around. "*The* daughter? The one that was in the papers?"

"Watch yourself, buddy. I've taken a shine to her and I won't take kindly to any disparaging remarks."

The man's eyebrows shot up, his right eye zeroing in on Tony. "Does she know who you are?"

"Not yet."

M.C. let out a slow whistle. "I don't envy you the telling of that tale."

"All the more reason for you to keep your knowledge to yourself. Now, go on. I'll meet up with you in a minute."

Tony, tall enough to see over most everyone else's head, kept Essie and the deputy in clear view. The man stood much closer to her than propriety allowed, and every time she took a step back, Howard took a step forward.

Tony was still too far away to hear their conversation, but there was no mistaking Essie's displeasure. Pressing through a clump of people reuniting with their loved ones, Tony finally reached them.

"Does your uncle know about this?" Howard was saying.

Essie caught sight of Tony and looked at him as if she were drowning and he was the only life preserver around. Howard glanced back over his shoulder and scowled.

"Pardon my interruption, Essie, but our guest has arrived." Tony slipped his arm around her, then touched his hat. "Deputy, would you excuse us?"

Not waiting for an answer, he applied pressure to Essie's waist and moved her toward the baggage car. "You okay?"

"Yes. I'm fine."

"What did he want?"

"Nothing. He saw us riding through town and wanted to see why we appeared so 'cozy.' His word."

"What'd you tell him?"

"That you'd received permission to court me."

"What did he say?"

"He was not pleased."

Tony frowned. "Why not?"

"Because a few months back I refused his suit. But I made it clear to him that I'd accepted yours. Really. So there's no need to hold me so close."

"We'll talk about it later," he said, keeping his hand right where it was. If the deputy was watching, Tony wanted to make sure he knew which way the wind blew.

⌘

Essie took a liking to M.C. Baker right away. He was around the same age as Uncle Melvin—younger than Papa but older than herself—and he didn't seem to mind that she was the one representing Sullivan Oil instead of her father.

They'd dropped his trunk off at the front desk of the Commercial Hotel and were now sharing a meal in its large dining room. Used to be, Essie would have known every person in the place, but with the way the town had grown over the last couple of years, most of the patrons were unfamiliar to her.

M.C. picked up his final roasted rib and peeled some beef off with his teeth. "How much you producing?"

"In '96 we produced only about fourteen hundred barrels," Essie said, dabbing the sides of her mouth with her napkin. "But by the end of last year, we'd produced almost sixty-six thousand—all within the city limits."

"They've since moved out of town," Tony said, "and have expanded their producing wells to three hundred forty-two."

"All cable-tool?"

"Yep." Tony sliced off a portion of chicken-fried steak. "And all flush production—no pumps whatsoever."

M.C. lifted his brows. "How far down's the oil?"

"Anywhere from nine hundred to twelve hundred feet," Essie said. "Between us and that oil, though, is black, gummy clay and soft rock. So it takes us a good bit of time to break it up."

M.C. swiped his plate with his bread. "My rotary will bust through that in no time. And we can speed everything up even more by pouring water outside the drill pipe."

"What good would that do?" Essie asked.

"The water will come back to us through the pipe. But it'll be carrying rock and mud with it."

She took a sip of tea, realizing the wisdom of what he was saying. "How long do you think it would take you to drill me a well?"

M.C. dragged his napkin across his mouth and leaned back in his chair. "I can drill a thousand feet in thirty-six hours for six hundred dollars."

She and Tony exchanged a glance. A frazzled woman Essie had never seen before took away their plates and replaced them with bowls of suet pudding, then hurried off to her next customer.

"When can you give me a demonstration?" Essie asked.

"I'll need a third down and Tony's help. That going to be a problem?"

She shook her head.

"Well, then. You show me where and I'll start assembling every-thing as soon as I can get a crew here."

"That would be wonderful."

With their business concluded, the talk turned more personal. M.C. caught Tony up with news of Beaumont. The two men had obviously become well acquainted while Tony was with Morgan Oil.

"Just heard yesterday that Miss Morgan's been betrothed to Norris Tubbs."

Jerking his head up, Tony stopped his spoon halfway to his mouth.

"You might remember her," M.C. said. "She's the old boss's daughter? Name's Anna, I believe. You know her?"

Tony narrowed his eyes. "I believe I've run across her a time or two."

M.C. nodded. "Nuptials are set to take place within the month."

Tony paled, and Essie wondered at his reaction.

"But she can't get married this month," Tony said. "Her father hasn't even been in the grave for six weeks."

"You know Darius—" M.C. leaned in as if imparting a secret. "He's the new boss-man now."

Lips thinning, Tony gave a succinct nod.

"Anyhow, he's not one to give much nevermind to any social conventions."

The tick in Tony's jaw began to beat. "This is a bit more serious than a society rule. He's marrying Anna off with undue haste and to a man three times her age."

"Appears so."

Tony set his spoon down on the table. His easy use of the girl's first name surprised Essie. Had they been sweethearts? Had she broken his heart? Was that why he had left Beaumont without so much as a reference?

"That's not what has the tongues wagging, though." M.C. shook his head and scraped his spoon along the sides of his pudding bowl. "Nope. The really big news is that Finch Morgan's new wife died."

Tony fell back against his chair.

Essie looked between the two men. Who was Finch Morgan?

M.C. lifted his gaze. "Don't ya wanna know what the cause of death was this time?" He pulled his napkin free from where he'd tucked it into his collar. "Gastric fever."

Tony's lips parted.

M.C. turned to Essie. "This will be the second one in just over a year."

She frowned. "Second wife to die?"

"Yes, ma'am."

Sympathy filled her. "Childbirth?"

"No, ma'am. They died of gastric fever."

She blinked. "*Both* of them?"

" 'Fraid so." He pointed his spoon at Tony. "I believe our boy here knew the family, didn't you, son?"

Tony rubbed the strip of skin just beneath his nose. "When did she die?"

"Last week."

Folding her napkin, Essie wondered again at Tony's familiarity with these Morgans. First Anna, then Finch, and now his deceased wife?

"Who exactly is Finch Morgan?" she asked.

"I'm not right sure of his exact connection to the family," M.C. said. "Tony'll know, though."

Tony combed his fingers through his hair. "He's first cousin to Darius Morgan."

"Maternal or paternal side?" M.C. asked, his eyes sparkling with mischief.

"Paternal," Tony ground out.

"I see," Essie said. But truth was, she didn't see. She didn't at all understand how Tony had such intimate knowledge of the Morgan family. Intimate enough to call them by their first names and intimate enough to know who was related to whom.

Then a more disturbing thought occurred to her. If Anna was Darius Morgan's sister, then she was in line to inherit Morgan Oil. And Essie was in line to inherit Sullivan Oil.

Her heart sped up. Was Tony a modern-day fortune hunter? Was he looking to woo the beneficiaries of oil tycoons until he found one gullible enough to fall for him?

Papa might not have old money the way the Morgans did—and therefore was not a tycoon—but in Texas, Sullivan Oil was by far the biggest producer.

She studied Tony's drawn face. One thing was certain. Anna Morgan was much more to Tony than the daughter of his old boss.

chapter EIGHTEEN

TONY HAMMERED Mrs. Lockhart's kitchen door with his fist. In the twilight, he could see the backyard was not kept nearly as nice as the front. Weeds filled the gardens, vines rode up the derrick's legs, a loose board shifted beneath his feet, and paint peeled off the porch railings.

The door swung open. "What are you doing here?" Mrs. Lockhart asked, ushering him inside. "Aren't you supposed to be training for the bicycle race?"

"I decided to stop here first. Is it a bad time?"

"No, no. Come in. Have you had your supper?"

"Yes, ma'am. I ate down at Castle's."

She tsked. "Sit down. I'll slice you up some fruitcake." She served them both a piece, poured two cups of coffee and joined him at the table. "Now, what's wrong?"

"Have you heard from your daughter?"

"Goodness, Tony, there hasn't been enough time for a response. Why?"

"I found out that Darius has arranged a marriage between my sister and Norris Tubbs."

"What! Who's Norris Tubbs?"

"Part owner of the H&TC Railroad. Both my father and Darius have been trying to get him in their back pocket for some time now. The man is old enough to be Anna's grandfather."

"Is there any chance whatsoever that your sister is amiable to the match?"

Tony scoffed. "She cannot stand the man."

Mrs. Lockhart drummed her fingers on the table. "Well, don't panic. Your father's not been in his grave even two months. Anna's betrothal is nothing short of scandalous, but she won't be able to marry for at least another ten months or more."

"They are to marry before the month is out."

"Impossible! How do you know?"

"I heard it today from a driller by the name of M.C. Baker."

She touched her throat. "Good heavens."

"I've got to do something." He jumped up from the table. "But short of kidnapping her, I can't think of a thing."

"Dear me." She watched him pace, a worried frown on her face. "In *Her Martyrdom*, Lady Charlewood sequestered herself in a convent. Perhaps—"

Tony whirled around. "This is not some senseless romance novel! This is my baby sister we are discussing, and I'll thank you to treat the topic with the seriousness it deserves."

The elderly woman straightened her spine. "How dare you take that tone with me, sir."

His shoulders slumped. "Mrs. Lockhart, please. I meant no offense. I'm merely trying to point out that—"

"If you want my assistance, you'd best watch both your tone and your tongue."

He said nothing.

"Sit down."

He returned to his chair.

"I see you brought my novels back," she said, eyeing the two books he'd set on the table upon his arrival.

"Yes, ma'am."

"Did you read *Marjorie's Fate?*"

"Yes, ma'am, I did."

"And what did you conclude?"

"That Dr. Letsom was a scoundrel."

"I see." She folded her hands on the table. "And what brought you to that conclusion?"

"He loved no one more than himself. He acted out of turn without thinking through the consequences. He ruined the woman he professed to love."

She took a sip of coffee. "And what of Miss Marjorie?"

"She was taken advantage of. How could a young, naïve thing like her have been expected to know what he was up to?"

"She knew the difference between right and wrong. She knew she was breaking the rules of society. She knew she was lying to her parents."

He leaned back in his chair. "What are you saying? It was her fault?"

"I'm saying they both made poor choices."

"All right. I'll agree with that."

"Good." She dabbed her mouth with a napkin. "Now, about your sister. I will wire my daughter and tell her I am coming to Beaumont on tomorrow's train. Meanwhile, can you get word to Anna to meet me at the First Baptist Church on Pearl Street two days from now at ten in the morning?"

He put his chair down. "What are you going to do?"

"I'll see for myself how Anna feels about this match. If she is as reticent as you say she is, I will tell her to sit tight for now, but to be ready for action the moment you or I send word. In the meanwhile, I am going to do some research."

"Research?" he asked. "What are you going to research? Your romance novels?"

"The very same."

Rubbing his eyes, he checked his irritation. "Have you ever met Anna before?"

"Of course, but only briefly."

"I'll give you a letter to take with you, then. Now, what about your daughter's husband, Archie? He's Darius's right-hand man."

Mrs. Lockhart frowned. "Archie is not anyone's 'right-hand man.' He is an employee of Morgan Oil. No more. No less."

"I didn't mean to imply Archie would be involved in anything untoward."

"I should think not. Nevertheless, I don't wish to jeopardize his job, nor put his loyalties to the test. So you can be assured I will be very discreet." She stood. "Now, I need you to go so I can begin my research."

"Mrs. Lockhart, I'm not sure that romance novels—"

She handed him his hat. "You may pick me up tomorrow morning and carry my bag to the train station for me. By that time, I will have several options for you to consider."

He stood with indecision. What other choice did he have? He could go to Beaumont himself and confront Darius, but that would solve nothing. His brother would go to great lengths to protect this coveted connection with Norris Tubbs, just like Tony would go to great lengths to protect his sister.

But Darius had the upper hand. He was Anna's legal guardian and had the ability to keep Tony from getting anywhere near her or Mother until it was too late. Darius would also have Tubbs' power and support behind him.

But he would never suspect Mrs. Lockhart. Tony doubted Darius even knew who she was. If he got wind of it, though . . .

Tony gave her arm a gentle squeeze. "You must be very careful. Darius isn't evil, but he's greedy. If you were found out, no telling what he'd do. At the very least, Archie would lose his job."

She nodded. "I'll be careful."

"You won't do anything without discussing it with me first?"

"Of course not."

"All right, then." He settled his hat on his head. "I'll come by for you first thing tomorrow morning."

⌗

With Mr. Baker in town, Essie had to forgo Tony's bicycle training. Instead, she and Papa had Baker, Uncle Melvin, Aunt Verdie, and Preacher Wortham over for supper. Papa had wanted Tony to join them, now that he was officially courting her, but she'd insisted that Tony train instead, even if she wasn't there with him. But what she really wanted was an opportunity to speak with Mr. Baker without Tony present.

Slicing an apple pie at the sideboard, she served up six plates while Aunt Verdie placed them on the table. The sheriff's wife was a handsome woman, her blond hair highlighted with silver. Having never had children, she had the hourglass figure that every woman in town coveted—a tiny, tiny waist with extremely generous proportions both above and below.

"My crew should get here within a couple of days," Mr. Baker said, "and then we'll be able to get started."

"I'll take you through the fields tomorrow, then," Papa replied. "We've started drilling outside the city limits now."

"That's what Tony was sayin'. "

Essie slid back into her chair. "Have you known Mr. Bryant for long?"

Mr. Baker looked at her with confusion, before his expression cleared. "Oh, you mean Tony? Well, I guess that depends on what you'd call 'long.' I've been in Beaumont off and on for a couple of years."

"Off and on?"

"Yes, ma'am. My brother and I have been drillin' water wells all over the state, but our families are in Beaumont and so we always return there between jobs. That's how I got to know Tony."

"I see." She scooped up a bite of pie with her fork. "You know his family, then?"

"Oh, I know who they are, but I don't know them personal-like the way I do him."

She frowned. How could he know Tony and not his family? That didn't make a bit of sense. Not in a small town like Beaumont. But she couldn't think of a graceful way to ask such a question.

"I'm surprised Morgan Oil didn't hire you to drill for them, what with you right there and all," Uncle Melvin said.

"Well, I reckon we were so busy with our water business that we didn't really think about drillin' fer oil until here recently when we heard they was using rotaries up in Pennsylvania—and very successfully, I might add. But once we got wind of it, we went straight to Tony."

"And did Mr. Bryant contract your services?" the preacher asked.

"No, sir. Before any firm plans were made, Mr. Morgan passed. And now, well, the new boss is still sorting out which end is up."

"Tony knows the Morgans quite well, then?" Essie asked.

Color rushed to Mr. Baker's cheeks. "I'd say that's a safe assumption, ma'am."

"Oh?"

He swallowed. "Yes, ma'am. He, uh, he worked for them." He glanced at Papa, then back at her. "You did know that, didn't you?"

"Oh yes, of course," she replied. "He said he ordered their equipment and such."

Mr. Baker visibly relaxed. "That's right. That's why I went to him about the rotary drill."

"And what about you? Do you know the Morgans?"

"No, ma'am. Just . . ." His voice tapered off.

"Just . . . ?" she prompted.

"Just from a distance, ma'am."

She dabbed her mouth with her napkin. "Mr. Bryant seemed upset about Miss Morgan's betrothal to Mr., um, Tubbs, I believe?"

Mr. Baker's eyes darted in two different directions. "Did he?"

"He certainly did. Were he and Miss Morgan close?"

With a large, stubby finger, the driller pushed the last bite of dessert onto his fork. "They went to school together, I believe."

Before she could continue her line of questioning, Aunt Verdie interrupted.

"The pie was delicious, dear," she said. "Every bit as good as your mother's."

The others at the table echoed her sentiments and Essie smiled her thanks.

Papa pulled his napkin from his neck. "Mr. Baker? Preacher? Melvin? Would you care to join me for a cigar?"

The driller shoved back his chair. "I'd be much obliged, sir." He turned to Essie. "The meal was mighty fine, ma'am. Mighty fine."

Thanking him, she stood and gathered their plates while the men retreated to the front porch. She realized many of her questions about Tony and his relationship to the Morgans could have been answered if her father had simply thought to ask Tony when he first brought up the idea of courting her.

But Papa had relegated that discussion to her and now it seemed a bit late to start inquiring about it. Or maybe it wasn't. Now that they were officially courting, it was only natural she'd want to know about his family and his past and, certainly, his connection to Morgan Oil.

"You have somethin' on your mind, Essie-girl?" Aunt Verdie asked.

Essie glanced out the window, trying to judge the time. "I was just thinking about Tony. Perhaps if we hurried with these dishes, I could still catch him before he left the bicycle club."

Her aunt's expression softened. "You run on, now, and see to that man of yours. I'll take care of these dishes."

"Oh no. I couldn't."

"It would be my pleasure."

Essie shook her head. "No, really. I wouldn't feel right."

Without further argument, Aunt Verdie cleared the table, and Essie made short work of the dishes. She was just finishing up when she spotted Ewing and Mr. Baker through the window. They'd come around from the front and moved into the backyard, deep in discussion.

Mr. Baker was clearly distressed. Ewing placed a hand on the man's shoulder, stopping him. The preacher glanced at the house, frowning, then said something to Mr. Baker. Both men bowed their heads.

∼⁊∽

Essie slipped into the clubhouse, surprised to see Tony was only on the Indian clubs. He should have finished with those long ago. He juggled them in the air with much more precision than Sharpley ever had.

Pushing aside thoughts of Anna Morgan, Essie allowed excitement over the upcoming race to fill her. She only wished she had more time to prepare Tony.

She'd been training riders for four years now, ever since she opened the club. She'd originally organized the race to bring in new members, but after reading everything she could get her hands on concerning the art of racing and training, she'd come to covet a winning trophy for Sullivan Oil, for her club, and for her town.

Tony caught the clubs, returned them to their bin, then dropped to the floor for push-ups. She stayed in the shadows, telling herself she just wanted to see if he did all one hundred of them. But she lost count after the first fifteen, distracted by the sight he made aligning himself parallel to the floor.

He lifted his body with quick, powerful movements. Arms flexing, legs stiff, toes together. Light from the sconces splashed onto him, highlighting the sweat glistening on his skin. With a final grunt, he lowered himself to the floor and lay on his stomach, unmoving.

She stepped from the shadows.

"Essie," he said, raising his head. "I didn't hear you come in." He pushed himself up and stood, leaving an imprint of moisture the length of his body on the wooden floor.

His dark hair fell in abandon around his face. His chest heaved with each breath, stretching the wet shirt across his shoulders and delineating his muscles in sharp relief.

Arms hanging limp, he rested his weight on his right leg, throwing his hip slightly off to one side. She pulled her gaze and thoughts from their wayward paths, only to be caught short by the intensity of his stare.

"I . . ." she began. "We . . . Papa and Mr. Baker . . . they, uh, they retired to the porch, so I thought I'd come check on you."

His breathing was the only sound in the quiet of the building. "I'm glad you did."

She swallowed. "I thought you'd be almost finished by now."

"I got a late start."

"Oh?"

"I stopped by Mrs. Lockhart's on my way."

She blinked in confusion. "Mrs. Lockhart's?"

"Have you seen her backyard, Essie? It's a mess. I think I might go by and clean it up some while she's gone."

"Gone? You went by her house and she was gone?"

"No, not yet. She's leaving tomorrow for a short visit with her daughter."

Essie shook her head. "I don't understand. Why were you at Mrs. Lockhart's to begin with?"

He shrugged. "I've been by to check on her several times since that night I first escorted her to your lecture. She's rather up in years and has no family in town."

Essie absorbed that bit of information. Mrs. Lockhart had been such a pillar of the community for so long, it had never occurred to her to think of the elderly woman as fragile or lonely. But she could understand how a newcomer might view her that way.

"Oh," she said. "Well, that's very thoughtful of you. And, no, I had assumed her front yard was a reflection of her back."

"Well, it's not. But I'll take care of it."

She nodded absently, trying to gather her scattered thoughts. "So what all have you done?"

"The first three sets of laps and some of my exercises. I was just fixing to do my last set of laps now."

"I see," she took a step back. "Well, go ahead. Don't let me stop you."

Nodding, he retrieved the bicycle leaning against the wall, swung into the saddle and began his regimen. The wheels whirred slowly, then picked up momentum with each passing lap. The faster Tony went, the more he crouched down, like a jockey riding a horse.

She soon found herself caught up in his progress, shouting encouragement and urging him to even greater speed. When he completed his final lap and crossed the imaginary finish line, she cheered. It was one of his best runs by far.

Releasing the handlebars, he sat up, a smile wreathing his face. Clasping his hands together, he shook them in the air like a winner, then continued to glide around the track once more before pulling to a stop beside her.

"Oh, I wish I'd had my stopwatch!" she exclaimed. "You were splendid!"

He sat straddling the bike, his feet planted on either side. "I do better when you're here watching." His voice was low, pleased.

"Well, it's no hardship to watch you, I can tell you that."

His expression changed immediately. Reaching out, he clasped her hand and drew her close. Her skirts bunched around his leg. The bike's crossbar pressed against her hip.

"You smell good. Like cookies," he said, raising her hand to his mouth.

Shivers raced up her arm. "Cookies?"

"You know, the kind with cloves. Icebox cookies." He turned her hand over and rubbed his lips against her palm. "They're my favorite."

She stared, fascinated with the difference between her white fingers and his tanned ones, while the dark stubble on his cheek caught against her fingernails.

"Unfortunately, I smell like I've been training for a bicycle race."

She felt his smile while watching the skin beside his eyes crinkle, his expression turning rueful. And though he did smell of a man who'd been laboring, she did not find the odor unpleasant. She managed to refrain from saying so, however.

"Would you like to go fishing?" he asked.

"Right now?"

His smile widened. "Tempting, but I was thinking of after church on Sunday."

She flushed and tried to step away, but he put a hand against her waist, staying her.

She lowered her gaze. "Yes, thank you. I'd love to go fishing."

Closing his eyes, he planted a kiss onto her palm. "Sunday it is, then."

Pulling her hand away, she pressed it against her stomach— whether to capture the kiss and keep it close or to calm the jitters inside, she didn't know.

She took a step back. "It's late. I suggest we call it a night. Why don't I start putting out the lights while you take care of the bike?"

He nodded and she turned, making her way to the far wall, all the while disconcerted to know that he stayed right where he was, watching her.

It wasn't until much later that night when she was home and tucked safely in bed that she realized she'd totally forgotten to ask him about his family and the Morgans.

Rolling over, she bunched up her pillow. No need to fret. There would be time enough for that while they were fishing.

chapter NINETEEN

ESSIE COULDN'T remember the last time building a rig had caused such a stir. Every boomer in the patch kept one eye on his job and the other on the Bakers' marvel.

Two days after M.C.'s arrival, his brother, C.E., descended on Corsicana with their crew of rig builders. Essie watched them with fascination. A tougher, stronger, meaner group of men would be hard to find.

Whiteselle's Lumber Yard delivered pre-sawed roughs, and M.C.'s crew attacked them like ants on a picnic lunch. They worked at a fast and furious pace, putting every other able-bodied man to shame.

Skillful, ambidextrous, and exceedingly strong, they laid down a derrick floor, then began to nail together the rig's legs. Dirt clouds churned so thick around the crew that she had to squint sometimes just to see.

When Essie made an appearance, the Sullivan Oil hands invariably stopped their work, but there was no stopping M.C. Baker's crew. They paid her no mind at all. She wasn't even sure they realized she was there.

As the derrick went up, the men raised their timbers with a pulley they called a "gin pole." Muscles bulged, sharp commands abounded, and a good deal of hazing occurred without anyone missing a step.

Essie watched one sweat-soaked man as he steadied a three-by-twelve-inch board in a corner of the derrick, then sank in a spike with three quick blows. Instead of a hammer, he used a long-handled hatchet with a round, serrated head opposed to the blade, hammering spike after spike with first his right hand, then his left.

Tony stood below him, then pointed up and shouted something, but she couldn't make out his words. In conjunction with M.C.'s arrival, Papa had pulled Tony from his roustabouting and promoted him to tool pusher for the rotary rigs, while Moss would remain tool pusher for the cable rigs.

Tony knew his tools backwards and forwards, but she didn't think he came close to deserving such a high position. He was, after all, a very recent employee, and they had several other men who had worked longer and were more deserving—if not, perhaps, as qualified.

She also didn't want people thinking the job had been given to him because of his relationship with her, though she worried that might have indeed factored into Papa's decision. And until she could find out exactly what had happened to him at Morgan Oil and what his connection to Anna Morgan was, she was determined to maintain an employer–employee relationship with him while in the patch. It wouldn't be easy, though.

The rig builder shouted something down to Tony, who, in response, threw back his head and laughed. The two shared a smile before Tony turned away from the derrick and caught sight of her. His face registering surprise, then panic.

He quickly glanced around to see if anyone was near her, then bore down on her, scowling. "What are you doing here?"

"I beg your pardon?" she said.

"You heard me." He snatched his hat off belatedly, pinching the crown between his fingers. "What are you doing here?"

His vehemence shocked her.

"I'm here to watch the construction of our new rig, Mr. Bryant. Was there something you needed?"

He shooed her with his hat. "I need you to leave. This is no place for a woman, and you are distracting the boys."

"Nothing seems to distract these boys. And even if I were, I own the company. Which means I can go wherever I please—and without having to explain myself."

"Lower your voice," he said. He grasped her elbow and propelled her toward the edge of the field where she'd left her bicycle. "I don't want you challenging me in front of the men."

She tugged against his hold. "Let go. I want to watch the rig builders."

He tightened his grip. "I'm afraid that's out of the question."

"It is not. Just who do you think you are?"

They reached the street and he jerked her bike up off the ground. "I am overseer of the rotary rigs. And I do not allow females of any sort around the patch—even part owners."

"You work for me, Tony, not the other way around. You do not have the authority to tell me where I can and can't go."

"I told your father I would not accept this position unless I had absolute power on the field. He agreed to my terms. If you have a problem with that, then take it up with him. But for now, you are to put your pretty backside on this bike and ride well out of harm's way."

"No."

He narrowed his eyes. "If you don't want me to sling you over my shoulder and bodily carry you all the way to your front door, then I suggest you get on this machine, and right quickly."

"You wouldn't dare."

He leaned in close. "Try me."

She didn't make any move to take the bike from him.

"You have to the count of ten. One . . . two . . ."

She could not believe he would actually do it. But, then, maybe he would. And if he did, the men would talk about it all over town, and any respect she'd garnered over the years would go up in a puff of smoke.

"Seven . . . eight . . ."

She grabbed Peg's handlebars. "I am going straightaway to discuss this with my father. We will see just exactly who is boss and who is not. I expect you to be in our office the moment your shift is over."

Without another word, she mounted the bicycle and, with all the dignity she could muster, rode toward home.

❧

Papa was not at home. Nor at the courthouse. Nor at the attorney's office. The longer she looked for him, the more irritated she became. He'd promoted Tony without consulting her. He'd excluded her from discussions with the Baker brothers. He'd contracted for three rotary rigs before even seeing if the first one was going to work.

Pulling to a stop in front of the jailhouse, she jumped from the bike, then stormed up the steps and through the door, bumping square into Deputy Howard.

"Whoa there, girl," he said, clasping her around the waist to keep her from falling. Warm breath from his mouth and nose touched her cheek.

She shoved against him. "Let me go."

He held up his hands in mock surrender. "Now, what's got you cross as a snappin' turtle on this fine summer day?"

"Men in general. You in particular." She scanned the room and found her uncle and father standing beside the sheriff's desk, staring at her in surprise.

She knew she was behaving badly, but she couldn't seem to rein in her temper. "I've been looking all over for you, Papa."

"Well, I'm right here. Has something happened?"

"Nothing catastrophic. Just a few things I'd like to get straightened out."

"Can it wait a minute? Deputy Howard is leaving for Austin this afternoon, and Melvin and I need to finalize a few things before he leaves."

"Austin? Why?"

"The annual Texas Sheriff's Association Convention starts Monday, and Melvin is going to send Howard in his stead."

"Oh." She tugged the bow under her neck and removed her bonnet. "Very well. I'll wait."

Howard moved away from the doorway. "I think I'll pick up those records from the courthouse on my way to the train station instead of getting them now."

"Fine," Uncle Melvin said, then turned back to Papa.

Howard sidled up to Essie, winking at her. She stepped to the right, putting distance between them.

"I like the opening sentence much better than the way we had it before," Melvin said. "Do you think the petition is strong enough now?"

"Oh, I think it's plenty strong. The question is whether or not the Association will back it."

Essie moved to the desk. "What is it?"

"Take a look," Melvin said, turning the document so she could see. "We want to ride the tide of the anti-lynching crusade led by that newspaper editor in Tennessee. If Billy John can get members of the Sheriff's Association to sign this petition, the state congress will be hard-pressed not to pass a law punishing those responsible for lynching in our state."

She glanced at the other papers on his desk but saw no evidence of the postcard she'd seen before. "You can't arrest an entire mob, can you?"

"Naw," he said. "But we could arrest the ringleaders and make an example of them."

Papa checked his pocket watch. "Well, if you don't need me any further, Melvin, I guess I'll see what it is Essie wants."

"No, no. You go on. Billy John and I can take it from here."

Papa ushered her out the door and to her bicycle. "Now, what is it that has you all worked up?"

She recalled the sting of Tony's dismissal afresh. "Tony refused to let me watch the rig builders. He practically forced me onto my bike and made me leave."

"Oh, I'm sorry, honey. I forgot to tell you to quit going out there."

"What?" She stopped pushing her bicycle to stare at him. "You agreed to that without talking with me first?"

He shrugged. "There wasn't time. Besides, he's the one running the site now. If he doesn't want any women out there, then that's his prerogative."

They continued down the street. "I'm not just *any* woman. I'm part owner and his boss, to boot."

"That may be so, but surely you see his point, Essie. The fields are getting rougher and rougher. Tony said you interrupt the work and distract the men, and depending upon what they're in the middle of, that can be extremely dangerous."

"What are you saying? That I'm never to go out to our fields again for the rest of my life?"

He chuckled. "I don't think we have to go quite so far as that. Just lay low for now until Tony has a chance to establish himself in his new position."

She blew out a huff of breath. "I wish you would consult with me before making decisions like this. You promoted Tony without due consideration. Grandpa or some of our other men should have been offered the position first."

"I don't know why you keep harping about this. If we were replacing Moss, then you'd be right." He shook his head. "We needed a tool pusher for our rotary rigs. None of the men but Tony had ever even seen one. Like it or not, he's the man most suited for the job."

She sighed. "That may be true, but something just isn't quite right. I can't put my finger on it. But he left Morgan Oil so suddenly, and he knows the Morgan family more intimately than he let on at first."

"You think he's lying to us about something?" Papa asked, clearly surprised.

"Withholding, maybe. He knows too much about that family not to have some personal tie."

Papa considered her words as they turned onto Eighth Street. "Well, let's put the shoe on the other foot for a moment. Moss or any of the men who report at the house know plenty about our personal lives."

She supposed he was right. But would Mr. Moss use her Christian name in casual conversation the way Tony had with Miss Morgan's? She couldn't imagine him taking such a liberty. Not unless theirs was a more . . . intimate acquaintance.

No, if Mr. Moss were to call her something other than Miss Spreckelmeyer, it would undoubtedly be in the form of a nickname. Thank goodness she'd escaped that unpleasant designation.

Essie showed Tony into the study. She'd forgotten he was coming by the house right after work. When she'd instructed him to do so, she'd thought to tell him in no uncertain terms that she would go out to the fields whenever she pleased. To have to concede defeat on the matter did not sit well.

He'd not taken the time to bathe or change. His clothes were splattered with mud. His face was covered in dirt. His brown eyes, however, shone brightly.

"I'd ask you to sit, but, well . . ."

He smiled. "I understand. You go ahead, though."

Papa was not at home, so she took his place behind the desk.

Tony moved to the window, leaning back against the sill. "The judge told me y'all bid on some land south of town."

"That's right."

"I went down there and looked it over. Looks like a ripe field."

"I certainly thought so."

"When will you know if you won the bid?"

"Anytime now."

An awkward silence settled over them.

Tony cleared his throat. "The rig builders should finish the derrick within another day or two, but that's going to cut into our fishing time. Would you mind if we postponed our date until next Sunday?"

She moistened her lips. Her plans had been to ask him about Anna Morgan while they were fishing, and she wasn't sure she could wait another week to satisfy her curiosity. Perhaps an opportunity would present itself between now and then.

"No, of course I don't mind," she answered. "Next Sunday is fine."

He hesitated. "Did you have a chance to talk with your father?"

"Yes," she said, clipping the word.

"Good. He told you about the masks, then?"

"Masks?"

"Yes. The cup masks."

"What cup masks?"

"I thought you talked to your father?"

"I did, but we discussed your request that I stay away from the fields."

He nodded as understanding dawned. "I am sorry about that. It's just that women—"

She held up her hand. "I'd rather not rehash it, if it is all the same to you. Now, what about these masks?"

"When we swab the wells, the sulphur gas that rushes up out of the hole is so strong it can knock a fella clean out. We waste a lot of time waiting for that gas to blow before letting the bailer down. So I was thinking, what if we got us some of those cup masks they use in the factories up north? We could just wear those and then we wouldn't have to worry about anybody keeling over. And it would save time, too."

She leaned back in her chair. "You know, Tony, you come up with more creative ways to spend money than anyone I've ever met. You just talked Papa into investing in three rotary rigs and now you want me to order masks?"

"Not just any masks. Cup masks. You know, the kind that look like pig snouts?"

"Pig snouts."

"Yes. They fit over the nose and mouth and prevent noxious gases from getting into your throat and lungs. For us, they'd also save time."

She sighed. "I appreciate what you're trying to do, but if the sulphur gas is truly as dangerous as you are suggesting, then cup masks would be used up in Pennsylvania. But no one uses them. No one. They simply get out of the gas's way when it starts to blow."

"So your answer is no?"

"I have to consider both the benefit and practicality of them," she explained. "And though they might help the men breathe, I cannot imagine the boomers wearing them. Think of how uncomfortable and hot they would be."

"They wouldn't wear them all the time. Only when the gas starts to blow."

She shook her head. "They could just as easily clear out of the way. I'm sorry. I simply can't justify the expense of masks for every man in my employ."

"Not every man. The drillers."

"We have over three hundred drillers, Tony. We can't just up and buy masks for all of them. Besides, we don't even know if they would work."

"Yes, we do. I had one sent out already and tried it. Works great."

She frowned. "Where did you get it?"

"I'm not sure where it came from. Your father ordered it."

Her lips parted. "When did he do that?"

"Couple of weeks ago."

"Good heavens."

"So what do you say?"

"I say we've been doing just fine for the last four years. I imagine we'll continue to do so."

"You don't even know what they cost and haven't seen them in action."

"I'm afraid I won't have the pleasure of seeing them in action, Mr. Bryant, since I'm no longer allowed on my own fields."

His lips thinned. "Is that what this is about? You're mad because you got your nose tweaked, so you're going to risk the health of the men for the sake of your pride?"

She shot up out of her chair. "That is quite enough. I don't know what makes you think you can address me in such a manner, but let me assure you that you cannot."

"Those masks can be a matter of life or death."

"I hardly think so. As I pointed out before, every oil patch in America has managed just fine without them."

"Does your father know you are refusing to buy them?"

"You go right ahead and run to him, since that seems to be your wont. But I guarantee you, this time he will say the decision is mine and mine alone."

Tony put on his hat. "Well, I guess we'll find out, won't we?"

"We certainly will. In the meantime, I expect to see you at training tonight. Be prepared for a vigorous workout."

"Not to worry, Miss Spreckelmeyer. I can handle anything you care to throw my way." Spinning around, he stalked out of the office and slammed the door behind him.

chapter TWENTY

ESSIE PLACED sugar cookies in a tin, the buttery aroma filling the room. The door opened and she glanced over her shoulder.

"Ewing," she said, smiling. "It's been a while since you've come in the kitchen door. And just in time for cookies. Would you like some?"

Hanging his hat on a peg, he nodded. "Don't mind if I do."

His reddish blond hair fell in abandon across his forehead, but his black clerical suit fit him with the precision of a well-tailored garment.

She handed him the tin. "Papa's in his study. I'd walk you back there, but I need to get to the clubhouse."

He set the cookies on the table. "Actually, I didn't come to see your dad. I came to see you."

"Me?"

"Yes."

She glanced out the window. "I'd love to visit, but Tony's expecting me."

He held out a chair. "He can wait."

She slowly untied her apron and hung it over the oven-door handle. "What's the matter?"

"Please, have a seat." Tension tightened the lines on his face.

Smoothing her skirts, she took the chair he offered, then watched as he settled in across from her.

"We've been friends a long time," he began.

"My stars and garters, Ewing. What on earth has happened to make you so morose?"

He took a deep breath. "How well do you know Tony Bryant?"

She blinked. "What kind of question is that? I'm courting him, for heaven's sake."

"Yes." He cleared his throat. "But what I'm trying to determine is, um, just how much you know about him."

"Who's asking?" she said, cocking her head. "My preacher, my friend, or my former suitor?"

His face filled with color. "I'd like to say your preacher, but I'm not sure that's the case."

"Then which is the case?"

"Your friend. Your friend is asking. Though, I don't think I'd have agonized over it quite so much if I hadn't been a former suitor."

She digested that bit of honesty, then pushed the tin of cookies toward him. "You've heard something you think I need to know. And whatever it is, it's unpleasant. Am I right?"

He nodded, breaking a cookie in half, then putting it in his mouth.

"Well, let's hear it."

He finished chewing and swallowed. "Tony Bryant is actually Tony Morgan. As in the Morgan Oil Morgans."

"What?" she asked, frowning. "What are you saying?"

"I'm saying he's the late Blake Morgan's younger son."

As she tried to sort through her confusion, one thought rose immediately to the surface. *That would mean Anna Morgan's his sister.* She slid her eyes closed, a sense of relief flowing through her.

"Oh, Ewing. I'd suspected his ties to the Morgans were more than he'd let on, but I'd imagined he was a spurned suitor of Anna

Morgan's and that he had ulterior motives for courting me." She shook her head. "And now to find out Anna's his sister, of all things."

She smiled at her foolishness and at Ewing, but his face did not reflect her relief.

"I don't think you're seeing the big picture, Essie. He's been lying to you. To the entire town."

"Oh, I'm sure there's a perfectly reasonable explanation. Just look at how I mistook his interest in me, thinking it was due to my being an oil heiress—just like Anna—when all the time she was his sister."

"I don't know. I mean, we both know your first instinct has always been to see the best in people—even when it's not there."

He gave her a pointed look, and she knew he was referring to a beau of hers from a few years back whom she'd grossly misjudged.

"That aside," Ewing continued, "why would a Morgan pass himself off as a nobody unless he wanted something?"

She gave him a cautious look. "Like what?"

Ewing rubbed his forehead. "Like a position with Sullivan Oil."

She hesitated. "Come to think of it, why would he need a position with Sullivan Oil when he has his own company?"

Ewing held her gaze. "Perhaps he was figuring to learn firsthand his competition's strengths and weaknesses."

She swallowed, her calm suddenly eclipsed by impending dread.

Setting his elbows on the table, Ewing linked his hands together and rested his chin on his fists. "And what better way to do that than by courting the owner's daughter and infiltrating the company at its highest and most vulnerable level?"

Her mind balked. She tried not to think the obvious, but it was becoming all too clear.

"Are you absolutely certain about this?" she asked.

"I'm not at all certain of his motives. Only that his real name is Tony Morgan."

"How long have you known?"

"I was told a couple of days ago," he said, lowering his hands.

"By whom?"

"Does it matter?"

She cringed. If Ewing had heard it from some busybody, then no telling how many others were whispering behind their hands about Essie Spreckelmeyer being courted, once again, for all the wrong reasons. "Who all knows?"

"I think only me and the person who told me."

"But I thought you heard it through the gossip mill?"

"I never said that. I was given the information in the strictest of confidences from an outsider. You have no idea how much I have struggled with whether or not I was at liberty to tell you."

"And no one else knows?"

"If they do, I've not heard a word. And I feel sure I would have. This would be way too juicy a piece of meat not to have every jaw in town gnawing on it."

She nodded, dreading the time when Tony's identity was eventually discovered. Not only would she be at the center of the townsfolk's speculations, but now that she had time to consider it, she realized they would not take kindly to being duped. Particularly not by a Morgan.

Ewing looked out the window. "I wonder if he had some nefarious reason for using a false name."

"What do you mean?"

He shrugged. "Well, a fella doesn't hide his identity for good reasons, that's for sure."

She frowned, then rose to her feet. "You did the right thing, Ewing. It would have been horrible if I'd been the last to find out."

"That's what I finally decided, too," he said, standing. "So what are you going to do?"

"Tell Papa."

"Would you like me to come with you?"

"No, I think it's best if I do it myself." She reached out with her hand. Ewing slipped his around it.

"Thank you," she said, squeezing.

"You all right?"

Nodding, she bit her lower lip. "I'll be fine."

"You don't have to put on a brave face for me."

"I know."

Hand-in-hand, they walked to the door.

He retrieved his hat. "Well, thanks for the cookie. And remember, I am your preacher. If you ever need a shoulder . . ."

She kissed him on the cheek. "If I ever need a shoulder, I think I'll come visit my friend Ewing, not Preacher Wortham. That is, if it's all right with you?"

"You know it is."

Closing the door behind him, Essie swallowed the hurt pushing against her. She would save that for later. Right now she needed to tell Papa.

∾

Essie knocked on the door of her father's study, then poked her head inside. "Can I come in?"

He waved her in without bothering to look up from the paper he was writing on. His gray hair looked as if it had been plowed into distinct rows. Even as the thought occurred to her, he ran his fingers through it again, reinforcing the furrows.

His jacket hung on the back of his chair. His four-in-hand tie lay in a puddle on the corner of his desk. The cuffs of his white shirt were smudged with ink.

She seated herself in one of the wing chairs across from him. After a few minutes, he put his pen in its holder and blotted the page. "Don't you have bicycle training tonight?" he asked, still skimming whatever it was he'd written.

"Yes, but I needed to talk with you first."

"Well, if you plan on hounding me again about Tony's position as tool pusher, I'm not up to it," he said, reaching for his pen and dipping it in the ink well.

"No. It isn't that."

"What is it, then?"

"I've just received some rather disturbing news."

He scribbled something on the bottom of the paper. "Go ahead."

"Tony Bryant is actually Tony Morgan, Blake Morgan's son."

Papa stopped writing mid-sentence and looked up. Being a judge, he was a master at disguising his feelings. But she knew him well and saw the surprise light his eyes before he quickly shuttered it.

"How did you find out?" he asked, returning the pen to its holder.

"Ewing told me."

"How did Ewing find out?"

"He wouldn't tell me."

Papa leaned back, the brown leather upholstery creaking. "Who else knows?"

"I don't think anyone, yet."

"Well, somebody does or else Ewing wouldn't have found out."

"He said it was an outsider who asked him to keep the information private." She hesitated. "Perhaps it was Mr. Baker? I saw them talking out in the yard that night they were over for dinner."

"Isn't exactly reassuring to find out our preacher can't keep his mouth shut, is it?"

Essie stiffened. "He was wanting to protect me. Surely in this case, breaking a confidence was the lesser of two evils. And why are we talking about Ewing when we should be talking about Tony and what to do about this?"

Papa rubbed his mouth. "I'm not planning on doing anything about it."

"What?"

"I like him. I always have. He's a hard worker. He's knowledgeable. He's innovative. And he had the good sense to court you."

She threaded her fingers together. "Papa. Surely you can read between the lines here. He isn't courting me because he has feelings for me. He's courting me to worm his way into our company."

"I don't think so, Essie. And it disturbs me that you do."

"It's the only thing that makes sense. What other possible motivation could he have for pretending to be someone he's not?"

"I'm not sure he sees it as pretending, exactly."

She raised a brow.

"His father disinherited him. Completely. Didn't give him so much as a penny. Left just enough for his wife and daughter to get by on and gave the rest to his first son."

"Oh, Papa. That can't be true. Mr. Morgan had plenty of money to spread around. It doesn't make sense for him to disinherit anyone, especially not his own son."

"All the same, that's what he did."

She frowned. "How could you possibly know all that?"

"The content of Blake's will is common knowledge among the men in my circle."

She tried to process what he was telling her. "But how do you know Tony is the son that was disinherited?"

"He's the second son."

"How can you be sure?"

Papa took a deep breath. "I've known who he was from the moment he stepped into my office that first day."

"What? He told you and you didn't tell me!"

"No, no. He never said a word about it. But I knew his father, Essie. We were on opposing sides of a bill I wanted passed once, back when you were just a little girl. He was a hard man with a lot of money. When the bill went in my favor, he took it personally and

I found, through no fault of my own, that I'd made a formidable enemy."

"But that doesn't explain how you knew Tony."

"The Morgan men all bear a striking resemblance to one another. Tony looks like his father. And his father like the father before him. There was no mistaking him. And even if I'd had any doubts, they were put to rest when he used the last name Bryant."

"Why?"

"His mother was a Bryant. I'd known her father for years. He hated the Morgans and refused to grant Blake permission to court his daughter. But Blake was still stinging from the loss of that bill and wasn't about to be told no a second time. So they eloped."

"Good heavens."

"And if that weren't enough, she was barely out of the schoolroom and he was twenty years her senior and still grieving over his first wife."

"What are you saying?"

"It wasn't a love match—at least, not on his part. He wanted a mother for his baby son and a wife to . . . well, he wanted a wife. And to be perfectly honest, I think his main reason for choosing Leah was because Alfred told him he couldn't have her."

"Oh, that poor girl."

He shrugged. "It was a long time ago. In any event, she gave him another son and then a daughter, but Blake left his fortune and his business to Darius, his first son, and nothing to Tony."

"Why? What did Tony do to warrant his father's wrath?"

"He had the unfortunate distinction of being the product of a loveless marriage. Blake didn't care any more for Leah's offspring than he did for Leah."

Essie couldn't begin to comprehend something so reprehensible, particularly when it was the man's own flesh and blood.

"What happened to Mrs. Morgan and Anna?"

"He marginally provided for Leah and Anna, though Darius holds all the power and the purse strings."

"But that doesn't explain why Tony would pretend to be someone he's not."

"Let me ask you this: If you'd known he was Blake Morgan's son, would you have hired him on?"

"I never wanted to hire him to begin with."

"Exactly. If he had any chance of getting a job in the oil patch, he had to be someone other than Tony Morgan."

She rubbed her forehead. Tony, her Tony, was the cast-out son of Blake Morgan? She tried to imagine her parents disinheriting her. The hurt and betrayal alone would be devastating.

"Why didn't you tell me?" she asked.

"I didn't mind his being a Morgan. I wasn't about to hold a grudge against him simply because his father hadn't cared for me. At the same time, I didn't want to show my hand too soon, just in case his motives were questionable. So I decided to sit tight and see what happened."

"And when he asked to court me? It didn't occur to you that I might like to know the identity of the man I was stepping out with?"

"I thought about telling you. But after praying about it, the Lord told me to be still. So that's what I did. You'd have found out here pretty quick, though."

She frowned. "Why do you say that?"

"I just learned that Darius Morgan outbid us on the mineral rights for that chunk of land south of town."

"No! You can't mean it. I didn't even know he was interested in it."

"Me either."

"And we lost?" She tightened her lips. "I can't believe it. And not only that, but now we're going to have to deal with Morgan Oil doing business right here in our own backyard."

Papa shrugged. "He has just as much right to it as we do."

"But . . . but we were here first!"

A sparkle entered his eyes. "Would it soothe your sense of injustice if I bought up some mineral rights in Beaumont?"

She thought about it, then smiled. "Actually, I think it would. You want to?"

He chuckled. "We'll see. In the meanwhile, Morgan's men will be pouring into town pretty soon and they'll be all too happy to tell everyone within hearing distance just exactly who Tony is."

She bit her lip. "Is Tony aware that you know he's a Morgan?"

"He has no idea."

"And you think it's really as simple as he wanted a job?"

"I do. From everything I've seen and heard, he's a fine man. I've been most impressed."

She hoped he was right. Oh, how she hoped he was right. "Do you think he knows about Morgan Oil's plans to move in?"

"I doubt it. It's my understanding he's been completely cut off from them. Besides, I just found out myself a couple of hours ago."

"Did you tell Uncle Melvin about Tony?"

"The very first day the boy arrived."

Slapping her hands against the arms of the chair, she pushed herself up. "Well. I guess I'll go on to the clubhouse. I'm sure Tony's wondering what's keeping me."

"What are you going to do?"

"First I'm going to train him for the bicycle race. Then I'm going to ask him straight out who he is."

chapter TWENTY-ONE

TONY JUGGLED the football with his thighs and feet, trying to see how long he could keep it in the air. The door to the clubhouse squeaked open and he caught the ball.

"Where have you been?" he asked.

Essie removed her shawl and hat and hung them by the door. "Something came up and I couldn't get away."

He pushed the hair out of his eyes. "Is it because you're still mad at me?"

"Mad at you about what?"

He hesitated. If she wasn't dwelling on their argument about her going to the fields, he wasn't fool enough to bring it up. "You aren't wearing your bloomers."

She glanced down at her brown skirt and white shirtwaist. "I didn't have time to change."

"What is it? What's happened?"

"We lost our bid for the mineral rights south of town."

"You're kidding." He frowned, yet took time to appreciate the sway of her hips as she approached. "Who outbid you?"

"Morgan Oil."

He froze. "Morgan Oil? Why would they bid on rights clear up in Navarro County?"

She stopped in front of him and took the ball from his hands. "You tell me."

Dragging his hand across his mouth, he looked around the clubhouse, trying to make sense of what she'd told him. "I have no idea. I didn't even know they were interested in it."

"No? Well, I'm glad to hear that, anyway."

He glanced at her sharply. "What's that supposed to mean?"

"Nothing," she said, moving to the bin against the wall and dropping the ball inside. "Did you put yourself through all the paces?"

"I did."

"You're completely through with your workout?"

"Except for our football match."

"Well, we won't be having that tonight." She turned around, facing him, then clasped her hands in front of her. "Just when were you planning on telling me your real name is Tony Morgan?"

Take the deuce. One of M.C.'s crew must have inadvertently said something. He'd been afraid of that. He'd hustled her off that field just as quick as he could. But it obviously hadn't been quick enough.

"I don't know, exactly," he said. "How did you find out?"

"That hardly matters, Tony."

"No, I don't suppose it does." He cleared his throat. "I've been wanting to tell you for quite some time."

"Then why didn't you?"

"I was afraid you'd question my motives."

"Motives for what?"

"For working for Sullivan Oil. For," he swallowed, "for stepping out with you."

"And what are your motives, Mr. Morgan?"

He started toward her, but she held up her hand. "Stay right where you are, sir, and answer my question."

"It's a really long answer. Can we go to your office over there and sit down?"

"I don't think so. Why don't you just give me the short version."

He massaged the back of his neck. "My interest in you is genuine, Essie. Very genuine. And asking for permission to court you was not something I did lightly."

He gave her a chance to respond, but she remained silent. The sconces cast a glow over her features. Her expression gave nothing away.

"I think about you all the time," he continued. "I think of all the places I want to take you and all the things I'd like to do with you, then I remember I have no money. No secure future. Not even a real name anymore." He blew out a huff of air. "Then I start worrying about how I'm going to support you. I've been scared out of my mind that if you ever found out who I was, you'd think I was using you to gain a foothold in your father's business. And I'm not. I swear I'm not."

She remained stoic. "What are you doing, then, Tony?"

"I'm trying to learn everything I can about the oil industry. I know a lot about the business side of it, but not as much about the everyday field work. So that's why I came here. To get a job with the largest producer of Texas oil so I could learn the ropes."

"Well, you've certainly managed to move up the chain of command rather quickly, haven't you?"

He crossed the floor, ignoring her attempts to keep him at bay. "I earned those positions fair and square," he said. "My success in the fields has had nothing to do with you and me."

"I'm part owner and sole heir to the Sullivan Oil enterprise. Of course it has to do with you and me. Do you take me for a fool?"

He grasped her arms. "Don't, Essie. Don't believe the worst, please."

"How can you expect me not to when you've done nothing but lie from the moment I laid eyes on you?"

"That's not fair. I've not lied about everything. Only about my name. It's just a name."

She pulled free of him. "Don't patronize me. It's much more than a name and you know it."

"All right. I was wrong to have lied. And I've known that for quite some time now. You have no idea how many times I've wanted to push the clock back and knock on your door for the first time as me. The real me."

She swallowed, her poker face disintegrating, the distress in her eyes apparent.

"Why didn't you just tell me?" she asked. "At least when we began to court. Couldn't you have told me then?"

He reached for her again, but she flinched, so he contented himself with lightly rubbing her arms.

"I wanted to," he said, "but don't you see? If I'd told you at that point, you would have sent me packing. You know you would have."

She turned her face away, and he could not resist pulling her to him. She felt so good. So soft. Whiffs of clove and sugar teased his senses.

He nuzzled her hair. "If you don't believe me, ask Mrs. Lockhart."

She jerked out of his arms and stumbled back. "Mrs. Lockhart? *Mrs. Lockhart!* What has she to do with this?"

"Well, she, she knows who I am," he answered, confused at her reaction.

"You told Mrs. Lockhart who you were and you didn't tell me?" she screeched.

"Not on purpose. She recognized me. What was I supposed to do?"

Essie spun around, no longer willing to face him. "Oooooh, I cannot even believe this is happening."

"What's wrong with Mrs. Lockhart knowing who I am?"

Essie covered her face with her hands. "Don't you see how humiliating this is? 'Poor little Essie Spreckelmeyer, the wallflower of Corsicana, finally gets herself a man because she comes part and parcel with the biggest oil company in Texas.' "

"Now, just a minute," he said, grabbing her arm and jerking her back around. "That's about the stupidest thing I ever heard and not a single soul would ever believe it. You're smart, you're pretty, you have a zest for living that others only dream about. You've accomplished more in your short life than most could accomplish in two lifetimes, you think nothing of risking your own skin to save somebody else's, and you make the best green corn patties I've ever tasted in my life. That oil company is nothing compared to you."

Her jaw slackened. "When have you had my green corn patties?"

"On the Fourth of July."

She stared at him, completely befuddled. "You think I'm pretty?"

"What fool kind of question is that? You're bound to own a mirror, so you know good and well you're pretty."

By slow degrees, her expression softened. "Thank you." Her gaze swept over him. "I think you're pretty, too."

He frowned. "Men are not pretty."

A smile crept onto her face. "Tony Bryant's pretty," she crooned in a soft, whispery voice.

It took him a moment to register she wasn't baiting him but was instead teasing him. And smiling. She wasn't angry anymore.

He let out a sigh of relief, then smoothed a tendril of hair behind her ear. "My name is Tony Morgan. Tony Bryant Morgan."

"Ahhh. That's right. I forgot. Tony Bryant *Morgan* is pretty."

"He is not."

"He is, too."

The light picked up the laughter in her eyes, the peaches in her skin.

"I'm sorry," he said. "I promise you this: I'll never, ever be anything but completely honest with you henceforth and forevermore."

Her amusement was slowly replaced with a touch of vulnerability. "Is there going to be a forevermore, Tony?"

Slipping his arms around her waist, he gently drew her close. "There will be if I have anything to say about it."

He lowered his lips to hers and kissed her. Not the way he'd have liked to, but the way he ought to. He tucked her more tightly against him, inhaling her scent, testing the way she felt in his embrace. Her arms snaked up around his neck, her fingers stroking the hair at his collar as she returned his kiss with the same enthusiasm she brought to most everything else she did.

Desire rushed through him and he forced himself to pull back. The yearning he saw in her eyes nearly undid him. Groaning, he pressed his face against her neck and helped himself to the tiniest of tastes before setting her at arm's length.

"I think we'd better head on home, Essie," he said, breathing heavily as he waited for the fog in her expression to clear. When it did, she gave him a tender smile, not at all embarrassed by her passion or his.

For the next two weeks, Tony hardly saw Essie outside their training sessions. Even then, with the date of the bicycle race drawing near, all her energies were focused on the track, not the courtship—though he did manage to steal a kiss or two.

Still, she broke their fishing date when an argument flared up amongst her organizers over who was to be the grand marshal for the bicycle parade. Some thought it should be the mayor, others thought it should be a wheeler.

He tried to take her to the soda shop, but she insisted she didn't have time; race headquarters needed to be set up downtown instead. On Saturday, the hospitality committee had proposed to greet guests at the front door of the Commercial Hotel with a white porcelain bathtub filled with punch and large cakes of ice. The preacher was none too happy about it.

He'd nodded coolly to Tony. And though Tony was careful to acknowledge the preacher's greeting, he accepted the fact that some folks were not as friendly as they used to be now that they'd discovered he was a Morgan.

"My congregation is scandalized at the very idea of using a bathtub in public," Wortham said to Essie.

"But a bathtub is perfect," she argued. "Think of all the filling and refilling of punch bowls we'd have to deal with otherwise, not to mention the chipping of ice."

"How 'bout using a horse trough?"

"A horse trough! I can't have our guests drinking out of the same thing their horses do."

"A coffin?"

"Ewing, would you please be serious?"

"I am. All my elders are breathing down my neck and a coffin is where I'm gonna end up if you insist on using that bathtub!"

"Listen, if you're so concerned with propriety, why don't you and your elders park yourselves in front of Rosenburg's Saloon and save a few souls instead of pestering me?"

In the end, she got her way, but it caused a strain between her and Ewing, and various members of her church took her to task on Sunday morning, though she didn't seem too terribly concerned.

Tony's relief at no longer having to hide his identity had filled him with an unprecedented sense of freedom—regardless of the censure bestowed by a few Corsicanans. Judge Spreckelmeyer had told Moss that he'd known all along Tony was a Morgan—which turned out to be the case—and that he'd thought it best if the boys judged him on his own merits before finding out who he was.

There was a bit of awkwardness among the Sullivan Oil hands for a few days, but M.C.'s crew had no such reservations. Since the other men on the patch held them in awe, their obvious respect went a long way in restoring Tony's standing in the fields.

Mrs. Lockhart returned from her second trip to Beaumont in just as many weeks, catching up to him on her bike in front of Castle's Drug Store.

"I need to talk to you," she said.

He assisted her off her wheel, took hold of the handlebars, then glanced up and down the street. "Shall we walk?"

As soon as they were out of earshot, she stopped. "Anna is being most uncooperative. She refuses to enter a convent. She doesn't find the idea of being swept out to sea by a pirate the least bit intriguing. And she claims you are the only relative she has that would be willing to stand up to Darius."

"You found a pirate?" he asked, shocked.

"Well, no. But I'm sure I could have."

He blinked. "I see. Well, Anna's got the right of it. Convents and pirates are not at all how I would have her proceed. And Grandfather Bryant would have taken her in, but he passed several years ago."

He turned the bike in the direction of Mrs. Lockhart's home and started walking again. "How's Mother holding up? Did Anna say?"

"Your mother has taken to her bed. She'll be of no help whatsoever."

"No. That doesn't surprise me."

"And I've a bit more bad news, I'm afraid."

He glanced at her. "What?"

"Morgan Oil is entering the bicycle race."

He stopped. "Our bicycle race?"

"The very same."

"But, Morgan Oil has never once accepted the invitation. It was only extended to us out of courtesy. Everyone knows we wouldn't accept."

She said nothing.

He narrowed his eyes. "Darius is clearly meddling. He's only entering because he knows I'm racing for Sullivan Oil."

"That was Anna's opinion, too."

"Has a wedding date for her been set?"

"August thirteenth."

The tick in his jaw began to pulse. "Come on. Let's get you home. For now, I've got to get through this race. But after that, I'm taking care of Anna. And Darius, too."

Half an hour later, he stormed into the bicycle club. A large group of women sat in a circle, hemming blue-and-white sashes for the assistant parade marshals.

Their chattering came to an abrupt halt at his entry, but he couldn't have cared less. He walked directly to Essie and snatched the sash she was stitching out of her hands.

"You're coming with me," he said.

"What's happened?"

"I'm sick and tired of playing second fiddle to a bicycle race. I want to go to the soda shop, and I want to go right now."

She pulled the sash back into her lap. "Don't be ridiculous. I've got more to do than I can possibly finish before Saturday arrives. I can no more go to—"

He reached down, pulled her to her feet, then leaned so close he could count her eyelashes. "Put that sash down, Esther Spreckelmeyer."

She narrowed her eyes. "Don't you bully me. I will not leave my members in their time of need."

"You wanna make a bet?"

Shirley Gillespie stepped beside them and reached for the sash. "Go on, Essie. You've been working ten times harder than the rest of us. A walk to the soda shop will do you wonders."

Essie tightened her hold on the sash. "I don't want to go to the soda shop. I want to hem sashes."

Shirley began to peel Essie's fingers away from the fabric. "We'll be fine. Won't we, girls?"

A chorus of affirmations filled the room, urging Essie to go. He could see it was a matter of pride now, and if nothing else, Essie had more than her fair share of pride.

He placed his lips next to her ear and whispered, "I want a kiss and I'm not waiting one more minute. So you can either come outside and give me one or I'll take it right here in front of God and everybody."

She immediately let go of the sash. "Good heavens." She glanced at her members. "Ladies, I'm afraid I must—"

"Go on, honey," Mrs. McCabe said. "You give that young man of yours a little attention."

"That's right," Mrs. Bunert said. "You'll find your man has to roar like a lion and posture and establish himself as king of the jungle. But don't let it trouble you none. We all know it's the lioness who's really in charge."

"It's the lioness who does all the work, you mean," Mrs. Gulick said. "While the 'king' lounges around and waits for his supper to get hunted, caught, killed, and laid at his feet."

Shirley gently pushed them toward the door. "Perhaps y'all had better get going."

Tony glanced around. "Actually, I'm thinking about changing my mind and helping with the sashes. The conversation has become rather . . . enlightening." He winked at Mrs. Zimpelman.

The women tittered. If they had been surprised to find out he was a Morgan, they'd been quick to come to his defense when townsfolk had a cross word to say about it. He didn't know what he'd done to earn their loyalty, but he was sure glad he had it.

Even still, he didn't linger. Clasping Essie's hand, he pulled her out the door, down the steps and around to the side of the building lickety-split.

Pressing her against the wall, he covered her mouth with his. Their kiss was long, wet, and pure heaven.

"I thought you were taking me to the soda shop," she murmured against his lips.

"I am." Holding her face with his hands, he kissed her again, running his thumbs along her jaw, her ears, her neck. "I've missed you."

"Mmmm."

When his passion began to outpace his good sense, he buried his fingers into her hair and pulled back, resting his forehead against hers.

"I can only afford one soda," he said. "You want a Coca-Cola or a Dr. Pepper?"

She smiled. "I like them both. It makes no difference to me."

"Let's go, then." Tucking her hand in the crook of his arm, he headed toward town, looking forward to sharing a drink in one glass with two straws.

chapter TWENTY-TWO

TIPPING HIS hat, Tony stepped off the boardwalk, allowing two women to squeeze past. Town was always crowded, but with tomorrow's parade and race, the streets, hotels, and restaurants teemed with people.

A wheeler darted between an oncoming carriage and a wagon. Drivers cursed and horses whinnied, but the rider gave them no heed. Turning south, he hugged the edge of the street, heading straight for Tony.

Tony jumped back onto the walkway and out of the way, accidentally jostling a farmer and his son.

"Excuse me."

The man had no time to respond before he was caught up in the movement of the crowd. The bicyclist whizzed past.

Glancing over everyone's heads, Tony spotted the Commercial Hotel another block up the road. In conjunction with City Hall, Essie's club was hosting a reception for the oil companies participating in the race. He'd received a telegram from his mother. She, Anna, and Darius would be attending. Fortunately, Anna's betrothed planned to stay behind in Beaumont.

Tony looked both ways, then loped across the street, avoiding horse droppings and dodging traffic. At the steps leading to the hotel, he paused to brush off the front and shoulders of his jacket. It would be the first time he'd seen his family since being disinherited.

"What's the matter? Worried they won't allow a field worker into the party?"

Recognizing his brother's voice, Tony glanced sharply over his shoulder. Darius approached the steps, sporting a new goatee, carefully shaped and trimmed. His Prince Albert suit, however, fit a bit too loosely. Seemed he'd lost some weight. On his arm, Mother stood in her widow's weeds. She frowned up at Darius before sending a sympathetic smile in Tony's direction.

"Tony!" Anna gasped, drawing his attention. A vision in white and yellow, she wore the diametrical opposite of Mother's black clothing.

He barely had a chance to take it all in before his sister launched herself into his arms. Managing to stay upright, he clasped her tightly while her feet dangled above the boardwalk.

"You have my word," he whispered, "you'll not marry Tubbs or anyone else unless you want to."

"Oh, Tony," she responded, her voice cracking.

He gave her a reassuring squeeze.

"I absolutely adore Mrs. Lockhart," she said quietly in Tony's ear. "Thank you for sending her."

"Anna," Mother hissed. "Would you please conduct yourself with at least some semblance of decorum. Get down. Tony, release her at once."

He lowered her to the ground and brought his mother's gloved hand to his lips, her familiar scent of lavender teasing his nose. "You are looking well, ma'am."

His words contradicted his thoughts, though. The severe black gown accentuated her drawn appearance and sallow coloring. Even the powder she'd used could not disguise the circles beneath her eyes. Were they testament to her grief or to her distress over the events following Dad's death?

"If you would, Dogbone," Darius said, his tone sarcastic, "be a good boy and follow a few steps behind us. I don't want anyone to think we're together."

"Enough of that, now," Mother said.

Darius placed his hand under her elbow and guided her up the stairs.

Tony watched them pass, then looked at Anna.

She rolled her eyes, holding Tony back out of Darius's hearing. "He's been an absolute beast. For a while now I've been wishing Dad had disinherited me, too. Then I wouldn't have to put up with our charming brother day in and day out."

❦

For a split second, Essie thought Tony had grown a goatee overnight. Then she realized it wasn't Tony at all, but his brother. She stood at the hotel's parlor door, receiving guests with Mayor Whiteselle on her left and his wife on her right. A good many folks had arrived already, and the pleasant hum of conversation drifted about them.

She was so caught up in studying Darius, she failed to notice the person ahead of him in line until the woman spoke.

"How do you do?"

Essie jerked her attention to the task at hand. "Ma'am. Thank you so much for coming, and welcome to the Corsicana Oil & Gas Bicycle Invitational. I'm Essie Spreckelmeyer."

"Miss Spreckelmeyer, at last. So nice to meet you. I've heard a lot about you."

Essie felt her face heat, silently cursing that blasted newspaper article. She never knew how to respond to references of this sort. Saying "thank you" didn't seem quite right, yet ignoring the comment wasn't acceptable, either.

"Ma'am. And you are?"

"Leah Morgan. I've heard my Tony is courting you?"

Essie's lips parted. This was Tony's *mother*? Good heavens. She was clearly much younger than Essie's parents, yet she looked so tired and downtrodden. Did she mourn for a man who never saw fit to love her back? Did she mourn for him the way Papa mourned for Mother?

She squeezed Mrs. Morgan's hand. "Yes, ma'am. Tony and I are indeed courting. I am delighted to make your acquaintance. I would very much like to find a few moments to visit later, if you are able. For now, however, please allow me to introduce you to our mayor's wife."

She made the introductions, noting that while Mrs. Morgan's black silk gown was fashionable, the style was quite severe.

"Would you look at that?" Tony's brother said, drawing Essie's regard. "Punch served out of a bathtub." He smiled at her. "How quaint."

His eyes were the same coffee color as Tony's. Same broad shoulders, same height, same hair, no dimple.

"You must be Mr. Morgan," she said. "Welcome to the Corsicana Oil & Gas Bicycle Invitational. I'm Miss Spreckelmeyer."

"Not *the* Miss Spreckelmeyer?" he asked, taking a step back and looking her up and down. "The one who is so well known for her participation in a bicycle, um, *competition* up north?"

He might look like Tony at first glance, but his skin had a distinctly yellowish tint to it, giving him an unhealthy appearance. And the warmth of his voice did not match the coolness of his eyes.

"Even more important, though," he continued, "the Miss Spreckelmeyer whom my half brother has taken such keen notice of?"

She glanced down the line. Tony and a lovely young woman were conversing with the mayor. He must have felt her regard, though, because he looked over and winked.

It was all the fortification she needed. She turned back to Darius with a genuine smile. "You are quite correct, sir. I am indeed being courted by your brother."

"I must confess," he said, taking note of the exchange between her and Tony. "I'm a bit surprised. Tony's interests have always run to girls fresh out of the schoolroom. Strange that he would suddenly acquire a taste for the more matronly type. Wouldn't you say?"

Shock momentarily held her silent before she realized he was deliberately trying to discomfit her. She smiled to herself.

"Well, Mr. Morgan," she said, leaning toward him conspiratorially, "you know what they say . . . there's no accounting for taste."

He lifted his brows.

"Please, might I introduce you to our mayor's wife?"

She handed him over to Mrs. Whiteselle, then turned as Tony and the young girl beside him finished with the mayor.

Tony reached out to her. She placed her hand in his as he leaned over and kissed her cheek.

"You look stunning," he said.

So do you, she thought. He had on his dark alpaca jacket, but the silk four-in-hand tie with a paisley pattern was one she hadn't seen before.

She tried to picture what changes his family might see in him after his summer away from home. His shoulders and chest had filled out from his work in the fields and their training in the clubhouse. The sun had added warmth to his skin, and though his trim waist wasn't visible beneath his suit, it would be in evidence tomorrow at the race.

A spurt of pride rushed through her. This handsome, wonderful man was *her* beau.

"I'd like you to meet my sister, Anna," he said.

The young woman smiled and Essie caught her breath. Flawless skin, large brown eyes, long, long lashes, and rich brown hair conspired together to form nothing short of perfection. And as if that weren't enough, she'd accentuated it all with a fabulous hat heaped high with white trim, yellow posies, and blue ribbons.

"It is so very nice to meet you, Anna. Welcome to the Corsicana Oil & Gas Bicycle Invitational."

"Thank you. Mrs. Lockhart had nothing but the nicest things to say about you."

Essie glanced at Tony, then back at Anna. "You know Mrs. Lockhart?"

"Oh my, yes. We are fast friends. Has she ever loaned you any of her books?"

Frowning, Essie lowered her voice. "Oh dear. I hope she hasn't been foisting those awful things off on you. They are a bit frivolous and not a little shocking."

"Do you think so? I hadn't really noticed. What do you think, Tony?"

He shrugged. "*Thorns and Orange Blossoms* wasn't so bad."

Essie stared at him, aghast. But before she could ask why in the world *he* had read Mrs. Lockhart's books, the next person in line stepped up.

⤲

"So then the mortician says, 'Yes sir, sheriff. It was a grave undertaking.' " Laughing, the mayor looked around at the men in their circle. "Get it? Grave undertaking?"

Tony smiled, beginning to see why the man was so well liked. Judge Spreckelmeyer, the sheriff, and a fella by the name of Mudge from Alamo Oil chuckled.

A burst of appreciative male laughter from across the hotel's parlor drew their attention.

"Appears your sister is the belle of the Welcome Reception," the judge said, clapping Tony on the shoulder.

Taking a sip of punch, Tony looked over the rim of his cup to where Anna sat surrounded by men. A couple of wheelers from some of the smaller oil companies, along with Preacher Wortham and Deputy Howard, all vied for her attention.

"Their efforts are doomed to failure, I'm afraid," Darius said, joining them.

"Oh?" Spreckelmeyer said, stepping back to make room for him. "And why is that?"

"She's betrothed."

"Betrothed?" Dunn asked. Tony could see the sheriff mentally counting up the three short months since his father's death.

"Yes. To Norris Tubbs."

"Norris Tubbs!" Spreckelmeyer exclaimed. "Of the H&TC?"

"The very same."

"But he's my age."

Darius pulled on his cuffs. "So he is."

The sheriff, the judge, and the mayor exchanged glances, then looked at Tony, but before he could say anything, Harley tugged on his coat.

"Hey, Mr. Tony."

"Well, howdy there, Harley. Where did you come from?"

"Me and some o' the boys have been helpin' Miss Essie lug ice and such. I was telling 'em about what happened that night when Bri was bit and wanted to show 'em your knife. Do ya mind?"

"Of course not." He pulled it from his pocket and handed it to the boy, watching as he raced over to a small group of schoolmates. The gangly youths in their Sunday-go-to-meeting clothes pulled at their collars and scratched their starch-covered chests while hovering near the refreshment table.

"Ah, looks like Finch has finally made it," Darius said.

Tony turned his attention to the entryway. Essie excused herself from the group she was attending and welcomed the newcomer. Finch made a show of bowing deeply and bringing her hand to his lips.

He didn't look like a man who was grieving over the loss of his second wife. He held Essie's hand too long, no matter how gracefully she tried to extract it, and then bent close, whispering something before pulling back, clearly amused by his own words.

Essie freed her hand and unobtrusively wiped it against her skirt.

She scanned the room, smiled at Tony, then proceeded to escort Finch toward the group of men. His suit was black with lace at his cuffs, accented by an elaborately tied ascot and patent leather bals. He always had been a bit of a dandy.

"Gentlemen," Essie said, "I'd like you to meet Mr. Finch Morgan. Blake Morgan was his uncle." She introduced her father, the sheriff, the mayor, and Mr. Mudge from Alamo Oil. "And you, of course, know these two."

Tony extended his hand. "I was sorry to hear about Rebecca."

Finch clasped his hand. "Thank you. I still can't quite believe she's gone."

"I confess to feeling the same way."

Finch pulled out a quizzing glass and peered at Tony more closely. "I see you finally stripped yourself of that ghastly moustache. When did you do that?"

"He did it the same day he was stripped of his inheritance," Darius answered. "Both lightened his load a bit, didn't they, Dogbone?"

Essie gasped and an awkward silence followed.

Tony rubbed the skin above his lips. "Funny how something that was such a part of me is so easily discarded. I find I hardly even notice its absence anymore."

Chuckling, Finch reached into his jacket and withdrew a silver cigarette case. Flipping it open, he offered mechanically rolled cigarettes to the men. Darius and Mudge each withdrew one from the holder, but the others declined.

"Well, if you gentlemen would excuse me?" Essie was wearing her blue gown, the one that had a really wide sash that hugged her waist and emphasized her curves. He'd first seen it the night she lectured her club on bicycle etiquette. It was one of his favorites.

Pink filled her cheeks at his obvious admiration before she excused herself again and turned away.

Finch struck a match against the wall, held the flame for Darius and Mudge, then himself.

"I'm afraid I haven't quite decided what to think about those pre-rolled cigarettes," the mayor said. "Do you really think the taste is worth the extra expense?"

"I find them far superior to the handmade ones," Finch answered. "What about you, Darius?"

"Oh, I'll not turn them down when offered, but in truth, a smoke's a smoke. They're all pretty much the same to me. Kinda like women. Right, Tony? It appears women are all pretty much the same to you, too, no matter how old they are."

Spreckelmeyer pulled his hands out of his pockets. The sheriff slowly straightened.

Darius had been trying to rile Tony since he'd arrived. Tony wasn't sure of his brother's game, but until he figured it out, he would hold on to his temper. Still, if Darius wasn't careful, it would be Spreckelmeyer's wrath he'd be facing and right soon if he kept it up.

Harley reappeared at Tony's elbow and handed him the knife. "Thank ya. The fellas liked it real well."

"Anytime, Harley."

"Hey, that's some kind of knife there, Mr. Morgan," Mudge said. "Can I see it, too?"

Tony handed it to him.

"Look at this, Mayor," he said, holding it up. "It has a fancy stag handle with the top shaped like a dog bone."

Spreckelmeyer and the sheriff also leaned in for a better look.

"I'm surprised you still have that old thing, Tony," Darius said. "I remember when Dad gave it to you." He laughed. "Now, there's an amusing story for you—"

Jeremy Gillespie busted through the parlor door covered in slush and skidding to a stop. He quickly scanned the room, spotted Tony and started toward him. He'd just reached their circle when he noticed Darius.

"That your brother?"

"Yeah. What's the matter?"

Jeremy returned his attention to Tony. "It's Crackshot."

"What about him?"

"Well, we'd tied a gunnysack around the top o' the bailer and let it down real slow-like, when the sulfur gas started to blow. So we all backed off, but Crackshot, he got a little impatient. I tried to tell him that sulfur'd knock him out. But he goes right back over there and starts swabbing all the while that gas's rolling down his throat."

Tony shook his head. "You'd think he'd have known better."

"Aw, you know what a loose screw he is."

Essie joined them, and Tony slipped his hand under her elbow. "Is Wilson all right?"

Pulling off his hat, Jeremy gave Essie a brief nod, then turned back to Tony. "He stood it for a while. Even started up with another jag when his knees just up and buckled."

"Oh no. What did you do?" Essie asked.

Jeremy shrugged. "I grabbed that cup mask Tony takes such stock in." He shook his head. "You should've seen me wearin' that thing all the while I was wrestling with that load o' human being, trying to get him far enough away so's I could push up and down on that big set o' lungs he has and pump some o' that stuff out of him."

"Where is he now?" Tony asked.

"Still lying there. But he's breathing."

Tony looked at the sheriff. "Can you find the doc and have him meet me out at the Agarita well?"

"Both me and Howard will look for him, but in this mess there's no telling where he is. You'd be better off takin' him to the doc's house before dark sets in. We'll meet you there."

"I'll go with you, Tony," Judge Spreckelmeyer said.

"No, sir. I don't want you out around that sulfur. And you'd be of more use looking for the doc."

The judge nodded and headed off with Sheriff Dunn.

"Jeremy, go get Ewing," Tony said. "He's over there with my sister, that woman in white and yellow."

"You think you'll need the preacher?" Essie asked, concern lacing her voice.

"I just want to be prepared. Either way, I'll come by the house tonight and let you know how he's doing. Harley, you stay clear of the field, you hear? I don't want you near the gas, either."

He started to leave when Essie grabbed hold of his hand.

"Be careful, Tony. That sulfur is . . ." She swallowed.

It wasn't just worry he saw in her eyes. It was something bigger. Something deeper. Something so sweet he couldn't possibly resist it.

And right there in front of his brother, his cousin, and the entire oil industry of Texas, he grasped her chin and kissed her flush on the lips. "I'll be careful."

chapter TWENTY-THREE

IT WAS almost midnight when Essie finally headed toward home. At the Welcome Reception, some of her club members had uncovered the plans of a small group of automobile advocates. They intended to overrun tomorrow's bicycle parade with their horseless carriages.

With a great deal of effort, Essie managed to track down this faction only to discover they had but one automobile between them. They were, however, quite intent upon using it.

"I'm a firm believer in progress, Mr. Roach," she'd said. "It is my opinion that though your automobiles are slow and prone to break down, they will one day be as common on the street as horse-drawn vehicles."

"Darn tootin', " he replied, spitting a wad of tobacco at his feet.

"I suggest a compromise."

His eyes narrowed. "I'm listenin'. "

"Your vehicle can bring up the rear of the parade, and after you have passed, the crowd can fall in behind you, cheering you all the way to the racetrack."

"No, ma'am. I wanna be at the front."

"I'm afraid that is quite impossible. The entire event is centered around bicycles and they must lead the way. However, we could arrange for one of our city councilmen to ride in the vehicle with you, making your automobile our grand finale and hinting of our bright and prosperous future."

Scratching his chest, he considered her for a moment, then thrust out his hand. "You got yerself a deal, little lady."

She spent the next hour trying to find a councilman who was still awake and who would be willing to miss the parade so he could ride in the caboose.

Opening her gate, she stepped through. The city had coordinated the race with the cycle of the moon to ensure as much light as possible during the evening hours of the event weekend. That full moon now shone down on Tony Bryant Morgan lounging on her porch steps. Her fatigue fled.

He didn't say a word as she moved forward, just patted the spot beside him.

"How's Mr. Wilson . . . er, Crackshot?" she asked, settling on the step.

"In a minute," he said, then gathered her in his arms and kissed her.

The scent of sandalwood and shaving soap surrounded her. He splayed one hand on her back, the other squeezed her waist. She tried to inch closer, but they were as close as their position would allow.

"Come here," he said, slipping his arm beneath her legs.

But before he could lift her onto his lap, she placed her hands against his chest. "Absolutely not."

He stilled, and she softened her words with a smile. "Much as I'd like to, it's improper and we both know it."

"Nothing will happen," he murmured, shifting over onto one hip so he could hold her flush against him.

She shook her head, the brim of her hat knocking against his forehead.

"Will you take off your hat, at least?"

She pulled back. "You don't like my hat?"

"I love your hat, but it's in my way."

"Which, in all likelihood, is just as well."

He brushed her cheeks with his knuckles. "It's also hiding your eyes from me and I want to see your eyes."

She tried to scoot back, but he was having none of it.

"Don't," he said.

"I wasn't going far. Just to the other end of the step, at least until my heart slows down a little bit."

He ducked under her hat and trailed kisses along her jaw. "It won't do you any good. I'll simply follow you over there."

"Tony, if we don't stop I'll have a difficult time staying, um, unmoved. So either you let me put some space between us or I will go on inside and we can talk about Crackshot tomorrow."

Sighing, he moved his hands from her back to her face. "All right. Just one more, then we'll talk."

And what a kiss it was. By the conclusion of it, Tony was the one who stood and put distance between them. Standing a few feet away, with his back to her, he tilted his head up toward the sky.

Millions of stars glittered against its black backdrop. Was this what Abraham saw when God made His promise? Stars so brilliant and numerous no one could doubt His omnipotence?

"Will you marry me, Essie?"

She jerked her attention back to Tony. He'd turned to face her, his hands jammed in his pockets.

"What?" she said.

He stepped forward, bent down on one knee and took her hand in his. "Will you do me the honor of becoming my wife?"

Her heart sped up. Her hands turned clammy. Her eyes filled.

The answer was on the tip of her tongue when she realized he'd never mentioned his feelings for her. Not ever. Not even once. Oh, she knew he enjoyed her company and that he was attracted to her. But she wanted more. Much more.

"Why?" she asked.

He seemed taken aback by the question. "Because I love you. Don't you love me?" His grip on her hand loosened and he started to pull away. "I thought you . . ."

She squeezed his hand and fell to her knees in front of him. "I do, Tony. I love you very much. And, yes. I would absolutely love to be your lawfully wedded wife."

A huge grin split his face. Scooping her up against him, he kissed her again. She wrapped her arms around his neck, answering his delight with her own.

When he finally pulled back, they were both having trouble breathing.

"Now will you take off your hat?"

"No," she said, smiling. "Not yet. Not until the deed is done."

He groaned. "What if I can't wait that long?"

Placing a tiny kiss on his chin, she removed herself from his embrace and returned to the step. "Now . . . how's Crackshot?"

And though her tone was casual, she could not calm the excitement and exhilaration she felt within. After all the years of singleness and all she'd been through, for the Lord to drop this man from the sky when she was least expecting it made her somewhat speechless.

Tony settled himself on the sidewalk, facing her. "He's not good, Essie. He woke up, and he can breathe all right, but he can't see."

She sucked in her breath. "What do you mean? Are you saying he's blind?"

"Yes, but we're hoping it's temporary. The doc has potatoes against his eyes and is keeping him in a dark room. As soon as Crackshot's kin can get here, though, Doc wants them to take him down to Galveston where he can swim around in the ocean with his eyes open."

"Will that cure him?"

"That's what they say. Only time will tell, though."

She covered her mouth. "I should have listened to you. If we'd had those cup masks, none of this would have happened."

"No, it has nothing to do with the masks. If Crackshot had stayed back like the rest of 'em, he wouldn't be laid out right now. My guess is, even if he had a mask, he would've been too cocky to wear it." Tony shook his head. "He has nobody to blame but himself."

She still couldn't help but feel guilty. "Will you make sure any doctors settle up with me?"

"I will." He stretched out his leg, then tapped her toe with his. "You sure were a long time coming home."

"Last-minute details."

He yawned.

"Goodness," she said, rising to her feet. "You need to get to bed and get some rest. I need you in tip-top shape for tomorrow's race."

Standing, he brushed off his backside. "Don't worry, ma'am. I'll be ready." He joined her on the porch. "I have a ring for you, Essie."

A ring? She clasped her hands together, still struggling to comprehend how she could go from organizing parade details to becoming betrothed in the span of an hour.

He fished inside his pocket, then removed a bit of cloth. Unfurling it in his palm, he cradled a diamond ring, barely distinguishable in the shadows of the porch.

"I don't need a ring, Tony," she said, her throat closing.

"Yes, you do. All the Morgan women wear a diamond." He reached for her left hand. "This one was my grandmother's."

She frowned. "I thought you were disinherited?"

"It belonged to my mother's mother and had nothing to do with my father."

He tried to take her ring finger, but she closed her hand around his.

"Don't you think we should wait?"

"For what?"

"Well, to, to talk with Papa. And the truth is, there are still some things we need to talk through. After the bicycle race is over and things calm down will be soon enough."

He frowned. "I don't want to wait until then. I want everyone in Texas to know you're mine and I want them to know it while they're all here in town."

She hesitated. "I do, too, Tony. But not until we've talked."

"About what?"

"Things."

"Well, you sure don't sound like a very excited bride-to-be. Are you sure you even want to do this at all?" His tone was sharp, wounded.

"I *am* excited. You can't imagine how thrilled I am."

He said nothing.

"Tony, it's just that, well—"

"Are you gonna marry me or not?"

"I am."

"Then give me your hand."

Biting her lip, she slowly lifted her left hand. He slid the ring on, the metal smooth, his fingers rough.

"It fits perfectly," she whispered. "Thank you."

"You're welcome." But his voice was clipped.

"I really am excited, Tony, and the ring is lovely."

"You can't even see it. It's too dark."

"I don't need to see it. Just having you give it to me makes it everything I'd ever want."

He stood stiffly for a moment. "Well, good night, then."

She clasped his hand. "I love you."

After a slight hesitation, he pulled her against him. "I love you, too. So much it scares me."

He kissed her thoroughly, then rested his forehead against her hat's brim.

"I didn't mean to be so clumsy in the asking, Essie. The question just kind of popped out."

"It was perfect."

"A fella only has one chance to ask his woman to marry him. He's supposed to have flowers and poetry and stuff like that. The only reason I had the ring with me was because Mother gave it to me tonight at the reception."

"She did?"

He nodded. "I asked her to bring it."

Essie stilled. "When?"

"When I knew I wanted to marry you."

"And when was that?"

"For a while now."

She laid her hand against his chest. The diamond on her finger caught the moonlight. "I loved your proposal and I love the ring. I'll cherish them both forever."

He brought her hand to his lips and kissed her palm. "Good night, love."

"Good night, Tony."

The diamond was huge. And beautiful. And hers.

Essie knelt beside her bed in her nightdress, moving her finger this way and that, watching the facets of the stone capture the candlelight and reflect it back at her.

She wondered if it would make rainbows on the walls when the sun hit it just right. Her grandmother used to have crystal prisms hanging in her front window. As a girl, Essie would jiggle them just as the sun was beginning its descent, then stand as tiny rainbows danced across the walls and the floor and even herself.

Tony said his mother had given the ring to him. That pallid woman she'd met briefly at the reception and who had innocently asked if Tony were courting her had, all the time, knowingly carried an heirloom that she would, by evening's end, relinquish forever to another woman. A woman she didn't even know.

What had she thought when Essie brushed her off so easily on to the mayor's wife? When Essie had been too busy filling a bathtub up with punch to sit down for a proper visit? Did she know Essie was thirty-four years old, ran a bicycle club, and was part owner of Morgan Oil's biggest rival?

She worried over Tony's earlier refusal to hear her confessions. At the same time, she wondered how critical it was for her to share those transgressions with him. She'd already confessed them to the Lord. He'd forgiven her and pronounced her clean.

Did that mean she wasn't obligated to ask for pardon from her fiancé? Was the Lord's forgiveness truly enough for her and Tony both? Maybe she wouldn't tell Tony anything. Maybe she didn't need to.

She folded her hands together.

Dear Lord, thank you for giving me Tony. I love him. I want him more than life itself. But I do not want him more than I want you. Give me wisdom. Guide me. Show me what you would have me do.

Opening her eyes, she admired her ring one more time before blowing out the light and crawling into bed.

chapter TWENTY-FOUR

THE MORNING of the parade dawned clear and beautiful with a smattering of clouds scattered like dandelion puffs in the sky. Essie fastened a cropped white jacket with large red buttons over her bicycle costume. She'd considered wearing her award-winning outfit but decided against it—not wanting to invite any questions about that unfortunate event.

Besides, there were still those who frowned upon the use of knickerbockers. Her shortened white skirt and matching gaiters were much more acceptable to the masses.

Lifting her latest purchase from its box, she settled the lacy white toque onto her head, then secured the hat with pearl-headed pins. Inspecting herself in the mirror, she fluffed the scarlet silk trim, the red ribbon roses, and the white ostrich tips spilling over the crown.

But it was her ring that again and again captured her attention as it flashed in the light. Lowering her hand, she held it out. With delicate craftsmanship, the platinum mounting displayed a rose-cut diamond encircled by eight tiny ones. She still couldn't quite believe it was hers.

The grandfather clock chimed nine. She quickly pinched her cheeks, then skipped down the stairs. Tony was already waiting in the parlor.

He held a beret, his brown hair mussed and windblown. The new racing outfit he wore hugged his tall, athletic form and left Essie short of breath.

"Good morning," he said, his voice low and intimate. "Is that a new hat?"

She nodded.

"I like it." He looked her up and down, his gaze snagging on her hands. "Somebody forgot her gloves."

She clasped her hands behind her, hiding them from view. "I didn't want to cover up my ring."

His eyes grew warm. "I like seeing it on your finger."

"So do I."

"Has your father seen it?"

"This morning at breakfast."

"What did he say?"

"He said it took you long enough."

Tony let out a breath and smiled.

"Didn't he mention anything about it when you arrived?" she asked.

"No. He just opened the door, told me 'good luck' and instructed me to wait for you in the parlor. I didn't know if he meant good luck with the race or good luck with you."

She laughed. "Probably both."

"I'd told him I was going to ask you, about the same time I asked my mother about the ring. Yet now he seems upset. Did he change his mind, do you think?"

"No. Believe me, I'd know if he didn't approve. I think his reticence is due to his just now realizing that once we marry I'll belong to you and not him."

They stared at each other across the parlor floor, thinking about her words and what they meant. Her heart began to hammer. It was really going to happen. She was really going to marry this man.

"The day's going to be extremely long and hectic," he said.

"Yes."

"This will probably be the only opportunity we have to be alone until late tonight."

"Probably."

"Would you mind terribly if I kiss you, then?"

Her eyes darted to the clock.

"I know it's early, Essie, but—"

She held up a finger, stopping his words, then closed the parlor door behind her and leaned against it. His Adam's apple bobbed.

She waited, but he made no move to close the distance between them. Apparently, if they were going to share a kiss at the shocking hour of nine o'clock, he didn't mind asking permission, but he wasn't going to start it.

Pushing off the door, she walked across the Axminster rug and slid her hands up onto his shoulders. "Don't mess up my hat."

After a long kiss, he placed her at arm's length. His face was flushed, his breathing ragged, his eyes dark.

She smiled. "Perhaps we'd better go?"

He nodded.

She let herself out of the parlor.

A bicycle built for two leaned against the white picket fence. Squealing with delight, Essie ran down the porch steps.

"Tony, look! Is it yours? Where did it come from?"

Catching her by the hand, he hauled her back. "It's not mine. It's on loan from Flyers. They agreed to lend it to us for the parade as an advertisement. I thought it would be the perfect solution to your grand marshal dilemma. I'm just glad it arrived in time."

"But there is no dilemma. The mayor is going to be the grand marshal. We've already decided."

"It might have been decided, but there's still dissension in the ranks. Those ladies of yours want a wheeler as the grand marshal and are only agreeing otherwise because you asked them to."

He opened the gate.

"So what did you have in mind?"

"The mayor on one seat, his lovely wife—and prominent member of the Corsicana Velocipede Club—on the other."

"Oh, Tony, that's perfect," she said, running her hand along the machine's sleek red frame. "I've never ridden one. Have you?"

"I rode it over here and I have to tell you, it's deuced embarrassing to ride without a partner."

"Oh, I hadn't thought of that."

He grasped the front handlebar and held out his hand. "Ma'am?"

She gazed longingly at the backseat. "You get to steer?"

"It's the gentlemanly thing to do. Plus, it gives you the better view. I only hope I can see over your hat."

She took his hand, then hesitated. "If I start, how will you mount? Plus, I can't steer. How are we going to do this?"

"You're the etiquette expert."

She worried her lip. "I don't see any way other than starting together."

He glanced up and down the street, then gave her a quick peck on the lips. "Together's my favorite way."

Being in the back not only allowed Tony to steer, but it also gave him an opportunity to admire a view he didn't get too often. He greedily took in Essie's long neck, gently sloping shoulders, and trim waist. His inspection continued and though her skirts ruffled in the breeze, he was able to make out enough of an outline to be pleased with what he'd discovered.

As they drew closer to town, activity picked up and he was forced to focus on his surroundings so as not to hit any potholes or run anybody over. Friends hollered out greetings. Others stopped and pointed, admiring the unusual machine.

All along Jackson Avenue, from Thirteenth Street on down, the people of Corsicana congregated in anticipation, even though the parade was still a good hour away. Tony and Essie weaved through a sea of brown suits and white dresses. Flags hung from second-story windows, red-white-and-blue banners draped from building to building along the parade route. The oil companies had strung up signs endorsing their riders in the upcoming race. Tony smiled at the sight of the Morgan name on the hand-lettered Sullivan Oil sign.

By the time they reached the starting point, a majority of the parade entrants had already gathered. Tony slowed the bike but before he could stop, Essie jumped off and began to organize the event.

She sent the city council members and the Corsicana Commercial Club off to clear the streets and stand along the parade path. She corralled the assistant marshals and asked Mrs. McCabe to give them the white duck caps the Slap Out had donated, along with the blue-and-white sashes her club members had hemmed.

She asked the bugle corps to warm up their trumpets, then attempted to organize the rest of the club according to bicycle brands. Mr. Sharpley arrived in a cart pulled by a wheeler, his leg cast wrapped in red-white-and-blue bunting. Essie spent several moments visiting with him before being called back to her task.

She was positioning a "giraffe" tricycle with its rider nine feet above the street when a group of about twenty young men, led by Jeremy Gillespie, rode up wearing bloomers.

Essie propped her fists on her waist. "Just what do y'all think you're doing?" she asked over the laughter of the crowd.

"Why, we're joinin' the parade," Jeremy said. "And don't you try and stop us, neither. We call ourselves the Bloomer Brigade and it's our mission to make sure any anti-bloomer fellas out there will behave, or else!"

She was no match for Jeremy's charm and after her experience in New York, she realized his mission might indeed be warranted. She sent him and the others on down the line, where the boys made a show of batting their eyes and calling out to the fans in falsetto voices.

She had most everyone where she wanted them and was arranging the women of the Corsicana Velocipede Club at the front of the line when Shirley Gillespie screamed, bringing silence to the immediate vicinity.

"Essie! What on earth is this?!" She grabbed Essie's left hand and held it in front of her.

Essie, already flustered from the activity, turned a deeper shade of red and pulled her hand from Shirley's grip. Shirley looked around her, locked eyes with Mrs. Lockhart and hoisted Essie's hand up again.

"Look!"

Every man, woman, and child within fifty yards looked at the diamond on Essie's finger. The women of her club swooped in around her, exclaiming, babbling, and vying for a better look. One by one they turned to Tony, wide-eyed.

He stood grouped with the other five racers and tugged on his beret. Smiles replaced the women's questioning expressions and they turned back to embrace their leader. She might never have broken free if the automobile hadn't chosen that moment to drive up, blast its horn and scatter her entire parade to the edges of the street.

It took her another twenty-five minutes to reorganize everyone before finally approaching Tony's band of racers.

"We're ready to begin, gentlemen," she said, careful to avoid his eyes, though her face again filled with color. "If you would fall in right behind the buglers, then you will be the first to reach the track and will have time to rest before this afternoon's race. Are there any questions?"

There were none. She glanced at him briefly. He winked. She blushed again, turned to the trumpet players and gave the signal to start.

⟜

Mr. Mitton's racetrack at the fairgrounds was one of the best mile tracks in Texas. It was run by the Navarro County Jockey Club and leased by the oil companies for the annual bicycle race.

Wandering through the pasture outside the gate, Tony perused the wide variety of exhibits. Bicycle manufacturers had every kind of bike on display: sociables, trikes and quadricycles, Warthogs, Spauldings, and Panthers.

He picked up a new racing bicycle to judge its weight, then spun the pedals to see if the wheels wobbled.

"A finer machine you'll not find anywhere in the country," the salesman assured him.

Tony tapped the steel tubing with his fingernail and listened.

"Mr. Tony!" Harley Vandervoort hollered, running up to him. "Howdy-do."

The boy's lips had turned blue from eating some kind of berry and he smelled like he'd been hanging around Mr. Mitton's thoroughbreds.

"Howdy-do to you, too. You having a good time?"

"I surely am. You gonna win that race fer Miss Essie today?"

"I'm going to try."

"I hear tell you're mashed on her and done asked her to wed up. That true?"

"Sure is," he said, chuckling, then looked around. "Where's your folks?"

"Ma's over there selling husk rugs with them other women, and Pa's whittling up stuff for the Men's Bible Group. What're you doing with that there bicycle?"

"Listening to its ring." He tapped it again with his fingernail. "Hear that? That flat sound means the tubing's not seamless but has been made from a strip of steel rolled and brazed along the seam."

The salesman sputtered.

Tony tipped his hat and guided Harley away. "You don't want a wheel with brazed tubing."

Brianna ran up with a saucer of ice cream piled on top of a waffle. "Howdy, Mr. Bryant."

"It's Mr. Morgan," Harley corrected.

"Oh yeah. I keep forgettin'. "

"Mr. Tony will be fine," Tony said. "You all recovered from your snakebite?"

"Oh yes, sir. I got me some fang marks on my ankle, though." She looked around, then leaned in close. "I charge the fellers at school a nickel to see 'em. I done saved up sixty-five cents already."

Tony frowned. "I don't know that you need to be showing off your ankles like that, Miss Brianna. That's not exactly proper."

"Shoot," Harley said. "It ain't like she's wearin' her hair up yet. Besides, she don't let just anybody have a peek. I got to give 'em the nod first."

Another youngster called out Harley's name, and the two took off before Tony could think of a response. He recalled Brianna didn't have a mother and made a note to himself to ask Essie to have a talk with her.

The League of American Wheelmen motioned Tony over to their booth and persuaded him to sign a petition demanding better roads, as well as laws protecting cyclists from teamsters and cab drivers who waged an unrelenting war against the machines.

Local citizens and merchants had set up tents to sell garden vegetables, fruits, breads and honey, floor rockers, agricultural implements, hops, boots, shoes, harnesses, and leather.

He was surprised to find Mrs. Zimpelman inside a booth filled with sterling vest chains, watch fobs, and buckles. He'd never met her husband and therefore didn't realize she was married to the silversmith. Before he could offer a greeting, however, a customer approached asking to see her selection of cuff pins.

Tony passed by M.C. Baker's booth and waved but didn't interrupt the brothers as they gave a demonstration of their rotary drill to curious onlookers. The rotary had been so successful in drilling through Corsicana's gummy clay soil that the boys had christened it the "Gumbo Buster."

A few of those very same boys just outside the Anheuser-Busch tent were trying to subdue one of their own who'd had more than he could hold. Deputy Howard shoved them aside, grabbed the rowdy and dragged him a few yards away, where he locked him up in what had become known as Howard's Hoodlum Wagon. Tony noted there were already a few others inside the mobile jailhouse sleeping it off.

The *aroogha* of an automobile's horn signaled the arrival of the final parade participants, followed by a wave of spectators. Tony headed back toward the track, making a point to stop at each oil company's exhibit on his way, even Morgan Oil.

"Well," Darius said as Tony approached, "if it isn't the cast-off who's doing everything he can to land on his feet."

Tony ignored him and offered a hand to Morgan Oil's racer. "Duckworth, good to see you again."

"Morgan." The man was small, like a horse jockey, but with thighs as big around as a woman's waist.

"I saw you practicing yesterday," Tony said. "Should be a good race."

Before Duckworth could reply, Darius interrupted.

"I hear felicitations are in order," he said, drawing deeply on a hand-rolled cigarette, the fire at its tip consuming the tobacco.

"That's right."

Darius flicked ashes onto the ground. "I know what you're doing," he said, his words and tone slicing through any previous pretense.

"And just what is it that I'm doing, Darius?" Tony asked with a sigh.

"You're placing yourself into a position of attack, with your sights on me and your gun cocked and loaded." Smoke trickled out of his nose. "I'm here to tell you you're wasting your time. I must say, though, you managed to insinuate yourself into Sullivan Oil rather quickly. Dad would have been proud—if he'd cared enough to be."

Tony turned to walk away and bumped chests with Finch. The man had sidled up behind him, blocking his path. And though his cousin gave the appearance of being soft, he had the Morgan brawn hidden beneath his dandified clothes.

Tony didn't excuse himself. Nor did he ask Finch to move. Just stared at him eye to eye.

Finch finally stepped back. "Care for a smoke?"

Tony ignored him and headed to the hospitality tent, hoping to find Essie. He wanted to check over his bike one more time before the big event.

chapter TWENTY-FIVE

STUMBLING ALONGSIDE the sheriff, Harley prayed his pa wouldn't hear about this. It was bad enough to be hauled across the fairgrounds by his collar, but if Pa were to find out, it'd be a whupping for sure.

"Crook?" the sheriff hollered, frog-walking Harley up to the Slap Out's booth. "I'm in need of a bar of soap, if you please."

But it wasn't Mr. Crook who approached the table. It was that spiteful ol' Mrs. Crook. She'd not been around much lately. Not since she'd whelped them two babies. And Harley hadn't missed her at all.

She didn't look like the witches he'd read about in some of them storybooks. No big nose with a wart or nothing. No stringy hair. No evil laugh. Matter of fact, she didn't look so bad for an old lady . . . until you got to know her.

"Any particular kind of soap, Sheriff?" she asked, eyeing the two of them.

"Whatever you got at hand will do—nothin' that tastes too good, though."

Her mouth formed a little *o*. "I see. Just one moment and I'll fetch you some."

"Mama?"

Harley could just make out the top of Mae Crook's head as she skipped over to her ma. "How come the sh'ff wants to eat soap?"

"It's not for him, Mae. It's for Harley," she said, heading toward the back of the tent.

The four-year-old girl grabbed the edge of the table and rose up on tippy-toes, her big brown eyes peeping over the top. "Won't ya rather have a licorice, Harley?"

"Not today, Mae," he said, making his voice sound real natural-like. "Today I think I'll have me a nice big bar o' your daddy's most expensive soap. Sheriff's treat."

The sheriff gave Harley's collar a twist, choking him some. Mae let loose of the table and climbed up into her mama's chair.

"I got me two baby brothers," she said. "Chester and Charlie."

"Sound like a couple o' crooks to me."

Keeping the grip he had on Harley's collar, the sheriff used his other hand to pinch the tender spot between Harley's shoulder and neck. Hurt like the devil, but Harley made sure he didn't flinch.

"Here we are, Sheriff," Mrs. Crook said, making a show of setting out not only a yellow ball of waxy soap but a tin cup of water to wash it down with.

The sheriff slapped a nickel on the table.

Mrs. Crook slid it back and gave Harley a look colder than a dead snake. "No charge."

Picking up the ball of soap, Harley tossed it in the air and caught it one-handed. "Why, thank ya, Mrs. Crook. That's right neighborly of ya. Ain't it, Sheriff?"

The sheriff pocketed his nickel, then grabbed the tin of water. "Let's go."

Harley had hoped to do this someplace private, but Sheriff Dunn just took him out behind the Slap Out's tent and handed him the cup of water. No doubt he wanted to make sure that soap lathered up but good.

"Swish."

Mae Crook lifted the back hem of their canvas tent and stuck her head out like some puppy dog. She might only be four, but Harley'd be jiggered before he'd carry on in front of her. He swished, lifted his chin and spewed the water out in a big ol' arc that spread out just enough to catch the sheriff in its wake.

Sheriff Dunn grabbed Harley's cheeks and squeezed. "Stick out your tongue."

He was tempted to "stick out his tongue," all right, but didn't dare. He opened wide. The sheriff didn't give him any quarter as he rubbed soap all over Harley's tongue and mouth.

The longer the sheriff scrubbed, the more Harley fought back the desire to gag. The slimy stuff smelled bad and tasted worse. Finally he couldn't stand it anymore and began choking.

The sheriff let go but didn't offer up any water. Harley leaned over, spitting out what he could.

"You gonna curse anymore?" the sheriff barked.

"No, by jingo, I'm not!"

The sheriff growled. Harley slapped his hand over his mouth, realizing what he'd said, but it was too late.

Dunn grabbed him and scoured his mouth all over again. When the sheriff finally let go, Harley fell onto all fours, choking, spitting, gagging.

"Any man worth his salt can make his point without using foul language," Dunn said. "If'n you wanna grow up to be half the man your pa is, you'd best be acquiring some better manners. You got that?"

"Yes, sir," he said.

Dunn tossed out the water and stalked away. Harley sat back on his feet, raking his fingernails over his tongue, trying to get the soap off. Residue trickled down his throat, mixing with the berries, ice cream, and taffy he'd eaten earlier. His stomach began to rebel.

A pair of very small, brightly polished boots entered his range of vision. He tamped down his bile.

"I brung ya some water, Harley," Mae said.

Accepting her offering, he rinsed and spit until he'd drained the cup. "Thanks."

"How come the sh'ff done that to ya?"

Harley stood and made his way to a shade tree. The little girl followed. "Your ma know you're out here?"

"She's gone home with the babies."

"Your pa, then? He know you're not in the tent?"

She nodded, making her black curls bob up and down like springs on a buggy seat. "I askt him fer these." She opened her fist. Two buttons of licorice nestled inside. "I knows ya like 'em."

He scrutinized her, surprised she'd asked her pa on his account. "You sure ya don't mind sharing?"

"I ain't sharing 'em with ya, Harley. I'm a-giving 'em to ya." She extended her chubby little hand.

He knew if it had been him who had the licorice, he wouldn't be sharing them with anybody, much less giving them away lock, stock, and barrel.

He took one of the candies. "You eat the other, Mae. Wouldn't be right fer me to take both."

They popped the candies into their mouths and sucked on them. The licorice went a long way in covering up the taste of the soap, though it still lingered.

They continued to suck, trying to make the treat last as long as they could, when four men slipped behind the hatmaker's tent a few yards away. Harley'd snuck around enough to recognize it when somebody else was doing the sneaking. He put his finger to his lips, warning Mae to keep quiet, inched the two of them behind the tree trunk, then peeked around the edge.

One of them was Mr. Tony's brother. Everybody was talking about how the two of them looked alike, but Harley disagreed.

This fella had eyes that reminded Harley of the Wanted posters in the sheriff's office, and his hands were cold and clammy when you shook them. Mr. Tony was nothing like that. The other three men wore racing outfits and had been in the parade. One wore a black sash, one a blue, and one a yellow.

"We ain't so sure we still wanna do this, Mr. Morgan," the one in the black sash said. He wasn't puny or nothin'. He just looked it standing next to Mr. Morgan. "I askt around and yer brother's well liked in these parts."

"Not only him," another piped up, "but the judge, too. Did ya know the sheriff is his brother-in-law? If'n we pocket Sullivan's man, it'll be more than the bloomer-gal and yer brother who'll be upset."

The third one nodded his head. "We want more money."

Mr. Morgan eyeballed the fellers one at a time, real slow-like. "I'm sure it would interest the League of American Wheelmen to find out you boys failed to ride the full and exact course in Kickapoo Creek's Six-Day Race."

The men exchanged glances. The one with the yellow sash took off his hat and scratched a bald spot that had previously been hidden. "You can't tell 'em that without implicatin' yerself."

"You think not?" Mr. Morgan pulled out his watch and popped it open. "The purse will remain the same. You pocket Sullivan Oil's wheeler, my man will take first, and we'll split the winnings between us, just as planned."

Baldy straightened his shoulders, puffing out his chest some. "We ain't doin' it, then."

Quicker than scat, Morgan grabbed the feller, yanked him close and read him the Scriptures.

Mae tugged on Harley's overalls. "I'm hot. Can—"

He clamped his hand over her mouth, shaking his head and hammering his finger against his lips. Her eyes widened, but she hushed up.

Harley held real still but didn't hear any signs they'd been nicked. Still, he didn't risk taking a look. Just kept him and Mae hidden behind that tree until he heard the fellers break up and leave.

After a minute of quiet, he pressed his hands against the bark and leaned just a wee bit over—just enough for one eyeball to have a look-see. Nobody there. He poked his head out. Still nobody.

Taking Mae by the hand, he hustled her back toward her daddy's tent. "You done real fine fer a girl, Mae. Shoot, fer a boy, even. Maybe when ya get a little older, if ya promise not to act like a girl, I'll take ya out fishin'. "

She jumped up and down. "Yes, by jingo! Take me fishin'. "

He pulled up short. "Don't ya be swearin' none, Mae. A feller worth his salt can say what needs to be said without swearin', fer gosh sake." Lifting the bottom of the Slap Out's tent, he shooed her under. "Go on. I gotta find Miss Essie."

She fell to her knees and scurried under.

"Mae?" he said.

She poked her head out.

"Thanks fer the licorice."

∞

"Now, remember," Essie said, tucking in the ends of Tony's red sash, "keep your body as close to the bicycle frame as you can. Legs in, chest down, head up."

"I will."

"Don't let the others run you wide on the curves or foul you with their elbows."

"I'll be careful."

"Pace yourself. Don't start out too fast, but don't let anybody get too big a jump on you, either."

Tony clasped her hand and squeezed. "Quit worrying, Essie. Everything's going to be fine."

"I'm not worrying. I'm just reminding you of a few things, is all."

He smiled. "Well, how about this, then: How about I go win this race for you?"

Butterflies churned in her stomach. "Do you think we have a chance?"

"More than a chance. A good chance." He looked over at the other cyclists talking with their trainers. "When I was watching them yesterday, Ethey Oil's man started out slow, then took off like a shot, but it was too little, too late."

"That may be, but Ethey Oil's not the one I'm worried about, nor El Filon de Madre Oil or even Tyler Petroleum. It's Alamo and Morgan Oil that will be your real competition."

"Mudge is known for launching a series of attacks, but he doesn't have the leg strength to endure it. He'll start falling behind toward the end."

"Maybe, maybe not. Some men accomplish feats in a race that they can't ever achieve during their training."

"Not this one."

"What about Morgan Oil?"

"Duckworth's good, but I think I can beat him. No, I know I can beat him. You wanna watch me?"

"I sure do."

"Then go on to the stands, woman. I'm fixing to win Sullivan Oil a race and me a hefty little purse." He leaned close and whispered, "If you kiss me real sweet, I might treat you to a soda with my winnings."

She lifted an eyebrow. "If I kiss you real sweet, you're likely to lose your head and not concentrate on what you're doing. Now, quit your lollygagging and go win me a race."

Everywhere Essie looked, she encountered the anxious faces of spectators who had placed their final bets and filled the stands to root for their champion. Excusing herself, she wove through a press of men, women, and children wearing scarves and hats with their oil company's colors.

A group of rowdies wearing Alamo Oil's orange sang the "Texas War Cry" to the tune of "Anacreon in Heaven." Another group, who smelled as if they'd made one too many trips to the Anheuser-Busch tent, booed the Alamo singers and a shouting match ensued. Essie hurried past, hoping to be well out of the way if their shouts turned into something more physical.

She finally reached the section of stands designated for the Corsicana Velocipede Club. Mrs. Zimpelman stepped back, allowing Essie room to move toward the front.

"Why, Miss Morgan," Essie said, surprised to see Tony's sister beside Ewing and Mrs. Lockhart. "You're wearing Sullivan Oil colors."

The girl had secured a charming straw hat to her head with a red scarf tied fashionably off-center underneath her chin. "Please, call me Anna. And I hope you don't mind, but I was afraid Darius might lose his temper if I started cheering for Tony while sitting in the midst of Morgan Oil supporters."

Essie grasped Anna's hand. "It is our pleasure to have you, and I know Tony will be touched. Will it upset your mother, do you think?"

"None whatsoever. It wouldn't do for her to stand here with me, though, so she chose not to come at all."

The Merchants' Opera House band began to play the "Flag of Texas" as two flag bearers marched onto the track, one carrying the Stars and Stripes, the other carrying the Lone Star. The six bicyclers followed, their wheels beside them.

A deafening cheer rose, then the grandstands swelled with song as the crowd robustly sang along with the band.

"Among the flags of nations,
There is a place for thee,
Flaunt up, thou bright young banner,
Flaunt proudly o'er the free."

The racers' bright silk sashes glistened in the late-afternoon sunlight. The man from Alamo lifted his hand and waved to the fans. But it was Tony who captured Essie's attention. He looked like a giant among the other men. Tall, self-assured, and singing the well-known song with gusto.

Her heart filled with pride and pleasure and excitement. These races had always been important to her, but this one was by far the most significant. Not only because Tony was Sullivan Oil's man but because he was *her* man.

The song ended and the crowd roared their approval. An official began to line the cyclists up. The anticipation in Essie slowly built with the sweetest suspense imaginable. What a week it had been. The frantic preparations. The Welcome Reception. The heart-tugging moment when Tony proposed. The bright, color-splashed parade. And now these last few precious, nerve-jangling moments.

"For heaven's sake, Essie," Mrs. Lockhart said. "Wave to that Vandervoort boy before he falls."

Essie looked in the direction Mrs. Lockhart indicated and saw Harley several sections over, leaning across the barricade and madly waving his arms. She waved back and held up crossed fingers.

He pointed to the track and shouted, but of course she couldn't hear what he was saying. She assumed he was pointing to Tony, so she smiled and waved to the boy again. His face turned frantic. He began squeezing past people in an effort to get to her, but when he tried to push past Katherine Crook, she pulled him up short.

Essie held her breath. Harley had a history with the Slap Out's proprietress and did not always think before he acted where she was concerned. But there was nothing Essie could do about it from here.

A quietness settled over the crowd, pulling her attention back to the track. Each man placed his right leg over the bicycle bar and rested his foot on the pedal. The official raised a gun toward the sky.

"One!"

Essie's hands grew clammy.

"Two!"

Her heart thundered.

"Three!"

Bang.

The sound reverberated through her. Spectators shouted and whistled. The riders shot forward and immediately converged on the inside line. Tony settled down over his handlebars and focused on the track ahead of him.

The riders took turns leading and falling behind, but Tony did exactly what they'd decided on in advance. He moved forward early and pushed a moderate pace rather than stay amidst the pack and fight off attack after attack.

Morgan and Alamo Oil would eventually bridge. When that happened, it would be survival of the fittest and she wanted Tony right up there with them.

At the halfway mark, the riders for Morgan and Alamo Oil began to pull forward, then suddenly became embroiled in a shoving match. Essie couldn't tell who pushed whom first, but their antics threatened to unseat Tony, who rode on their left.

Mr. Duckworth, the Morgan man, grabbed Mr. Mudge by his sash and nearly jerked him off his machine.

Mudge lost his balance and zigzagged, while Tony, Mr. Duckworth, and the three other competitors whizzed by him. The remaining group of five stayed fairly close until about three-quarters of the way around. Duckworth, in a green sash, began to push toward the front.

Get ready, Tony, she thought. *Get ready.*

In a burst of speed, Ethey Oil pushed ahead of both Tony and Duckworth, but neither of those men gave chase, knowing the man would never be able to sustain his lead.

Sure enough, the Ethey man began to slow and pulled directly in front of Tony. Before Tony could go around him, however, Tyler Petroleum came up on Tony's immediate right.

No! Essie thought, as El Filon de Madre Oil rode up behind him, the three men pinning Tony in a box. Duckworth came around on the outside and took the lead.

Utter pandemonium broke loose in the stands. Spectators screamed, banners waved, whistles pierced.

"What's happening?" Anna asked.

"Tony's been pocketed," Essie shouted over the noise, frustration welling inside her. "The other riders are conceding the race to Morgan Oil and are trapping Tony to keep him from competing."

"But why? Why would they do such a thing?"

"The usual reason," Essie answered. "For a percentage of the purse."

Anna sucked in her breath. "Can't the official do something? Surely he realizes what is happening."

"Yes, he knows. And though pocketing may be unethical, it isn't illegal."

Essie rode the wave of her emotions along with the Sullivan Oil supporters around her as they alternately expressed shock, anger, and, finally, fury.

"Is there anything Tony can do?" Anna shouted.

"Yes," Essie said helplessly, "but it's very dangerous and we never trained for it. I just never expected such a thing to happen."

Grabbing the railing in front of her, she watched the racers continue to move in a clump. Never had she felt so impotent. And with a knot of concern in her throat, she turned to the one source she knew could do anything, no matter what the situation.

Help him, Lord. Please. Won't you please help him?

chapter TWENTY-SIX

OUTRAGED, TONY gripped his handlebars more tightly. He'd seen a jockey pocketed once in a horse race, but it hadn't occurred to him it could be done in a bike race.

He wasn't about to concede defeat now, however. Breaking out of the pocket would require a cool head, and he was running out of time.

Pushing his anger aside, he quickly assessed the men surrounding him, then began to shore up his nerves. If he was willing to gamble with his good health, he just might manage it. He had to. Essie had never won before and he wanted to be the first man to win it for her. Just like he'd be the first man—the only man—she'd ever know in the biblical sense.

The Tyler man on his right eased off to the outside, presenting an enticing opening. But Tony checked his impulse to shoot through, realizing Tyler could close the pocket at any time and dump Tony in the dirt.

Instead, with heart hammering, he inched forward until his front wheel just barely overlapped Ethey Oil's rear wheel. Maintaining a constant rate of speed, Tony gave a quick twist on his handlebars, slapping Ethey's wheel and knocking it toward the inside of the track.

The Ethey man responded just as Tony anticipated, involuntarily overcompensating to the outside and momentarily swerving out of Tony's path. Accelerating, Tony shot through on the inside and escaped.

The crowd exploded with noise. Duckworth glanced over his shoulder, then hunkered down. Shutting out as much of the world as he could, Tony settled into a crouch, zeroed in on Duckworth's rear wheel and concentrated on catching up to it.

Help me catch him, Lord. Help me win this for Essie.

The gap between them shortened, but his legs burned, his back ached, and he was running out of track. He pedaled harder, his feet flying, his wet shirt clinging to his back. The finish line came into view. Duckworth glanced back again, giving Tony an opportunity to gain a few more rotations of the wheel.

His front tire pulled within inches of Duckworth's. Tony veered to the outside. *Faster. Faster.* The only sound that came to him was the purr of tires.

He passed Duckworth's back tire, his pedals. Closer. Closer. Almost even with him. The finish line hurtled toward them. Tony curled up and pushed as hard as he could.

They were so close, Tony didn't know who'd won and was going too fast to stop. People poured over the barricade and onto the track, sprinting toward the two riders. Those left behind shouted, whistled, stomped their feet and rattled cowbells.

No political rally, prayer revival, or holiday parade ever sounded so loud. The wooden beams supporting the grandstand trembled. Tony finally managed to slow enough to stop. He jumped off the bike just as hordes of men bedecked with green ran past him and surrounded Duckworth, congratulating him, patting him on the back, hefting him up onto their shoulders.

Disbelief, disappointment, and frustration crashed down around Tony, threatening to buckle his knees. He'd lost. He couldn't believe it. He scanned the stands for Essie but, of course, couldn't find her.

Instead, he found Darius. On the track, not ten yards away, accepting handshakes and congratulations as if he'd earned the privilege.

Tony should have known Darius wouldn't leave the outcome to chance. Too much was at stake—for both of them. Darius wanted to demonstrate his supremacy over Sullivan Oil in general, and Tony in particular. Tony had wanted to win the thing for Essie and the town of Corsicana.

Anger at being stripped—again—of something that rightfully belonged to him burst through the tight control Tony had heretofore been able to manage. Like a bull who'd been teased with a red cape one too many times, he charged, a war cry bursting from his throat.

Darius's startled expression before Tony slammed into his gut gave a momentary bit of satisfaction. But not nearly enough. Following his brother into the dirt, Tony made the most of his advantage and drove his fist into Darius's jaw. Blood spurted from his brother's mouth.

Hands from countless strangers pulled Tony off of Darius and up onto his feet.

He flung them off. "Get back!" he shouted. "This is between me and him. *Back away*, I said."

Whether no one wanted to be the first to persuade him otherwise or if the men had simply found something new to bet on, Tony didn't know and didn't care. All that mattered was that the crowd formed a circle around the two men, leaving Tony free to even the score with his brother.

Pushing himself into a sitting position, Darius touched a hand to his mouth. "You knocked out one of my teeth!"

"I've barely begun, big brother."

Darius removed a hanky from his coat pocket and pressed it against the place where his tooth used to be.

Tony nudged Darius's boot. "Get up. And for once in your life do your own dirty work instead of paying somebody else to."

Folding his feet underneath him, Darius began to rise. "Look, Tony. I'm not going to fight you just because you haven't learned how to lose with grace."

Tony grabbed Darius's lapels and snatched him close. "I didn't lose. You cheated."

Darius grinned, the black gap in his teeth giving Tony great satisfaction.

"I didn't do anything illegal," his brother said. "And let's admit it, that's not what has you so riled up. It's that I, once again, have come out on top."

Tony shoved him. Hard. Pedaling his feet, Darius stumbled back and would have fallen if the crowd hadn't been there to catch him.

"There isn't a person present," Tony said, "who doesn't know you won because you stooped to chicanery."

The crowd propped Darius back up. With great nonchalance, he dusted the dirt from his sleeves. "And there's not a person present who doesn't know the only reason you're in a higher-up position with Sullivan Oil is because you got underneath Essie Spreckelmeyer's skirts."

Tony exploded with fury. Leaping forward, he slammed another fist into Darius. Before he could follow him to the ground, though, strong hands grabbed Tony and jerked him back.

"What the blazes do you think you're doing?" Sheriff Dunn roared. He gave Tony a hard shake. "You better get out of my sight, Tony Morgan, and stay out before I throw you in Howard's wagon and keep you there until you rot."

Tony's vision cleared. He stumbled back, taking stock of his surroundings. The once uproarious crowd stood in silence. Finch knelt beside Darius. Others made room for Dr. Gulick as he shoved his way to the front.

Within the circle of gawking men stood Essie, hands covering her mouth, his grandmother's ring winking in the sun.

Turning, he walked away. Away from what he had done. Away from Darius. Away from her.

❦

Essie knocked on Room 314 of the Commercial Hotel, then wrapped her shawl and her composure about her. The door swung open.

"Essie," Anna said, widening the door. "Come in."

Crossing the threshold, Essie glanced around the sitting room. Tony's mother, dressed in black, stood with her back to the room, holding open a panel of blue-and-gold damask drapes at the window. Darkness obscured any view she might have had, though, and instead reflected the woman's frail image like a mirror.

The golden striped settee was vacant. One of Mrs. Lockhart's romance novels was open and flipped upside down on a side table. The wing chair beside it held an indention in its cushion.

"Tony's not here?" Essie asked.

"We've not seen him since before the race," Anna said, closing the door.

"How's Darius?"

"Cut lip. Black eye. Nothing too serious. He was complaining more about some stomach ailment that's been grieving him lately. He's really angry about his missing tooth, though."

Essie nodded.

"Do you mean to say you've not heard from Tony, either?" Mrs. Morgan turned away from the window, worry lines making deep creases between her brows.

"I'm afraid not."

"Oh dear." Anna glanced at her mother, then back at Essie. "Can I pour you something?"

"I'm sorry. I can't stay. I need to find Tony."

Mrs. Morgan stiffened. "Is he in some kind of trouble?"

"Not that I know of, ma'am. I'm just worried because he didn't come out to the house tonight. I . . ." She swallowed. "I thought he would."

The two women stared at her.

"Well," she said, backing toward the door, "if you hear from him, would you tell him I'm looking for him?"

"Of course," Anna said. "Where are you going now?"

Essie opened her mouth to answer, but tears clogged her throat. She didn't know where to go. They didn't have any "special place" just the two of them went other than the bicycle club, and he certainly wasn't there.

She'd sent Jeremy to check in all the saloons. He'd insisted it was a waste of time, convinced that Tony didn't drink, yet he still did as she bid. But with no luck.

She'd been to his boardinghouse, Castle's Drug Store, the Slap Out, and now here. Where on earth was he?

Swallowing, she took a deep breath. "I guess I'll try the jailhouse next."

"The jailhouse!" Mrs. Morgan exclaimed.

"Only because my uncle is the sheriff," Essie assured her. "It's very likely that he'll know where Tony is. I'm sure he's fine, ma'am. I just, well . . ."

"You're upset," Anna said. "And understandably so. Of course you want to find him." She grabbed her hat and tied it on. "I'll help you."

"No," Essie said. "It isn't necessary."

"Nonsense. We can cover twice the amount of territory if we work together. Just tell me where you planned to go after the jailhouse?"

Anna grabbed her wrap and slung it over her shoulders. "Don't wait up, Mother. I will very likely be quite late."

She followed Essie out the door and down the stairs into the hotel lobby.

"I honestly don't know where I'll go, Anna. And I'd hate to—"

"Well, ladies. This is a surprise."

"Ewing," Essie breathed, whirling around at the sound of his voice. "Oh, I'm so glad you're here."

The preacher nodded politely at Anna, then turned to Essie. "What's the matter?"

"I can't find Tony anywhere. Have you seen him?"

"I'm afraid I haven't."

She listed the places she'd already searched. "I was just heading over to the jail to see if Uncle Melvin had seen him. Anna offered to help, but it's so late and she doesn't know the town. I don't want to send her off by herself."

"Not to worry," he said. "I'll be glad to assist. Have you tried your house?"

"Not for the last hour or so."

"Okay. Miss Morgan and I will check there while you head to the sheriff's. We can rendezvous at the Slap Out."

∽

Essie leaned Peg against the railing in front of the sheriff's office. Uncle Melvin would not be pleased to see her out this late, especially with the town full of so many strangers bent on extending the day's festivities into the wee hours.

But she was desperate to find Tony. To let him know she loved him and the race didn't matter. She also needed to assure herself that he was safe and unhurt, for though Darius hadn't struck Tony with his fists, he'd delivered blows just the same. He'd simply delivered them with words.

She cringed again at Darius's coarse accusation. And she was just human enough to confess she'd been every bit as outraged as Tony. All the same, she was glad Melvin had shown up when he had.

Stepping into the office, she noted two of the cells held a handful of men sleeping off their inebriated states.

Deputy Howard dropped his chair onto all fours and rose to his feet. "Well, well. Look who's out past her bedtime."

"Where's Uncle Melvin?"

"Here and there. You need something?"

"I'm looking for Tony. Have you seen him?"

Howard circled around his desk. "What's the matter? Worried yet another man's gonna leave you high and dry?"

She froze. What exactly was he intimating? That he knew something about Tony she didn't? Or that he knew something about her past that he shouldn't?

"A simple yes or no will do, Deputy. Do you or do you not know where Tony is?"

He leaned a hip against her uncle's desk. "No, can't say that I do."

"And Uncle Melvin? Do you know where he is?"

"Nope."

"Thank you." She turned to leave.

"There is one thing before you go." His hand brushed against the figurine she'd given her uncle years ago and set it to wobbling. Making a grab for it, he snatched it up before it could fall and break. Turning it over in his hands, he examined it, then slowly scratched underneath the figure's raised arm with his dirty thumbnail. "Seems we have a mutual acquaintance."

Her first instinct was to ignore him and keep going, but some sixth sense made her turn back around to face him.

"I met him while I was in Austin at the Sheriff's Association Convention." His thumb moved to the open neckline and chin of the figure. "His name is Adam Currington."

Her breath caught. She glanced again at the men in the cells. One snored. The others lay sprawled out in various positions, either asleep or unconscious from too much drink.

The deputy looked up. "Ever heard of him?"

She said nothing.

" 'Cause he sure as shootin' has heard o' you."

Swallowing, she forced down her panic. Surely Adam would not have betrayed her deepest, most carefully guarded secret. He might not be an honorable man, but he wasn't cruel or unfeeling.

"Mr. Currington's a sheriff now?" she asked.

Howard chuckled. "No, no. I ran into him at a—while I was uptown, not at the convention."

"How do you know him?"

"I'd only just met him that evening. I entered a local establishment and settled myself down by a few friendly lookin' fellas, one of whom was Currington. When they found out I was from Corsicana, they asked if I knew that bicycle gal from the papers. Before I could answer, Currington piped up, saying he knew you . . . quite well."

She kept her expression carefully blank.

He encircled the statuette in his hand more securely and began to rub his stubby finger across its chest. "Since you and he are so, um, close, you prob'ly know liquor seems to loosen his tongue a mite. Makes him say things that would be best kept to himself."

Apprehension welled within her.

He slid his thumb down the figurine and began caressing the hem of its skirt. "When I think o' the mistake I almost made with you." He shook his head. "I can't bear the thought of lettin' another man fall into your trap."

"My trap?"

He set the china ornament back on the desk, then directed his full attention to her. "Oh yes, Essie. I know all about ya. I'd heard the rumors, o' course, but Currington, who was evidently run out of this town on a rail a few years back, confirmed every tale I ever heard and then some."

Her lips parted. She'd thought Adam Currington was beyond hurting her anymore. She began to realize, however, that was not the case, as a fresh sense of betrayal rose within her yet again.

"And I think it's my civic duty to warn your *fee-yon-say* so he doesn't suffer the same fate." Standing, Howard hitched up his trousers. "O' course, if you could convince me that Currington was lying . . . or maybe take a stroll with me one evening real soon so we could, um, *discuss* the matter . . ."

She gasped. "How dare you!"

"Oh, keep yer knickers on." He leered. "Though it won't bother me none if'n ya don't. Either way, I'm free on Tuesday. Perhaps I could meet ya out behind yer place, say, around midnight?"

Shoving the hurt aside, she straightened to her full height. "You are wasting your breath, Mr. Howard. You'll find I'm not one to quail in the face of a bully."

"That so?" He walked to the big window fronting the office. "Wonder what the townsfolk would think about both their judge and sheriff harboring a strumpet?"

She sucked in her breath.

"Wonder how many members you'd have left in that club o' yours if'n the matrons of this town learned the truth about their leader?"

Whirling around, she charged to the door. "I will not listen to this."

He sidestepped in front of her, thrusting his arm across the doorway and blocking her way. "You will listen, you uppity little tart."

"All I've to do is tell my uncle and you'll be out of a job."

"You do that and I'll see your reputation ruined before you can spit three times."

"I doubt anyone would believe you."

"You think not? Not everybody around here kisses the ground your uncle and father walk on. And you can be sure their reputations would suffer plenty. They are, after all, elected officials by the trusting citizens of this fine town. And don't underestimate what yer beau's reaction is going to be, either. Not too many men I know of want used goods."

She tried to duck under his arm.

He grabbed her and slammed her against the wall. "I want a piece of what you gave Currington."

"Release me this minute, and if you threaten me again I'll not only tell Tony, I'll tell my uncle and father, too. Just watch me if you don't believe me."

He studied her as if gauging her sincerity. "You tell Tony and you can kiss your wedding day good-bye." He ran a finger from her ear to her chin. "Besides, there's no need to tell anybody anything. It's just one little stroll I'm wantin', Essie. Which is no more than you gave Currington." He loosened his hold, stepped back and winked. "See ya Tuesday, sugar."

chapter TWENTY-SEVEN

COASTING TOWARD home, Essie took note of the late—or early—hour. The first light of dawn had touched the sky and set off a chain of events she ordinarily delighted in. A yellow-and-pink sky framed the hundreds of stark, towering derricks that formed Corsicana's landscape. Songbirds flitted from rig to rig and tree to tree, announcing that this was a day the Lord had made and all should rejoice and be glad in it.

Rejoicing was the furthest thing from her mind, however. She, Anna, and Ewing had spent the entire night looking for Tony. But without success. And as troubling as that was, it was her confrontation with the deputy that had unsettled her the most.

She refused to be blackmailed by him. But if she didn't do as he said, he'd reveal her secret to the entire town. Were that to happen, the effects on her father and uncle could be devastating—not to mention what Tony's reaction would be.

The only thing to do, then, was to call Howard's bluff and confess to Tony. And the sooner the better. That was turning out to be a bit difficult, however, seeing as she couldn't find him.

The knot in her stomach tightened. Where was he? Anna said it wasn't like him to disappear like this and not tell the family where he was going. Her mood softened a bit at the thought of Anna. What a surprise she had been. Not at all the pampered little rich girl Essie had expected. Hardheaded, passionate, and fiercely loyal to Tony, she'd been tireless in their search for him.

And Ewing. *Preacher* Ewing. Essie smiled. As a youngster, she had spent many a day with him hunting all manner of creatures. And all those hours of hunting together had come back in a rush, allowing them to work with efficiency and thoroughness. Yet even then they couldn't locate Tony.

Where is he, Lord? Where is he?

Surely he wouldn't have left town. Would he? But she could think of no other explanation. There wasn't a rock in all of Corsicana that she, Anna, and Ewing had left unturned.

Opening her gate, she dragged herself down the walkway and leaned Peg against the porch.

"Where have you been?"

Squealing in fright, Essie jumped back. She glanced up on the porch, then felt a rush of joy and relief, quickly followed by anger.

"Tony!" She raced up the steps. "We've been looking all over for you. Where on earth have you been?"

"Where have *I* been? I've been right here. For hours—once I cooled off, that is. Wondering where the devil *you've* been." He pointed at the front door. "I spent forever throwing rocks at your window, until one actually broke the glass and went all the way through. Nobody could've slept through that. And that's when I realized you weren't home. I've been waiting for you ever since."

He still wore his racing outfit minus the red sash and beret. His hair lay in disarray. A full night's growth of whiskers shadowed his face.

"Well, if that don't beat all," she said. "There we were looking every which way, and you were right here on my very porch the entire time. Anna and Ewing must have just missed you when they came by here to check."

"Anna? Anna stayed out all night, too? And in Ewing's company? She can't be doing that, Essie. What were the two of you thinking?"

She propped her hands on her waist. "Don't you dare lecture me, Tony Bryant Morgan. I've just spent the longest night of my life looking for you and I'm not about to take any sass over it. You had the three of us worried to death."

"About what?"

"About where you were. And how you were. And if you were okay." She ran her gaze over him. "Are you? Are you okay?"

"I'm hungry."

She smiled. "Anything else?"

"My knuckles are pretty sore."

She walked to him and lifted his scuffed-up hand to her lips, anointing it with a kiss. "Come inside and I'll take care of this for you." She moved to the door and held it open. "You coming?"

"It's awfully early for me to be paying a call."

"Probably so, but I think it'll be okay. Just this once."

Bone tired, Tony lowered himself into a bentwood chair at Essie's kitchen table. She lit a fire in the stove, set a pot on to boil, then grabbed a couple of cloths and a bottle of arnica.

Placing her rag over the mouth of the bottle, she tipped it upside down, dousing the cloth with liquid, then held her palm out. "Let me see your hand."

He rested his hand in hers while she pulled a chair up beside him and began to dab the cuts and bruises.

"I'm sorry, Essie."

She looked up. "For worrying me?"

"For losing the race."

"I don't care about that silly race, Tony." She returned her attention to what she was doing.

He knew that was a lie, but he didn't feel like arguing. She moistened her rag again.

"Did Anna say anything about Darius?" he asked. "Is he okay?"

"He's mad about his tooth and has a black eye, but other than that, sounds like he'll recover just fine."

After wetting the cloth time and again, she finally upended the tincture and poured it out onto the rag.

"I haven't fought him since we were kids," he said.

She attended a particularly tender spot, but he held himself still, careful not to show any signs of discomfort.

"He never even swung back," he said. "Not once."

She gently cleaned some dried blood from his knuckles, set the rag down and blew on the places she'd doctored.

"I wish you'd say something."

She looked up at him, her blue eyes soft. "I love you."

His throat started working.

She put the stopper back on the bottle.

"Essie?"

"Hmmm?"

"I love you, too."

She smiled. Not a big, hearty smile. But a small, quiet one. Like she was being told something that she already knew.

Leaning over, he took hold of her waist and pulled her onto his lap. "Will you marry me soon? I don't want a long engagement."

"I'll marry you whenever you say the word."

Gathering her close, he kissed her. Only, this kiss wasn't hot with passion like the one yesterday morning. This one was slower. Gentler. More of a sharing. Of her heart. Of his love. And it affected him even more than the other one.

"Essie Spreckelmeyer! Get off that man's lap this *instant*!"

Essie jumped to her feet, color rushing to her face.

Judge Spreckelmeyer stood in his nightdress, his pale, white shins and bare feet poking out the bottom. He looked back and forth at the two of them. "Has he been here all night?!"

"No!" she said. "I mean, not exactly. Not like you mean."

Standing, Tony picked up the cloth and tincture of arnica and handed it to her. "I was on your porch, sir."

"All night?"

"Yes, sir."

"With Essie?"

"No, sir. Alone."

He looked at Essie. "And where were you? Why are you still wearing yesterday's clothes?"

"I was with Anna and Ewing. We were looking for Tony. I didn't realize he was here waiting on me."

Spreckelmeyer set his mouth into a stern line. "Well, I don't care what age you are or whether the two of you are betrothed. His staying on our porch all night and coming inside the house before I've even made a trip out back simply isn't done, and you know it!"

"Papa—"

"You're absolutely right, sir," Tony said, interrupting her. "I apologize. It won't happen again." He turned to Essie. "I'll stop by later to pick you up for church."

She slammed the medicinals on the table. "Now, wait just one minute. Nothing improper happened, Papa. That kiss was the first time he's so much as touched me since yesterday morning. I won't have him running off with his tail between his legs like he's done something wrong."

Tony clasped her hand. "I did do something wrong, Essie. I came inside the house while your father was sleeping and at an hour no decent fella should."

Her lower lip curled down in a sweet pout. "I was gonna make you breakfast."

The picture of her cooking for him at the brush of dawn filled his mind. "The first time you make a morning meal for me, Essie, your name will be Mrs. Morgan." He leaned over and kissed her on the cheek. "I'll pick you up at the usual time." Stepping toward the archway, he nodded at Spreckelmeyer. "Sir."

The judge stepped out of the way and Tony left the house, his spirit renewed, his step light.

~

Knocking on the Spreckelmeyers' doorframe a few hours later, Tony peeked through the screen, wondering which hat Essie would be wearing to church. He heard a door slam, then her booted feet run to the top of the stairs.

To his surprise, she jumped onto the banister, slid down on her backside, and landed square in front of him, her smile happy and wide, her hat tall and sassy.

Shoving open the screen, he stepped in, grabbed her around the waist and kissed her just as he'd been thinking about doing ever since he'd left this morning.

"I wanted to do that the first time I ever saw you sliding down that thing," he murmured against her lips.

She ran her fingernails along the nape of his neck. "I don't think you would have received the same response from me then as you are now."

He chuckled. "No, I guess not."

Spreckelmeyer's study door opened and Tony released her, putting a proper distance between them.

Essie tugged on her gloves. "Tony's here, Papa. You ready?" She glanced up at her father's silence.

He wasn't even close to being ready. He was only in shirt, trousers, and suspenders. No vest. No tie. No jacket. No hat.

"Papa? Are you feeling poorly?"

305

Before he could answer, the sheriff stepped out into the hall as well. He wasn't dressed for church, either. In fact, he looked as if he'd never even gone to bed.

With the town as full of rowdies as it was, it wouldn't have surprised Tony. But since he'd moved to Corsicana, he'd never known the sheriff to miss a Sunday service. Not once.

"What's the matter?" Essie asked.

Tony considered making a polite withdrawal, but whatever news they had to give, it clearly wasn't good and he wanted to be with her when she received it.

Spreckelmeyer must have guessed as much, because he indicated the four of them should move into the parlor and take a seat.

Tony escorted Essie around a green-and-gold ottoman before settling her on the settee beneath a huge painting of an English fox hunt with hunters in full riding habits, restraining their anxious horses.

Joining her, he threaded his hand with hers.

Spreckelmeyer and Dunn sat in chairs opposite them. Neither said a word for several moments. The sheer white curtains along the front wall stirred, but the breeze was not sufficient enough to be felt inside the room.

"You're scaring me, Papa," Essie said as the silence stretched on. "What is it?"

Spreckelmeyer rested his elbows on his knees, then looked up at Tony. "Son," he said, "your brother was found dead in his hotel room this morning."

Essie gasped.

"What?" Tony asked, frowning and confused.

Spreckelmeyer said nothing, just looked at him with compassion and sympathy.

Tony turned to the sheriff. "I don't understand."

"He's dead, Tony."

Shock, disbelief, and bewilderment stacked up so fast, he couldn't even think of where to begin. "How? He's in excellent health."

The older men looked at each other, their glances telling.

White-hot panic shot through Tony. "Sweet saints above." His breath stuck in his throat. "From that punch? He died from that punch I gave him yesterday?"

"No, no," Spreckelmeyer said.

Relief poured through Tony, but he still felt sick to his stomach. "Then how? How did he die?"

"He was murdered."

Tony's lips parted. "Murdered? What are you talking about?"

The sheriff cleared his throat. "He was stabbed."

"Stabbed?" Tony shook his head. "That can't be. How did that happen? Who did it?"

"I don't know yet."

Essie squeezed Tony's hand. He felt the blood drain from his face. "My mother and sister? Were they harmed?"

"No."

He expelled a breath. "Have they been told about Darius?"

"Yes."

He released Essie's hand and stood. "I need to go."

The sheriff stood, as well, and put a hand on Tony's shoulder. "They're all right. Preacher Wortham is with them."

Tony frowned. "But Wortham has church this morning." The absurdity of him worrying about who was going to preach the Sunday service sounded strange even to his own ears. But if the others in the room thought so, they didn't give any indication.

"Bogart's gonna take care of it for him."

Tony stared at him.

"Bogart was our preacher before Ewing," Dunn said. "He retired a few years back."

Shaking his head, Tony made another effort to pass the sheriff. "I still need to get to my family."

Dunn increased the pressure on his shoulder. "In a minute. I think it would be best if you got all the details now. No need to upset the women with this kind of talk."

Desire to comfort his mother and sister pulled at Tony, but he saw the wisdom of the sheriff's words. He looked at Essie.

Nodding, she patted the spot beside her. He sat back down, trying to make sense of what the sheriff had told him. Stabbed? Darius had been stabbed? To death? But how? Why? By whom?

He knew Darius had enemies. Knew his brother could be underhanded. Still, he couldn't imagine Darius doing something so nefarious it would motivate someone to kill him in cold blood.

But someone had. And whoever it was would have to be mighty strong. His brother might not have fought back yesterday when Tony was going after him, but he'd most assuredly have fought back if someone was trying to kill him.

"Do you have any suspects at all?" Tony asked.

Dunn slowly nodded. "One."

"Who?"

The sheriff swiped his thick gray moustache with a leathery hand. "You."

Essie gasped a second time.

"*Me?*" The idea was so preposterous, he couldn't even process it. "Why? Because of that stupid race?" His anger started to build. "You think I'd kill somebody—my own flesh and blood—over some stupid bicycle race?"

"No. I don't think it had anything to do with that race."

"Then what possible reason can you have for suspecting me?"

"You mean besides the fact that you have now inherited the entire Morgan fortune and the oil company that goes along with it?"

All powers of speech fled from Tony.

"Besides the fact," the sheriff continued, "that you can save your sister from a marriage you've been very vocal about opposing but had no way of stopping—before now, that is?"

None of what the sheriff was saying had even occurred to Tony. But, of course, Dunn was right. Tony was next in line to inherit. And with that inheritance came all the power, resources, and privileges he needed to take proper care of his loved ones. And Essie, too.

Dunn leaned back in his chair. His blue eyes sharp. Perceptive. Intelligent. Deep grooves surrounded them from years of squinting into the bright Texas sunlight.

"I'm not gonna pretend like I don't want it," Tony said. "I do. I'd always assumed part of it would be mine." He drew down his eyebrows. "But I don't want it so badly that I'd kill a man for it. Especially not my own brother. We had our differences, but I never wished him dead. Never."

"Uncle Melvin," Essie said, her voice soft, calm, "I do not for one minute believe that you think Tony did this awful thing. And even if you did, there is no crime in inheriting the Morgan fortune. Granted, it doesn't look good, particularly on the heels of the scuffle the two of them had yesterday. But it isn't enough to accuse him of murder, and I'm devastated to think you would stoop to doing so."

Her voice cracked on the last few words. Tony slipped his hand back into hers.

Dunn moved his attention to her, his distress evident. "You know I would move a mountain for you if I needed to, but this is not something I have total control over. I have rules to abide by. Procedures to follow."

"You have no proof that he did it," she said, anger and hurt edging her voice.

Dunn and Spreckelmeyer exchanged a glance.

"Essie," Spreckelmeyer said, "Darius was stabbed with a stag-handled knife shaped like a dog bone."

chapter TWENTY-EIGHT

ESSIE'S BREATH caught.

Tony fell back onto the cushions of the settee. "My knife? Darius was stabbed with *my* knife? The one my father gave me?"

Uncle Melvin's cheeks sagged, weighing his frown down even farther. "I'm afraid so."

"But I haven't seen my knife since I showed it to that Alamo fellow, Mudge, at the reception Friday night." He sat up. "You were there. Harley had just borrowed it and given it back, when Mudge asked to take a look at it."

Uncle Melvin gave no indication as to whether he recalled the incident or not.

Tony looked over at Papa. "Before I had time to get it back, Jeremy came in with news of Crackshot and I left without it." He scooted forward, sitting on the edge of the couch. "I missed it almost immediately because I needed it out at the rig when we were tending Crackshot."

"You never asked Mudge to return it to you?" Melvin asked.

"Of course I did. The very next morning when I saw him at the parade. But he said he'd left it at the Commercial, thinking I'd go back there to retrieve it."

"And did you go back to the hotel?"

"Yes, but no one there had seen or heard a thing about it."

Essie had held her peace for as long as she was going to. She knew her father and uncle didn't really suspect Tony killed his brother. She also knew they were elected officials and had to follow the due course of the law.

So she had sat there and let them accuse Tony, interrogate him and scare him half to death. Enough was enough.

"What are we going to do, Papa?" she said. "Both of you know he didn't do it. Anyone could have picked up his knife."

Papa rubbed his forehead. "It's not that simple."

"It is."

"No, it's not. Besides, the decision isn't mine to make."

"You're the Thirty-fifth Judicial District Judge. If you say there's not enough evidence, then that's an end to it."

He lowered his hand. "Not this time. Not when the accused is my future son-in-law. Maybe if the two of you weren't already betrothed, I could do something. But now, if we don't make this arrest, no one will believe in Tony's innocence. They'll think Melvin and I manipulated the facts to suit ourselves. And that's just the type of thing that incites lynch mobs."

Her heart jumped into her throat. "You're going to arrest him?" She swerved her gaze to Melvin. "You are thinking to actually take him to the jailhouse and put him in a cell?!"

"Where were you in the wee hours of last night?" Uncle Melvin asked Tony.

A tick began to hammer in Tony's jaw. "Sitting on the front porch there."

"This front porch?"

"Yes, sir."

"For how long?"

"From about midnight to dawn."

Melvin shot Essie a quick glance before returning it to Tony. "Alone?"

Essie stiffened.

"Yes, sir."

"Did anyone see you there?"

"No, sir."

"The whole night long? Not one single person happened by?"

"A straggler or two happened by. But it was dark and I was sitting in the shadows. I wasn't about to holler out a greeting. It would have ruined Essie's reputation."

Her uncle stood and approached the fireplace. His back to them, he propped his hand on the mantel. "Where were you before that?"

"I walked down to Two Bit Creek to cool down after my fight with Darius. Then I came here."

"What did you do then?"

"Threw rocks at her window."

He whirled around. "What?"

"I was trying to wake her up. I hadn't seen her since my fight with Darius and I knew I'd never get to sleep unless I talked to her first."

"So you snuck around back and threw rocks at her window?"

"Yes, sir."

Melvin took a step forward, pointing his finger. "Don't you ever do that again!"

Papa heaved a sigh. "Melvin, you are digressing."

"Are you forgetting what happened last time, Sullivan?"

"Melvin—" Papa growled.

Essie jumped to her feet. "Can we please just stick to the issue at hand?"

Her uncle looked at her. "Did you go out there and meet him?"

"I wasn't even home!"

"Has he done that before?"

"Of course not."

"Well, if'n he ever does it again, I assume you will not dignify him with a response?"

She stormed around the chairs. "I most certainly will respond. Nothing short of desperation could motivate Tony to wake me up in the middle of the night, and I'd answer his call like *that*," she said, snapping her fingers.

"Desperation? Desperation for what?" her uncle barked.

Papa surged to his feet. Tony jumped clear over an ottoman and shoved her behind him, placing himself between her and her uncle.

"Listen here, Sheriff. You got something to say, then you say it to me, but you leave Essie alone. I don't care if you're the sheriff, her uncle, or her last living relative. Nobody talks to my woman like that. *Nobody*. You understand?"

"And just what're ya gonna do about it, Morgan? Stab me with your knife?"

Essie gasped.

"That is enough!" Papa roared.

Her uncle and Tony stood chest to chest.

"Stop it, Melvin," Papa said. "I mean it."

Melvin took a step back but didn't relax his stance.

"You too, Tony."

Tony fished around for her hand. She slipped it inside his. He took a step back, keeping her partially behind him.

"Say what you have to say, Sheriff," Tony said. "But I'm done chitchattin'. "

Uncle Melvin hardened his features. "You wanna know what I have to say? I say you're under arrest, Anthony Bryant Morgan. For the murder of your brother, Darius Morgan."

Essie lay curled up on her bed, crying to the Lord for help. Her first instinct had been to go out and do something. Anything. But what could she do?

Melvin had forbidden her to go to the hotel until they'd removed the body. He wouldn't even let her go and offer condolences to Anna and her mother.

Tony didn't want to make any more of a spectacle than necessary as he went to the jailhouse and asked her to stay behind.

Papa had gone to send a telegram to a judge from another district. It would be unethical for Papa to sit in judgment on a case that involved his future son-in-law.

And Mother was gone, of course. Out of reach.

Essie pressed a handkerchief to her mouth. *Oh, Lord. I need my mother.*

Aunt Verdie had tried to be there for Essie since Mother's death, but Essie was closer to Uncle Melvin. She ran her finger over the Florentine stitches on her pillow slip. Going to her uncle now, though, was out of the question—particularly when she was so disappointed in him.

She had many women friends from church and the bicycle club, but what could they do? Nothing. Not one blessed thing.

And then, she realized, Christ was still her groom. He hadn't left her simply because she and Tony had decided to get married.

But as she lay on her bed, no words of prayer came to her. No Scriptures. No memorized verses. No nothing. So she'd simply cried, beseeching the Lord and repeating the only prayer she could think of.

Help. Please, Lord. Help.

She was so tired. So empty. When had she last been to bed? At some point she must have dozed off, for the sound of someone knocking on the front door downstairs jolted her awake.

Too tired to move and not up for visitors, she stayed in her bed.

The door opened. "Essie?"

It was a woman's voice.

"Are you home, honey?"

She heard the creak of the stairs, but she still didn't answer. The footsteps came down the hall and stopped at her bedroom door.

She rolled over and tears engulfed her eyes. "Mrs. Lockhart."

The elderly lady came in, sat on the edge of the mattress and opened her arms. Essie moved into them and sobbed. The slightest hint of camphor rose from Mrs. Lockhart's clothing.

"There, there, dear," she said, patting Essie on the back. "That's it. You have a good cry, then I'll tell you what we have planned."

Essie took a trembling breath and leaned back. "We have a plan?"

"Well, of course. But finish your cry first. You'll feel much better for it."

Essie dragged the hanky across her eyes. "I want to hear our plan."

Mrs. Lockhart stood up and held out her hand. "Come, let me do your hair first."

"For what?" Essie swung her legs over the side of the bed.

"For the emergency meeting of the Velocipede Club."

"But I didn't call an emergency meeting." Essie sat down on her vanity stool and began to remove the pins from her hair.

Mrs. Lockhart picked up the brush. "Shirley called it. We are due to convene in thirty minutes."

∞

Wearing a white shirtwaist, brown skirt, and simple straw hat, Essie entered the Velocipede Club with Mrs. Lockhart. Afternoon sunlight streamed in through the windows lining the upper edge of the building. It appeared as if the entire female membership was present and every single one of them was talking at once.

Mrs. McCabe and Mrs. Zimpelman caught sight of her first. One by one the women quit speaking until the earsplitting noise trickled into total quiet. Essie looked over the sea of faces regarding her with concern and affection.

When she'd asked the Lord for help, she never imagined He'd send angels disguised as bloomer-girls. Tears piled up in her throat, making it almost impossible to swallow.

Shirley strode to her and clasped her tight. "Oh, honey. Don't you worry about a thing. We'll figure something out."

And in a rush, the entire group crowded about her, reassuring her and pulling her to the chairs that had been set up.

Shirley moved to the podium and hammered on the gavel. "Order, please."

The women settled and gave their attention to Shirley.

"As you know, our beloved member and Essie's much-anticipated fiancé has been placed in the jailhouse for something we all know, beyond a shadow of a doubt, our Mr. Morgan would never do."

"He certainly wouldn't."

"Don't know what the sheriff was thinking."

"Inexcusable is what it is."

Shirley rapped the gavel again. "Because of Mr. Morgan's relationship with Essie, the sheriff and judge don't have the legroom they usually do under these circumstances."

"Such a mess."

"Poor Mr. Morgan."

"We've got to get him out of there."

"Verdie, can't you do something about the sheriff?"

Aunt Verdie was here? Essie twisted around but was unable to find her in the crowd.

"Ladies!" Shirley said, shushing them. "Please. We are wasting time."

The women quieted.

"Now," Shirley continued, "leaving Mr. Morgan's fate to some strange judge or, worse, Deputy Howard, simply will not do." She lifted her chin. "Therefore, I move that we, the women of the Corsicana Velocipede Club, take on the task of rescuing our Mr. Morgan."

A beat of concern broke through Essie's daze. Rescue? They were going to break Tony out of jail?

"I second the motion," said Mrs. Gulick.

"All those in favor say 'Aye.' "

"Aye."

"Opposed?"

Essie opened her mouth, but before she could interject a bit of caution, the door opened. Anna, Mrs. Morgan, and Ewing stepped inside.

Shirley smiled. "Mrs. Pickens, as Membership Chair, would you please go and welcome the Morgans and Preacher Wortham?"

The proprietress of the Flour, Feed and Liquor Store jumped to her feet and escorted Anna and her mother—both in black—to some vacant chairs, Ewing close behind them.

"We appreciate your coming," Shirley said, "and we offer our condolences. However, I feel compelled to warn you, our conversation today will be open and frank and perhaps upsetting to you as we discuss the circumstances surrounding Mr. Morgan's death. Are you sure you're up to staying?"

Anna looked at her mother, who dabbed her eyes with a handkerchief, then nodded.

"Very well. Then, as there was no opposition to our motion, the floor is open for discussion. Before we start, however, I respectfully suggest that the most effective and upright way to accomplish our goal is to find out who really did kill Darius Morgan. So we must first try to ascertain who would profit from his death." She scanned the audience. "The floor recognizes Mrs. McCabe."

The coroner's wife stood, her usual jolly expression nowhere in sight. "Mr. McCabe has laid out many a man in his day. Those who died in a similar fashion to Mr. Morgan were most often the victims of," she held up her fingers, ticking off the reasons, "explosive anger—due to cheating at cards and such. Or accidents—cleaning out guns and that sort of thing. Reckless behavior while under the influence of intoxicants. Sometimes jealousy—usually involving a woman. And occasionally, premeditated, cold-blooded murder."

"Have you spoken to Mr. McCabe since he's seen the body?" Shirley asked.

"I have."

"And what is his opinion?"

"Premeditated, cold-blooded murder."

Fans fluttered and whispers ricocheted throughout the room.

"The floor recognizes Miss Davis."

Young Victoria stood, casting a quick glance at Ewing, then blushing prettily. "Mr. Morgan was quite wealthy. Isn't it possible that someone who worked for him or who had unsatisfactory business dealings with him might have held a grudge of some sort?"

"Excellent point. Are you recording all this, Mrs. Blanchard?"

The club secretary nodded, busily scribbling in her record book.

"The floor recognizes Mrs. Lockhart."

"In *The Shadow of Sin*," she began, using her cane to push to her feet while those in attendance suppressed a groan, "Mr. Goodenough found his young wife in the arms of Mr. Huffstutter and planned an elaborate scheme to murder them both in their sleep. Of course, he ran into difficulty when—"

"Thank you, Mrs. Lockhart," Shirley said, gently interrupting. "As Mrs. McCabe pointed out earlier, jealousy can, indeed, be a powerful motivator. Mrs. Vandervoort? I believe I saw your hand next."

Essie listened as each woman had an idea for motive, and as the list lengthened, her optimism wavered. The possibilities were endless, but of all those presented, none were as compelling as the motives assigned to Tony.

"Last one," Shirley said.

Anna Morgan rose. "I believe that there is one motive we are overlooking, and that would be my motive."

The women stilled.

"Darius was forcing me into a marriage I did not want. I had just as much motive to kill him as Tony did. Anyone who knows our family well knows that Tony and I are very close. If something were to happen to Darius, and Tony were to inherit, that would solve all my worries."

Ewing jumped to his feet. "Miss Morgan, though your hypothesis sounds reasonable at first, there isn't a soul who would actually believe you capable of such a thing. The idea is ridiculous."

"No more ridiculous than believing Tony did it."

Ewing scowled at Shirley. "I will not permit that ludicrous supposition to be entered into the minutes."

"If we are going to do this right, the list needs to be thorough," Anna argued. "Keep it in the books."

Essie glanced back and forth between the two.

Shirley cleared her throat. "There are no right or wrong suggestions, Preacher Wortham."

"Then I did it!" he said, slamming his fist against his chest.

Mrs. Bogart gasped.

"Don't be absurd, Ewing," Anna said. "You'd never even met Darius before Friday."

"Well, I can tell you this: I don't want you to marry that old boiler you're betrothed to. So that gives me just as much motive as you, now, doesn't it?"

Anna's features softened. "You don't want me to marry Mr. Tubbs?"

"Well, of course I don't."

She bit her lower lip. "Well, I don't believe I'll have to."

Ewing blinked in confusion. Essie smiled.

Shirley folded her arms. "Are you two quite through?"

After a slight hesitation, Anna nodded, slid a hand beneath her skirts and sat. Befuddled, Ewing plopped down beside her.

"Now," Shirley continued, "I suggest we try to gather a bit of evidence based on some of these suggestions. Mrs. Blanchard? Let's start from the top and begin making assignments."

The secretary stood. "Number one. Someone who worked for him or who had unsatisfactory business dealings with him."

Shirley tapped the lectern with her fingernail. "That's going to be difficult. We'll need access to Mr. Morgan's personal files and records." She looked at Anna. "Would that be something you or your mother could get your hands on somehow?"

"Yes," Anna said. "That part would be easy. We simply take a train back to Beaumont and raid Darius's desk. The problem will be what to do with the papers once we have them. Neither Mother nor I would know where to begin."

"Essie?" Shirley asked. "You would be able to, wouldn't you?"

"Perhaps," Essie said. "But is there any reason we can't have Tony go through them? He's apt to be much more familiar with the Morgan ventures."

"Excellent idea. And it would make him look less guilty and more a martyr to have him resort to doing his work within the cell."

"I agree," said Mrs. Zimpelman. "As a matter of fact, I recommend he also continue his work for Sullivan Oil. The men he oversees could go to him daily with their reports and for their assignments."

"Will the sheriff allow that, do you think, Mrs. Dunn?" Shirley asked.

Aunt Verdie smiled. "You leave the sheriff to me."

Ewing stood. "That's all well and good, but Miss Morgan and her mother cannot do what you ask of them. If the murderer really is a business acquaintance, he will not allow these women to simply walk off with the evidence. No, the scheme is much too dangerous."

"Oh dear," Shirley said, then looked at Anna. "Don't you have a cousin who could escort you?"

Anna shook her head. "Finch is determined to stay here. He doesn't think Sheriff Dunn and Judge Spreckelmeyer will be impartial and he wants to make sure 'Tony gets his due.' So we wouldn't want Finch to accompany us or even to hear of our plans. He's very loyal to Darius."

"But all the Morgan papers are rightfully Tony's," Essie said. "Your cousin wouldn't have any choice in the matter."

"It would still be best to keep our plans to ourselves."

"I'll go with them," Ewing said.

Essie lifted her brows.

"Not only can I provide them with escort and protection," he said, "but I can help them carry the documents back here."

"That's very generous of you, Preacher Wortham," Shirley said. "Thank you. Mrs. Blanchard? What's the next motive on our list?"

"Jealous husband."

"Oh my." Shirley scanned the crowd. "Miss Morgan? Can you or your mother shed any light here?"

"I'm afraid not," Anna said. "Darius was not stepping out with anyone. As far as him seeing someone he oughtn't, I'm afraid I have no idea about that."

Mrs. Lockhart rose. "I have a daughter in Beaumont. I will contact her and see if I can determine who Mr. Morgan's romantic interests were."

By the end of the hour, several women had been assigned a motive to investigate. The rest compiled a schedule for delivering meals to Tony.

Before the meeting adjourned, all members pledged themselves to secrecy. Even Aunt Verdie and Ewing. In order to keep the women's plans from being hindered, the menfolk needed to be kept in the dark.

As the meeting broke up, Essie stayed in her seat and looked down at her ring. A ring worn for over four decades by another woman, yet even still it sparkled. She wiggled her finger, allowing the sunlight to catch in the diamond's prisms.

Somewhere long, long ago, this stone had been nothing more than a lump buried in the ground. But with hard work and great perseverance, it was mined, cleaned, cut and polished. Then treasured by the woman who wore it.

And now the man God had prepared for Essie had placed it on her finger. A good man. An honest man. A man who'd been forsaken by his father.

But he would not be forsaken this time. Not by her. Not by his friends. And not by his heavenly Father.

She stood. There was work to be done and she aimed to do her share.

chapter TWENTY-NINE

M.C. BAKER stepped into the jailhouse. "Howdy, Sheriff. I'm here to see Morgan."

Melvin slapped his pen on the desk, splattering ink all over his papers. Tony'd had more visitors in the last two days than any one prisoner in the history of Melvin's entire tenure as sheriff. He'd spent so much time letting folks in and out of Tony's cell that he hadn't accomplished one single thing.

Grabbing up the keys, he strode to the back of the building. Tony sat behind an old table, pen and ink in hand, lantern sputtering in the breeze. Melvin couldn't believe he'd let Verdie talk him into allowing all that stuff into Tony's lockup. She never interfered with his work. Never. Until now.

Yet Verdie and every other woman in town was treating Morgan as if he were a native Corsicanan or something. And it was all due to the fact that he was Essie's betrothed. Melvin had at first figured the women would try to convince Essie to break the betrothal. Instead, they'd aimed their displeasure at him, the man who had kept them safe and secure for the past three decades.

Oh, he didn't think Tony had done the killing. He'd merely lost his temper back at the Spreckelmeyers' house and as a result had treated the boy a bit harshly. Still, he couldn't outright ignore the evidence that pointed to him or it would bring down censure from every man in town and many of those in the state's capital. That might be preferable, however, to the censure of the women of the Corsicana Velocipede Club.

He drove his fingers through what was left of his hair. If he had any prayer of finding out who did the actual killing, though, he was gonna have to be allowed to get some work done.

Unlocking the cell, he jerked it open and scowled at his prisoner. "I'm getting mighty tired of jumping up and down like a jack-in-the-box every other minute. If'n I leave this durn thing open, will you stay put?"

The average person might have missed the momentary surprise on Tony's face, but Melvin had made a career of watching for subtle nuances in a man's expression.

"Yes, sir," Tony answered. "I give you my word."

Melvin nodded once. "Well, all right, then." He turned to Baker. "Go on. Everybody else has."

Baker entered the cell and began to review the day's business with Tony.

Melvin returned to his desk and looked over his notes. A vast number of the folks who had entered town for the bicycle race had left, leaving behind the locals and the oilmen. For all he knew, the killer had come and gone, too. But until he knew for sure, he'd do everything he could to piece together what had happened. He didn't want to be known as the sheriff who'd allowed the killer of one of the wealthiest men in Texas to get away without a trace. He also didn't want Essie's fiancé hung if he wasn't the guilty party.

He again examined the list of every guest at the Welcome Reception, where Tony'd left his knife, along with every employee of the Commercial Hotel. He'd questioned the men who'd attended the reception, particularly Mudge, who'd been knocked out of the race by Darius's man.

But after the race, Mudge had nursed his disappointment in Rosenburg's Saloon and passed out, spending the whole of the night in plain view. The other men in the race had plenty of folks confirming how they'd spent their evening, as well. Melvin scratched through name after name on the guest list. Those who had a motive didn't have an opportunity, and those who had an opportunity didn't have a motive.

He had a few more people at the Commercial Hotel he wanted to talk with, though. Not only the ones who were working the night of the reception, but those who'd discovered Darius's body in his room early that morning. He also wanted to find out if anyone had seen Darius's sister and mother coming or going during the time in question.

Baker bid good-bye to Tony, then tipped his hat to Melvin before leaving. Darkness fell and crickets took to serenading his small office.

Melvin turned up the flame of his lantern. "So what do you think, Morgan? Anything new occur to you as far as your brother's concerned?"

Tony looked up from his papers. "I really don't know what to think, Sheriff. My mother and sister brought a bunch of Darius's papers back from Beaumont today and I've been studying them. Everything looks to be in order. He's let go of an employee here and there, but nothing that would incite a person to murder."

"How recently have those folks been dismissed?"

"Since my father's death at the beginning of the summer."

Melvin nodded. "Well, make me a list of their names and I'll send it over to the sheriff of Jefferson County and have him look into it."

Howard walked in, saw the cell door open and quickly palmed his gun. "What's goin' on?"

Melvin shook his head. "Put your gun away before somebody gets hurt. I was just tired of opening and closing his cell a hundred times, so I decided to leave it open."

Keeping his gun trained on Tony, Howard stealthily made his way to the back of the office. Tony lifted his hands.

"Would you put that thing away?" Melvin repeated.

Howard ignored him until he had the cell door firmly closed and locked. Releasing the hammer on his pistol, he returned it to his gun belt. "Seems a mite careless to leave his door open like that, Sheriff."

Shrugging, Melvin stood. "Suit yourself. Now that you're here, though, I'm gonna make a run over to the Commercial."

"You find out something new?"

"Nope. Just snoopin'. I'll be back directly." Grabbing his hat, he strode through the door.

❧

Essie stepped into the sheriff's office, then stopped cold at seeing Deputy Howard alone with Tony. Her hands grew clammy. For the past two days, she'd wrestled with herself about whether or not to tell Tony about Howard's threats and the reason behind them. But that was a discussion she preferred to have in private. Something sorely lacking under the present circumstances.

She'd debated telling her father or even Uncle Melvin but found that for the first time in a long, long while, it wasn't either of them she wanted to share her troubles with. Instead, she wanted to go to another man. Her man.

She smiled at him through her worries and he rose to his feet. Circles shadowed his eyes and some color had faded from his sun-washed skin.

"I've brought you a little something to eat," she said.

Howard stepped around his desk. "Why, thank you, Essie. I appreciate that."

She stiffened. "I was talking to Mr. Morgan."

Hitching up his trousers, Howard sauntered over to her. "Well, I don't reckon he's hungry right now. Them women from yer bicycle club have been making sure he's the best-fed fella in all of Navarro County. Me, on the other hand, I've not had me so much as a bite to eat since noon." He stepped into her space. "You got something fer me, Essie?"

"My name is Miss Spreckelmeyer."

He lifted the corner of the napkin covering her basket. She swatted his hand.

"Easy, now. I was only taking a peek." He lowered his voice to a level Tony wouldn't be able to hear. "But I don't mind waiting, Essie. It is Tuesday, after all, and if'n you wanna give me a peek of what you got later on tonight, well, that's just fine by me."

"Step aside," she said.

"Not just yet, sweetheart." He grasped the napkin and whipped it off. "I can't let you take that into his cell without making sure of its contents. Wouldn't want you to slip our prisoner a weapon or nothin'." He rifled through the basket, then picked up a peach and took a bite out of it. "Ummm. That tastes mighty sweet. You sure you wanna waste all your sweet stuff on him?"

She slipped out from between Howard and the wall, then walked over to her uncle's desk and snatched up the keys.

Howard followed and grabbed her wrist. "I'm not sure you should be goin' in there. The prisoner might be dangerous and I'd hate for something to happen that would, um, compromise you in the town's eyes."

"I believe I'll take my chances," she said, shaking off his grip.

Howard smiled, removing the keys from her grasp. "That's what I'm countin' on, girl. That's what I'm countin' on."

Tony stood at the bars, frowning as he looked at the two of them.

"Get back," Howard said, approaching him.

Tony moved to the back of the cubicle. Howard opened the door, then locked it behind Essie when she stepped inside.

Instead of returning to his desk, though, Howard leaned a shoulder against the cell and ran his finger along one of the bars.

"Would you excuse us, please?" she said.

"Don't mind me, Miss Spreckelmeyer. I'm only doing my job and standing guard. Just carry on. You know, like you would if nobody was around to see."

His words hung in the air and she didn't know what to say or do. She couldn't tell Tony about Adam with the deputy standing there. And she couldn't not tell him, either.

"Maybe I should come back when Uncle Melvin's here," she said to Tony.

He took her hand and pulled her to the other side of the table. Putting his back to Howard, he leaned against the table, his broad form blocking her from the deputy's view.

"What is going on?"

"Long story," she whispered.

"You're gonna need to speak up," Howard said. "I can't hear ya. Unless, of course, you want me to join you." His chuckle made her skin crawl.

Tony studied her a moment. "Your uncle's at the Commercial Hotel," he said quietly. "Find out when he'll be here and come back then. And from now on, only come when he's here."

Her shoulders wilted. "But I don't want to go. I just got here."

"Quit your whispering," Howard said.

She heard the keys rattle in the lock. "Here," she said, handing Tony the basket of food. "I'll be back later."

He squeezed her hand. "I love you."

Howard threw open the door.

Essie hustled around the table. "Thank you, Deputy. I'm ready to leave now." She sailed through the door of the cell and out of the office before he had a chance to waylay her.

Essie waited until nearly midnight, then made her way to the sheriff's office, careful to stay under the cover of the wooded areas, even though it was a more circuitous route. She knew it was the deputy's turn to spend the night at the jailhouse. She also knew he'd be slipping out in hopes of meeting her behind her house.

With any luck at all, his absence would give her enough time to tell Tony everything. About Howard blackmailing her. About Adam. About her past.

Give me the strength, Lord. Give me the words.

The jailhouse was dark when she arrived.

"Who's there?" Tony said when she opened the door.

"It's me." She struck a match and lit the lantern on Melvin's desk.

Tony rose from his cot, his hair tousled. "What are you doing here?"

"We need to talk."

"Has something happened?"

"Howard's blackmailing me." She grabbed the keys to the cell.

"No," Tony said. "Don't open the door. If someone were to come in, I don't want them to think you're trying to bust me outta here or, worse, that we were doing something that would compromise your reputation. Just leave those where they are and we'll talk through the bars."

She returned the keys to Melvin's desk.

Tony held out his hand. "Come here."

Running to the cell, she slipped her hands into his. The bars separated their bodies but not their hearts. Not their souls.

"I miss you," he said.

"Me too." She leaned against the door. "I don't like being barricaded from you. I want to be in there with you or you to be out here with me."

He brought her hands to his lips. "You better tell me what's going on. I expect Howard to be back any minute and I don't want you here when he arrives."

She nodded. "While Howard was in Austin a couple of weeks ago, he ran into a man who used to work for Sullivan Oil." She stopped, unsure of what to say next.

"Who was he?"

She moistened her lips. "Just a man. A man who, um, makes a habit of going from town to town and preying upon women who can't see that his charm has but one goal. A very unsavory goal."

Tony nodded. "I understand. What has that to do with Howard?"

"Well, this man told Howard some things—private things—about me . . . and him."

"What do you mean?" Tony asked, frowning.

Her heart tripped. *Help me, Lord.* But no words came. Only incredible remorse and shame and fear. Before she could summon up a gentle way to say what needed to be said, his jaw slackened and his eyes widened.

"What are you saying, Essie?" he whispered.

She swallowed. "I'm saying that this man seduced me and told Howard about it, and Howard is using that to blackmail me."

Tony's hands relaxed their hold, but he didn't completely let loose of her. "What do you mean by 'seduced' you?"

Moisture rushed to her eyes. "I mean that he ruined me."

"By force?" he asked.

She slowly shook her head.

He let go of her and stumbled back. "You—you've been with another man?"

"Once. It was a long time ago. He means nothing to me. I was foolish—"

Tony turned his back, braced his hands on the table and hung his head.

"I'm sorry, Tony. I, he, it was . . ."

Tony gripped the edge of the table, his knuckles turning white. "Why didn't you tell me?"

She didn't know what to say. Explaining there had never been an opportune time sounded hollow even to her ears. "I should have."

"You're right, you should have." His voice was hoarse.

Oh, don't cry, Tony. Please don't cry.

"Tony—"

"Go away."

"Please. I tried to tell you. Not once, but twice. Yet each time—"

He whirled around. "You should have tried harder. Insisted, in fact—*before* I put that ring on your finger." He pointed toward the west. "You gave that man something you can never give again, Essie. Something that rightfully belonged to me. Why is it that every important thing that belongs to me—my inheritance, my father's approval, my woman's virtue—is given to someone else?"

"Tony, I—"

"Get out!" he shouted. "Get out now!"

Tears flooded her eyes. "Just like that? You don't even want to give me a chance to explain what—"

"There is nothing you can say, Essie, to change the fact that you will come to our marriage bed soiled."

She sucked in her breath. "Oh yes, there is." She removed his grandmother's ring from her finger and held it out to him. "If there is no marriage bed, I can't very well come to it 'soiled,' now, can I?"

He slapped the ring, knocking it from her grasp and onto the floor somewhere. Though his hand had barely grazed her fingers, the sting of his rejection went much deeper.

She longed to explain, to make amends, but his eyes were shuttered and a barrier much more formidable than a few steel bars now stood between them.

Fortifying herself with calm resolve, she picked up the lantern and returned it to her uncle's desk. She could feel Tony's gaze boring into her, but she resisted looking at him. She blew out the flame, plunging the room into darkness. After a bit of fumbling, she found the door.

"Good-bye, Tony," she whispered. "I'm sorry." Then she clicked the door shut behind her.

chapter THIRTY

ESSIE WENT straight from the jail to Uncle Melvin's house, staying well away from the streets east of Beaton. Tony might think her loose, but she wasn't. And she may have to accept his condemnation, but she needn't put up with Howard's perfidy in the meanwhile.

She knocked and didn't have to stand on the Dunns' front porch for very long before Melvin swung open the door. "Essie! What's happened?"

"I need to talk to you."

"It's the middle of the night."

"Your deputy is blackmailing me and has asked for sexual favors in exchange for his silence."

His face registered shock. "He *what*?!"

"May I come in now?"

He widened the door.

"Mel?" Aunt Verdie said, her voice filtering down from upstairs somewhere.

"It's business, Verdie," he hollered. "Go back to sleep."

Essie followed him to the kitchen. A room she'd spent many hours in as a child, a haven that held memories of laughter and love.

Lighting a lantern, he looked up and saw her tear-streaked face. He sucked in his breath, anger flushing his face. "I'll kill him. I'll kill him with my own hands. Sit down, baby, while I get Verdie to come down here with you."

She touched his arm, stopping him. "Please. Can we just talk for a minute?"

"He's hurt you and he's gonna pay. There's nothing to talk about."

"I've been able to hold him at bay. Nothing's happened . . . yet."

"He hasn't touched you? Hurt you?"

"No."

"Then why are you crying? Why are you here at one in the morning?"

"I'm here at one in the morning because the deputy said he would be waiting for me behind the house tonight and I was afraid to go home. I was crying because I went to the jailhouse and told Tony what was happening. Which then led to me telling him about Adam. Tony, he, he—" The tears came again.

Melvin reached for her, enfolding her in his embrace. "Oh, honey."

"He doesn't want me anymore. He told me to get out of his sight."

She couldn't believe this was happening again. *Why, Lord? Why? After everything I've been through. After accepting my singleness and living in it joyfully. Why would you dangle Tony in front of me only to snatch him away? Haven't I been tested enough?*

After a few minutes, Melvin released her, built a fire in the stove, then put a pot on to boil. She laid her arms on the table and rested her head within them.

Moments later, Melvin put a handkerchief in her hand and joined her at the table.

"Start at the beginning," he said. "Tell me everything."

After seeing Essie safely to her house and checking the grounds surrounding it, Melvin headed to his office. All was dark and quiet when he arrived. He lit the lantern, hoping to wake his prisoner from a sound sleep. But Morgan sat on the edge of his cot, elbows propped on his knees, his head in his hands.

Just the sight of him caused Melvin's anger to rise all over again. Unlocking the cell door, he flung it open. Tony raised his head, the splotches on his face giving evidence to the young man's devastation. But Melvin hardened his heart. Tony wasn't the only one devastated this night.

"You've got some kinda nerve," Melvin said. "Sitting in here accused of murder like a common criminal, yet passing judgment on one of the sweetest angels God ever placed on this earth. And did that angel pass judgment on you when I hauled your lousy backside to this jail? No. No, she did not. That gal never doubted you for a minute. And how do you repay her?" Melvin took a step inside the cell. "By throwing her love right back in her face because she made a mistake."

"A mistake?" Tony asked, incredulous. "Do you know what she did?"

"I know all about it."

"And you call that a *mistake*?"

"Yes, I do."

"Well, I'd call it a lot worse than that."

"Is that so?" Melvin narrowed his eyes. "Well, sir, let me ask you a thing or two: Are you without sin? Can you throw the first stone?"

Tony didn't answer.

"I didn't think so."

A tick in Tony's jaw pulsed. "And that's supposed to make everything all right? Because I'm human and haven't led a sin-free life?"

He jumped to his feet. "She was mine, Melvin. *Mine.* And she gave that no-account something that belonged to me and nobody else. She had no right!"

"She had every right. I'm not defending what she did. I'm not saying it was honorable, but it was her gift to give and she gave it. Are you so puffed up with yourself that you can't come down off that high horse and forgive her?"

Tony scrambled around the table.

Melvin drew his gun. "I wouldn't."

Tony froze. The two stood facing each other, both breathing hard.

"I'm gonna put away my gun," Melvin said, releasing the hammer, the sound loud in the quiet room, "but while I got your attention, let me remind you of something. Everything you have belongs to God Almighty. Your inheritance. Your freedom. Your family. Your woman. Your very life. So quit whining about losing what 'rightfully belongs to you,' because the truth of it is, ain't none of it belongs to you. It belongs to Him. And the sooner you realize it, the sooner you'll quit wallering around in this sorry state you're in and start being thankful for whatever blessings He's decided to bestow on you." He shook his head. "And one of those blessings, son, is a sweet little gal by the name of Esther Spreckelmeyer. Heaven knows you don't deserve her, but for whatever reason, you got her. And you might wanna think long and hard before you go throwin' my baby out with the bathwater."

The door to the office opened.

Howard entered, paused, then closed the door behind him. "Sheriff. This is a surprise. What are you doin' here? Is everything all right?"

Melvin unbuckled his gun belt and set it on Tony's table, gun and all.

Howard frowned. "What're ya doing? Morgan can reach those from there."

Melvin walked toward Howard, rolling up his sleeves. "Give me your gun, Billy John. And your badge."

"What?"

"You heard me. Let's have 'em."

"What are you talking about?"

"I'm talking about the fact that you're fired and I want your gun and badge before I beat the tar outta you for threatening one of the finest citizens of this town."

Howard chuckled. "Come on, Melvin. Quit foolin'."

"Do I look like I'm foolin' to you, Billy John?" Melvin stopped in front of him.

Howard glanced at Tony. "Listen, I don't know what lies Morgan's been feedin' you, but I haven't threatened anybody."

Melvin swiped Howard's gun from its holster, cocked it and pressed it against the deputy's chest. "Give me your badge."

"You do this, Dunn, and I'll tell my grandfather. You sure you want to cross the secretary of this fine state? You sure you want me to tell him how you risk the safety of this town—our entire county— by favorin' murderers?"

Nudging Howard's jacket aside with the gun's nozzle, Melvin raised his other hand and ripped the star off the deputy's shirt. "You tell your grandpa anything you like. Now, take off your gun belt."

Howard hesitated, then unbuckled his belt and let it drop to the floor.

Melvin stepped back, opened the pistol's cylinder and emptied it.

"You even gonna tell me who I supposedly threatened?" Howard asked.

Melvin set the empty weapon on his desk. "Yes, sir. I'm firing you because you had the audacity to threaten a woman in my town. But this," he said, swinging his fist around and planting it deep into Howard's gut, "is for making the mistake of threatening my niece."

Howard was younger and prided himself on being fast with his fists, but Melvin hadn't been sheriff for thirty years without learning a thing or two about how to handle himself in a fight.

The boy didn't have a prayer. Melvin's size, strength, and experience overpowered him in no time. Howard shielded his face and head with his arms, then curled up against the wall.

"That's enough, Melvin," Dunn heard someone say. He felt himself being pulled away.

"No more, Sheriff," the voice said. "No more."

Winded, Melvin looked over to find Tony holding him back.

"No more," Tony repeated.

Melvin nodded, his own body immediately cataloging all the places Billy John's fist had connected with during the scuffle. His eye, his jaw, his shoulder, his ribs.

Tony knelt beside Billy John. "Howard? You okay?"

"Leave me alone," he slurred, pushing Tony away and bringing himself to his feet. He sneered at Melvin through eyes beginning to swell shut. "You've made a big mistake, Dunn. A big mistake."

"Get outta my town, Billy John," Melvin said.

"I'll leave when I'm good and ready to leave. Maybe that's now. Maybe it ain't. But you can't kick me out. I haven't broken any law." He glanced briefly at Tony. "But then, you don't care about that, do you, Sheriff? You only care about protectin' the criminals and running off the upstanding citizens, don't ya?" Without waiting for an answer, he stumbled out the door.

⌘

Sunlight poured through the jailhouse window. A breeze that carried a hint of lilac on it rustled the papers on Tony's table. Rubbing his forehead, he tried to concentrate on his work, but his grandmother's ring—Essie's ring—kept distracting him.

He'd found it in the corner of his cell and had set it on his desk. Picking it up for the hundredth time, he discovered he enjoyed touching it simply because she'd touched it, too.

Melvin's words kept ringing in his head, but he had a hard time accepting them. Because if what Melvin said was true, then Tony had nothing and God had everything.

And there were some things Tony wanted. He wanted to be proven innocent and freed from jail. He wanted his inheritance. He wanted his father to be proud of him. He wanted his wife to be pure. No, he wanted *Essie* to be pure.

But he would never have his father's approval and he would never be Essie's first. He might never win his freedom and, thus, never be able to enjoy his inheritance.

So he was back where he started. With him having nothing and God having everything.

Don't you have enough already, Lord? Do you have to have what belongs to me, too?

But deep down he knew no matter what he did or didn't do, he had no control over any of it. But God did. And the only viable solution was to give it up to Him.

And why not? How much worse could it get? He swallowed, immediately realizing it could get a whole lot worse. He could lose Essie for good. Lose his life for good.

But even if he didn't get her back, or if he hanged for the murder of his brother, he would at least have the comfort of knowing he'd left the decision-making up to God and not to himself.

Blowing out a breath, he silently relinquished his control and laid it at Christ's feet. And in doing so, realized he might not ever have made his earthly father proud, but perhaps he had his heavenly Father.

The knot he'd been carrying around in his chest eased some. A shadow crossed the door to the sheriff's office. He glanced up.

"Russ!" he exclaimed, jumping to his feet. "Walker!"

With his cell wide open, it was hard to stay put, but he did, allowing Dunn to greet the men first.

"Sheriff," Tony said, "this is one of Morgan Oil's finest drillers, Russ O'Berry, and my family's attorney, Nathaniel Walker."

Dunn shook the men's hands. "I'll need you to leave your weapons out here, fellas."

Tony lifted his brows but said nothing. Men had been coming and going for days now without being relieved of weapons. Shoot, Dunn had even let Tony start shaving with a razor blade every morning.

Still, he could understand the sheriff's caution. Not only were these fellas strangers, but Russ was a virtual giant. With his driller's hat and boots, shoulders like an ox, and a chest like a locomotive, he'd give anyone pause.

Tony smiled. He hadn't realized how much he'd missed Russ until just this moment.

Russ handed over a pistol and a bullwhip. Walker wasn't carrying.

"Won't you come into my parlor?" Tony asked, indicating the two ladder-back chairs in front of his table.

Russ chuckled, extending a hand. "Here I been picturing you in some dark, dank cell and look at ya. Even jail cain't keep you down. How are ya?"

Tony clasped his best friend's hand and slapped him on the shoulder. "Well, I've been better, but I'm mighty glad to see you." He turned to Walker. "Good of you to come, Nathaniel."

"You shaved your moustache."

"I did."

"Yes, well." He pushed his spectacles farther up on his nose. "I'm sorry it took me so long to get here, but there were a lot of papers to draft and prepare."

"I understand."

The three of them settled.

Tony looked at Russ. "How are Iva and the kids?"

341

"Iva's sassy as ever and the kids are missin' their 'Unk Tony.'"

"Well, don't you leave town without letting me give you some sarsaparilla sticks for 'em. I'll send out for some today."

"They'll love that."

Tony smiled. "How are the fields?"

"They're pretty much running themselves these days." He proceeded to give Tony a rundown on the wells in Beaumont—which were producing, which were drying up, and which were still being drilled. Throughout the conversation, Walker removed some papers from his satchel, fidgeted and cleared his throat.

Finally Tony turned to him. "You have something there for me?"

"Yes, I do." He handed Tony the papers. "You need to sign in all the places I've indicated."

Tony nodded. "I'll read them today and have 'em ready for you in the morning."

Walker hesitated. "Well, I was hoping to get them back right away."

"Oh?"

"Yes, I, um, need to return to Beaumont."

Tony thumbed through the documents. "I'd like to oblige you, Nathaniel, but it'll take a while for me to sort through these. Even if I could finish them by tonight, it'd be after the evening train's already left."

"They're just standard papers, Tony, transferring everything from Darius's name to yours."

"I understand. I'd still like to read them, though, before signing."

"I see. Well," he said, clearly affronted. "I guess I'll have no choice but to come by first thing in the morning, then."

Tony nodded. "I appreciate your understanding, sir. Meanwhile, Finch is staying at the Commercial. I know he'd love to see you."

"Tony Bryant Morgan!" Mrs. Lockhart marched into the office, slamming her cane down with each step. "Just what in the Sam Hill is going on?"

She was wearing her bloomers. The really poofy ones. And charging into the jailhouse like a schooner in full sail.

The men quickly rose to their feet.

She pulled up short and gave Russ the once-over. "Well, now. Aren't you the kind of fellow who could carry his bride out of a fire? You married?"

"Yes, ma'am," he said, casting Tony a sideways glance.

She sighed. "Well, of course you are."

"Mrs. Lockhart, may I present my friend Mr. O'Berry, and my attorney, Mr. Walker."

She waved her cane at Tony. "Don't you try to distract me, young man. I want to know where Essie's diamond ring is."

"I'm a bit occupied right now," he answered. "Perhaps you could come back a little later?"

"It's all right, Tony," Russ said. "We don't mind. Besides, we'd like to know about this diamond ring, too. Wouldn't we, Walker?"

Walker blinked. Tony groaned.

Russ placed a hand on the back of his chair and held his other out to Mrs. Lockhart. "Please, ma'am?"

Accepting his hand, she settled herself in the chair as if it were a throne. "Now," she said. "Where's her ring?"

"Right here on my desk."

"Don't you know whether you're on your head or your heels? It's supposed to be on her finger. Why isn't it?"

"Mrs. Lockhart—"

She slammed the end of her cane on the floor. "Do not patronize me, sir. In *Love's Chain Broken*, you will remember Mr. Tittle and Miss Vermilyea treated the elderly Mrs. Coughenburger with disdain, yet if they had just taken but a moment to heed her words, much of their pain and misery would have been avoided. Tell me you remember that part?"

Tony felt his face heat. "Yes, ma'am. I remember."

Russ's eyebrows shot up to his hairline.

"Then you will also recall that in *Her Only Sin*, Miss Klingenfluss was gravely misunderstood?"

"Yes, ma'am."

"And Mr. Longanecker had to do a great deal of groveling to get back in her good graces?"

"Yes, ma'am."

She folded her hands on top of her cane. "So what are you going to do about that, then?"

Russ, Walker, and the sheriff all stared at him.

He cleared his throat. "Grovel?"

She smiled. "I think that would be the best course of action."

Tony nodded. He'd already come to terms with the Lord and had planned on coming to terms with Essie—even before Mrs. Lockhart arrived. He still loved his fiancée and wanted his ring back on her finger. Wanted her as his wife. The question was, did she still want him?

chapter **THIRTY-ONE**

FIVE DAYS had passed since the Velocipede Club last convened. In the meanwhile, Essie's members had taken quite a shine to sleuthing. No need for Mr. Holmes or Dr. Watson in this town—not when they had the ladies of the Corsicana Velocipede Club. But now the novelty had worn off a bit, and the women found themselves hitting one dead end after another.

Graying clouds blocked out the morning sunlight but produced a cooling breeze through the clubhouse's high windows. Members filed in, their voices quiet, their expressions gloomy. Shirley called the meeting to order and one by one the women stood and reported what they'd discovered about Darius—or rather, what they *hadn't* discovered.

Essie smoothed her glove over each of her fingers. Since she'd given Tony his ring back, she'd begun to wear her gloves again, thinking it would keep her from noticing her bare left hand. But it hadn't. She missed his ring. And she missed him.

All the women knew she and Tony had had a "tiff," as they called it, but none knew the reason. Most assumed it was due to his being in jail, and they were none too happy with her for not standing by his side. Little did they know it was Tony who'd renounced her, not the other way around.

She was sorry she'd given the ring back, though. If she'd realized it would create such turmoil and division in the club, she wouldn't have. Her decision to break their engagement was in no way a reflection of her belief in his innocence.

So she'd minimized their estrangement. Told the ladies it was her way of teaching him a lesson. They shook their heads and explained there were plenty of ways to do that without removing the ring, but now that the deed was done, they advised she not take it back too quickly, else all would be for naught.

So when Tony sent her a message via Harley Vandervoort requesting she come by at her earliest convenience, she'd prevaricated. Not just because the ladies expected her to, but because she wasn't quite ready to face him again.

"Mr. Tony wants to see ya," Harley'd said as he waltzed into her office at the Velocipede Club.

"He does?" she'd asked, putting down her pen.

"Yep. Said fer you to come by soon as ya could."

She'd glanced at the door, resisting the urge to leap to her feet and run all the way to the jailhouse. But what would she do when she arrived? Nothing had changed and they couldn't say what needed to be said with anyone else listening in.

Howard wouldn't be there, of course, not since Uncle Melvin had dismissed him, though she'd heard he was still in town. And he'd wasted no time in announcing to any who would listen that she'd had an affair with Adam.

She hoped no one would believe him—that they'd attribute his tales to sour grapes over losing his job. But with all the new people in town, not everyone knew her. So he might be able to persuade some.

Still, she couldn't discuss the matter with Tony. Not under the current circumstances, for even her uncle's presence would embarrass her. And with Howard spreading rumors, she dare not sneak out at night to rendezvous at the jailhouse.

Besides, it was a little irksome to be summoned in such a high-handed manner. As if Tony did, in fact, expect her to drop everything the moment he crooked his finger.

She'd picked her pen back up. "I'm not sure I can go, Harley. I have an awful lot of work to do."

His eyes widened. "But he has somethin' powerful important to tell ya. He ain't gonna like it if'n you don't come."

"Tell him to write it down, then."

That had been two days ago. He'd sent Harley around three more times, but with nothing more than further curt invitations. She'd politely, but firmly, declined.

"He's gettin' kinda testy about all this, Miss Essie," Harley'd argued. "He says I weren't to leave unless I had ya in tow."

"In tow?" she asked, stiffening. "He expects you to *tow* me down there? Were those his exact words?"

Harley started backing up out of her office. "Don't worry none. I ain't gonna make ya do nothing you don't wanna."

"You most certainly aren't. And let me give you a little advice, young man. If you ever decide to woo a lady, you do it with gentle persuasion. You do *not* demand she do this or that, and you definitely don't have her towed somewhere."

"What's pur-sway-shin?"

"When you try to make someone change their mind about something."

"Now, how's Mr. Tony supposed to do that when ya won't even talk to him?"

She blinked. "Well, I don't know. With a kind note? Maybe something poetic? Seems to me he could figure it out, considering all those silly romance novels he reads."

She sighed. She should have known better than to lose her patience. Harley was far from discreet, so every person in town knew she'd not only refused his requests, but that, according to him, she'd demanded romance.

It wasn't romance she wanted, however, but divine intervention. So she hadn't quit praying. Or quit loving him. Or quit trying to help find the real murderer.

"We've come full circle, then," Shirley said to the group. "We're no closer now than we were on Sunday."

Essie reined in her thoughts and looked around the room, but no one had observed her inattention. Mrs. Bogart worked her fan. Young Miss Davis picked at a snag in her skirt. Mrs. Owen shooed a fly.

"Perhaps we're taking too much for granted," Anna Morgan said. Her mother had not returned with her to Corsicana but had stayed behind in Beaumont, too distraught to venture out again. So Anna had taken up residence with Mrs. Lockhart.

"What do you mean?" Shirley asked.

"I don't know, really," she said, sighing. "What do you think, Mrs. Lockhart? Has there ever been a horrific state of affairs in one of your books where things were not as they seemed?"

Essie closed her eyes, trying to suppress her exasperation. They were not going to find the man who murdered Darius Morgan by examining romance novels.

"Well," Mrs. Lockhart said, tapping her cane, "in *From Out of the Gloom*, everyone thought Mr. Bumpus had been strangled, when, in fact, he'd been poisoned. But the killer made it look like strangulation to confuse the authorities."

Essie gripped her hands together and kept her mouth firmly closed, reminding herself it was Mrs. Lockhart who had comforted her in her hour of need. Mrs. Lockhart who'd taken in Anna. Mrs. Lockhart who'd made sure meals were delivered to Tony on a regular basis. Essie would, therefore, be still and let the dear woman refer to as many books as she wanted to.

"Actually," Mrs. McCabe said, "it's interesting you should bring that up. When my husband laid Mr. Morgan out to rest, he mentioned to the doctor that the deceased's stomach was inflamed and his skin rather yellow."

Shirley frowned and turned to the doctor's wife. "Is that normal for someone who's been stabbed, Mrs. Gulick?"

"Indeed, it isn't."

"What was Dr. Gulick's response to your husband's remark, Mrs. McCabe?"

"Well," she said, "he sort of laughed and jokingly said perhaps Mr. Morgan had been poisoned with arsenic. I thought nothing of it at the time, because it was so clearly obvious that Mr. Morgan had been stabbed. I mean, blood was everywhere."

Moaning, Mrs. Bogart turned white and swooned. The ladies sitting next to her exclaimed and jumped up, one supporting the elderly woman's head, another putting her fan to vigorous use and yet another patting the woman's cheek.

"Oh dear," Shirley said. "Seems our conversation has upset Mrs. Bogart's sensibilities. Does anyone have smelling salts?"

The next few minutes were spent reviving Mrs. Bogart, while Essie's heart began to hammer. Even though the basis for Mrs. Lockhart's suggestion was a romance novel, Essie could not dismiss it out of hand. Not after hearing the comments of the doctor and coroner.

"For argument's sake," Shirley said, continuing even though Mrs. Bogart had not yet fully recovered, "let's pretend Mr. Morgan's death was due to poisoning. Well, if that were the case, why in the world would the killer go to the trouble of stabbing him?"

"Because he needed to implicate Tony," Essie said, eagerness stirring inside her. "And that meant using his knife and leaving it where the sheriff would be sure to find it."

Mrs. Zimpelman shook her head. "Then why not just stab Mr. Morgan to death and leave the poison out of it?"

Mrs. Bogart fainted again. Miss Davis alternately fanned the elderly woman and wiped her brow with a handkerchief.

"Perhaps the killer is of small stature," suggested Mrs. Pickens, her bug eyes overwhelming her reedlike face. "Mr. Morgan was a very large man and, I would imagine, rather hard to subdue in a fight."

"But doesn't it take a while to poison someone?" Shirley asked.

"Not necessarily," said Mrs. Gulick. "There was that woman over in Walker County who put arsenic in her husband's eggs. He died within the hour."

Excitement began to buzz throughout the room.

Shirley rapped the gavel on the lectern. "Mrs. Pickens? Who's purchased arsenic at the Flour, Feed and Liquor Store lately?"

"Well, heavens to Betsy, any number of people. Mr. Flouty bought some rat poison. Mr. Pennington, some paint. Deputy Howard, some paste." She lifted her bug-eyed gaze to the rafters as if visualizing the patrons who visited her mercantile. "The Buntings are putting up new wallpaper."

Shirley gasped.

"Oh dear," she said, wringing her hands. "I didn't mean to—"

Shirley held up her hand. "It's all right, ma'am. I'm quite sure my parents didn't poison Mr. Morgan with their wallpaper." A smattering of giggles flitted throughout the room. "Still, it is best to be thorough with your recollections. Please continue."

Mrs. Pickens listed at least a half dozen more names, none of whom were at all likely to have murdered Darius.

"We need to ask the Crooks," said Mrs. Vandervoort. "Perhaps someone bought something from the Slap Out."

Mrs. Pickens stiffened. "I'm sure if there was arsenic to be had, the person in need would have come to the Flour, Feed and Liquor Store. As a matter of fact, even that Mr. Morgan bought soap and arsenic to kill the bedbugs in his mattress."

Essie's lips parted. Silence blanketed the room.

"What?" Mrs. Pickens asked, looking from one woman to the other, then her eyes all but popped right out of her head. "Good heavens, I don't mean *our* Mr. Morgan. I meant the other one."

"The dead one?" Shirley asked, confused.

"No, no. The other one. The Frenchified one."

"Finch?" Anna asked. "Finch Morgan?"

"Yes, I believe that's his name."

Anna shook her head. "It wouldn't have been him. He was Darius's constant companion. They were more like brothers than cousins. He would never have wanted Tony to inherit."

"What about Deputy Howard?" Aunt Verdie asked.

"An unpleasant man, for certain," Shirley said, "but what possible motive could he have?"

"It is no secret he's been sweet on Essie," Mrs. Lockhart said. "Maybe he implicated Tony to get rid of his competition?"

The ladies murmured to one another.

Essie cleared her throat. "Mr. Howard knew full well he had no chance with me even had Tony never stepped foot in our town."

"Well," Shirley said, "let's meet again tomorrow morning to discuss this further. In the meanwhile, we will ask Mrs. Pickens to check with Mr. Pickens so we can be sure we haven't overlooked anyone. And Mrs. Vandervoort? If you would visit the Slap Out and see what you can find out from the Crooks, we'd be most appreciative." She struck the lectern with her gavel. "Meeting adjourned."

∞

Essie opened the door to find Harley on her front porch. His boots were scuffed, one of his stockings had slid all the way down, and dirt-encrusted knees peeked out from beneath his short pants.

"This is fer you, from Mr. Tony," he said, handing her a note card, now smudged with dirty fingerprints.

"Tony wrote this?"

"Yep. And he made me cross my heart, hope to die, that I'd not let anybody read it but you."

"I see." She slid her finger under the wax seal, breaking it open, then unfolded the piece of paper.

Dearest Essie,

In the tale of *Lord Birmingham's Daughter,*
Miss Dye thought her beau didn't want her.
He exclaimed, "That's not so!"
She said, "Tallyho,"
Then came back and he did like he oughter.

Yours, ABM

She bit her lip but was unable to suppress her smile.

"Uh-oh," Harley said. "Yer not gonna give in to him, are ya?"

She tilted her head. "I thought you wanted me to. Don't you like Mr. Tony?"

"Oh yes, ma'am. I like him plenty. But I just figured out that if you go see him, he'll quit payin' me two pennies to bring you messages, and I've made ten cents in three days. Besides, my ma said you wouldn't give in easy. She says the fellers in Miz Lockhart's books like stuff better when they hafta work fer it."

"Good heavens." She widened the door. "Come on in and wash your hands. I've some warm cookies on the cooling tray."

"Yes, ma'am!"

He ran to the kitchen, but she slipped into Papa's study, sat down at his desk and took up his pen.

Dearest Tony,

I enjoyed your limerick very much. However, I have it on good authority that Lord Birmingham's daughter never appeared too eager. Since you hold this tome in such high esteem, I will maintain my distance but look forward to future correspondence.

ES

～

"You needn't stay in Corsicana any longer, Russ," Tony said a few days later, leaning his arms on the table. "Spreckelmeyer says it looks like he's going to have to take me up to Fort Smith for a trial sometime next week and we should be able to clear everything up then."

"Fort Smith?" Russ replied, spinning his chair around and straddling it. "Isn't that where Hanging Judge Parker presides?"

Tony hesitated. "You know, I think it is. But Melvin didn't mention it."

"Well, that's not good. Darius is still dead. He was killed with your knife. You're the only one with a motive. So how exactly do ya figure this judge—or any judge, for that matter—will let ya go free?"

"Because I didn't do it."

"Sure looks like ya did, though."

Tony rubbed his eyes. "There's talk now that Darius was poisoned and the knife was just a decoy."

"Yeah, I heard that. I also heard it weren't true. Heard instead, the sheriff made the whole poison thing up on account of his niece." He shook his head. "That Howard fella's done nothing but harp about how Dunn treats ya more like a guest in here than a prisoner, and there's plenty of roughs who are willing to listen to him."

Tony looked around his cell—the pillows and quilts on his cot, his shaving implements on a stool, the table covered with books and papers, a basket of cookies from the women, the cell door wide open. The only things lacking were curtains for the barred window and a rug for his feet.

"What are you suggesting?"

"I dunno, Tony. I just got an uneasy feelin', is all. There's a trace o' unrest in town. And Finch ain't helpin' any, either, what with the way he's making Darius out to be a candidate for sainthood."

Tony sighed. "That can't surprise you."

Heavy footfalls clumping up the stairs outside drew Tony's attention. An oilman with skin leathered from the sun stepped into the jailhouse, the slush from his boots leaving imprints. He was one of the men brought up from Beaumont to begin work on the new piece of land Darius had bought. Crossing the room, the man glanced at the sheriff, looked Tony up and down, then turned to Russ.

"The boss is lookin' fer ya."

"Finch?" Russ asked.

"Yep. And he ain't gonna be none too pleased to find out yer in here with Mr. Darius's killer."

Russ rose slowly to his feet. "Finch isn't my boss or yours. Mr. Morgan here is. And he's no murderer. Once he's had a trial, that'll be clear enough."

"That ain't the way we see it." He lifted his hand to keep Russ from speaking. "Now, we ain't holdin' it against ya, Russ. Not with you and Tony goin' back as fer as you do. But ever'body knows he done it."

The sheriff rounded his desk, stepping between the oilman and the cell. "You've said your piece. Best move on outta here now."

The man pushed a plug of tobacco from one cheek to the other with his tongue. "The boys don't like it, Sheriff. Man like him killing his own blood. He don't deserve to live, much less be treated like some highfalutin guest." He spit, missing the spittoon by a good foot. "Don't imagine they're gonna put up with it fer much longer."

"They're gonna put up with it until the law takes its due course, and you can tell 'em I said so."

He took Melvin's measure, then spit again. "Whatever you say." Moving his gaze past the sheriff's shoulder, he locked eyes with Russ. "You comin'?"

"I'll be there in a minute."

Russ and Melvin didn't move until the oilman retraced his steps and was well out of sight.

Melvin let out his breath.

"How long's that been going on?" Tony asked.

"Been like that since I arrived in town and is only gettin' worse." Russ turned to face him. "So if it's all the same to you, I'd like to stick around awhile. Keep my eye on things."

"What about the wells back in Beaumont? What about Iva?"

"Iva and the kids'll be fine. And don't you worry none about Morgan Oil. Archie's top-notch. He'll keep everything going back home."

∽

Dearest Essie,
 I dream of the girl in big hats.
 Who hunts frogs and snakes but not rats.
 Will she slide down the rail
 And visit the jail,
 And stay for a nice little chat?
       Forever yours, ABM

chapter THIRTY-TWO

ESSIE SAT with the other members of the Velocipede Club, content to let Shirley run the meeting. Being the banker's daughter had always given the young woman a place of distinction within town, but it wasn't until she married Jeremy that she had gained the confidence she displayed now.

Gone were the frilly ruffles and flounces and oversized bows. In their place were sensible and modest shirtwaists and skirts. Some of that, Essie knew, was due to the fact that Jeremy refused to take money from his father-in-law, so Shirley couldn't afford to dress as she had before. Yet Shirley had never been happier. And there was no denying she was still the prettiest girl in the county.

Essie glanced at Anna sitting beside her in her mourning attire. If there was ever anyone to rival Shirley's beauty, it would be Tony's sister. But she was so different from Shirley. Her brown hair and olive complexion were in stark contrast to Shirley's blond hair and pale, pale skin.

Anna looked at Essie and smiled. They'd spent quite a bit of time together this past week. Enough for Essie to recognize that the girl came alive as soon as Ewing appeared on Mrs. Lockhart's doorstep. It hadn't gone unnoticed in town, either, that he'd become a frequent visitor of the elderly woman now that the girl was staying there. Essie slipped her hand into Anna's and squeezed.

Perhaps the girl would one day become Essie's sister by marriage. That is, if Essie and Tony reconciled. And with the poems he'd sent, a kernel of hope had begun to stir within her.

Even if he was willing to forgive her indiscretions, however, they had the murder charge to face. What if the new judge pronounced Tony guilty?

Please, Lord. Even if he doesn't marry me, I don't want to see him condemned for something he didn't do. Please help us find the culprit, Lord. Please.

She drew her attention back to the meeting at hand.

"Do you have a report for us, Mrs. McCabe?" Shirley asked, nodding to the coroner's wife in the second row.

Mrs. McCabe stood. "Mrs. Gulick and I both checked again with our husbands and we are quite certain now that Mr. Morgan was poisoned. When he and our Tony Morgan got into fisticuffs, Dr. Gulick was called in to treat Darius Morgan's injuries."

"That's right," said Mrs. Gulick. "But my husband said he spent more time treating things that weren't the least bit related to the fight."

"Like what?" Shirley asked.

"All kinds of things," Mrs. Gulick answered. "The man complained of severe stomach cramps, burning pains in his hands and feet, dizzy spells, and irritating rashes. My husband didn't know what to think of it at first."

"But after he was killed," Mrs. McCabe said, "and my Percy brought up the yellow color of his skin and the swollen stomach, that's when they started to suspect poisoning."

Shirley frowned. "Then he died of arsenic poisoning?"

"No, no," Mrs. McCabe answered. "The stabbing is what killed him. But Dr. Gulick said that even if he hadn't been stabbed, he wouldn't have been much longer for this life."

A sudden outburst of conversation buzzed throughout the room.

"Do you suppose it was the same person who did both?" Mrs. Vandervoort asked over the noise, silencing the exchanges.

"I don't know," Mrs. McCabe answered.

The women once again began to discuss the possibilities amongst themselves.

Shirley hammered with her gavel. "Does the sheriff know about this?"

"He does."

Mrs. Blanchard stood. "I suggest we try to find out how the arsenic was administered. That may give us a clue as to who was doing the poisoning."

Aunt Verdie rose, her simply cut gown highlighting her exaggerated hourglass figure. "I had the same thought earlier this week. Melvin rarely discusses his work with me, especially when it concerns such unpleasantness. But now that Deputy Howard is no longer about, I was able to look through Melvin's desk at the jailhouse." She slipped her hand into the hidden pocket of her skirt and pulled out a small bound book. "I managed to find his notes."

A smattering of applause circulated.

"He made a list of the items he'd found in Mr. Morgan's hotel room. I tried to narrow it down to items that might have had arsenic in them. Unfortunately, I couldn't find a thing. No cup, no whiskey bottle, no food, no nothing." Aunt Verdie licked her finger and flipped through several pages. "Would you like me to read what all he found? The list is quite lengthy."

Shirley bit her lower lip. "Before you do that, let's consider the different ways arsenic can get into a person's body, other than swallowing it. Anyone have any ideas?"

"What if it gets on your skin?" asked Miss Davis. "I mean, could the murderer have put it in Mr. Morgan's shaving cream?"

"I'm not sure," said Shirley. "Do you know, Mrs. Gulick?"

She shook her head. "I'm afraid I don't. I know it can be inhaled, though."

Shirley turned back to Aunt Verdie. "Is there anything on the sheriff's list that could be inhaled?"

Aunt Verdie bent the sides of the book back, cracking the spine. "Well, let's see. There were cigarettes in the ashtray."

Shirley's expression lit up. "Couldn't someone have mixed arsenic with the tobacco?"

Essie and Anna exchanged a glance as several of the members murmured with excitement.

"No," Aunt Verdie said. "No, that isn't possible. Says here they were those new mechanically rolled cigarettes. There wouldn't be any way to get the poison inside those."

"Mechanically rolled?" Anna asked. "But Darius didn't ordinarily smoke pre-rolled cigarettes, at least not unless Finch was around to offer him one."

Squinting, Aunt Verdie held the book out at arm's length. "Well, Mel's notes say there was not only an ashtray, but a silver case full of 'em inside the pocket of a jacket that was slung across a chair." She looked up. "According to this, it was your brother's jacket."

"But I don't understand," Anna continued. "Are you certain there's nothing about a pouch of tobacco?"

Aunt Verdie flipped back and forth between some pages. "'Fraid not. It does say that Mrs. Morgan and Finch stayed by Mr. Darius's side throughout the doctor's exam, and both she and Finch stayed with Darius until he was resting peacefully—making them the last ones to see him alive."

"Excuse me," said Mrs. Zimpelman, the silversmith's wife. "Does it say what the cigarette case looked like?"

"Why, yes." Aunt Verdie ran her finger down the page, then stopped. "It says the case was: 'silver, engraved scrolls, crest with lion with ax in raised paw.'"

Mrs. Zimpelman gasped. "Why, that's the case I sold to Mr. Morgan—Mr. Finch Morgan—on the day of the bicycle race. I remember because we don't have very many cases, since very few people smoke mechanically rolled cigarettes. So when he came by our tent looking for one, I had to sort through several of our crates to find it."

"Why would Finch need another cigarette case when he already has one?" Anna asked. "And what was it doing in Darius's coat pocket?"

The women sat in silence, trying to decide if what they'd discovered had any significance at all.

"What if you rubbed the arsenic on the outside of the cigarette?" Mrs. Vandervoort asked. "You know, the part he puts in his mouth and inhales?"

"Mrs. Gulick?" Shirley asked.

"Well, I don't see why that wouldn't work," she said.

"Wouldn't he notice the powder?" Anna asked.

"Not necessarily."

"Is it possible," Shirley said, "that Mr. Finch Morgan poisoned Mr. Darius Morgan?"

"I can't imagine him doing such a thing," Anna said. "He and Tony have never seen eye to eye. Finch would never want Tony to inherit anything."

Disappointment assailed Essie, then she felt guilty about it. She harbored no ill will toward Finch Morgan. She simply wanted to find the real culprit.

"Wait a minute." Anna slowly straightened. "Now that I think on it, both of Finch's late wives died of gastric fever."

"Gastric fever?" Shirley asked. "Both of them?"

"Yes, and their sicknesses were very similar to what Darius had been experiencing these past couple of months—dizzy spells, headaches, yellow skin, a pain in their stomachs. That kind of thing."

"Well," Shirley said. "What do you think, Mrs. Gulick?"

"Sounds an awful lot like arsenic poisoning to me."

"But why?" Anna argued. "What possible reason could Finch have for wanting his wives or, more to the point, Darius dead? He and Darius were practically attached at the hip."

"I don't know," Shirley answered. "But I'd sure like to have a look at the cigarettes in that case. Is there any way you can get your hands on it, Mrs. Dunn?"

"Oh, heavens no. Melvin keeps everything like that locked up. He's already frantic about his notes being 'misplaced.' I haven't any idea how I'll get them back to him without him finding out I took them. Mr. Morgan—our Mr. Morgan—already knows I have them. He, of course, was there while I was searching Melvin's desk. He hasn't said a word, though."

"Nor will he," said Mrs. Lockhart. "Give the book to me. I'll tell the sheriff I picked it up by accident with a stack of novels I'd laid on his desk."

"Do you think he'll believe you?" Essie asked.

"What choice does he have?"

Shirley nodded. "All right, ladies. We're getting closer. I just know we are. Your assignment for today is to see if we can determine where Mr. Darius Morgan's pre-rolled cigarettes came from." She slammed the gavel onto the lectern. "Meeting adjourned."

∞

Dearest Essie,
    I love you with all of my heart,
    There are things I would like to impart.
    You mean so to me.
    I beg leniency,
    For acting a fool and an upstart.
    Please come back to me.
                Yours alone, ABM

∽

The brisk wind whipped the treetops and made steering Peg a challenge. But Essie persevered. She'd wanted to look her best the next time she saw Tony, but after reading the sweet limerick she had waiting for her upon her return from her meeting, she'd simply turned right around and remounted her bike.

It wasn't until she reached town that the clouds began to gather and the wind played havoc with her hair. Her navy skirt slapped against her legs. Her hat strained against its pins. Increasing her speed, she tucked her head down, hoping to reach the sheriff's office before the rain began. She'd just dismounted when a raindrop plopped onto her sleeve.

She rushed up the steps and across the threshold, then pulled up short.

Tony jumped to his feet. "Essie. You came."

She had an unobstructed view of him through the open cell door. My, but she'd forgotten how handsome he was. So tall. So broad. So much a man. His brown hair was tousled, his shirt wrinkled. Bluish shadows beneath his eyes pointed to his weariness and the strain he'd been under.

A pang of guilt rushed through her. She should have come sooner. She should have realized what a shock her revelation had been and extended him some latitude—particularly considering all he was going through.

He took a step from behind his table and tentatively opened his arms. Lifting her skirts, she ran to him. He caught her tight against him, holding her, kissing her, murmuring to her.

"You came," he whispered. "You came."

"I'm sorry," she said.

"Shhh," he replied, kissing her again.

He slowly let her down, so that her toes touched the floor, but he didn't release her. "Don't ever leave me again."

"I won't," she said. "I won't." And this time, she kissed him.

Uncle Melvin cleared his throat.

Good heavens. She hadn't even realized he was there. Hadn't so much as greeted him. She tried to pull back, but Tony wouldn't let her go.

"Would you excuse us, Sheriff?" he asked.

Uncle Melvin stiffened. "Now, just a—"

"Please, Uncle Melvin?" she asked, looking at him over her shoulder. "Please?"

Red filled his face. "Essie, I don't . . ." He searched her expression, then sighed and pointed a finger at Tony. "You will act with the utmost decorum?"

"Yes, sir."

"Essie?" he barked, turning his frown onto her.

"Of course."

After a slight hesitation, he shuffled over, closed the door to the cell, locked it and left.

Tony scooped her up, sat on his chair and settled her in his lap. Now that the initial rush was over, his next kiss was slow and, oh, so sweet.

He pulled the pins from her hat, removed it and set it on his desk. "I have missed you."

"I've missed you, too."

"I'm sorry I said those things."

"It all came as a shock to you. I completely understand."

"Forgive me?" he asked.

Nodding, she brushed his cheek with her palm. "Do you forgive me?"

He tunneled his fingers into her hair, holding her head firmly and bringing his eyes close to hers. "Yes. Yes, I do, Essie. It is forgotten and we will never speak of it again."

Moisture filled her eyes. "I'm so sorry."

"No, I'm sorry. I was in no position to throw stones."

She kissed him again, wrapping her arms around his neck. Desire poured through her. She squirmed.

Groaning, he pulled back. "Will you still marry me?"

"Yes."

Reaching across the table, he grabbed the diamond ring sitting on his papers. He slipped it onto her finger, then kissed it. "I don't ever want you to take that off again. Not ever."

"I won't."

When their kisses were no longer enough to satisfy her, she pulled away and stood. His eyes were dark, his breathing heavy. Every fiber in her body wanted to return to his arms.

"Where are you going?" he asked.

"If I don't put some distance between us, I'll have a hard time doing what I promised myself I'd never do again—at least, not until I'm officially wed."

"Then go get Ewing and let's get this thing done."

She widened her eyes. "And what would we tell our children when they asked where we got married?"

He smiled. "That they were conceived in the jailhouse?"

Her lips parted.

Chuckling, he grabbed another chair and pulled it next to his. "I'm jesting. Sort of. Now come sit down."

"Is it safe?"

"I'm not sure," he replied.

She took the seat on the opposite side of the table. He moved his around next to hers.

"How have you been?" he asked, grabbing her hand. "What have you been doing all this time? Tell me everything."

She watched him bring her hand to his mouth and kiss each finger individually.

"I've been trying to keep from thinking about you," she said, "but didn't have much success. What have you been doing?"

"Writing poems."

She smiled. "They were lovely. I'll treasure them always."

"You will not. You will throw them away immediately. If anyone ever sees them, my reputation in the oil patch will never recover."

"Well, since your reputation in the patch directly affects Sullivan Oil's productivity, your secret is safe with me."

He hesitated. "Essie, honey, you do realize that if I'm freed I can't work for Sullivan Oil anymore, don't you?"

Shock struck her motionless. "What?"

"I'm head of the Morgan estates now. I'm no longer the second son. I'm the only son. I have to go back to Beaumont. We both do. Permanently."

She tried to pull her hand away, but he held tight.

"I can't run Morgan Oil or any of the rest of it from here," he continued. "Surely you realize that."

"But . . . but I've lived here all my life."

"I know. And we'll come back. Often. It's only a train ride away."

"My father."

"He and I have talked at length. He fully expects this, and if you'll think back, ever since we started courting—which was right about the time we began converting to rotaries—he started taking over the running of Sullivan Oil again."

"My uncle." She swallowed. "I don't know anyone in Beaumont. I'll be an outsider. An interloper."

"Folks are a little different in Beaumont. They don't expect you to have been born and bred in their town. New people come in all the time and are accepted as if they'd lived there all their lives."

"But . . ." Tears began to sting her eyes. "What about . . ." She took a trembling breath. "What about my bicycle club?"

His face filled with compassion. "I'm sorry, Essie. You can maintain ownership of it, but you can't bring it with you. You'll have to leave it behind."

She placed a fist against her mouth, blinking rapidly. But she could not hold the tears at bay.

He reached for her waist and pulled her back onto his lap. "I'm sorry, love. I'm truly so very sorry."

She turned into him and sobbed.

"It may never happen," he said, stroking her hair.

She hiccupped. "W-what?"

"There's a good chance I'm going to hang on behalf of whoever killed Darius."

She sat up. "You can't believe that."

"It's a very real possibility, Essie. And you should prepare yourself for it."

She shook her head, swiping moisture from her eyes. "No, I won't. I refuse to. You are innocent."

"Innocent people are hanged all the time."

"Not in my world, they aren't."

"Nevertheless, there's no sense in worrying about moving to Beaumont or even saying our vows until after the trial is over."

Her body began to tremble. "Are you saying that if you're convicted, you won't marry me?"

"I can't, Essie. Don't you see?" He rubbed his hands up and down her arms to calm her. "Even if I didn't hang, you would be marked as the wife of a criminal. You'd have to deal with that stigma the rest of your life."

"I don't care."

"I do."

"But you haven't done anything!"

"That won't matter if I'm convicted."

Giving up her club and moving to Beaumont suddenly seemed trivial compared to the possibility of losing Tony. Refusing to even consider it, she pressed the butt of her palms to her eyes to dry them. "Then we need to make sure that you're not convicted." Squaring her shoulders, she focused on that very matter. "Now, can you think of any reason Finch would want to kill Darius?"

"My *cousin* Finch?" he asked, surprise lacing his voice. "He would have nothing to gain by Darius's death. Only mine."

"Yours? Why yours?"

"Because Finch is next in line to inherit after me."

"Finch is? But what about Anna? Or your mother?"

Tony shook his head. "The will was quite clear on that. Dad wanted his fortune to remain in the hands of a man. A Morgan man, that is. Not whoever married Anna. Her husband was to receive a dowry and Mother was awarded a stipend, but neither were to inherit."

Uncle Melvin knocked—actually knocked—on his own office door before coming in.

But Essie hardly noted it and instead jumped to her feet. "My stars and garters."

Melvin moved to the cell and unlocked the door.

"What is it?" Tony asked.

"I've got to go, love." She leaned over and pecked him quickly on the lips.

"Your hat," he said.

"There's no time." Then she ran out the door and into the rain.

chapter THIRTY-THREE

SOAKED WITH rain, Essie burst into the Velocipede Club. Shirley was giving a group bicycle lesson to five older girls from the State Orphan's Home.

She took one look at Essie, then turned back to her pupils. "Please practice mounting and dismounting by riding from wall to wall five times. You may begin."

Essie tried to wipe her face with her handkerchief, but it was just as soaked as she was.

"What's happened?" Shirley asked, escorting her into the privacy of the office.

Essie grabbed a towel from the shelf and pressed it against her face and neck. "I think Finch killed Darius and made it look like Tony did."

"Why would he do that?"

"If something happens to Tony, Finch is next to inherit the Morgan fortune."

Shirley took a moment to process Essie's words. "Are you saying that Finch killed Darius in hopes that Tony would be the one hanged for the deed, leaving him as sole heir?"

"That's exactly what I'm saying."

"I don't know, Essie. It sounds awfully risky. What if he went to all that trouble and then Tony wasn't implicated?"

"Finch made sure he was."

"How?"

"By using Tony's knife." Essie shook out her skirts, splattering water onto the floor. "He was standing right there that night when Harley gave Tony his knife back and Mr. Mudge asked to see it. He could have easily slipped it into his pocket after Tony left and Mr. Mudge laid it down."

"Darius wouldn't have been an easy man to stab."

"No. But remember, he had suffered a beating in addition to those dizzy spells and things that he'd complained to Dr. Gulick about."

"What about the arsenic?"

"Like Anna said, Finch and Darius were 'inseparable,' which would have given Finch plenty of opportunity to sneak the poison into Darius's food, drink, or whatever was handy."

"We also know Finch purchased some arsenic and soap to 'rid himself of bedbugs,'" Shirley added.

"As well as buying the cigarette case found in Darius's coat pocket," Essie said. "Perhaps it had been a congratulatory gift for winning the race. Except, Finch laced the cigarettes with arsenic. Darius accepts the gift and smokes one of his new cigarettes. The poison weakens him even further. Finch kills him with Tony's knife and then leaves it where it would be found."

Shirley stared at her for a moment. "That's an awful lot of ifs. I'd hate to be hasty and accuse him unjustly."

"So would I. But you must admit, it fits."

"What should we do?"

"I think we take what we know to Uncle Melvin."

"I agree," Shirley said. "Do we wait until after our meeting tomorrow?"

"No. I think we need to do it now. Today."

"Should we call an emergency meeting first?"

Essie pulled the pins from her hair and toweled it off. "If we do that, I'd have to publicly accuse Finch. And if he didn't do it, I will have done him a grave injustice."

Shirley took a deep breath. "You're right. I guess it would be best to let the sheriff do the accusing."

❧

Tony listened from his cell as Essie tried to convince her uncle that Finch was Darius's murderer. She laid out the means by which he did it, along with his motive and opportunity. Tony's initial reaction had been denial, but the more he thought about it, the more the idea had merit.

Melvin leaned back in his chair. "What do you think, Morgan?"

Essie turned toward him. Her hair was plastered to her head from being caught in the rain earlier. And though the bad weather had passed, her gown had to weigh thirty pounds as wet as it was. As far as he could tell, she didn't even realize her state of dishevelment. Her face was earnest, her cheeks rosy. Her eyes were alive with hope and trepidation.

Tony leaned against the bars. "When our family's lawyer brought me papers to sign after Darius's death, Finch had asked him to change them so that he would have the authority to run the Morgan estate while I was incarcerated."

"Doesn't make him a murderer."

"No, but he's had two wives die in two years. Both of gastric fever, which is just a fancy way of saying a swollen stomach. Doesn't arsenic inflate a person's stomach?"

"Yeah," Melvin drawled. "Matter o' fact, it does. But Darius was stabbed."

"He was also poisoned," Essie said.

"True, but it was the stabbing that killed him. You think Finch has the constitution to do something like that?" Melvin asked Tony.

He rubbed his mouth. "Not really. I'd be mighty surprised."

"Where are the cigarettes?" Essie asked.

Melvin cocked his head. "How is it that you know about the cigarettes?"

She swallowed, then stood up straighter. "I looked through your notes."

He dropped his chair legs onto the floor. "And just when did you do that?"

"This morning. Mrs. Lockhart shared them with me."

Jumping to his feet, he leaned forward. "What's she doin' with them, and who else has had a gander at my notes?"

Essie didn't respond.

"Answer me, young lady!"

The steps outside creaked and Harley burst through the door, skidding across the wood floor and stopping just short of Melvin's desk. "You gotta do somethin', Sheriff! We got trouble."

Melvin frowned. "What kinda trouble?"

"A lynch mob."

Essie gasped. Tony stiffened.

"A lynch mob?" Melvin asked, his tone questioning. "Corsicana hasn't seen one single lynching in its entire history."

"Well, look out yer window if you don't believe me."

Melvin stepped to the window. "Sweet saints above."

"What're you gonna do?" the boy asked.

Hurrying to Tony's cell, Melvin closed its door and locked it. "Harley, go to the church and tell Preacher Wortham what's goin' on. Tell him to round up as many men as he can and to get over here lickety-split."

Tony's heart jumped into his throat as Harley scurried out the door.

"And stay away from that mob!" Melvin hollered just before the door slammed shut. He grabbed his rifle and scooped up some spare bullets from his desktop. "You need to get outta here, Essie."

Yanking open the top drawer, she grabbed a key and unlocked the storage room. She disappeared momentarily, then came back out. "Where are the extra rifles?"

"Quit wasting time, Essie," Tony said, gripping the bars. "You've got to move. Now."

"I can't just up and leave y'all here. Not with a mob coming. Now, where are the rifles?"

"That blasted roof started leaking again and I had to move them out," Melvin said. "Now, I need you to go find your pa, just in case he hasn't already heard, and have him round up the Sullivan Oil men."

Standing in indecision, she glanced at Tony.

"It'll be all right," he said.

Melvin gave her a push. "Go on, girl."

She tripped across the threshold, then ran down the steps as he bolted the door behind her.

He and Tony locked eyes.

"You won't be able to hold 'em, you know," Tony said.

"I'll hold 'em. Ain't nobody lynching no prisoner of mine."

chapter THIRTY-FOUR

ESSIE PUSHED several cartridges into her rifle. "Find as many of the women as you can, Shirley, and meet me by the hanging tree."

"You can't go out there alone," Shirley said, handing Essie another cartridge from the box.

"Nor can I spare the time it would take to get the girls." She cocked the lever, seating a round. "If we're lucky, the mob won't make it to the cottonwood tree. But if the men can't stop them at the jailhouse, I want to be waiting for them at the other end." She placed a hand on her friend's arm. "Don't let me down, Shirley."

"I won't, Essie. We'll be right behind you."

೧೪೦

Tony heard the crowd of men well before they reached the jailhouse. The sheriff positioned himself at the window, his rifle aimed at the crowd. "They're here, son," he said over his shoulder, "but don't worry. Help's a-comin'."

Before Tony could respond, a voice from outside pierced the air.

"Give us your prisoner, Sheriff!"

"You know I won't do that, Howard," Melvin hollered back. "I'm under orders to protect him and I aim to do just that. Now, you boys just go on home before somebody gets hurt."

"We're takin' him, Sheriff. We're takin' him and seein' that justice is served."

The crowd hollered and cheered.

Melvin cocked his gun. "Not another step, Howard, or you'll be the first to go."

"That wouldn't be very smart, Sheriff, shootin' the grandson of Texas's secretary of state."

Melvin looked down the site of his rifle. "My prisoner isn't going anywhere."

Footfalls rushed up the steps. Melvin opened fire, startling both Tony and the crush outside. The pack fell back for a moment, leaving Howard writhing in agony on the stoop.

Word quickly passed through the throng in front of the jail and down the street that the former deputy had been shot. Then, as if an unseen flag had been dropped signaling the start of a race, men stampeded the jailhouse. Some jumping through the window, others busting through the door.

Melvin fired, wounding at least a dozen before the mob seized him by the shoulders, disarmed him and hurled him back.

The screams of the injured echoed in Tony's ears, blood pouring from their wounds. Melvin was cut off from Tony's view as the mob surged forward, stepping on and over the fallen men as if they were sacks of potatoes.

At first it seemed as if the crowd of roughs were strangers to Tony, but as they dragged him from his cell, he saw their leaders were from Morgan Oil. Men who'd done Darius's dirty work for him. Many with shady pasts. Darius had provided a haven for men of their ilk—roughs who were loyal to his brother, even if it wasn't for edifying reasons.

Tony could smell the alcohol on their breaths. He fought and kicked and bucked but was only rewarded with beatings and rougher treatment as he was dragged down the street toward the big cottonwood tree on the outskirts of town.

⚭

The two armed riders waiting for the mob gave them pause. Tony's left eye was swollen shut, but his right still worked fine and shifted to a man and a woman on horseback. On the left was Russ O'Berry, the best friend Tony'd ever had, sitting atop a horse at least ten hands tall. He sported a pistol in one hand and a bullwhip held casually within his other. To his right was Essie Spreckelmeyer, aiming a loaded rifle at the hearts of Tony's captors.

His stomach clenched. What the blazes did she think she was doing here? The crowd slowly drew to the base of the tree, becoming unusually quiet in order to ascertain the dangers posed from this unexpected quarter.

Russ scanned the crowd. "Afternoon, Horace. Norman. Paddy. I reckon you know Tony here hasn't had a trial yet?"

The mob was supposed to provide anonymity. This recital of specific names caused a disconcerting murmur to pass through the crowd.

"Our argument ain't with you, Russ," one of the roughs called out, "so just git outta the way 'fore we string you up, as well."

Faster than a striking snake, Russ stung the rowdie across his cheek with the bullwhip, leaving him with a red mark but no broken skin.

"I ain't goin' nowhere," Russ said, controlling his horse with his thighs. "And if anybody makes a move, my whip'll slice a whole lot deeper."

The man's eyes blazed while he touched his cheek, but he remained silent.

"Now, release the prisoner." Russ's voice rang with authority.

The crowd fell back in disorder, but the men holding Tony kept their grip firm.

A voice from the back cried out, "String 'im up! The woman, too!"

The mob gained a new surge of momentum. Tony's heart hammered. Where were the men Melvin had sent for? He struggled, then pitched forward, while several shots sent hats flying. A hush spread over the assembly.

Tony glanced up. Russ covered the crowd with his pistol while Essie began to reload.

Through the tight mass, Ewing pressed forward. "Stop this at once!" he cried. "Let Morgan go!"

The butt of a wooden bat descended onto the preacher's head. He crumpled to the ground. Essie gasped, momentarily losing focus.

The crowd immediately took advantage of her distraction and surged forward, pulling her from her horse. Russ couldn't shoot without the risk of hitting her. His whip lashed out, and though several men screamed, the throng managed to catch hold of the whip's tail and jerk, tearing it and the pistol from Russ's hold and spooking his horse. He inflicted some damage with his boots and fists but was no match for the number of men who dragged him from his saddle.

"We want a hangin'!" the men began to chant. "We want a hangin'!"

The atmosphere took on that of a distorted carnival. A boomer in well-worn denims slung a rope across a great limb of the giant tree while someone else slipped its noose over Tony's neck. Rough hands threw him up on Essie's horse. Others held her and Russ back.

"No!" Essie screamed. "Please! He's innocent! Let him go!"

Russ flung men from his body like a dog shaking water from its fur, only to have another swarm of rowdies wrestle him to the ground over and over until he had no fight left in him.

In that moment, a tremendous fear gripped Tony. Not for himself, but for Essie. For Russ. And for Russ's family if something happened to him.

He dared not think of what the mob had done to the sheriff. For nothing short of death would have been able to keep him away.

The sun began its descent, beating down on the ruddy faces of the rowdies who'd worked themselves into a greater frenzy than before. Nothing could save Tony, his best friend, or the woman he loved. Nothing but God Almighty himself.

Sacrifice me, Lord, but save the others. Please.

"Quiet!" someone roared. "I wanna hear his neck snap!"

The throng whooped and the ground shook with suppressed violence.

Tony braced himself. A quiet fell upon the gathering. After a couple of seconds, Tony realized the ground was still shaking, not from the agitated crowd but something else entirely.

He, along with all those present, looked to the east as over a hundred riders on horseback galloped up and quickly surrounded the rioters. A huge cloud of dust enveloped them.

When it began to settle, the silhouettes of armed men and women slowly took shape, their expressions serious, their weapons primed. Tony looked over the faces of his rescuers.

Grandpa, Jeremy, Moss, and a multitude of other men who worked for Sullivan Oil. The Baker brothers and their crew of rig builders. Men who worked for Morgan Oil but weren't in Darius's back pocket. The sheriff, the judge, and the women of the Corsicana Velocipede Club—Shirley, Mrs. Lockhart, Mrs. Dunn, Mrs. Vandervoort, and a dozen more. His gaze stopped on Anna. Did she even know how to use that weapon she was holding? But her attention was completely focused on the crowd.

"Release Miss Spreckelmeyer and Russ O'Berry!" the sheriff ordered.

The men holding Essie and Russ did not respond. Several guns swerved toward them, taking a bead on their hearts. They let go and raised their hands.

Russ quickly recovered his bullwhip. The men gave him a wide berth. Essie scrambled to Tony's horse, grabbing its reins and holding it still.

Tony looked down at her, then saw Finch for the first time. His cousin broke through the crowd and moved to the horse's flanks. He raised his hand to strike the mare when his wrist was caught midair with the whip and jerked back in an unnatural direction.

He screamed as the bones in his wrist broke, still unaware that Russ had saved his life, for several guns were seconds away from riveting Finch with bullets.

The assembly stilled, not wanting to draw the attention of the armed men—or women.

"Corsicana is a good, wholesome town," Melvin roared. "And I, for one, will not stand still while you besmirch its history with a lynching."

"But this man murdered his own brother in cold blood!" Finch shouted, cradling his broken hand.

"I have a dozen women here who say otherwise," Melvin responded.

The crowd murmured.

Tony kept his gaze pinned to Finch, uncomfortable with the man's proximity to Essie. From the corner of his eye, he saw Judge Spreckelmeyer slide off his horse and circle round Finch from behind.

"These gals have some mighty convincin' evidence that it was his cousin, Finch Morgan, who killed Darius," Melvin continued, spitting to the side. "And not just him, but he maybe killed his wives, too."

The shock of this unexpected news rippled through the crowd. Russ quietly approached Tony, while Finch and the rest of the mob were preoccupied.

"They're lying," Finch shouted, reaching across his body for a knife.

The judge pressed the barrel of his gun into Finch's back. "Raise your arms, Morgan. Nice and slow."

Finch lifted his left arm. "I can't raise the right," he said, pushing his words through clinched teeth. "My hand is hanging by a thread."

Spreckelmeyer patted him down, relieving him of his knife. Russ quickly released Tony's bound hands.

The mob's thirst for blood shifted its focus. "Hang Finch Morgan!" they began to chant. "Hang Finch Morgan!"

Tony slipped the noose from around his neck and swung off the horse. "Get Essie outta here *now!*" he said to Russ.

Russ grabbed Essie, but the crowd was already surging toward Finch. Pulling her against him, Russ readied his whip. Tony stood in front of her, effectively sandwiching her between the two of them.

The sheriff swung his horse to the front, raised his rifle toward the sky and fired.

The crowd quieted.

"I'll be taking Finch up to Fort Smith for a hearin', so you can rest assured justice will be served."

"Let's save 'em the trouble!" somebody shouted.

Melvin stilled his prancing horse. "Well, now, much as I'd like to oblige you, I'm afraid I'm bound by oath to do otherwise. If it makes you feel any better, though, Hangin' Judge Isaac Parker will be waiting for us."

The mob cheered.

"Right now, though, we'd like everybody to go on home and settle down a bit. Show's over."

There were some token protests, but being surrounded by a hundred armed men and women dampened the crowd's enthusiasm. With more encouragement from the sheriff and his posse, the gathering began to disperse, then changed courses altogether when Mr. Rosenburg hollered, "Free drinks at my place fer the first fifty patrons."

Tony turned to Essie.

"Ewing," she said.

"I'll go find him," Russ offered, then headed to the spot where Ewing had fallen.

"You all right?" Tony asked her.

"I think so," she answered, her voice shaking. "You look awful, though. Does it hurt terribly?"

He touched his cheek and eye. "I'm fine. Could've been a lot worse."

"Is anything broken?" she asked, running her hands along his chest, arms, and hands.

"I don't think so." He threaded his fingers through hers, putting a stop to her examination. "What possessed you to take on that mob with nothing more than Russ and a rifle? You about scared me to death."

"I knew the women would come as quickly as they could. I just decided not to wait on them." She smoothed a tuft of hair sticking out from his head. "On my way here, I ran into Russ and he insisted on coming with me."

He shook his head. "Well, I can tell you this, no one will ever again be able to say you're marrying a younger man."

She frowned. "What?"

"I aged ten years seeing you up there. That makes me thirty-eight and you just thirty-four."

She smiled, but before she could respond, the judge and sheriff interrupted.

"Essie?" her father said. "You all right, honey?"

"I'm fine," she said, hugging them both.

"Is Ewing okay?" Tony asked.

"He will be. Your sister, Russ, and a couple of the older women are taking him home and seeing to his injuries."

"What about Howard?"

"The mob left him for dead, but the bullet didn't hit anything vital," Melvin said. "I have him recuperatin' in a jail cell while the doc tends to the others who were wounded." Melvin looked Tony up and down. "What about you? You all right?"

Tony held out his hand. "Much better than I was a few minutes ago, thanks to you and everybody else. I wasn't sure what happened to you after the mob rushed us."

Melvin nodded. "They stuck me in a cell and left several men to guard me. You know who freed me before my men could get there?"

"Who?" Essie asked.

"Your band of bloomer-gals. That's who."

She brightened. "How'd they do that?"

"Same way them suffragettes did in *A Woman's War*."

Her jaw went slack. "*A Woman's War*? You read Mrs. Lockhart's books, too?"

"Shhhh," he said, looking around, then signaled Grandpa over. "Gather up several men and escort Essie, Tony, and the rest of the ladies home." Someone shouted the sheriff's name and he excused himself.

"I want you to go on to the house with Essie," the judge said to Tony. "I don't want you staying in the boardinghouse until things settle down."

"Yes, sir," he said. "You think they'll sentence Finch to hang?"

"I'd say it's almost certain."

The depth of Finch's misdeeds overwhelmed Tony, flooding him with sorrow. Thoughts of Darius, Finch's wives, and their shortened lives left him feeling dejected. What a waste.

Spreckelmeyer squeezed Tony's shoulder. "Well, at least one good thing came from this."

"Sir?"

"Well, Anna."

"Anna?"

"Yes. If it hadn't been for all this mess, why, she and Ewing might never have gotten married."

Tony looked at him blankly. "Married?"

"Why, sure. She was afraid if the worst happened, she'd have to honor her marriage contract with Mr. Tubbs. Ewing told her that'd be mighty hard to do if she were already wed. So I married those two up this afternoon."

"What?" He looked at Essie. "Did you know about this?"

"No," she said, eyes wide. "This is the first I've heard."

Spreckelmeyer chuckled. "Well, now, with all that's been going on, that's not so surprising."

Tony scanned the crowd, then remembered Anna and some of the others had taken Ewing home to see to his injuries.

Grandpa approached with a couple of horses. "You two ready?"

In a bit of a fog, Tony helped Essie mount, then swung up onto his horse. The Sullivan Oil men surrounded them and proceeded to escort them to the Spreckelmeyers' house on Bilberry Street.

"Where's Finch?" Tony asked Grandpa.

Grandpa spit a wad of tobacco onto the ground. "He's got him an escort, too. Straight to the jailhouse."

chapter THIRTY-FIVE

ESSIE WOKE early, anxious to check on Tony. She hastily donned a shirtwaist and skirt, then hurried down the stairs. Tony and Papa sat at the kitchen table. From the looks of the almost-empty coffee-pot, they'd been there awhile.

"What are you doing out of bed?" she asked Tony. New bruises had materialized and his right jaw was swollen, though both eyes were open now.

"It looks worse than it feels."

Papa stood and picked up his coffee cup. "I'll be in my study if you need me." He pecked her on the cheek and left the room.

Songbirds heralded the morning and a bit of eastern sun touched the window. She could see Tony had made good use of the bathwater she'd prepared for him last night. His hair was clean, his swollen face shaven, and she could smell a faint hint of sandalwood.

"Are you hungry?" she asked.

"Not really. I've a belly full of coffee right now. What about you?"

She shook her head, then poured herself a cup. "How long have you been up?"

"Awhile."

She leaned against the counter. "Did you sleep all right?"

"Yes. It was good to be in a real bed again."

"I imagine." She blew on her cup. "I'll have Jeremy or someone collect all of your things from the jail."

"I can do it."

"No. I don't want you near there. Not anytime soon, anyway."

He studied her. "How long you gonna make me wait for a good-morning kiss?"

A weightlessness seized her tummy. "Your jaw's swollen. Won't it hurt?"

"Not unless you plan on punching me."

She smiled.

He stood, then ambled toward her. "I like waking up in your house." He took her cup and set it down. "I'd like it even better if I were waking up in your bed."

She swallowed.

He slipped his arms around her waist. "Good morning, love." Then he kissed her. Softly. Gently. Sweetly.

It didn't take long, however, for passion to rush in and burst open the gates of desire. He clasped her more tightly against him, splaying his hands wide on her back and waist. She slid her arms around his neck.

He flinched and she jerked back.

"Oh," she said. "I'm sorry. Did I hurt you?"

"No," he said. "I guess I'm just a little more sore than I thought." He slipped his hands into hers. "Come sit down at the table with me." He held her chair, then settled in across from her. "Have you made any plans for the wedding?"

"Not yet. I've been spending most of my time trying to prove your innocence."

"And I certainly appreciate that." He squeezed her hand. "But now that we have that behind us, I was wondering if you're going to want a big wedding?"

She shrugged. "It's not so much that I want one, it's more that I'll get one by default. My father's the Thirty-fifth Judicial District Judge, and we know most every person in the county."

He nodded. "Maybe *big* wasn't the right word. I think I meant fancy. Are you going to want a fancy wedding?"

She considered his question. As a young girl, she'd imagined her wedding in a thousand different ways. Sometimes she'd seen herself wearing a lavish beaded gown fit for a princess. Other times she'd visualized a wedding in an outdoor glade fragrant with colorful blooms. She'd even imagined galloping off in the sunset with some handsome cowboy. But those childhood fantasies didn't hold the same appeal now that they did then. Since her betrothal to Tony, the details of the ceremony had become secondary to the commitment she was making to God and to him.

"You know," she began, "I think I can honestly say I don't care one way or the other. So long as it's you who I'm exchanging vows with, most any kind of wedding will do. Why? Do you want a fancy wedding?"

He took a deep breath. "You know what I'd really like?"

She shook her head.

"I'd really like to get married today."

Her lips parted.

"And not just because I'm ready to enjoy all the benefits awarded to married couples—though I'm certainly looking forward to that with great anticipation."

She felt herself blush, though he didn't suffer the same affliction.

"The other reason I'd like to accelerate the exchanging of vows is because I need to return to Beaumont. My family's business interests go well beyond Morgan Oil and have been languishing since Darius's death. I really need to go home."

She looked out the window at the legs of the oil rig in their yard. "Well, I can certainly see you needing to straighten out your affairs.

And though a hasty wedding sounds extremely tempting, I'm not sure that's the best solution."

His shoulders slumped.

"Don't misunderstand, Tony. I'm impatient, too." She took both of his hands into hers. "But I have to think about Papa and all my friends. If I'm going to live away from them the rest of my life, then I think I should stay here for just a few more weeks and plan a modest wedding where everyone will have a chance to say good-bye. I also need to tie up my loose ends at the Velocipede Club and prepare Shirley to take over."

"Are you going to change your mind about marrying me?"

"No." She squeezed his hands. "In three weeks, I will be yours and I will go wherever you go."

Pulling her to her feet, he kissed her. Roughly, deeply, right there in the kitchen where anyone could walk in.

"I love you, Essie."

∽

Throughout the next three weeks, she found that her hometown, the town that was as much a part of her as her right hand, no longer held the luster it once had. Not without Tony in it.

She sought out Anna's company more than anyone else's because she somehow felt closer to Tony when she was with Anna. But Anna was a new bride herself and busy settling in with Ewing, whose injury had not hindered the honeymoon at all, she guessed, considering how happy the two of them looked whenever she caught sight of them.

And this last week had been nothing short of miserable for her. Why, oh, why hadn't she told Tony to come for her sooner?

But finally her wedding day had arrived. And Tony would be coming in on the ten o'clock train. Even then, though, she wouldn't be able to see him until the ceremony. She didn't for one minute believe in bad luck or good luck or any such nonsense, but Mrs.

Lockhart had been adamant. In *Clarabel's Love Story*, Clarabel had seen her groom before the wedding, and that marriage had lasted only three days.

Dragging her hope chest into the center of the bedroom, Essie ran her hand across the ornate wooden trunk. She'd been ten when her mother began filling the box with family heirlooms that would be Essie's when she married.

She slowly lifted the lid. Her grandmother's white-on-white embroidered bedspread, some lace tablecloths, and curtains all lay folded and wrapped in tissue. From her great-grandmother, she had a full set of silver tableware with engraved handles. From Aunt Verdie, a cut-crystal punchbowl and cups.

Linens hemmed and embellished by Mother and by Essie's own hands lay underneath handkerchiefs, tea towels, and hosiery. Chemises, corset covers, and dressing sacques.

And on the very top, her nightdress. Made especially for her wedding night. The tissue crackled as Essie folded it aside and lifted the gown from the chest. Tiny white rosettes were sprinkled among three rows of rice stitches decorating the neckline. Lace trim ran along the sleeveless straps. Only one delicate ribbon held the garment closed.

She slipped her hand beneath the bodice, disconcerted to find the gossamer fabric so sheer, so clingy. She swallowed. She'd only worn this gown once before. The night she'd decided to remain unmarried for the rest of her life. The night she'd decided to have her Lord and Savior as her one and only Groom.

And yet now He'd sent her a flesh-and-blood groom. One who would give her children. Who would grow old with her. Who would see her in this gown this very night.

I'm glad I wore it for you first, Lord. Because even though you've sent me a groom, you will always be first. In my heart. In my marriage. In my life.

◦◦◦

Four hours later, after the ceremony and wedding meal, Tony waited for his wife at the bottom of the stairs. Her bedroom door opened, but it was Mrs. Lockhart who came out. He smiled again at her bright purple gown with pink trim, then took the steps two at a time to assist her descent.

"I'm still unhappy with you, sir," she said as he slipped his hand under her arm. "A bride should be taken on a train to Niagara Falls for her wedding trip."

"Essie didn't want to go to Niagara Falls," he said.

"Doesn't matter. You're the man. You're the one who should be deciding these things."

"And I did decide. I decided to take her to Enchanted Rock in Llano County."

"On a bicycle!"

They reached the bottom of the steps, and Tony smiled at the woman who'd taken him under her wing the very first time she'd seen him.

"Not ever," she continued, "not even in one of my novels, have the bride and groom traveled away on a bicycle." She leaned in close and whispered, "Where on earth will you spend the night? You can't think to be with your bride for the first time on nothing more than a bed of grass!"

He tweaked Mrs. Lockhart's nose. "I shall not discuss such things with you, ma'am. For shame."

"Well, someone needs to talk some sense into you. It's not too late," she said, squeezing the sleeves of his jacket. "You can send your friend with the bullwhip to the train station right quick to secure you some tickets."

The bedroom door opened again. Anna, Shirley, and Mrs. Dunn came out of the room backwards, hovering in front of Essie. Finally she came into view and his heart sped up.

Her bicycle costume was the same blue as her eyes, her straw hat surprisingly simple, with a wide ribbon band that matched her outfit. He took an involuntary step toward her.

She placed her gloved hand on the balustrade.

"Wait," he said, then patted the rail. "This way. I want you to come to me this way."

Mrs. Dunn gasped.

Smiling, Essie hopped onto the banister and, with bloomers ruffling, slid straight into Tony's waiting arms.

"Hello, Mrs. Morgan," he said, pulling her against him.

"Good afternoon, Mr. Morgan."

He kissed her firmly on the lips. "Are you ready?"

"I am."

He lowered her to her feet. She hugged the women good-bye. The sheriff, judge, and preacher stepped into the foyer. Anna kissed Tony's cheek, then moved next to Ewing while Essie's uncle enfolded her into his arms.

"Be careful, Essie-girl," he said. "Do you have your pistol?"

"Yes," she said, pulling back. "We'll be fine."

Turning to her father, she stepped into his embrace.

"Ah, Squirt," he said. "I wish your mother could have seen you today. You were the prettiest bride I ever did see."

Lifting up on tiptoes, she kissed his cheek. "I'm the happiest bride you ever did see."

He squeezed her tight, then let her go and held out his hand to Tony. "Take good care of her, son."

"I will, sir. And we'll come back through Corsicana on our return trip toward the end of the month."

"I'd like that." He sighed. "Well, you have a passel of folks out there waiting for you. Y'all'd best get going."

Tony offered Essie his arm and opened the door.

They stepped out onto the porch. The yard and street were full of wedding guests. Friends of his. Friends of hers. Friends of their families. They cheered and whistled.

Clasping Essie's hand, Tony looked at her. "Here we go."

They ran down the steps and walkway under a shower of rice. Russ opened the gate and they rushed through.

"Oh, Tony!" she exclaimed. "It's a *side-by-side* bicycle built for two!"

"That's right," he said, helping her mount. "I don't want you in front of me or behind me. I want you right beside me. On our wedding trip and for the rest of our lives."

He kissed her, amazed that if his father hadn't disinherited him, he would never have come to Corsicana. Would never have met Essie.

At the time in his life when he thought he had nothing, when he thought his cup was empty, his heavenly Father was selecting the finest of wines to pour into Tony's cup until it overflowed.

Essie pulled away slightly and flushed. The whistles and hoots of the crowd penetrated Tony's consciousness as folks on the street parted for them, waving, calling out good wishes and throwing the last of the rice.

Winking at Essie, Tony took a quick glance behind them to be sure their clothing and supplies were still secured to the machine, then jumped onto his seat and pushed off.

EPILOGUE

BEAUMONT, TEXAS
JANUARY 10, 1901

TONY CROSSED the curving veranda of his three-story home and entered a side door with six-month-old Sullivan on his hip.

"Let's go find Mama," Tony said, hanging his hat on the hall tree before heading to the reception room.

Essie stood beside an easel that held a diagram of an automobile. Her new wide-brimmed hat trimmed in blue velvet slanted fashionably to one side. A number of ladies sat grouped around her.

"You're back early," she said, glancing at Tony.

The baby waved his pudgy arms and kicked his legs upon seeing his mother. Tony handed him to her, noting again Sullivan's blond hair was the same color as Essie's, though his nose was red and runny.

"How was your drive?" she asked Tony, pulling a handkerchief from her pocket and swiping Sullivan's nose.

"Exhilarating," he answered, then turned to greet Essie's guests. He recognized the senator's wife, Mrs. Lockhart's daughter, and Russ's wife among the throng. "How do you do, ladies? What are y'all up to this fine afternoon?"

"We're discussing the features of the new Locomobile," Essie answered, loosening Sullivan's coat and tickling him beneath the chin. She grinned as he squealed with laughter.

"Yes," said Iva O'Berry, smiling at Tony mischievously. "Your wife has invited us to be part of her Beaumont Ladies Automobile Club and she's going to teach us how to drive."

He snapped his attention to Essie. "What?"

"That's right," continued Iva. "Today she's explaining that the wooden body of the Locomobile rests on three full-elliptic springs. The boiler and engine are below the seat of the body, and the feed-water tank is below the rear of the body."

His lips parted.

A huge boom from somewhere outside rattled the windows of the house.

"What in the world?" Essie said, absently patting the baby's back.

Tony glanced out the tall windows facing east. "Sounded like a cannon or something."

The women stirred.

"Essie?" he asked, returning his attention to the matter at hand. "May I see you in the library for a moment?"

"Certainly." She looked at her ladies. "If you'll excuse me, I'll be right back."

With a calm he didn't feel, he escorted her beneath the majolica glass light fixture and past the gingerbread spool design portals separating the hall from the stairwell.

"You're back," his mother said, stepping into the hall.

The baby opened his mouth in a huge yawn.

"Oh dear. You've worn the poor little thing out, Tony." She held out her arms. "Come, my sweet, and let's go to the nursery, where Grandmama can get you out of your coat, then rock you to sleep."

Essie relinquished her son, and Tony marveled again at the delight his mother took in the baby. She'd regained much of her former glow and vigor since becoming a grandmother.

"Thank you, Mother," Tony said, but she was already on her way up the stairs, singing softly to Sullivan.

Tony opened the heavy sliding doors to the library, inviting Essie to enter with the sweep of his hand. Stained-glass windows with the faces of Dickens and Longfellow welcomed them.

He slid the doors shut.

"I was going to tell you," she said before he could even turn around.

"When?"

"When I knew I had enough ladies interested."

He rubbed his eyes. "Essie, women are not supposed to drive. I only taught you because you are not like most women."

"And I love it! It's fabulous. I think it a crime to forbid other women to drive. So many of my friends want to learn. That's what gave me the idea of forming a club."

"No."

"What?"

"No," he repeated. "The men of this town will ride me out on a rail if I let you teach their wives to drive."

She crossed her arms. "That's what everyone in Corsicana said about the bicycle club, too."

"Essie—"

"I'm forming the organization, Tony. I've all that money from the sale of the Velocipede Club and I want to invest it in an automobile club for women."

"Using my car as its teaching tool?"

"Using *our* car."

"They'll wreck it."

"No, they won't. I'm an excellent teacher."

He suppressed a groan. The menfolk were going to kill him. Russ, especially. He thought it a great joke that Essie was such a tomboy and took tremendous pride in ribbing Tony about it. But he would be furious if Iva took up driving.

"In *Thrown on the World*," Essie said, "Miss Moffitt became a shoe cobbler when her father lost his eyesight—a craft supposedly suitable for men alone. Yet she helped many of her lady friends make a way for themselves."

"Miss Moffitt also blew up the barn."

Essie rolled her eyes. "She was a bit careless. I'm much more levelheaded."

Someone hammered the front door's knocker with excessive force. "Mr. Morgan! Mr. Morgan!"

Tony slid open the doors and stepped into the hallway just as Iva answered the door.

A teener in dungarees and covered with oil stood dripping on the front porch. "Mr. Morgan! Come quick. One of the rigs on Spindletop Hill is gushin' clear up to the sky!"

Essie grabbed his hand, her eyes alive with excitement.

"I'll send word back as soon as I can," he said, pulling her to him and planting a kiss on her lips. "We'll talk about the auto club later."

"Be careful," she said.

Grabbing his hat and coat, he rushed out the door and headed toward Spindletop, wondering how he was going to tell the men of Beaumont that before the year was out, their wives would very likely know more about automobiles than they would.

AUTHOR'S NOTE

I had such plans for incorporating all the exciting developments of the oil industry's early days—the building of the first oil refinery in Corsicana, the shipment of the first batch of refined oil in Texas, the clever marketing strategies the early oilmen used to promote their product. Yet Essie and her bicycle club simply took over the story and, before I knew it, the novel had ended and I didn't get to include all that wonderful history I'd so thoroughly researched. At least we managed to go from being rope chokers to mud drinkers! (Cable-tool boys to rotary boys.) The oil companies I used were all fictional, but the Baker brothers did, in fact, introduce their rotary drill to Corsicana, thus revolutionizing the Texas oil industry.

Being the daughter of an oilman, the wife of an oilman, a Texan, and a former resident of Corsicana, it has been a delight to write these last two books. I shall always be particularly fond of my *Trouble* books and of all the friends I made while researching them.

Next, we're off to Seattle in the mid-eighteen hundreds. So get ready to rewind back a few years and watch for a brand-new story in June 2009. Until then, come by and visit me on my Web site (*www.IWantHerBook.com*). I have a blog, a chat room, games, contests, email, and a lot of readers just like you, waiting with open arms. See you there!

Love at First *Fight*?

Lady Constance Morrow finds herself held against her will aboard a ship bound for the American colonies—a ship filled with "tobacco brides" and felons. Drew O'Connor, a determined Colonial farmer who is nearly as headstrong as Constance, wins her as his bride but soon realizes their marriage of convenience has become most inconvenient indeed.

A Bride Most Begrudging

What Is *The Measure of a Lady*?

Rachel van Buren arrives in Gold Rush San Francisco with two wishes: to protect her younger siblings and to return east as soon as possible. Yet both goals prove more difficult than she could imagine. Rachel won't give up without a fight though, and soon all will learn an eloquent but humorous lesson about what truly makes a lady.

The Measure of a Lady

She Has One Mission: Find a Husband

As Essie Spreckelmeyer nears age thirty, she decides the Lord has left her to find a husband on her own. After writing down the names of all the bachelors in her small Texas town, she closes her eyes, twirls her finger, and...picks one. But convincing the lucky "husband-to-be" is going to be a *bit* more of a problem.

Courting Trouble

Looking for More Good Books to Read?

You can find out what is new and exciting with previews, descriptions, and reviews by signing up for Bethany House newsletters at

www.bethanynewsletters.com

We will send you updates for as many authors or categories as you desire so you get only the information you really want.

Sign up today!